Silver Threads

Tom Ralston

TOM RALSTON

PlashMill Press

Published in Scotland and the United Kingdom in 2008
by PlashMill Press

First Edition

A CIP catalogue record for this book is available
from the British Library.

ISBN-13: 978-0-9554535-5-7

Printed and bound by CPI Antony Rowe, Eastbourne

PlashMill Press
The Plash Mill
Friockheim
Angus DD11 4SH
Scotland.

I dedicate this book with love and thanks to my wife, Ina, who has had to live with me as it all took shape, and to my two precious daughters, Caroline and Gillian. Thank you for encouraging me to continue with it when it would have been so much easier to give up.

To my mother, who polished my shoes and who always wanted the best for me and to Rod Fleming, my long-suffering publisher and editor.

Thank you all for your help, patience and understanding.

Tom Ralston

Prologue

*T*he *Arun class Lifeboat's engines were screaming at full power when she struck the rock. Her instruments showed that she was travelling at an indicated speed of almost nineteen knots.*

The impact of her thirty-one tonnes grounding was made infinitely worse by the fact that she was surfing down the face of a huge gale-driven, breaking sea when she struck. This made her true speed closer to twenty-five knots, or thirty miles per hour.

Nothing that the genius of man could conceive would withstand such a cataclysmic collision.

The rock smashed through her keel and starboard bilge and into the survivors' compartment below and forward of the wheelhouse. Her momentum drove her relentlessly over the rock. She destroyed herself as she went; the rending and crashing horror continuing through the engine room until finally the trail of devastation stopped right aft, in the battery space.

The immediate damage to her fibreglass hull was indescribable; it had been broken and shattered into millions of shards.

Both of the turbo-charged 500 horsepower diesel engines had been sheared from their mountings and had driven forward into the tank space, howling and shrieking in their death agony. Their incursion into this space completed the destruction of the diesel fuel tanks, which had already been partly torn from their mounts by the shock.

The heavy batteries were torn from their restraints and were smashed into unrecognisable pieces against the forward bulkhead of the aft cabin, plunging what remained of the boat into complete darkness.

The noise that accompanied this destruction was unbearable.

On deck, the wheelhouse was almost torn from its mountings. Her mast and radar scanner went clear over her starboard shoulder, landing in the welter of broken water and foam that marked the domain of the rock.

Her life raft was thrown out of its holder into the maelstrom where, as it had been designed to do, it automatically inflated. The emergency position-indicating radio beacon, just about the only thing to remain in working order among the devastation, began its unfeeling electronic cry for help. This beacon and the small flashing light on top of the life raft were automatically switched on when their sensors made contact with the sea.

The next wave washed the shattered remains of what had been, just moments before, a proud and invincible craft, over the rock and into deeper water. There the seas took their revenge over the boat that had defied them for so long, surging and foaming freely through the waterlogged length of her. The flotation provided by the polyurethane foam that filled some of the shattered compartments was enough—barely—to keep her afloat.

Six men were aboard her that night.

The mechanic, thirty-four year old John Morrans, was the only paid member of the crew.

He was a lorry driver, making local deliveries of coal when not involved with his great love, the Lifeboat. Married, he had three children upon whom he doted. He was very big and powerful but as is usual for men of his size, he was an amiable lad, well respected by all his shipmates for his professionalism. He had been doing one of his regular safety checks in the engine room and was bent over the forward end of the starboard engine, checking the bilge pump, when she struck.

He felt very little pain, dying instantly as the screaming diesel smashed his body into pulp on its way over him and into the tank compartment. His blood turned the inrushing sea bright red—a colour that was soon diluted as the sea flooded the entire space below deck.

Eddie Smith was a fish worker who had just recently joined the crew as a deckhand. He was just nineteen years old and took great delight in describing himself as being, 'not married, but working hard at it.' He had been feeling seasick and not a little afraid, and had gone out on deck for some fresh air.

The sudden impact had thrown him hard against the safety rails that were fitted around the side of the boat. He had no time to feel fear as the heavy life raft--on its way overboard-- struck him a tremendous blow on the head. He too, died instantly. Attached to the boat by his safety harness, his body was washed around on the deck at the whim of the swirling sea.

The other deckhand, Jim Roberts, had been feeling sorry for his mate, Eddie, and was on his way aft through the wheelhouse to go out on deck to comfort him.

Although only a few months older than Eddie, he felt responsible for him; after all it was he who had talked him into joining the crew. Until Eddie joined, Jim had been the youngest on the boat.

Jim also was unmarried. He, like Eddie, was fortunate enough to die quickly, his spine smashed by the impact when he was thrown violently backwards against one of the seats.

The radio operator, Robin Stevens, was one of the older men aboard. Originally from Fraserburgh, he had married a local girl with whom he had become acquainted when he was fishing out of Mallaig. After they married, they had settled there. They had two children, grown up now, and Robin had come ashore and now worked for one of the fish auctioneers.

Robin died as quietly as he had lived. He had been sitting at his radio equipment, facing the port side of the wheelhouse, and had—as usual—been wearing his seat belt.

He was thrown sideways with enough force to break his neck.

The second coxswain, Ally Cowie, forty-five years old and married with three children, had been standing beside his coxswain. He was a successful fisherman, and owned the boat he fished. His father had been coxswain of the first lifeboat to come to Mallaig. He was facing aft, bent over the dimly lit chart table, confirming their position by converting the electronic data which appeared on their navigating system, on to the chart.

Ally's head was driven backward into the radar screen and he was rendered immediately unconscious. Unfortunately, his death was not quick.

He came to his senses lying amid all the chaos, jammed underneath the mass of debris that had been thrown forward by the force of the impact. In his greatly weakened state he was unable to extricate himself, and drowned slowly in the mercilessly cold sea which was now freely washing around the inside of the wrecked wheelhouse—a place which just moments before had been dry, warm, and safe.

His last thoughts were of his wife Mary, and the knowledge that she and their children would at least be well looked-after financially by the Lifeboat service, was of little comfort to him in his dying.

Francis MacDonnell, the coxswain, was twenty-six years old. He too was a very successful fisherman. He was not married but although he did not know it—and now never would—his long time girlfriend, Mairi, had just discovered that she was pregnant. Francis had been driving his boat before the storm as hard as his knowledge of the sea allowed—conscious that the seamen who had called for help would be desperate to see his lights appear through the gale-driven rain.

He had been uneasy for the last few moments; perhaps he had sensed that the boat's motion had changed somehow, and had known that this might be due to their going into shallower water. Wanting to make certain that they were well clear of the rocks that he knew were in the area, he had just asked Ally to re-check their position. He had been wearing his seat belt, but had untied it in order to turn toward the chart table behind him.

He was thrown forward and upward by the impact that killed his crew and wrecked his boat.

The top of his skull was shattered when it struck one of the metal uprights of the forward windows, and he died before he could wonder what he had done wrong.

The shattered hulk drifted into deeper water now, just north of the rock that had wreaked such devastation. Though completely waterlogged, it would float for a long time yet—a temporary tomb for the men who had so proudly manned her.

The gale continued, unsated by their sacrifice, and still the radio beacon persisted with its plaintive electronic cry for help.

Chapter One

The beginning.

There was nothing to warn Bill that the day he viewed from his bedroom window as he rubbed the sleep from his eyes was one that would change his life forever.

Yes, the warmth of the morning foretold what would be—for Campbeltown—a rare heat. The early sun beamed low over the Loch through a blue, cloud-free sky, promising that the day would soon gain in temperature, as it gained height. Yes, he felt a strange sort of calmness, a feeling that—if he had thought about it at all—he would have put down to the fact that he knew just what he was going to do with his new day.

Apart from the weather, the only other thing which was unusual, and over which he could rejoice, was that his normally noisy young brother, Donald, was still sound asleep. The only evidence that he was there at all was the sight of his mop of tousled black hair sticking out of the short gap between pillow and blanket.

Bill crept quietly downstairs as soon as he had pulled on a pair of suitably old and comfortable, short breeks.

He tiptoed as quietly as he could out of the front door and across the open landing to the toilet, which his family shared with the people next door. There he sat for a time, reading from the squares of newspaper placed there by his mother. Toilet paper was a long way off in the future. The cache on the other side of the toilet belonged to the people next door and Bill occasionally took a perverse delight in using some of their paper! He then went back inside the house to give his hands and face the usual young lad's perfunctory 'lick and a promise' from the brass cold-water tap at the black cast-iron kitchen sink.

"What are you doing up so early on a Sunday morning? Could you not wait till a decent hour before getting everyone roused? You're not going to the Sunday school with these trousers on, you'll affront me. Go and change them right now! Where do you think you are going at this time of day anyway?"

This mixture of question and instruction came from his bleary-eyed mother, Jean, as she surveyed her elder son from the warm comfort of her set-in bed in the kitchen. This tirade, of course, announced that she was now wide awake—a fact that dismayed Bill greatly

"Would you like a cup of tea and a slice of toast, Mam?" asked Bill, hoping that the offer would make her forget to question him further on his intentions. He lit the gas ring and grill on the old cooker while he spoke and then, as he started to fill the kettle he continued, "How many herring did Dad catch last week?"

This was a further attempt to allay the suspicions that he could see growing in his mother's eyes.

"Yes, I'd love a nice cup of tea and toast. And how would I know what herring he had? I didn't get a letter yesterday and even if I did, it would have been posted in the middle of the week. What are you up to anyway? It's not like you to be up so early in the morning, especially on a Sunday."

"I just thought that you could have been speaking to someone who might have known what the fishing was like," Bill continued. "Is this grill ready to put the bread under, or will I let it heat up a wee bit yet?"

"Let it heat a wee bit, it'll be red hot when it is ready—and don't cut that bread too thick, I don't like your usual doorstep slices!" The last was added as Bill took the loaf from the chipped white enamelled breadbox, and started rummaging in an untidy drawer in the kitchen table for the breadknife.

"I asked where you are going. Don't think I've forgotten!"

Seeing that further prevarication was useless, Bill reluctantly faced his mother and told her, as nonchalantly as he could, that he had arranged to go off early to Kilchousland—a favourite sandy bay which lay to the north of Campbeltown—for the day, with his pals.

"You can go to Kilchousland after Sunday school but not before, and that's final!"

Bill knew that protests would gain him nothing when his mother spoke in such tones, but he couldn't help trying.

"But Mam it'll not be worth going then," he whined. "We're walking from here on the shore road, along by Macringan's Point. It's a five-mile hike and if I don't get away soon, it won't be worth my while going at all. Please Mam, just this once?"

"You heard what I said. The kettle is singing now, it'll soon be boiling. Put the bread under the grill; it's hot enough now."

The beauty of the morning seemed somehow to have dulled suddenly and tears of self-pity were not far away, but Bill did as he was told.

"Look," said his mother, weakening—as mothers always do—when she saw the glistening tears start suddenly in his eyes, "I'll make you a nice piece, and you can go as soon as you come home but you have to go to the Sunday school first, and that's definite."

Sensing a possible compromise and hoping to lessen the blow to his plans, Bill pleaded; "Let me go straight from Sunday school, Mam, without coming home. I can take the piece with me and it'll save a lot of time. My pals will be at Kilchousland hours before me, as it is."

His mother reluctantly agreed to this, having first extracted a promise that he would take care of the new breeks into which he now had to change, and that he would not go swimming without supervision—"You're only twelve, far too

6

young to be in the water on your own."

A knock on the door heralded the arrival of his bosom pal Robert, a lad whose parents were not so enthusiastic about their son's religious instruction. Robert had no brothers or sisters, so Bill filled this gap in his life.

Bill quietly explained his predicament to Robert as they stood on the doorstep. "I wasn't worried too much about missing Sunday school, Rab, but my Mam says I have to go. I thought she'd forget, or that I could sneak out before she wakened."

"Tell her you're going, and then just plunk it, Bill!" was his friend's whispered solution to the problem.

The thought of dodging the commanded Sunday duty was something that instantly filled Bill with a dread of Divine retribution, an understandable reaction from one whose Scripture teacher's faith was firmly based upon the Calvinistically wrathful and jealous God of the Old Testament. Taking a day off was perhaps forgivable—only just—but lying to his mother on top of that would surely lead to punishment of the direst sort, from on high.

"No Rab, I'd better not. I'll maybe see you at the shore later. You just carry on."

After Robert had left, Bill finished his breakfast chores, a task for which he now spitefully wished he had never volunteered.

When he had finished and while his mother was sipping her tea, he climbed slowly back upstairs to his sparsely furnished attic bedroom, from whence he wistfully gazed over the roofs of the houses that lay between him and the still blue waters of the Loch. The air above the houses, he saw, was already beginning to shimmer slightly in the morning heat. Life was very unfair, he reasoned, as he indulged himself in the bittersweet descent into the mire of self-pity.

Tears were once more not far away.

God, if he were an understanding God, would never have sent such a perfect day on a Sunday, he argued. The more he thought along these lines, the more rebellious he became. This God, he now clearly saw, had deliberately devised all of the hateful things in Bill's life.

School—a waste of time!

Homework—an extension of his enforced incarceration in school! Why could he not do that which he desired above all else, leave school and be a fisherman? What was the worth of some dim remembrance of Shakespeare's plays, to a fisherman?

Stupid mathematics had never caught one single herring!

These mutinous thoughts gave sustenance to the seed that had been planted by Rab, and thus grew in his young mind the thought that—for the first time ever—he would take the enormous step of defying not only his mother, but his God also. To strengthen his rebellious resolve, he worked at convincing himself that he was not really doing anything wrong, and that he would make it all up to his Maker in due course. One day off, that was all that he desired.

The fateful decision made, he felt cheered but strangely apprehensive as he took off the old breeks and put on a better pair. He went back downstairs to where his mother had got out of bed and was busying herself around the small kitchen, clad in a threadbare woollen dressing gown.

"You're early enough for Sunday school, Bill," was her critical comment as he appeared.

"Comb your hair, and let me see you. I hope you washed at the back of your ears, young man! Hmm, your shoes could do with a lick of polish. Take them off. I won't have folk saying that you went out of this house dirty."

She too had been having remorseful thoughts to herself in the hour since her first-born had gone upstairs. She was torn between her love for him and the desire to please him, and her knowledge that the 'right thing' had to be done. She sat now on a low stool, bent and started to polish his shoes lovingly.

Bill looked down on his mother's head as it moved in time with her busy care-worn hands, and a great and hurting feeling of love came over him. How could he possibly harm someone who cared so much for him? 'Honour thy father and thy mother,' was the instruction in the Good Book. He knew instinctively that she had, with the enforced long absences of his father at the fishing, been both mother and father to him and Donald.

The peace of this tender moment was shattered by the noisy arrival of his brother into the kitchen. Too young for Sunday school, Donald—with his usual brotherly desire to torment his sibling—announced how sorry he was that "Poor Bill," as he put it, would miss some of the rare sunshine.

"You'll enjoy being inside in the nice cool church though," he concluded just before his mother stopped him.

That verbal assault from his brother was enough to tip the scales once more, in favour of plunking the Sunday school.

"There's your penny for the collection, and there are your pieces, I put a nice bit of cheese on them," announced his mother. "Take care of these good breeks now, you should really come home and change them by rights, but I'll trust you this time. Make sure you are back before teatime, or you'll be in big trouble and remember, no swimming unless there are grown-ups there."

Bill ran back up the stairs to the bedroom. Beside his bed was the small tin box that contained all his treasures. A small penknife and a hand magnifying glass were transferred into his pocket—he rarely went anywhere without them. He glanced into the wee diary—three years out of date now—into which he had laboriously copied all the wise sayings that had impressed him and helped form his young mind. His hope was that chance would lead him to find something that would justify the course to which he was now all but committed.

'The moving finger writes, and having writ moves on; nor all thy piety and wit can call it back to cancel half a line, nor all thy tears wash out one word of it,' he read from the first page he looked at.

Dismayed, he turned to another, only to see the old Arab proverb, *'Take what you want,' said Allah. 'Take what you want—and pay for it.'*

That's all a load of stupid old rubbish, thought Bill defiantly, as he threw the book back into the box. He didn't need anyone's approval for his actions. He was old enough to make up his own mind!

Downstairs again, he pocketed the sandwiches that his mother had made for him, but had to run the gauntlet of her embrace before gaining the waiting world outside.

"Take care, son, and remember to be home on time." The words wounded him as he thought of his forthcoming treachery to her.

The north-facing outside stairs led down into a large back courtyard that was bordered to the east and west by high walls. Opposite the dismal grey back of the tenement building the single-storey washing houses stood; one for every four families. There his mother did the washing every Tuesday. These wash-houses completed the enclosure of the back yard.

Bill ran across this yard below his mother's kitchen window, through the close that led to the front of the building, and on to freedom.

Down the brae he ran, forcing himself to abandon all his misgivings, and instead to think only of the pleasures which lay ahead.

He passed his maternal granny's house on the brae and then, as the ground levelled off, he turned left into the street where his other granny lived. Still he stayed on course for the Sunday school lest his mother—or more likely his brother—was watching from the bedroom window of their house.

Out of sight of his home Bill slowed to a stroll, beginning to feel the heat, which the clear sky had been promising.

There were few people around yet. It was too early for any of the Protestant worshippers to be about, and all the good Catholics were already at their devotions. He would have to get a move on however, he reckoned, before the people who lived in the big houses along the shore on the north side of the Loch took to the road on their way to church. It would be just like his luck to run into someone who would question him on his intentions. Maybe one of the Sunday school teachers lived along there and would comment on his sighting, to the lady who took his class.

These guilty thoughts sped his feet again and he ran, with the effortless ease of youth, along the road bordering the Loch, towards the path to Kilchousland. Not till he had gained this path and had passed all the houses, did he once more slow to a dawdle and take note of all that was going on around him.

He stopped to watch a busy kestrel hovering over some gorse bushes on the inland side of his path looking, he thought, for a late breakfast or an early lunch. A skylark, invisible high above, poured out its heart in song. The seabirds, he noted, seemed on the other hand to be affected by the heat as they floated aimlessly on the lethargic water at the mouth of the Loch—a Loch whose glassy surface was devoid of any trace of even the faintest air of wind.

Reaching a burn that was bridged by a single plank of wood Bill drank from its yet cool waters and lay down for a spell on the soft young bracken that grew beside it. Lulled by the whispering of the slow moving water close by his resting-place, he dozed quietly.

The Church bells wakened him.

Even from two miles away, Bill recognised the deep, sonorous, comforting baritone of the Lochend and the Longrow Churches. The Lorne Street and the Highland Parish bells were a little more highly pitched, and the Free Church had a sort of urgency about its tenor call that was at odds with the heavy somnolence of the day.

The sounds also awakened the feelings of guilt that lay not far below the surface of Bill's conscience, but with some effort he quickly consigned them whence they had come.

He unwrapped the sandwiches that his mother had so recently made, and munched on one of them thoughtfully.

There was something bothering him.

Not remorse for what he was doing, nothing to do with the fact that he was in defiance of his mother and his God. No, this was something that, in his drowsy state, he just couldn't recognise.

He shook himself, took another drink of water, and continued slowly on his way toward Kilchousland, still slightly troubled. Though he had no way of realising it, the fateful moment, his time of change, was very near now.

The morning air grew still warmer as the sun climbed, and the urgency of Bill's resolve to join his pals waned somewhat under its beneficent but soporific rays.

He wandered slowly down to the rocky water's edge hard by Macringan's Point, and sat on the rock bordering a shallow tidal pool, gazing over the burnished sea towards the great whale-like mass of Davaar Island, which stood silent guard over the entrance to the Loch.

The peace and beauty of the scene, when added to the heat-induced lethargy, caused his thoughts to slowly wander back over the events of the morning and he wondered if his Maker would somehow punish him for what he now clearly perceived as his wickedness.

He recalled the dark evening last winter when he, idle in company with some of his pals, had openly defied God by repeating aloud all of the profanities they had often heard, but had never until then articulated. He had waited in trembling fear for a bolt of lightning from heaven to strike him dead for his sins that night and he recalled his great relief and puzzlement, when nothing happened.

He lay down on his stomach by the sea pool, gazing into its cool waters, watching the baby fish as they, startled by his movements, darted to new positions they perceived as being safer. Now they hovered again under the sheltering fronds of seaweed, their tiny fins shimmering in the reflected sunlight. Cautious crabs, their presence betrayed only by their stirrings, lurked—trusting in their camouflage—on the sand close by the stones under which they would scuttle for shelter at the first sign of movement anywhere.

What happened next was something that Bill would never quite come to terms with in his lifetime.

He lay still, in a state somewhere between sleep and waking, his mind barely active. Why, he wondered, were the wee fish scared into hiding? He felt sure that they had some sort of intelligence but their heads were so tiny compared to his, that any brain they possessed must be minuscule.

The answer—that this behaviour was bred into them—eased into his somnolent mind without any conscious effort on his behalf. He sensed that this was the correct reply to the question that his subconscious thought had posed.

'I wonder,' he asked himself, 'If I would get answers to the other problems that bother me?'

Slowly and lazily he reviewed his life to date. What were the major doubts regarding his future?

School came immediately to mind. Why did he have to continue learning those things that he knew full well would be of no value to him in his life as a fisherman?

Answers to the unspoken questions formed quietly within his mind. He became certain that he would leave Campbeltown and would be a successful fisherman. He also gained the realisation that he should work harder at school. Learning was important.

Long afterwards, thinking on the events of the day Bill could never be quite sure of all that happened that warm morning. Perhaps it was all a part of this mysterious 'growing up' he had heard about. At the time it happened he felt quite relaxed, and knew somehow that this inner 'voice' was a gift of some kind. Later on he would not be certain if he had fallen asleep in the hot sun and dreamed it all or—and this he would come to think was much more likely—if he just happened to be 'tuned in' to something in his inner mind, some ancient long-forgotten power. In time he would learn more of the gift of 'second-sight' and would believe that he had been given an insight to this mystic power.

Bill woke up so gradually that he wasn't sure when the dream-like state ended, and conscious thought began again. It was still hot where he lay but his rocky couch now felt hard and uncomfortable so he sat up, and then stood.

When he looked around he saw that he was still alone on the shore, but towards the Brown Head on the Arran coast he could now see two sails shimering in the heat, the only signs that he was not alone in the world. The boats he saw were drifting with the tide rather than sailing, he reckoned, but such was his love for the sea that he would have given a lot to be there with them, drifting or not.

Bill put his hands into his pockets.

This was a mistake. His idle fingers found the unaccustomed shape of a penny piece, the one his mother had given him for the collection plate. The find brought him back to the present with a jolt!

He wondered if this whole episode with the voice was a result of worrying over his disobedience to his mother, and his fear of what the outcome of plunking the

Sunday school might be. Had the voice been real, or had he imagined the whole episode?

He reckoned that the best thing he could do in order to get back to normality was to continue on his way to Kilchousland—it wasn't too far away now. There, hopefully, he would meet up with Rab, and the rest of his pals.

Bill set off briskly on his interrupted walk along the shore, his mind still in turmoil over what had happened to him.

Why and when would he leave his place of birth to go somewhere unknown? Would he have a choice in the matter, or would it all just happen? The more he thought about it the more he became convinced that it was all a dream, and that he would gradually forget it.

These thoughts filled his mind to the exclusion of just about all else until the sound of happy young voices at play made him realise that he was close to his pals, a realisation that put all of these deep thoughts out of his mind for some time to come.

Off came the good breeks and the shirt and naked, in the confidence that his pals would not be in the water in the buff if there were any spying eyes around them, he joined the others in one of their favourite summer pastimes of feeling with their feet for the wonderfully camouflaged flounders which might be lying on the sandy bottom. The rest of the hot day passed in the innocent play of children who had not yet been indoctrinated into the wicked ways of the world, and it was with great reluctance—and empty stomachs—that the happy band finally got dressed and set off on the long walk home.

During the rest of that summer Bill wondered on several quiet occasions, just what had happened to him as he lay on the rocky shore, but of course he never reached any conclusion other than that it must be part of 'growing up.'

Autumn came, and the lengthening nights brought different attractions, games in which all the children who lived in and around the tenement joined. Almost all of these games were started by forming two teams, one of which—the hunters—sought to catch and then secure members of the opposition in the den, which was usually agreed to be the doorway of the Co-operative shop just across the road from their homes.

The tenement was ideally placed for this kind of play. Whilst the front of it looked on to the street that led to the town, the rear was bounded, behind the washhouses, by a hill whose steep slopes were liberally adorned with bushes and small trees, terrain which was well suited for the concealment of young fugitives. Almost the only shortcoming of this playground was that it was too close to home and because of this they were never out of earshot of their mothers' unwelcome call to "Come home, it's bedtime."

This was the time when the first awakening of feelings for the opposite sex started to develop in Bill's young mind. No education was given on this subject either at home or in school, so all the knowledge that he and his peers gleaned came from older boys and was, Bill would later discover, more often than not figments of their informants' over-fertile imaginations!

What was certain was that during the games they played he now sought out the company of certain girls to whom he had gradually started to feel greatly attracted, girls who had—not so long ago—been thought objects worthy only of derision, by him and his pals.

One of them in particular, Sophie Smith, appeared to respond more actively than any of the others to his innocent advances. She laughed more loudly than anyone else when he joked, cheered him on when he played football and more importantly, she seemed as keen as he was to cuddle cosily close together when they were hiding from their would-be captors, in a dark corner, during a game of hide and seek.

Surely she didn't feel the same strange urges as he? Did she feel the great warmth that seemed to him to be generated between them in the dark closeness of their as yet innocent embrace?

Girls, he reasoned, would never think the same dark thoughts as the ones that invaded his mind during that delicious period between waking and sleeping, as he lay in his warm bed. What did girls really look like, he wondered? What was the mysterious physical difference in their bodies? Did Sophie know more of this mysterious sex business than he did and if so, would she be prepared to share this knowledge? He wished that he had had a sister. That would have removed his ignorance on the physical difference, he thought—and then was immediately filled with shame at having had such base imaginings.

Part of the answer came one day from the most unlikely source.

Rab and he were exploring a wood near their home, accompanied by Kate, Sophie's big sister. Kate was two years older than either Rab or Bill, and usually sought the company of more mature boys.

"I'm just going behind this bush for a minute; don't you be peeking," she announced.

Something in her voice gave the lie to this admonition. Rab and Bill avoided eye contact as they followed her and then stood and looked on in embarrassed amazement as Kate squatted beside the bush, pulled down her underwear, and proceeded to urinate.

Bill was shocked at first by what appeared to be a total lack of any appendages in the area between her legs, but bending for a closer look revealed that there was in fact that thing—more an omission than anything else in Bill's opinion—to which the older boys had slyly referred.

"I told you not to look!" she cried in what was obviously mock anger and, having waited until they had seen all there was to see she then continued—"You will have to do the same now, I want to have a look at you."

Rab and Bill took to their heels at that and fled, pursued by Kate's mocking laughter.

It was an incident that they hid deep in their minds and never referred to again, but now they both knew just what the physical difference between the male and female bodies consisted of. They were no wiser however as to just what the strange urges in their blood meant, or of how these differences could be exploited.

Winter came.

With the cold and rainy West Coast weather that accompanied this season, there was less scope for playing outside.

Because of the enforced absence of his father at the fishing, Bill spent a great deal of his formative time with an old fisherman, Donald Black, who lived alone in the same tenement.

'Ban' is Gaelic for 'white' so Donald, because of his strong mop of white hair, was called 'Ban' by all his acquaintances. He had never married, but had an almost inexhaustible amount of patience with his young friends. He was a large man, who had obviously been very powerful in his youth. His huge red beak of a nose gave rise to the rumour that he was very fond of whisky, but in all the time that Bill spent with him, he saw no evidence to support this theory. Ban lived alone in a sparsely furnished room-and-kitchen, the door to which was in the close that served as entry to the back of the tenement.

Although Ban's habit of occasionally hanging some of his washing out to dry at his front window scandalised some of the ladies who lived in the tenement, their real problem was with his hobby, which involved keeping ferrets in his coal store! Ban used them when catching rabbits, a pastime that he pursued less often with his advancing years.

"Did you see these long-johns and semmits hanging right beside the close-mouth yesterday? It's an absolute disgrace!"

This was a common complaint when two or more of the gossiping tenants met, and was often followed by a long discourse about the ferrets—of which the ladies seemed to have an unreasonable fear—and what they perceived as his lack of personal cleanliness.

Ban's dress varied little from day to day. He habitually wore stout boots on his feet and his heavy trousers were of the variety known locally as 'fearnoughts.' They showed not the faintest vestige of a crease down the centres of the legs and were constructed of such heavy material that they gave the impression that they would stand erect by themselves. The entrances to the voluminous pockets, into which Ban's hands were habitually deeply buried, were, unlike normal trousers, parallel to the waistband. An ancient navy blue fisherman's jersey completed the rig that remained almost the same regardless of season, although he would don a well-worn tweed jacket on a cold winter day. His flat cap seldom left his head. On a warm summer day, when he was asked if the jersey was not making him feel very hot, he would smilingly reply, "If it keeps out the cold, it'll keep out the heat too!"

In Ban's company Bill gained a great deal of knowledge that would serve him well in his life as a fisherman, and also absorbed much of the ancient culture and folklore of the fishing community into which he had been born.

He learned the basics of net mending, and was able to splice ropes with confidence long before he left school.

Learning the art of mending nets was accomplished with the help of an old piece of netting that Ban had obtained somewhere. He would simply tear holes in it and tell Bill to "get on with it now!" When he became reasonably good at making simple repairs, Ban introduced him to 'stilters.' This was when a mesh that consisted of four sides was corrupted, either by design or by accident, and now had either five or three sides.

A stilter, or as Ban's accent would have it, 'steelter,' was used when taking a gore out of a net. A triangular piece of net would be cut from a regularly shaped panel, and both sides were then mended together. A gore, Ban explained, helped to shape the net into a bag, when in the water. If one was made accidentally when, for example, putting in a new piece of netting, it would cause problems that would require a great deal of work to correct.

The taboos of life at sea were well explained to him also, and this learning would stay with him for all of his life.

Salmon, pigs, rats and rabbits, were all forbidden words, being replaced by 'red fish,' 'dourkeys,' 'long-tails' and 'bunnies.' Here he heard for the first time the oft repeated tale of the young lad who, when the teacher wrote 'pig' on the blackboard during a spelling lesson in the primary school replied, "Dourkey!" when asked what that spelt. His father, he explained to the baffled teacher, would be very unhappy if he was to say the other word! Swan Vestas matches and white handled knives were banned from fishing boats, as were ministers of religion and most women—red haired ones being considered particularly unlucky. The bad luck that would certainly be brought on by the accidental spilling of salt had to be forestalled by throwing a pinch of the spill over one's right shoulder, but one had to use the left hand to do so. If anyone turned back to their home, having forgotten something, they had to sit for a few moments before leaving the house again. To pick up the item that had been forgotten and to leave with it immediately would certainly bring bad luck.

"And see when you've finished eating a boiled egg," said Ban, "You need to put holes in the bottom of the empty shells. If you don't the witches will paddle out to sea in them in a storm, and sink fishing boats!"

If a jersey was by chance put on back-to-front, it had to remain that way. Taking it off and replacing it the proper way would bring bad luck. If something was accidentally broken, two matches had to be broken at once. Breakages, Ban told Bill, always came in threes.

When going to sea, turning the boat 'widdershins,' or 'against the sun'—in other words anti-clockwise—in the harbour, was to be avoided at all costs. Shoes, particularly new ones, must never be placed on the table and sticking a knife into the mast was just as certain to bring a gale as was whistling, aboard the boat. If a proscribed word was accidentally used, grasping metal of some form whilst at the same time crying out—"Cold iron!"—might possibly compensate for the sin.

Bill was also made aware of the age-old respectability of the fishing profession.

"Where did the good Lord go when He wanted Disciples, eh?"

Ban often asked this rhetorical question and Bill soon learned not to answer it immediately, thereby giving Ban the opportunity he sought—to provide the answer himself. "I'll tell you where He went, He went to the Sea of Galilee where He knew He would find fishermen; that's what He did, and don't you ever forget it!"

Ban was, in common with most of his breed, a very superstitious man, and he also had a deep-seated belief in the supernatural. This might have appeared to be in conflict with his professed Christianity, but in fact it showed the simple acceptance of his upbringing. There was a definite, if somewhat mixed-up link between his forbears' primitive Pagan beliefs, and his current claim to being Christian. He moved easily on the strangely common ground between Christian spirituality and the ancient religions. Bill saw instances of this for himself in his Catholic friends when they blessed themselves. More often than not this was as much as a good luck invocation, as in prayer.

Ban talked of ghosts or 'bockans,' as his Gaelic upbringing would have him say, in a comfortable, matter-of-fact sort of way. They seemed to be a familiar, in-built part of his everyday life and he acted as though everyone else shared his beliefs.

He took great delight in sitting round his meagre coal fire in the dim gaslight that he retained in preference to the new-fangled but colder-seeming electric light, on a dark winter night with some of his many friends, regaling them with tales of the supernatural. This delight was only surpassed when another around the fire would take up the role of storyteller, especially if they recounted one that he had never heard before or—more likely—one that he had heard, and had forgotten.

Bill used to crouch quiet and unseen on the perimeter of these gatherings, absorbing the deliciously frightening atmosphere. One night he was alone with Ban.

"Tell me one of your bockan stories," he pleaded.

"No, you are far too young for that," replied Ban. "Your mother wouldn't be pleased with me if she heard that I was filling your head with stories of bockans."

"Do you really believe in ghosts, Ban?"

"Well now, my boy, that's a big question for a wee man. I would just say that you'll find out all these things for yourself when you get older. Just you keep an open mind, and remember that nothing is impossible, and that no-one knows everything."

"But Ban, I have heard a lot of stories in here, are they all just a lot of rubbish?"

"No, they're not all rubbish. I've told you that there are some things in this life that we cannot explain very easily. Just you bide your time and you'll find out what is what."

Bill sat quietly for a while, looking pensively and deeply into the glowing coals of the fire. Funny, he thought, how they took on all sorts of strange shapes—swirling and changing as you watched.

"You're very quiet," said Ban after a while. "Is there something bothering you?"

Bill thought for a long time before answering. The fact that he had never heard Ban mock anyone, nor take advantage of his or her inexperience helped him to decide that he would confide his doubts.

"Something strange happened to me last summer, Ban, and I'm not sure about it. I've wondered about it for a long time now, and it bothers me a lot. Will you not laugh at me if I tell you what happened?"

What on earth is coming here, wondered the old man. He resolved that whatever it was, he would respect the feelings of the young lad who sat staring into the fire.

"No, my boy. You know I'm not in the habit of laughing at anyone, nor of telling tales about them."

Bill waited for a long time, and then he spoke. He told old Ban exactly what had happened on that summer day when he had plunked the Sunday school.

"Am I going daft, do you think?" he concluded, turning his worried face to Ban at last.

There was a silence that seemed to Bill to last forever, then the old man spoke.

"I believe I know what might have happened to you, my boy, but you are not to bother about it. Some people are given a gift of second sight, which means that they can sometimes foretell the future. I'm not saying that this is what happened to you, exactly, but perhaps when you are in the correct frame of mind you will be allowed a wee glimpse of what may be to come. If that is correct—and I don't say that it is, mind you—you must never misuse that gift. You won't be able to call it up when you want to. It will come whenever you are in a certain frame of mind, or when something is bothering you a lot. You may be able to control it more as you get older, or perhaps you will lose the power altogether. The old people knew far more about this sort of gift than we ever will. Maybe it is a good thing that this knowledge is being forgotten, I don't know. Just you listen to what this voice told you. I'm sure it didn't suggest anything that will harm anyone at all, and I'd be willing to bet that it never will. You should stick in at the school though, and make the most of your time there. If there are better opportunities somewhere else when you leave school and go to the fishing then don't hesitate, off you go!"

Bill listened intently to what he was being told. It all made more sense now. Somehow it was in line with what he already intuitively felt, and it was reassuring that Ban did not suggest—as Bill had feared he might—that the lad's mind was suspect in some way.

Another long silence ensued, punctuated only by the crackling of coal on the meagre fire.

His next question to Ban, "What do you think of lassies?" provoked a great cackle of laughter before the reply came.

"Now then my boy, it is about time you were away home to your bed. You've bothered an old man enough for one night."

Ban also introduced Bill to the special language used by fishermen when they hailed another boat as they as they passed in the night.

"Puckle tonight?" was a common hail to another boat, to discover whether or not they had been lucky.

Answers varied from "A wheen o' baskets," which meant just a few baskets, to the giving of a definite quantity—for example "A couple of hundred baskets."

"Two or three baskets," was usually said in a glum manner, as it was less than "A wheen"!

"A wee puckle," could really mean anything at all, but if it was said in a smug tone, it meant that the one questioned was well fished, but was not about to reveal the exact amount!

Ban cackled with delight as he recalled the occasion when a pair of Carradale boats was fortunate enough to have caught more than a thousand baskets, early one evening. They almost immediately discharged this fine shot to a 'klondiker'—the fishermen's nickname for the trawler-sized boats that followed the fleets around, buying up the catches on the grounds, either boxing or salting the herring into barrels before taking them to market. When they had finished discharging, they dropped their anchors for a few hours sleep before resuming fishing.

They encountered a pair of Campbeltown boats in the dark hour before dawn and were hailed, "Puckle tonight?"

In all innocence the man forward on the boat so questioned replied accurately, "A thousand and fourteen baskets."

Ban fairly chuckled as he recalled that there was nearly a riot that morning because the Campbeltown man was able—even in the dim morning light—to see that the boat being interrogated was not loaded, and so was led to believe that the Carradale fellow was being sarcastic!

Bill gained practical experience of the fishing profession on the odd occasion when he was taken, against his mother's wishes, to sea for the night on his father's boat. He would be the first to confess that much of his time on these trips was spent hanging over the rail being sick, however, and that he was rarely able to keep awake much beyond midnight!

On one never-to-be-forgotten occasion when his brother and his mother went to spend a week with his aunt in Greenock, he chose to spend the entire week at sea. They were fishing out of Tarbert and the weather was glorious. It was summer and the nights were short, so Bill became acclimatised to the change of being awake all night and sleeping in the daytime. At that time he felt like a real fisherman, following his father up the pier to the sales ring in the mornings with the sample of their catch, feeling vastly superior to those whose luck during the previous night's fishing had not been so good.

Schooling went on as usual, but to the great delight of his teachers and of his mother, who still nursed fading hopes that her son would enter the ministry or some profession other than fishing, Bill now displayed a more healthy approach to learning. If learning would help him in his chosen profession then he would stick at it, he reasoned.

Chapter Two

Bill left school without a backward glance, just before his fourteenth birthday, and many years would pass before he gave proper credit to the band of dedicated teachers who had tried their best to instil a degree of learning into his often-unwilling brain.

A fisherman! That is what he was now!

A compromise had been arranged between his parents. His mother, who had fought hard to stop him becoming a fisherman, had realised that she had lost the battle to keep him at school and had bowed to the inevitable. She insisted, however, that he should not go on his father's boat and in deference to her wishes her husband, John, had arranged that Bill should start his chosen career with one of the oldest and most respected fishermen in the town, Archie Blair, aboard the *Bengullion*. This, his mother reckoned, would mean that there was less chance of sacrificing both husband and son to the sea's anger. Such tragedies were not unknown in fishing communities when a boat was lost with men from the same family in her crew.

In the months before he left school his mother went through the ritual of knitting a blue woollen jersey for him. This age-old, love-driven task commenced by her getting Bill involved in what to him was the boring task of holding the hanks of finest Irish wool between his outstretched hands, while she wound it into balls. These jerseys were all made to the knitters' own individual pattern. On too many occasions the bodies of lost fishermen had been recovered from the sea after the ravages of time and the attentions of crabs and fish had rendered them unrecognisable. They were returned to their loved ones for burial after one of the knitters—who had recognised the pattern—had wailed a name over the still-wet garment.

As his jersey slowly took shape, Bill had to stand immobile in silent protest whilst his mother measured it against his still-growing body.

Sea-boots were next. These leather, thigh-length boots were a major expense to the family, and Bill was taught how to apply many coats of dubbin—a trusted preservative—to them in an effort to keep the ravages of the salt sea at bay.

His canvas oilskins—locally called a doaper—and his sou'wester had to be hung out to dry after each waterproofing coat of a mixture of linseed oil and varnish. The correct mix was vital. Too much varnish and it would crack, allowing water to pass through. Not enough varnish, and the oil would remain for only a short time; slippery on the doaper's surface. This mixture gave off a particular smell, which would become so imprinted on his memory that he would never forget it.

Sea-boot stockings, thick knitted in black and white oiled Shetland wool, which also had its own very distinctive smell, completed his sea-going wardrobe.

The age-old system of allocating crews' duties was grossly unfair in many peoples' minds. It dictated that the youngest member of the crew had to cook. This task was carried out in addition to his other duties as a deckhand and, as no formal training in cooking skills was available, the learning of the basic culinary art was a skill that had to be picked up as one went along.

It was January and fishings in the Clyde were poor so Bill's first trip was to be to the 'North,' the local name for the winter fishing grounds in the Minches. This meant that, as shops were scarce where they would be fishing, the boat had to be provisioned for at least two weeks. January weather in the North was notoriously bad, and Bill was secretly a little wary of just how his stomach would cope.

Nothing in Bill's education had prepared him for the intricacies of purchasing food on a large scale. Ordering stores that would feed six men for two weeks, was therefore completely beyond him. Fortunately the under-manager in the local Co-operative shop was an old hand at the game so, under his benevolent guidance, the food was ordered and packed into large cardboard breadboxes, to be taken by barrow down to the boat. Once there, the boxes had to be lowered down to the deck and then manoeuvred down the narrow hatch that led to the forecastle. There they were unpacked and stowed in the lockers below the bunks and under the seats. Dozens of tins of meat, beans, peas and other vegetables, tinned fruit, condensed and evaporated milk—all these were piled high in the lockers that Bill was told were the most vulnerable to dampness. Dry tea, coffee, salt, flour and oats and other items that would suffer most from water, were placed in the dubious dryness of the locker nearest the fire.

The empty cardboard breadboxes were much sought after for lining the men's bunks in the forlorn hope that they would keep the ever-present dampness at bay. It was not long before Bill had decided for himself that this seeming comfort was short lived, all they really did was absorb and retain the dampness they were meant to repel!

Coal, fuel for the tiny stove on which almost all of the cooking would be done, and which was the only form of heating on the boat, was lowered down the same hatch and stowed in a locker below the benches that ringed the forecastle.

Bill was then warned that he must never break up the larger lumps of coal by hitting them with an axe or hammer, while they lay in the locker. This, he was told, would cause the planks on which the coal rested to spring away from the frames to which they were nailed, thus causing leaks. He had first to lift the coal in his hand and then hit it—not a good idea when one was in the midst of cooking, and when clean hands were desirable!

Fresh meat was kept in the hold, the coolest place on the boat and the paraffin, fuel for the single burner Primus stove, was kept in the engine-room.

The final task before sailing was accomplished by carrying fresh water in a ten-gallon can from the tap on the pier, and filling it into the main water tank. The carrying tank was finally lashed—filled with water—on deck, under the crew's supervision. This, they explained, would ensure a supply of cold drinking water for the men on deck.

When he had the stores all safely stowed, Bill looked around him at the forecastle that was to be his home now. It was roughly triangular in shape, around fifteen feet long and ten feet wide at the after end, narrowing to a point forward. There were six bunks, three on each side. Below the forward top bunks were the cupboards that held the myriad of tins and jars that he had taken aboard. There was a wooden bench on each side fitted with lifting lids that gave access to the dank storage space underneath. The whole forecastle was varnished, but this had been long stained dark by the smoke from the small fire that stood against the aft bulkhead, and from the pipes favoured by the older men. A stoutly built sliding wooden door in the aft bulkhead, led into the hold.

A wooden table was screwed to the floor (Bill was soon to learn to call this floor the platform) of the forecastle. When its collapsing leafs were raised they formed an extended triangular shape that roughly matched that of the forecastle.

There were two round enamelled basins lying beside the stove. One, the white one, was slightly the larger and was reserved for the weekly ritual of washing and shaving. This usually took place in the hold where the men took turns to strip to the waist and soap themselves well. Rinsing was done with a wet cloth! There was neither bath nor shower in Bill's home, but habitually he and his brother bathed every Sunday evening crouched up in the old zinc bath, in front of the fire. This bath—kept under the set-in bed in the kitchen—was filled with water that had been heated in pots and kettles on the gas cooker. Now he would get a bath only when he got home, and that might be five or six weeks hence. He was lucky at that, he was told. The East Coast drifter men who fished out of Yarmouth and Lowestoft in the autumn, also had to wait until they got home, and they were usually away for around three months!

The other basin, a brown one, was used for holding the water for washing up the cooking utensils, plates, and cups, knives and forks. A small tin that had once contained peas hung by a piece of twine that was tied to a rusting nail, beside the basins. Nail holes had been punched all around it so that it looked like a colander, and it contained the remains of a bar of Fairy soap. This tin was held over the dishwashing basin, and the hot water for washing the dishes was poured through it, thus creating 'sapples'—suds.

Bill was instructed to check carefully before emptying the used water overboard from this basin. It was not at all uncommon for spoons, knives or forks to be thrown out with the water.

He was told of his predecessor who, one fine summer afternoon as they lay at anchor, emptied overboard the basin that still held an unnoticed spoon.

"Twinkle, twinkle, little spoon. Knives and forks will follow soon," he was alleged to have recited as he watched the spoon flicker in the sunshine on its way toward the seabed!

Knives, forks and spoons were contained in a narrow drawer that was situated under the centre section of the table, and the cups and plates were held in one of the cupboards on the port side. However, Bill was soon to learn that one soup plate served for a complete meal.

For example, soup would be eaten from this plate and then, after a good scraping with the spoon, the meat, potatoes and vegetables would be piled on to it. When that course had been finished, it would then be filled with tinned fruit, often topped with thick custard—creamy, as it had perforce to be made with evaporated milk. The more fastidious among the crew might 'clean' their plate with a slice of bread before putting the sweet on it. They then ate this bread, of course. Waste not—want not indeed! The reply when Bill commented on this apparent lack of hygiene was, "Well, it'll all be mixed up in your belly anyway, so why not save on the washing up?"

Any newspapers that were taken aboard, he was told, had to be kept, as they were used to stop plates sliding in all directions on the table when the boat was being thrown around in bad weather. The newspaper was spread on the table, and then dampened. Plates were then placed on top of this makeshift tablecloth. They were also used as toilet paper!

Bill was to sleep in the bottom bunk aft on the starboard side, directly below the skipper's. This bunk was the nearest one to the vertical wooden ladder that led up through the sliding hatch, to the deck. Because of its position it was prone to be soaked when anyone left the hatch open and spray came aboard, so it was not a popular one. The men would take suitcases aboard with changes of clothes. These were kept in the bunks except of course when they were occupied; then they cluttered the linoleum-covered platform.

The 'toilet' consisted of a five-gallon tin—that had contained lubricating oil—which usually dwelt on deck behind the wheelhouse. A few minutes work with a hacksaw or a chisel removed the top. Then around three-quarters of the exposed edge had a piece of bicycle tyre lashed to it. When required it would have half of a bucket of seawater emptied into it before it was taken down to the warmth of the engine room. Most of the old daily newspapers were consigned there and the user would perch on it until his business was done, reading a page of the paper before putting it to its ultimate use. It was then taken on deck and the contents dumped overboard—to leeward—before it was rinsed and replaced in its usual abode.

The appointed day for sailing dawned and Bill awoke to the sound of gale-driven raindrops spattering on his bedroom window.

His mother, mindful of the anguish she had seen in the eyes of others whose sons had been lost to the sea and hopeful to the last, suggested that there was far too much wind for the boat to sail and reminded Bill tearfully that he didn't have to go—he could always go back to school again.

These loving pleas fell upon deaf ears. Bill knew his destiny, and was anxious to be away.

The boat sailed that morning headed North through Kilbrannan Sound for the Crinan canal, a route that would save the stormy passage through the strong tides that race around the Mull of Kintyre. Bill's excitement at being at last at sea was soon replaced with another feeling, one that was to become a frequent companion to him for several years, as seasickness took charge. As soon as they had cleared the sheltered waters of the Loch and had passed Macringan's Point, where Bill had his strange experience, the boat started to roll. This stirred up all the dirty bilge water, releasing a horrible stench—which was not improved by the habit of half of the crew who were addicted to smoking the malodorous thick black or—just as bad—bogey roll, pipe tobacco!

Sympathy had no part in the makeup of his shipmates. They had all been down the same path, and they knew that the only way to overcome the illness was to attempt to ignore it and get on with the job.

Bill prepared potatoes for the lunch, retching pitifully into the same bucket as held the peelings. Food was the furthest thing from his mind but he had been told what to do, and there was nothing for it but to obey.

The rest of the trip north, with the exception of the blessed calm of the four-hour passage through the canal, passed in a seasick haze. Bill took no real interest in what was going on around him, or in the magnificence of the scenery through which they were sailing until at last they turned into the slightly calmer waters of Loch Nevis, their chosen hunting ground.

Bill had long known that the relatively new practice of catching herring by ring-net was not yet universally accepted, and that there were still places where any deviation from the age-old method of drift netting was definitely frowned upon.

"Will we get into any bother here with the locals over our nets?" he asked of Dennis, a stocky pipe-smoking deckhand, and the oldest man on the *Bengullion*.

"No," answered Dennis, his old, pale blue, sea-wise eyes searching restlessly around the loch for any sign that herring might be shoaling beneath the spume that covered its wind-riven waters, "You won't get any bother here. The locals don't really like us too much, but I think they will be using our nets soon, themselves. It is only when we go further north and west, that we'll have to be careful. They can be a wicked lot up there, but despite that, we are all after same thing—the Silver Darlings." Then, anticipating Bill's next question he continued: "That's the nickname for herring. Aye, they're the silver thread that binds us all together in the long run."

"Where's the harbour here, Dennis?" asked Bill as he gazed at the desolate rocky mountains which bounded the Loch, ground upon which only heather grew, and which appeared to be devoid of any habitation.

"Harbour?" snorted Denis. "There's no real harbour here. If we catch any herring, we'll take them to the luggers (another name for klondikers) at Tarbert. No, not the Tarbert in Lochfyne," he continued with a smile, once again anticipating

Bill's next question.

"There's a wee bay called Tarbert up ahead of us. That's where the luggers lie, and that's the only harbour you'll see here. The railway has just opened up in Mallaig and there is a pier there, but that was built for steamers taking railway passengers to the Islands. There's nothing there but a few crofts, and a scatter of houses built for the railway workers. Maybe some day we will be sending herring by rail, but I just cannot see it myself. No, luggers are the only way forward."

"There's another small pier of sorts in a bay well to the south of us called Arisaig, but there's nothing but two or three houses there. No more questions now. I'm looking to see if there are any gannets or herring gulls about; we're here to catch herring, not for geography lessons," he added with a good-natured grin.

Bill went forward and lay on the deck with his head cocked over the rail. He gazed at the bleak prospect that lay before him. The barrenness of the hills in their winter drab around him was strangely at one with the leaden grey of the water below, but was totally at odds with the green fertile hills of his homeland, Kintyre. He allowed his mind to wander as he lay there and gradually, despite the cold, a feeling of peace and contentment came over him. He gradually drifted off into the same sort of trance-like state that he had experienced a few years ago. The feeling of having arrived at his new home, grew within him.

"Hey, boy, is that kettle near boiling? We're due a cup of tea, are we not?"

The cry from old Archie, the grizzled skipper, brought him abruptly back to earth, and he scuttled guiltily below to tend his fire. As he waited for the kettle to boil he reflected on his experience of a few minutes ago and remembered old Ban's words to him. Yes, he felt certain that he was somehow fulfilling his destiny in coming to this spot, and he felt better than he had done since he came aboard—was it only two days ago?

The wind strengthened quickly again as darkness fell, and before long their neighbour boat—ring-netters always worked in pairs—put on the dim lights at the side of his wheelhouse. This was the recognised sign, in the days before radio, for the two boats to come together for a discussion. It was soon agreed, when the boats were close enough to allow the skippers to chat, that the strength of wind had made the night unworkable and that they should go to anchor—a decision that was generally welcomed by the freezing men on deck.

That night, before turning in, Bill gazed around the dimly lit, smoky forecastle. He lay lazily on his elbow, right forward at the apex of the varnished den—once bright, but now dark-stained with the years of smoke, idly scanning his crewmates.

Archie Blair, the short stocky middle-aged skipper, was puffing on his pipe as he perused a tattered old chart. He wore an old pair of one-legged reading spectacles that seemed almost to defy gravity as they perched near the end of his large nose. Even though he was at rest, he still exuded an air of authority. This was the man upon whose expertise all their livelihoods—and lives—would rely. Archie had been married for many years but had no family.

Malcolm McKay, who looked to be not very much older than Bill and who was just as slightly built, sat hunched over his skinny knees, gazing into the glowing coals of the fire, drawing deeply on a Woodbine cigarette as he did so. He was married and had reluctantly left his young wife to look after their two children, the elder of them being just two years old. Malcolm constantly talked of getting a job ashore where he could witness and be part of their growing up but he was, like the rest, a fisherman born.

John Anderson, the tall thin engineer, had his elbows on the rickety table as he intently scanned his oil-encrusted fingernails. He had lank black greasy hair, and Bill wondered mischievously if it was like that because of the oil he worked among.

Alec Blair, a cousin of the skipper's, though a fair bit taller and more heavily built than his kin, had his eyes shut as he reclined upon the locker, resting his balding head on the edge of his bunk. Bill was not at all fond of this man. It appeared as though the only time Alec spoke to him was when he had a criticism to make on some aspect of his cooking. No other member of the crew ever commented on these remarks but Bill knew from their reactions that they did not approve of his constant carping.

Verbal ill-treatment of young men was commonplace on these boats. Bill had more than once heard the tale of the young cook who had fled on deck in tears and had sought solace in the wheelhouse with the skipper. Questioning revealed that one of the crew had used the word 'bastard,' when chastising him. The skipper, a good living man, stopped the boat and went below.

"Who called the cook a bastard?" he demanded of his crew.

The reply, "Who called the bastard a cook?" passed into the legion of stories on fishing that would be told and re-told wherever fishermen congregated.

Old Dennis O'Hara also sat at the table. His short-stemmed pipe was reeking as he read a cowboy novel; his reading glasses, like Archie's, perched precariously on the end of his nose. He was Bill's favourite, the only one of the crew to have shown any real kindness to him since they had left home. The oldest man aboard by some years, he sported a thick shock of white hair that was matched by the beginnings of the beard that he, in common with all the others, who had not shaved since they left home, was sporting now. He suffered from some ailment that caused his hands to shake very badly. Bill was later to watch with growing apprehension as Dennis had his weekly shave. He first of all sharpened the open razor that he used, by stropping it on a leather belt then, having washed, he applied shaving soap to his face with a sparse-haired brush. Bill's interest intensified into open-mouthed horror as Dennis, satisfied with the lather he had worked into his bristling beard, took up the aptly named and lethal looking cut-throat razor in his trembling hand. This razor shook—seemingly unstoppably—until it made contact with the old man's face then it was drawn quickly down in one smooth swoop. Bill was quite certain that some day Dennis would cut his nose clean off his face!

Bill was to learn much from this man. In the summer months he would lie forward with him on the foredeck for most of the short nights, head leaning out over the side, eyes fixed on the water below, looking for herring in the 'burning,' as Denis called the phosphorescence in the sea.

Herring were startled by the passage of the boat above and their quick movements stirred the phosphorescence so much that it caused a lightening in the darkness beneath, referred to by Dennis as 'a change in the water.' Trails left by individual fish near the surface were easily spotted, but great experience was required to detect the presence of a shoal that lay deep—the change in the water was not easily recognised. In order to cause more movement in the herring some men would bang the anchor stock on the rail of the boat to frighten the fish, but Dennis relied on an old wooden mallet.

Many times his call to the skipper of, "Ease her down!" would be followed by the question to Bill: "Did you see that, boy?" Too often, Bill had missed the sign that old Dennis's experienced eye had spotted.

"Right lads, it's time for bed. The wind could ease, and we'll be off to sea, so you'd better get some sleep while you can." This instruction came as Archie stood up, stretched himself and replaced the chart in the rough rack that had been formed by nailing pieces of wood between the timber frames that supported the deckhead above the cast-iron stove—the driest place in the boat.

Pipes were knocked out and cigarette ends thrown in the fire as the crew one at a time crawled into their bunks, having removed only their footgear and, in some cases, their jerseys.

"You'd better break some kindling and put it beside the stove to dry, boy," said old Dennis in a kindly tone. "The fire will be out before we get up—that's if we sleep all night." The last was said with a wink to Bill and a sly glance towards Archie's bunk.

Bill woke early, saw that it was daylight, and went on deck to see what the new morning had to offer. The wind had moderated a bit although it was still quite strong, and daylight revealed to him that they were anchored among a small fleet of perhaps a dozen similarly sized boats, lying in a bleak narrow bay on the south side of the loch. There were half a dozen large steam drifters at anchor there also, and from the empty barrels piled high on their decks, Bill recognised that they were the boats belonging to the curers who would buy their catches. Ashore there were six or seven small but sturdily built stone houses; smoke trails from their chimneys betraying the fact that the occupants were up and about even at this early hour. A tiny stone-built church nestling close to the shore completed the settlement.

Above the houses there were strange looking parallel lines on the hillside. Bill later discovered that they were the singularly ill named 'lazy-beds' in which grew potatoes, the staple diet of the hardy people who lived there. Clawing the meagre covering of earth into a central drill formed the lazy-beds. The crofters then carried seaweed up the hill and added it to the growing medium. This helped to overcome the lack of natural nutrients in the soil to a degree, but Bill was never able to ascertain why they were called lazy-beds, after he discovered just how much work was put into their construction and maintenance.

The haunting smell of burning peat pervaded the morning air.

One of the houses had some sort of sign hanging outside, but it was too far away for Bill to see whatever was written on it.

After breakfast—a thin feast of porridge, followed by bread and butter, all washed down by yet more of the strong tea which the crew demanded—Archie ordained that the crew should haul the net forward from its usual position on the port quarter and overhaul it, mending the small holes in the well-used cotton.

Bill, he said, should go ashore by getting a lift in one of the small punts that were dotted around the bay and see if there was any salt mutton—a favourite feast of his—for sale in the wee shop.

"See if you can get any of their home-grown tatties to go with it, and keep your ears open to hear if anyone has seen signs of herring, or if any have been landed anywhere!" This was the final instruction before he went on deck with the rest of the crew, leaving Bill to wash up the pots.

Jim MacInnes, the cook aboard their neighbour boat, hailed Bill and joined in his quest for a lift to the shore but almost an hour had passed before they were able to attract the attention of a swarthy man who was rowing past in a tar-coated old dinghy, and successfully begged a lift ashore. They were barely able to understand the thick Irish brogue of the fellow, and their embarrassment initially caused them to monopolise the conversation by telling him of their trip north. In turn, they learned from the rower that for the past seven days there had only been a few crans of herrings caught by drifters in Loch Hourn, just north of Loch Nevis.

Bill felt a strange sense of adventure as their small craft approached the land. He felt almost as though he was an explorer about to claim the country for his own.

They scrambled ashore on the rocky, wrack-strewn beach and helped Paddy, as they had laughingly christened their new Irish friend, to haul his boat a few feet up from the water's edge, then ran light-heartedly up towards the houses.

Jim stopped outside the house that had the sign attached, and read the legend on the bright enamelled sign: 'FINEST SCOTCH WHISKY.'

"This must be the shop. It's a pity we haven't any cash, or we could go back to the boat drunk. What would our skippers say then?" Jim joked as he ventured into the dark interior.

"Now then lads, how can I help you?"

This booming question came from behind the rough counter, and as their eyes grew more used to the gloom they saw a veritable giant of a man, bearded and wearing only a rough woollen shirt over his tweed trousers; trousers which were kept up by a lashing of fine rope around his middle.

Jim started to list his requirements, but the shopkeeper was intent on gaining more knowledge of his young customers.

"Just sit down on the barrels there, but watch you don't fall in among the salt herring," he commanded, laughing uproariously at his own joke. "Would you like a wee drink of milk? I fear you are a mite young for anything stronger."

Then, cups of warm milk in hand, they were subjected to a long list of questions.

"Where are you from?"

"What are the names of your boats?"

"Are they ringers?"

"Will there be any more boats from the Clyde arriving soon?"

"Have you any herring aboard?"

The list of questions seemed endless and Bill was glad to let Jim handle them, mainly because he was as yet still ignorant of the common parlance that existed within the fishing industry.

He rose from his perch on the barrel, empty cup in hand, and began to wander aimlessly around, examining the cluttered contents of the so-called shop, the like of which he had never seen before. There appeared to be just about everything on earth in there, all piled higgledy-piggledy on the rough earthen floor, and he idly picked through them at random.

"Can I help you?"

The question, put in the beautifully accented soft Highland accent of one who was more at home speaking Gaelic, should have been easily answered, but when he turned and looked at the girl who had spoken, he was struck dumb by what he saw.

She stood easily by the end of the counter near the door, smiling at him. She was nearly as tall as he was, and seemed around the same age. Her shining jet-black hair, pinned at the back of her neck by a comb, hung down below her waist. Her complexion although viewed only in the dimly lit shop interior, was without blemish.

Her face was oval shaped with high cheekbones, framed to perfection by her hair.

She had a very firm chin below full, red, glistening—but unadorned—lips, lips that promised the world as they smiled but her eyes—oh her eyes!

Black they were. Piercing black orbs, which Bill instinctively knew would haunt him for the rest of his days. They looked into the very soul of him, and he felt that they drew all the life from him yet gave the promise of more—much more—in return.

She wore a long plain black dress, belted tight around her waist.

Her waist was so slim that Bill felt as though he could span it with his hands, but his eyes were irresistibly drawn above, to the twin orbs of her bosom. Unaccented, they swelled the fabric in a manner that displayed what seemed to Bill's yearning eyes to be the most beautiful curves that Nature could ever have bestowed upon anyone.

Her pale hands, resting on the rough counter top, were long and Bill—in a moment of weakness—imagined them stroking his rough cheek.

Why had he not washed his face before he came ashore? Why had he not combed his unruly mop of hair? Was his jersey clean? What would this vision of loveliness think of him and the boat smell of him that must even now be assailing her pale nostrils?

"Do you want something?"

The girl smiled as she asked the question. The wisdom instilled in all of her gender since the days of Eve, recognised the devastating effect she had upon the lad who stood open-mouthed before her, but she wanted more of him.

"Oh yes, eh tatties—if they're your own—oh yes, and do you have any salt mutton?" stuttered Bill, his mouth dry and unmanageable.

"Yes we do. I'll serve you if you don't mind; my father seems to be busy with your friend. What is his name?" she concluded with a smile, which lit Bill's world with stunning brilliance until he realised that she had asked about Jim—not him!

Instantly jealousy raged behind his eyes, blurring his vision and slurring his voice as he answered.

"That's Jim. He's just a cook. I'm a deckhand and I'm going to buy my own boat as soon as I can. My name is Bill. What's yours?"

The lies about his status as a fisherman came easily as he tried in a gruff and amateurish way to somehow endear himself to the vision that stood before him.

"My name is Theresa, Theresa MacDonnell. I was born further up the Loch but I live here in Tarbert during the herring season. I am working for my father just now, but I want to become a doctor. I'll have to study very hard to get there, but I am determined that I will succeed."

She spoke more kindly to him now, recognising that she had caused him hurt by making him jealous and, partly to make amends, she smiled and continued, "What is the rest of your name and where do you come from?"

Her suppliant tone and the radiant smile made Bill regret having allowed his anger to show through, and the thought that he might have hurt her feelings, was almost beyond bearing.

"My full name is Bill Martin, and I am from Campbeltown, well Dalintober actually. That is a wee place just across the loch from Campbeltown. I am a fisherman, but you would have guessed that already, I'm sure. You are the most beautiful girl I have ever seen, and I'm sorry I got angry. I—I wasn't expecting to see someone like you in a wee place like this."

It was now Theresa's turn to become embarrassed. She instinctively knew that the compliment he paid her had come directly from an innocent heart. The glow of her already lovely complexion became enhanced even further by the faint flush which diffused upward from her beautiful neck.

"My father will come over soon. Will you be here again?" she murmured almost beneath her breath.

"Oh yes. Will I see you again?"

Theresa turned and, apparently having forgotten her promise to serve him, went towards the door in the back of the little shop then stopped, hesitated and turned, smiled, and looked long and full, straight through Bill's eyes and into the very heart of him.

"Yes, Bill. You may be very sure of that."

With that she was gone.

Everything that happened in the next minutes would forever be blurred in Bill's mind. All he could clearly recall was the face of the girl in the shop, but somehow he managed to get the few errands that he had come ashore for, before he wound his way, with many a backward glance, to the water's edge.

"What do you think of this place then? Barren isn't it?"

Bill didn't really hear Jim's question until it was laughingly repeated.

"Well I suppose it is, all right, but there's not much scope for anything here except fishing. There aren't many facilities, are there? Not even a proper shop," was the best reply he could muster.

"No, but there's one braw looking lassie, eh?" countered Jim. "I saw the effect she had on you, my lad. You'd better watch yourself; it's herring we're here to look for, not girlfriends!"

The pair didn't have very long to wait until another small punt was launched off the beach—there seemed to be a constant coming and going of such craft—and they were able to cadge a lift back to their respective boats. On the way out, Jim coached Bill on all the gossip he had picked up from the shopkeeper, gossip which old Archie would need to know; all of which pointed to the fact that the few herring that had been caught recently, were all from the Loch Hourn area.

"You are very quiet Bill," Jim laughed, after a spell of silence. "Are you in love or something?"

"Don't be daft," replied Bill, his blushes giving the lie to his denial. He seemed to be unable to forget those piercing dark eyes, and the slow smile on the beautiful lips.

Aboard his boat again, he told his skipper all the fishing news that he and Jim had been able to glean.

"Right lads," said Archie. "Let's get the anchor up now, and get the net laid aft again. If there are herring in Loch Hourn, it's time we were under way. We'll go alongside our neighbour and see if he agrees."

The trip north along a slightly less forbidding, and somewhat more arable coastline than had been seen in Loch Nevis, took not much more than an hour, then they turned east again into Loch Hourn, a place that to Bill seemed to be a carbon copy of the place they had just left. The wind had eased away, though the cloud-streaked sky was promising that it would return again soon.

"There's not much sign of life here," commented John sourly, as he gazed around the barren seascape.

"I thought we could only catch herring in the dark, with the ring net," said Bill.

"What would we do if we found some now?"

"Oh no, it doesn't need to be dark," replied old Dennis. "We can take them in daylight. If we find herring in shallow water in a loch, we'll nab them if we can get our big toe on the bottom." Then he continued, anticipating the question he saw dawning in Bill's eye, "That means if the water is shallow enough for the bottom of the net to reach the sea bed. Then the herring cannot swim out below the sole rope. They'll spot the net, you see, in the daylight and if they can, they'll dive away from it. If we did see any in the deep water, you're right, we probably couldn't catch them but we'd come back after dark, and it would be a different story then!"

"I can't see even a gull. I would say that you were being kidded on at that shop, young Bill; there are no herring here," added John. "I'd bet my life on it. There's not a boat to be seen either. You'd better get below and get some grub on the go; I'm so hungry that my belly thinks my throat has been cut!"

Bill did as he was bid; he felt downcast at the thought that he might be held somehow responsible for what he now feared would be a fruitless journey.

Fortunately he had not wasted all of his time in sightseeing on the short trip north between the two Lochs. He had been preparing vegetables for the pot of broth he planned for lunch or 'dinner' as the midday meal was called. The finishing touches to this—prepared to what he could remember of his mother's recipe—would not take long.

More coal went on to the fire, bringing what were to become the habitual noisy protests from the crew on deck, that they were being smoked to death.

"Right lads, dinner's ready, come and get it!"

This demand brought the cold and hungry crew clattering below into the warmth of the tiny forecastle.

Bill went on deck and asked old Archie if he wanted to go below for his broth, hoping that he would accept and would leave Bill in the wheelhouse, in sole command!

To his disappointment however, Archie declined the offer saying; "No, not just now. We're just going to go through the narrows. There are rocks about; I'll wait till we get into the upper Loch. We can slow down then and one of the boys will take her. I'm afraid there are no herring here though, there's not a sign to be seen."

Seeing Bill's disappointment and remembering his own keen young days he added: "You and I will get our dinner together when they've finished, and we'll get more peace to eat it, too."

Bill went forward and lay on the foredeck, gazing down into the brown brackish waters. He had looked all around with his sharp young eyes, and noted with disappointment that the only gulls around were pecking among the rocks at the water's edge. They were feeding on small crabs, Bill guessed. There was not one gannet—a sure sign that herring were about—to be seen. No herring here was his doleful thought.

"Right Bill, time for you and me to get some grub!" The welcome call came from Archie as he came forward, having been relieved on the wheel by Malcolm, his second in command and despite his youth, the unofficial mate of the *Bengullion*.

"Let's get some food inside us; we'll need it to keep the cold out. Just keep her going dead slow, Malcolm—I doubt we're on a wild goose chase here."

The last came with a sly glance at Bill, before dropping out of sight below deck.

Bill joined him and the others, having eaten, made their way back on deck.

"That's a good plate of broth, boy. Just the stuff to stick to your ribs," said Archie between slurps of the thick brew.

This unusual compliment cheered Bill up greatly. At least he could do something well, he thought.

"What is there in the water up here that makes it fizz, Archie?" questioned Bill.

"Fizz? Where did you see the water fizzing?"

This was blurted out loudly as Archie dropped his spoon into his almost full plate, his eyes seeming to pop out of his head as he glared at Bill.

"Just before we came below," Bill managed to answer, wondering just what he had said wrong.

Archie roared a Gaelic oath as he dived for the ladder out of the forecastle.

"What's wrong with you men? The boy is the only one among you that seems to have eyes in his head. Hard round with her Malcolm, there's solid herring back there, the boy saw them putting up!"

Bill, still not knowing just what all the fuss was about, hesitantly followed Archie on to the deck.

"What's 'putting up'?" he asked John when he could trust himself to speak.

"That's bubbles that come from herring when there are great shoals of them," John answered. "I don't know what causes it. Some people say that they come from the herrings' swim bladders. Are you sure you saw that?"

"Yes I'm sure. I don't know about putting up, but I saw a lot of wee bubbles coming up to the surface just not far inside the narrow bit of the channel."

Their neighbour, who had been following them, had also turned and was slowly heading after them.

"Stand by; they're putting up solid here!"

The urgent instruction came from Malcolm who had returned to his usual place on the foredeck when Archie returned to the wheelhouse.

To Bill, the next few minutes seemed filled with madness.

John dived for the buoy that was attached to the end of their net, and waved it in the air as a sign to their neighbour that they were about to shoot.

Alex took his place on the starboard quarter by the corks that kept the top of the net afloat. His task was to oversee the safe shooting of the net, and to ease the passage overboard of the five white buoys, or 'bows' as they were called. They were evenly spaced around the two hundred and fifty yards of the 'back-rope'—the rope on the top of the net, to which the corks were attached.

"It's just about slack water. I'm going to make a wee ring, we don't want to get too many herring in one go," called Archie.

"Away with her now!" was the next instruction as the skipper—heeding the calls from Malcolm who was still watching the water intently—gauged the boat to be in the best position to surround the shoal with the net.

Malcolm dropped the buoy and first few fathoms of rope into the water, beginning the shooting process.

"First bow."

"Second bow."

"Centre bow."

"Second last bow."

"Last bow."

These calls from Alex as he helped the buoys over the side, told Archie how much of the net had been shot and concluded with the shout—"Net's away!" when the last few feet were running over the stern.

Their neighbour, meantime, had steamed quickly to the buoy that marked the end of the net, picked it up and made fast a heavy rope—called a sweepline—to the eye in the rope to which the buoy was attached.

Normally the two boats would have towed the net—which was now in a neat half-circle behind them—for a few minutes, but old Archie called, "Meet us right away!"

The two boats came together quickly; starboard shoulders together, the rubber tyres that lined the sides taking the impact. The net now described an almost perfect circle or 'ring,' which is where the descriptive words 'ring net' came from.

"How did you feel them?"

The question came from Dan White, the skipper of the *Silver Birch*, their neighbour boat.

"The boy saw them putting up," answered Archie. Although this reply filled him with pride, it sounded unnecessarily sarcastic to Bill's untrained ear, but he was to learn that it was indeed normal. The question—"How did you feel them?" would be answered in a variety of ways.

For example, if the herring had been detected at night by their phosphorescent glow in the summer months, the answer would be, "We saw them in the water!" a reply which would sound even more sarcastic!

"Well done young fellow!" roared Dan. You've been keeping your eyes open. That's more than can be said for this team aboard here!"

The work of recovering the net began.

Bill's place was pulling the back-rope; Archie was beside him, hauling the net.

"Look, look! They're buzzing between the soles!" Malcolm roared.

This meant that the herring were within the ring, but were probably desperately trying to escape below the sole—the leaded bottom rope of the net—causing bubbles to rise to the surface as they did so.

"Up with these soles as fast as you can, heave up on the springs!" roared Archie.

The spring rope that led to the winch, which was situated amidships, was cracking loudly under the strain, but this noise was drowned by the excited cries from all hands as the first herring was spotted—meshed in the net nearest the soles. Others soon followed this solitary specimen, all of good size, and then the water started to boil just inside the narrowing circle described by the back rope—which was now starting to dip below the surface. The buoy at the centre of this ring was also beginning to show the weight of herring, by sinking deeper in the water. This provoked the call—"Up with the corks!"—which demanded increased efforts by Bill in his place aft and by Jim, who was hauling his end of the back rope on the foredeck.

At last the herring were 'dried up,' ready to be brailed aboard the boats and the *Silver Birch*, which until now had been pulling gently on a tow rope attached to the *Bengullion*'s starboard side so as to keep her out of her own net, was able to come round and start taking the herring aboard.

The two boats lay port side to port side with the net between them, a glistening harvest of silver boiling in the water that separated them.

Bill's allotted task was to stand forward pushing with a pole to keep the two boats apart, a task that was easy on this day of little wind, but one that he was to learn would require a great deal of effort when there was a breeze blowing.

The teasing then started—the light-hearted tormenting of men from whom the burden of uncertainty had been lifted and who knew that they had done a job skilfully, and would be well rewarded for it.

"Aye aye, youngster, you have the eye for the herring. God help them when you get a boat of your own," called one.

"God help the lassies if he is as deadly with them as he is with the herring!" This comment brought a laugh from the rest, but added a deep blush to Bill's cheeks.

"He has the eye of a hawk," called another, though this provoked the usual laughing retort of, "Aye, a shite hawk!" from someone else.

"Leave the boy alone," cried Dan. "If it wasn't for him, we wouldn't have a scale. You did well, my lad. Just you take no heed of them."

The brailer, which was a piece of heavy netting shaped like one of Jim's sea-boot stockings, had the open end attached to a metal hoop. This was dragged through the now densely packed herring. The hoop was then lifted aboard and jammed above the circular manhole in the deck. The metal plate that was normally in place over this hole had been removed. The winch lifted the closed end, thus emptying perhaps three crans of herring at a time through the manhole and into the waiting hold.

Suddenly there was a wild cry from Dennis—"There's the king! Get him lads, quick now!"

This cry sparked intense activity among both crews until one of them succeeded in flicking a herring over the corks, to freedom.

"What was all that about," asked Bill, who had watched in amazement.

"Did you not see that herring was far bigger than the others, and had a sort of redness about him?" replied Alec. "That is a king herring, and it is a very bad thing to kill him if you can avoid it. Some folk say that all the other herring will leave the place where their king was killed, and you won't get any more there for years. You should always keep your eye open for Himself when you are brailing—just in case."

Gradually the net was emptied of its silver haul, and there were but a few left when the two boats holds were filled to capacity. Those that remained were given to the gulls which had appeared as if by magic, at the first sight of a herring.

"Where are we going with them?" asked Dan.

"I suppose we'll have to go back south to Loch Nevis, there are no curers here," answered Archie.

"Aye, you're right," replied Dan. "I think we should go over to the Skye shore though, and go south as far as Sleat Point before we head east for Tarbert. There's nothing to be gained by letting all the other boats know where we got this shot. We won't tell any lies though, we'll let them think for themselves and if they jump to the wrong conclusion and head off for the Skye lochs, that's up to them!"

The two boats lay alongside until both crews had hauled the *Bengullion*'s net back into its usual position on her port quarter, and had got both boats ready for the short passage back to Tarbert. Only then did Bill's empty stomach remind him that he had left his dinner on the table, barely touched. He had the presence of mind however, to ask Archie if he had time for the plate of broth he had abandoned on the table—was it only a couple of hours ago?

When the boats had been prepared for the open sea, a task which included spreading and tying down a heavy canvas cover over the wooden hatch boards that had been laid in place over the open hold, they set off out of the loch. Because the boats now sat much lower in the water, the rubber tyre fenders were also lifted aboard. Had they been left out, they would have caused much more spray to come aboard as the waves struck them. There was also the risk of losing the fenders in heavy weather, when they would be vulnerable to the surging seas.

Northwest was the course they steered when they reached the mouth of the loch, towards the Isle of Skye. The Cuillin Mountains could be seen for a time in the distance, but the visibility was fading quite quickly as they neared the land, and the skyline soon disappeared in the murky gloom.

They altered course to the south-west when Archie thought they were close enough to the land and ran parallel with the shoreline of Skye for well over an hour and then, when they were near Sleat Point, the southernmost tip of Skye, they turned to the east again, heading for Loch Nevis.

The knowledge that they would soon be in sheltered waters pleased Bill no end because the wind had begun to freshen again from the southwest, and the deeply laden boats were making heavy weather of it. The water that swept freely across the decks justified the care that had been taken with their preparations for sea.

They rolled their way into Loch Nevis and calmer water shortly after darkness had fallen. Soon they saw the sparse dim lights in Tarbert Bay and went cautiously in, tying up this time alongside one of the luggers into which they hoped to discharge their catch.

The punts were very soon coming alongside bearing the curers, buyers who were eager to see the quality of the herring.

Bill was amazed by their attitude. For men who had been without supplies of herring, they appeared to be utterly uninterested, and openly critical of the quality.

"Aye, they're gey thin and spent, hardly worth the salt we'd have to use on them!"

Thus began one buyer, a thin and surly man, speaking with what Bill was later to learn was an east-coast accent.

The covers and hatches had been removed by the crew, opening the hold to display their wares, and this remark prompted another buyer to pick up the smallest herring he could find and sneeringly comment, "They're not the biggest I've ever seen, by a long way."

"They're gey soft too," commented another, displaying one as he spoke. He had been surreptitiously rubbing the herring's belly between thumb and forefinger, in order to soften it!

The boat's lights that had been turned to shine into the open holds accented the silver sheen of the beautiful fish—some of them still kicking—and the comments of these men were in Bill's mind, unfair and totally out of place. He waited eagerly for Archie or Dan to take them to task.

"Ach well, they're just as good as anything you'll see tonight, aye and tomorrow night too if this wind doesn't ease—and I don't think it will!" was the only reply from old Archie as he puffed smugly on his pipe.

Then Dan spoke. "Right lads, if nobody wants our herring we'll just get the hatches and cover back on. There are five luggers lying idle at Kyle and the sooner we get under way, the sooner we'll get up there. I'm sure they'll be able to do something with the herring that are too small and soft for these guys. Two or three hours will see us there."

"Nobody said they didn't want them, skipper," protested one of the buyers who had not spoken thus far. "I certainly could be doing with them, or at least with some of them." He finished with a sideways glance at his fellow merchants.

"What on earth is going on, John?" whispered Bill. "Do they not want herring? How does Dan know there are luggers at Kyle?"

"Quiet now boy," answered John quietly. "This is the usual performance. Of course they want them; they just don't want to pay for them! They're trying to get them as cheaply as possible. Dan doesn't know about luggers at Kyle or anywhere else, but he's gambling that this lot don't know either!"

Bill's attention was drawn from the narrowing huddle of buyers that encircled the grizzled skippers, by a loud hail from the darkness.

"That's a braw shot you've got there, boys, your boats are fine and heavy. Where did you get them?"

A blue painted boat emerged from the murk and came into the circle of lights that surrounded the two laden ringers and the lugger, her foredeck lined with her oilskin-clad crew.

"Don't you dare say a word now Bill," warned John. "Leave all the talking to the skippers."

"Well now Ian, it's nice to see you again. You're looking well." This was the opening remark from Dan, who obviously knew the questioner.

"It's yourself, Dan—and Archie too. It's grand to see you both. That's bonny herring you have. We'll need to get a fry from you; we haven't had any for a wee while now. Were you in one of the Skye lochs for them?"

The skipper of the blue boat had come forward out of his wheelhouse, and was gazing enviously at the full holds that lay before him.

"Well Ian," said Archie. "We decided that we weren't going to tell anyone where we got them. It will take us a good few hours before we get the herring discharged—that is if we sell them here. We might go up to Kyle with them." He said this with a sly glance at the watching merchants—"And all we want is an even start with everyone tomorrow. The way the weather is shaping though, it isn't going to make any difference. It's a poor night outside now, and you wouldn't be able to work where we got them, even if we did tell you—and we're not going to! But you help yourselves to a fry, that's no problem."

The definite manner in which this was conveyed, convinced the newcomers that further questioning would be useless, so Ian forced a laugh and replied, "I suppose you're right, Archie. I'd probably do the same myself. I hope you get a good price for them, though I doubt it—this miserable shower of buggers would rob their grannies if they thought they'd get away with it."

Having taken his frustration out on the hapless merchants, he stamped his way aft and into the wheelhouse, put the boat's engine into gear, and soon disappeared into the gloom.

One of the buyers, sensing that the fishermen were not about to give in easily, and aware that the herring offered before him might well be the last for a few days, spoke up in a conciliatory tone.

"Right then skippers, we could argue about this all night. Come on away down to my cabin. We'll have a dram and I'm sure we can agree on a sensible price for your shot. You are as keen to sell them as I am to buy!" He pointed aft on the lugger they had chosen to tie up to, as he spoke.

The two skippers muttered quietly to one another and then with a show of reluctance, agreed to talk further. They then, accompanied by all of the buyers, clambered aboard the indicated boat and disappeared below.

John went aft and disappeared down the hatch into the engine room to carry out some maintenance task—probably adding some oil to the crankcase, a task that the Kelvin diesel demanded at regular intervals.

Bill wandered forward to where Dennis sat, conserving his energy, as he often said in defence of his fondness for the supine pose!

"How much will we get for this shot, Dennis?"

"I don't know, boy," answered the man. "It depends on what sort of bargain the skipper strikes with the buyers. They'll probably settle for about three pounds a cran, I'd guess."

"A cran is four baskets, isn't it?" asked Bill, indicating one of the wicker baskets that lay on top of the hold. "Why do they sell the herring here by the cran, when it is by the basket at home?"

"You are a terrible boy for questions," Dennis replied, laughingly. "That is just the way they measure them here. There's nothing strange about it nor can I tell you the reason, it is just the way it has always been."

"Right, Dennis, if we get three pounds a cran, we have about two hundred and forty cran here between us. How much will we get each?"

This brought a cackle of spluttering laughter from Dennis, who had been puffing on his old pipe which was, as usual, held upside down in an improbable attempt to keep the rain from the tobacco.

"We can never be sure of that until we have the money in our hands, boy. First of all, the gross is split half-and-half with our neighbour. Then each boat's expenses come off. All the grub you bought and all the fuel we have burned getting here—aye and all that we'll blow out of the exhaust before we see home again—that fuel has all to be paid for. After that, what is left is divided into eight-and-a-half shares. The boat gets a share; there's a share for the engine, and another for the net. The crew and the skipper get a share each, and you get a half share. When you have served your apprenticeship, you'll get a full share like the rest of us. Now that is easily enough counted but we'll be fishing here for probably six weeks, so if we don't get any more herring, all of this shot will go in expenses, so we'll get nothing! That's the way it is with the fishing, lad. No herring—no pay. You know that well enough, I'm sure"

"I see," said Bill, trying to hide his disappointment. "We're sure to get more herring though, there were lots of them in Loch Hourn, weren't there?"

"Listen, boy," said the old timer. "You can be sure of only one thing at the fishing, and that is that nothing is certain. Perhaps we killed all the herring that were there. If not, maybe the ones that were left have swum away out into the Minches by now. Just you go and make a wee cup of tea. When we start discharging this lot, we won't get another one until we've finished."

Bill obediently scuttled off to see how the kettle—which was always simmering on the stove, was doing. He had hardly got below when Jim joined him.

"Now then, Bill," began his mate, with a sly grin. "How does it feel to be so close to her again?"

"What do you mean?"

"Fine you know what I mean. Don't try to kid me on. You are well pleased to be back here again. Will you be going back ashore in the morning to see if she is still in the wee shop?" he added slyly.

"I suppose I will, Jim. I am going to keep back a fry of herring for them, just in case. She is a lovely lass all right; I don't think I've ever seen bonnier. What do you think?"

Seeing that Bill was taking his teasing to heart stopped Jim in his tracks. "Are you serious about her? Surely not, you've just met her."

"I said that I have never felt this way before about a lassie—just kind of funny inside."

Jim thought about this for a while and then asked, "Do you realise that she will be a Catholic?"

"How do you know, and does that really matter?" replied Bill angrily.

"Well no, it doesn't matter to me, but they're nearly all Catholics up here. She is bound to be a Catholic too, with a name like Theresa. That's the name of a Saint. Catholic girls are all called after Saints. If you ever wanted to marry her you'd have to join their Church too. Not that I'm saying you want to marry her," he added hurriedly when he saw the angry glint in Bill's eye.

"That's the kettle boiling. I'll make the tea, Jim. Tell the men that it's ready when you go on deck. It's time you made a cup for your crew too. You won't get another chance until this lot is discharged!"

With that, Bill made it plain that the conversation was over. Although Jim was nearly a year older than Bill, the pecking order had already been established. Jim, despite his youth, recognised somehow that Bill was perhaps special in some way.

Dan and Archie were not long in appearing, the gleam in their eye and the aroma of a decent whisky on their breath, betraying that they had been well entertained.

"Right lads, that's it settled now. We've got a fair price for them. Let's get this shot of herring discharged. The sooner we get them away, the sooner we'll get out and catch some more. We'll be namely at the milk-carts in Campbeltown tomorrow." This was a reference to the fact that the milkmen often acted—in the days before local radio—as news-carriers. "Aye lads, your wives will be out with two shopping baskets when they hear about this!"

This short, good-natured preamble heralded the beginning of what to Bill was the hardest work he had ever undertaken. He was assigned to the hold where he had to shovel the herring into baskets, using a metal scoop that had been designed for the job.

It was backbreaking labour, involving constant bending and straightening as he filled the baskets. He also had to scrape and shovel to keep the deck at his feet clear of herring. This was to stop him standing on—and therefore damaging—the precious fish.

He was kept hard at it for nearly five hours without break, and great was his

41

relief when finally the last basket was hoisted from the hold to the traditional cry of "Tally!"

Then the hold had to be washed down and the removable wooden boards which had formed the lockers, and which had been thrown on deck as the herring were discharged, had to be washed and put back in place. While the hose was being used in the hold, the 'Whale' pump had to be in almost constant use emptying the dirty water and scales from the bilges.

Only after this was he free to come up on deck, remove and wash his oilskins and crawl down into the forecastle, aching all over, to tend the fire and kettle for the tea that was even now being demanded.

The crew came down one by one into the heat of the forecastle and quaffed mugs of steaming tea liberally laced with streams of the sweet condensed milk they favoured.

Archie, the skipper, was the last to appear.

"Hurry up now lads and get the boat ready for the sea, we're away back up to Loch Hourn to see if there are any herring left there. We should make the best of it whilst our luck is in."

Bill greeted this announcement with dismay, although he wisely said nothing. He would have loved a few hours in his warm bunk, and had been hopeful of getting ashore to see Theresa, but he had learned enough in his short spell aboard to realise that Archie was right.

He waited below with his skipper, delaying washing the dishes until the old man had finished his tea.

"I hope you kept a meal of herring boy, they'll go well with the tatties you got ashore here."

"Oh aye, Archie, they're out in the hold there," he answered, not adding that they had been destined for Theresa. "I'll gut them when we get under way."

"I don't think we'll do much in Loch Hourn, there's far too much wind now. We'll never hear herring playing with the racket it'll make coming down off the mountains. You'll be dead beat boy," he added in a kindly tone, smiling at Bill as he spoke. "You'll get a good doss when we get the anchor down, and that time isn't too far off. You did a good job today; we'll make a fisherman of you yet. Now," he continued, rising and making for the ladder that led up on to the deck, "Hurry up and get these dishes washed before we get outside into the motion."

During the short steam out of the loch and back up the shore to Loch Hourn, the weather was wild enough to convince everyone aboard that anchor was the only safe place for them. They anchored in a sheltered bay on the south side of the Loch and it was with a sense of profound relief that Bill finally crawled into his small but cozy bunk, a haven from which he would not emerge until the following day was well dawned.

After breakfast the crew hauled the net forward so that they could lay out the small holes that seemed to appear as if by magic. The wind was still blowing, so they laid the holes down into the sheltered hold where they would be mended in comparative shelter.

While they busied themselves there, Bill busied himself brushing up the dried herring scales that had fallen from the men's boots. This was to be a never-ending task as long as they were catching fish. When he had finished that, he set about making yet another pot of broth, dicing up the carrot and turnips as small as he could, just as his mother had instructed him. He could hear her now... "The smaller you cut the vegetables, the sweeter the broth will be"!

His thoughts were interrupted by the flurry of activity that greeted the arrival alongside of another Clyde ringer. This was a boat from Tarbert.

"Aye, Archie, you had a braw shot yesterday, but I doubt that'll be the last from this Loch for a spell. Some of the Kyle men must have come in here after you were under way, and they say they heard them clapping."

"Oh damn, is that a fact, Robbie?" answered Archie in a somewhat agitated tone, as he clambered aboard their visitor's boat, and went aft to greet the skipper. "Did anyone else hear it?"

"I don't know, but the men who told me seemed to know what they were talking about all right."

The two skippers joined in an earnest conversation in the wheelhouse, newly lit pipes filling the confined air with blue smoke until the haze rendered them almost invisible!

Bill sought out Dennis at once. He realised from Archie's reaction that something of great importance had been said, but just what it might be, was beyond him.

"What is going on, Dennis? Why is Archie so upset? What did that man mean when he said something clapped?"

"Now then, boy, just go easy. It was the herring that clapped. You see—I don't know what makes the noise, but very often men hear this loud 'crack' in a loch at night. Nobody knows what causes it, though some say it is a whale that is jumping right out of the water, or banging its tail on the surface. Whatever it is, it very often clears all the herring out of a loch—just like that! Time will tell. Now get below and see if the kettle is nearly boiling. You and your questions are giving me a sore thirst."

This was all said in a smiling, good-natured way. Dennis might have been old, but he still remembered his own learning time, and he did enjoy passing on his many skills to one who was so obviously keen to absorb them.

Seeing that Dennis was in an expansive mood, Bill decided to broach the subject of religion. He knew that Dennis was a Catholic, the only one aboard the *Bengullion*. Bill had been thinking about Jim's pronouncements on Theresa's Catholic background, and wanted to find if they were correct or not.

"Dennis," he began hesitantly, not certain of what reception he would get to the question he would now pose. "Dennis, I'll make the tea but could I maybe ask you about something different, first? It's very important."

"You're an awful lad for questions; I don't think I ever heard the beat of you yet.

Aye, ask away, but one question only. If I can help, I will, but I need tea soon!"

"Well you see, Dennis, it's about religion. What would happen if a Protestant married a Catholic? Would it be all right?"

Dennis took out his pipe and filled it slowly. He knew enough about Bill now to realise that this was not just an idle question so he thought for a long time as he lit his pipe, before he gave his answer.

"Now, Bill, you've asked a big, big question here, and I don't know that I can answer it as easily as you might think. I'm not an expert on these matters, but I will tell you as much as I am sure of. I know you don't ask questions without good reason. If a Catholic girl were to marry you for example, in a Protestant Church, the wedding would not be recognised by her Church. They would say that she was living in sin, and she wouldn't be able to make her confession, nor could she take communion. To make it right you would have to become a Catholic, and marry her in the Catholic Church and you would have to promise that all your children would be brought up as Catholics. Does that answer your question?"

"Aye, Dennis, but surely that isn't fair?"

"Fairness doesn't enter into it at all my boy," answered Dennis in a kindly voice. "You see, if I wanted to go to a friend's wedding in a Protestant Church, I would have to ask my priest for permission. That is the way it is at the moment. I dare say it will change in the future, these things usually do, but we cannot change them now. Is there something bothering you?"

"Well aye, Dennis, but it's not important yet. I'll tell you later if it gets important. Thanks for your help—I'll away and make the tea now!"

Chapter Three

This was how Bill's real education and his indoctrination into the ways of fishing for the king of fishes, the herring, began. Countless communities had been founded upon the herring fishing industry; fortunes had been made—and lost—by the men who traded in herring and wars had been fought over them. As someone later pointed out to Bill, there were literally dozens of songs that had been written about the herring. Bill was unable to respond to the challenge to name one song that had been written about the cod, haddock or hake!

Although in summer months herring could be found just about anywhere in the seas in daylight whilst they were feeding on the surface, in winter they sought the shore. This they did possibly to escape predators, although some said that they came to eat the seaweed, and this was where the ring net came into its own. The shoals were swimming tight against the rocks, and could be trapped with relative ease—provided the net was not torn to shreds on one of the many jagged rocks that lay hidden beneath the surface.

Bill learned the importance of getting to know where the vulnerable cotton nets could safely be shot—knowledge that had been hard earned in the past at the cost of many hours spent mending torn nets.

They fished all through the long weary winter venturing west, with mixed fortunes, to the isles on the far rim of the Scottish seaboard, isles with magical sounding names; Eriskay, Vatersay, Mingulay, Barra and the Uists.

He learned about the Minches in all its moods. The wild south-westerly gales and the grey mountains of sea that hissed viciously as they passed, and the driving rain that invariably accompanied them; the bitterly cold north-easters; and the rare calm days when the intense and utterly incomparable beauty of the islands more than made up for their remoteness. They cast a spell that would not ever be lifted.

On the rare days that were dry and warm enough to permit it, nearly everyone took their blankets, pillows, and the kapok filled mattresses on deck and draped them over the mast in what was in truth, a vain effort at drying them. Inevitably they would be soaked again within a very few days. On seeing the bedding hanging up old Willie, one of the crew of the *Silver Birch*—a man who claimed to have been round the world many times when he was in the Merchant Navy—would point at the drying clothes. "This lot reminds me of the Chinese laundry boats in Shanghai!" he would cackle

Bill had the worst bunk on the boat for getting wet. Very often the hatch was accidentally left open, allowing the spray or the rain to land on his blankets. However when he at last got into a long-coveted top bunk he was horrified to discover just how much water leaked through the poorly caulked seams of the deck, landing directly on him. He developed the habit of keeping his oilskin sou'wester on the narrow shelf at the foot of his bed and would cover his head with it when drips woke him up!

He learned also from the great treasure trove of traditional knowledge that was common among fishermen of that era; how some men had the gift of removing herring scales from their companion's eyes by licking them out with their tongues.

Another, much more dangerous practice he heard of was that of cleaning out boils with a lemonade bottle! This operation was carried out, he was told, when the sufferer's boils seemed to have become properly ripened and would—in a kinder environment—be ready for lancing. In the rough and ready way of the fishermen, an empty glass lemonade bottle would be filled with steam from the boiling kettle and would then have its open end quickly clamped over the offending sore. As the steam condensed, so a vacuum was formed over the boil, which would then void its poison into the bottle accompanied—so Bill was told—by the screams of the patient. When the man in charge of this operation gauged that enough pus had been drawn, he would smash the bottle with the hammer he held ready, thus releasing the vacuum. Bill silently promised himself that he would never allow this seemingly barbaric operation to be carried out on his person!

He suffered badly from sore and hacked hands until they became as calloused and hard as his shipmates'. One very breezy moonlight night they had many blank rings. He was told that this was common because when the moon was bright, the herring became very wary and as a result, were notoriously hard to catch. The exhausted Bill was delighted when at last they went to anchor, but his pleasure soon turned to dismay when Archie set the alarm to go off in just three hours. They were going to try again when the moon had gone down, in the darker time just before daylight broke.

When the alarm went off, Bill's eyes felt as though they were glued together and when he got out of his bunk he discovered that trying to open his fists—they had become tightly clenched as he slept—was nearly impossible because of the pain this caused.

Old Dennis, seeing his distress, said softly to him, "Get you up on the deck and piss on them. Believe me, that'll help." Had this advice come from anyone else, Bill would not have heeded it, but he did as Dennis had advised and it certainly did ease the pain a little. The only comment on his actions came from John as he passed on his way aft to start the engine. "Mind and wash your hands well before you make the tea, boy!"

Their long sea-boot stockings were often hung to dry on the length of string that was stretched above the stove, competing for space with the dishcloths that usually occupied this position. When taken from this string they were comfortably warm to put on. Bill learned the truth of the oft-repeated cry, "First up, best dressed!" when someone appropriated his warm stockings leaving cold, damp ones in their place. It was not at all uncommon for one or more of these stockings—dislodged by the boat's movement—to fall on to the hot surface of the stove, the singeing smell often being the first indication of the incident!

Bill learned that sometimes the herring rose almost to the surface, and one jumped clear of the water—perhaps to escape a predator. This action, when the splash was heard on a calm quiet night, betrayed the presence of the shoal beneath, to the keen ear of a listening fisherman. Occasionally many such fish jumping would disturb the surface of a calm sea. This was most often seen and heard when the first morning light appeared in the sky and the herring shoal left the shore, swimming fast to seek the safety of the deep. This was called 'rushing,' or 'playing off.'

One night his excited shipmates summoned him from his tea-making task, to witness something that was very rarely heard. He came on deck to hear a great rushing sound, like a mighty river in flood. It was on their starboard side but as he listened, the noise subsided, only to be replaced by an equally great noise right ahead of them. It was caused by vast numbers of herring jumping well clear of the water. Boats were shooting all around them and by morning, the entire fleet was heavily fished.

Bill was to experience this phenomenon rarely during his lifetime. Its cause would remain a mystery to him, but he did notice that it seemed only to occur on nights that were calm and had a heavy, almost oppressive atmosphere to them.

These were also the weather conditions that favoured the hearing of the 'cheepach.' This very high pitched whistling noise was like the chirping of chicks and was so highly pitched that the ability to hear it was reckoned to disappear with age.

Bill was never to know the real origin of this noise. Some said that air currents produced it, some that it was made by the tiny storm petrel as it skimmed over the waves. Whatever the cause, it certainly portended the onset of bad weather.

"When you hear the cheepach cry, chains and anchors you may stand by," was the traditional call from older men when the noise was reported by one of their keen-eared younger shipmates.

Bill learned rudimentary navigation by poring over the tattered charts and old nautical almanacs, questioning his shipmates until they lost patience with him. He learned how to box the compass to the quarter point, something that very few of his contemporaries could do.

Elementary care of engines he learned by getting on the right side of John, the engineer, by occasionally helping him to polish the brass pipes that festooned the engine, and by assisting whenever John was changing the lubricating oil, a notoriously dirty and unpopular task.

He learned the art of 'wiring'—where a two-kilo lead weight was attached to a length of thin piano wire. This weight was lowered into the water and was dragged along behind the slow moving boat. When it passed through a shoal of herring the wire hit them and the man whose hand held it, felt the resultant taps. The nature of the bottom could also be determined by letting out more wire, thus allowing the lead to touch the ground briefly. Regularly, the lead would become wedged into a rock. This would lead to frenzied cries, "Come astern!" from the man aft, as wire was stripped from his reel. The wireman's job, although a very responsible one, was not popular as it involved standing immobile and alone, right aft. This was a freezingly cold occupation on a typical winter night and aboard the *Bengullion*, was usually entrusted to Dennis's vastly experienced hands.

Their catches were almost all landed to the klondikers at Castlebay and Lochboisdale. The herring were salted and packed into barrels aboard these ships, in preparation for their export.

Almost all of the fishermen agreed that they greatly preferred Castlebay to Lochboisdale. Although the latter was a much safer harbour, offering excellent shelter in really bad weather, it presented a bleak face to the sailor approaching from the sea.

The Castlebay people also seemed much more approachable than their northern neighbours were. The sandy bays that surrounded the harbour were more picturesque and clean looking than the smelly, muddy inlets that prevailed on the shores around Lochboisdale.

Bill's natural curiosity and determination to gain all the knowledge that he could, helped him to learn fast, coached by men who were masters of their art, but to his sorrow they did not return to Loch Nevis, so he did not see any more of Theresa. Nor was he able to find anyone who knew anything of her or her family.

He wondered about her, often. How would her family make a living if, as he had heard, Mallaig might start to make a name for itself as a herring landing port? How would her father fare if all the boats deserted Loch Nevis for Mallaig? Had she, he wondered, left home to make her way in the world and gone—as she had said she would—to become a doctor?

He did not see the any real evidence around Barra or the Uists of the dislike he had been told was felt by the local fishermen, drift net users to a man, for the type of nets that the ringers used but he heard of the activities of the men who lived further north, in Lewis and Harris. These men made it quite clear that proponents of the new method of catching herring were not welcome, and would not be sold provisions or fuel at any of the ports on these islands.

He did witness the interest of some of the locals, mainly the Eriskay fishermen, in the nets carried by the Clyde men and thought—correctly as it transpired—that it would not be long before such nets were used by these islanders.

In early March, when the Minch season ended, they made their way home to the Clyde to pursue the herring now shoaling to spawn at Ballantrae Banks, off the Ayrshire coast, and at the Brown Head at Arran.

Despite the fact that he was now able to get home every weekend, and that his mother saw to it that he had clean clothes to wear every week, he longed, in his quiet moments, for the lonely wastes of the north that he had somehow come to love.

Girls were attracted to him; his body had started to fill out, showing signs of the powerful man he would soon become, and they seemed to recognise that he was in some mysterious way, special.

Bill had little time for them. He consciously compared them to Theresa, and found them wanting. In any case, he knew that his destiny was not to be realised with these shallow girls of the south. No, north was where his heart—and his destiny lay!

At last, after much soul-searching, Bill decided that he would write to Theresa.

Many half-written efforts were consigned to the fire before he was satisfied, and he posted the letter with a heartfelt prayer that she would answer—that is if she ever got it! He was not, of course, sure of where to contact her, but thought that he should address it care of the General Merchant's Shop, Tarbert, Loch Nevis. This rather grand address would, he reckoned, endear him to Theresa's father!

Several weeks went past, then one Saturday his mother smilingly handed him a letter postmarked Inverness.

"This was written by a girl, I'll bet," she teased. "There's a lovely perfume on it!"

Bill ran upstairs to his bedroom to open it, thanking his lucky stars that his brother was out. At least he'd get peace to read the letter.

From it he learned that Theresa was now at school in Inverness, preparing for her entry to University. The delay in answering, she wrote, was because her mother had forwarded his letter to Inverness.

He read on—"*I would love to see you again Bill, I think of you every day. Would you please send me a photograph of yourself in your fisherman's jersey, and I'll send you one of me?*

I want to become a doctor, and this will mean studying very hard indeed, and for a long time. It will cost my parents a lot of money too.

I will write to you but if you don't get as many letters as you would like, it is because I am studying hard. I will remain faithful in my thoughts of you and I know although we only met for a few minutes, that we were designed by God to be together. I would love to meet you once again, but that is not possible just now. Time will pass very quickly though, I am certain, if we try to discipline ourselves.

I am sure that our destinies are as one, and all I would ask is that if you decide you want someone else, that you let me know.

I don't think I will ever want anyone but you.

I have put my lips where the X's are at the foot of this page.

The contents of this letter created feelings in Bill that he never knew existed. His mind was in total uproar. He longed beyond belief to see Theresa, yet common sense told him that this entire affair was crazy. After all, he had only met her briefly. She had, he reasoned, practically told him in this letter that she loved him. He put his lips softly on the spot where she had indicated her own dear lips had been so recently, his emotions in complete turmoil.

As time went on however, he began to realise the sense in her reasoning. He had to carve out a place in the hard world for himself—and for her. Not for him were the easy pleasures of alcohol and girls. There would be plenty of time for relaxation when he had achieved all his ambitions.

Though he did not realise it at the time, her letter had the effect of channelling his efforts towards bettering himself. He would show them all just how it should be done!

In the meantime he did as he was told, however, posing self-consciously in the photographer's studio in Campbeltown clad, as requested, in his best blue jersey and matching trousers. The resultant photographs he sent direct to Inverness, with a short note in which he told her that he would try his very best to exist without hearing from her on a regular basis although he stressed that his longing for her was almost beyond bearing.

To his great delight a letter arrived soon afterward, with a photograph of Theresa. It had, she told him, been taken on the lawn of the boarding house where she stayed in Inverness. He could clearly see the vivid beauty of her eyes, eyes that seemed to smilingly watch him, and to declare her heart to him. This photograph and her letters became his greatest treasures, and went everywhere with him

Chapter Four

Three years passed, years in which Bill threw himself heart and soul into his job, learning much about fishing. These years were times of good fishings in the Clyde, which sadly meant that he spent very little time in the North. He did keep in touch, religiously writing to Theresa every weekend, but he deliberately kept his letters light-hearted. Her replies, in a similar vein, were the subject of much anticipation. Then, on a fine day in early June, at a time when the fishing was slack, reports of good catches of herring being landed at Barra filtered through to the Clyde ports.

Bill was delighted to hear this news and his joy knew no bounds when the skipper, Archie, announced that he should order stores for the North—they were off to try their luck among the Gaelic speakers once more!

This time, the weather being good, they sailed around the Mull of Kintyre—north past the islands of Gigha, Islay, and Jura. The waters between Jura and Scarba were home to the notorious great tidal races that powered the Corrievreckan whirlpools, hazards that had, he was told, swallowed up many small boats in the past. Then they sailed through the winding reaches of the beautiful Sound of Mull to the low grey lowering Ardnamurchan Point, the most westerly point on the British mainland. Then the course was set to the north and west, past the low-lying Isle of Coll and on to their destination, Barra.

Bill, who had by now of course overcome his bouts of seasickness, enjoyed the scenery as they sailed north, leaving the fertile green hills of Kintyre behind as they wound their way past increasingly stern and barren hills to where he believed his heart and his future belonged.

Bill grew to love this fishery off Barra. It was completely different to the others in that they pursued the elusive herring in deep water and in daylight. This was possible because the fish gathered near the surface to feed upon the prolific rafts of plankton that Bill saw, red-glinting in the warm sea.

Their quarry's presence was often betrayed by the attentions of feeding flocks of hungry gannets, beautiful birds that wheeled to and fro on high, busy in their quest for food until they poised, hovering arched in mid-air, beaks pointing their prey before folding their wings and plummeting straight down to disappear into the depths, with hardly a splash to mark their brief foray into the domain of the herring.

Bill loved to watch for these beautiful birds and learned how to interpret what he was seeing. A gannet that hovered for a time with both its long beak and its tail pointing straight down—or 'two-ply' as the old men said—before diving was surely after herring. The bird, he was told, was seeing a shoal of them and was waiting until one detached itself, as it was unwilling to dive blindly among the dense shoal.

Shooting around the spot where the bird was 'looking well' caught many shots of herring. An angled dive or 'skaving lick,' on the other hand, usually meant the prey was a fast-moving mackerel.

Sometimes, when they chanced upon a gannet sitting low in the water they would pursue it until the poor bird, in order to lighten itself enough to permit flight, spewed up some of its stomach's contents, thus revealing just what it had been feeding on.

They watched for whales and 'sailfish,' as his shipmates called the harmless basking shark. The presence of these slow swimming monsters, some of them thirty feet long, that fed on the same plankton as the herring, often revealed the shoaling fish below.

If a net accidentally encircled the sailfish, it could suffer a lot of damage. Bill learned that a small can of diesel oil was always carried on deck, and the contents drizzled overboard as the net was shot, if there were sailfish close by. As soon as the sailfish smelt the diesel they dived deep to be clear of it, and so went below the net also.

On the other hand, the sighting of a whale was always welcomed. Some of them fed on the herring shoals and it was not unknown for herring to be seen rolling off the whale's back as it surfaced. When being spoken of by fishermen, whales were invariably prefixed by the definite article. He had heard and laughed at the tale of the Carradale man who, on being asked by the crew of a passing boat if he had seen the whale anywhere replied, "No. Did you lose one somewhere?"

Their catches were landed either directly to the curers at their piers in Castlebay, or into the klondykers owned or chartered by some of the herring buyers. These ships, mainly drifters or trawlers requisitioned for the job gathered, sometimes at Lochboisdale in South Uist, but more commonly at Castlebay, in Barra.

A conversation between two herring buyers overheard by chance one day was to have a profound influence upon Bill's life.

He was lying in the heather, drowsy in the sun, one Sunday afternoon—they never then fished on the Sabbath—above one of the piers in Castlebay, when he gradually became aware of the conversation that was taking place on the shore below him.

"I'm telling you straight, the trains'll be the death of the likes of you and me, Dod. They'll soon get all the fresh herring they want anywhere in Britain just hours after they're landed. Who'll buy salted herring when they can get fresh, tell me that?"

"I don't agree at all, Eck. There have been trains running in and out of Yarmouth for years now. Have they killed off the herring exports, eh?"

"I'm not saying that it will kill it off next week, Dod. But you mark my words, it'll die. Soon rather than late!"

"Ach away with you, man, you're just havering," retorted the man addressed as Dod. "There has been an export trade to Russia for hundreds of years now. Are you telling me that they will run trains from Mallaig to the Black Sea or the Baltic—or maybe even to the West Indies next?"

"Aye well now, maybe you think your smart answers will stop the trains from running herring to London, but I don't," said Eck quietly. "They are already doing that from some of the Clyde ports. You will do as you see fit, but I doubt if my son will be following me into this trade. I'm telling you straight, fresh fish is the thing of the future, and you mark my words. I'll be thankful if I get another five years at this job, and don't ask me what I'll do after that! There's just not going to be a living in it."

After the pair had taken leave of one another, Bill lay quietly wondering about what he had heard. He had learned early that it was not always wise to heed the words of another too closely. Men, especially men who were rivals—be they fishermen or buyers—very often lied to one another.

Still, he believed that he had overheard an honest exchange of opinions between two canny men about something that could have a profound effect upon his future, so he determined then that he should somehow make it his business—and soon—to find out just what were the facts behind the discussion.

The opportunity to find the answers to many of the questions that vexed him was to come sooner than he could have anticipated.

They were steaming south from Castlebay late one fine afternoon when John, the engineer, troubled by the colour of the smoke from their exhaust and the slightly rough sound coming from his beloved Kelvin, told Archie that he would need to stop the engine to investigate further.

Their neighbour, seeing them stop, came alongside and Donald, engineer on the *Silver Birch*, joined John in his investigations in the hot engine room. The rest of the crews lay at their ease on the foredecks of their respective boats yarning to one another, their restless eyes still scanning the water and the skies around them, for signs of herring.

Bill and Jim took the opportunity their enforced stop gave them to drop baited hooks over the side in an attempt to catch something appetising for their crew's suppers, but their attempts had not had time to bear fruit before the two sweating men emerged from their tasks in the engine room below.

"I doubt, Archie, that the fuel pump is on its last legs," John announced, his face grave. "I wouldn't like to trust it any further; it could pack up at any minute."

"Are you sure? Where on earth will we get spares, or a new pump? There's not much chance of anyone in these islands carrying anything like that," said Archie, his face glum as he contemplated the loss of fishing time—and the expense involved in the repair.

"We could wait for a long time for one to be sent from Glasgow. You know how unreliable transport can be here."

"Aye, Archie, I don't know what to say about this," said Dan from the wheelhouse of the *Silver Birch*. "I'm afraid it'll be a towing job all the way to Oban. That'll take a good while, aye, ten or a dozen hours, even if this weather holds, but you daren't risk damaging the engine by running it."

The latter part of this statement was made as the speaker squinted skyward, looking for possible signs of wind.

"What about Mallaig?" commented Dennis, from his usual perch just forward of the forecastle hatch. "There's a train running between there and Glasgow. We could maybe get a new pump sent up that way? That would be quicker, would it not?"

"That sounds like a good idea, Dennis," said Archie, his face brightening visibly as he saw a possible solution to his new-found woes. "What do you think about that, Dan? Do you think you could tow us there?"

"Aye, no bother, Archie, and in a lot less time than we would take going to Oban," said Dan. "If John and Donald think it is not wise to run your engine, we'll take you there."

The two crews busied themselves by good-humouredly rigging a towline. Two ropes were used, joined in the middle by one of the rubber tyres that lined their starboard sides—this would cushion any jolts suffered during what was likely to be an eight-hour tow.

Bill and Jim wound in their fishing lines as the men worked.

"You'll get a look at Mallaig now, Bill," remarked Jim, in whom Bill had confided some of his thoughts. "Aye and maybe you will find out something about a certain dark-haired young lady too!" He ducked as he finished speaking, just in time to avoid the piece of herring bait that Bill had just removed from the hook, and had thrown at his friend in mock anger.

As soon as they had the tow rigged, they got under way. They started off slowly, gradually increasing speed until Bill commented to Alex that they didn't seem to be travelling much slower than if they had been using their own engine.

Bill woke up in his bunk with a start, having been asleep for a luxurious six hours, unable at first to comprehend how it was that the boat was making way through the water, rolling slightly, but with no engine noise.

As memory of what had happened dawned on him, he scrambled from the warmth of his bunk and climbed up on deck into the as yet cool dawn of a glorious day.

They were about halfway between the island of Rhum and Mallaig, he saw, and ahead lay the hills of Morar, gloriously lit by the rising sun.

"You're up early. It's not time for breakfast yet, boy," called old Dennis, his head leaning out of the wheelhouse window, pipe reeking as usual. "Is that not just a perfect morning for you. It's a pleasure to be at the sea on a day like this. Come and steer the boat for a wee bit, she's easy to steer when we're getting towed."

Bill didn't need a second bidding, but went aft and into the wheelhouse at once. He loved to steer the boat, with the kick of the wheel sending its feel of the sea to his sensitive hands, giving him a feeling of power.

"Where is John, he is supposed to be on watch with you, and what is all that smoke on the shore ahead of us, Dennis?" he asked after a few minutes at the wheel.

"More questions again!" exclaimed Dennis. "John is in the engine room doing something to the pump, but I don't know what all the smoke is. Maybe it is something to do with the railway. Either that or it will be from kipper sheds. I heard that there were a few of them on the go here now. They say that there is a good demand in London for fresh Mallaig kippers, and now that the railway is working, there's no problem getting them there fresh. Just you steer away for a spell. We'll have to stop outside the harbour and get strapped up alongside our neighbour before we go to the pier. You can give the rest of the crew a shout before we get there. We'll need their help to get the tow rope stowed away and anyway, the skipper will want to be on deck for berthing. You won't need to make breakfast until we get alongside. We'll all get peace to eat it, and I heard that there is a baker's shop there now. If that is correct, you'll maybe be able to get some nice fresh rolls for us. That'll be a rare treat."

As they drew closer, Bill saw that Dennis was in fact correct in his surmises. Some of the steam and smoke came from a pair of locomotive engines which lay panting, ready for action, just south of what could only be the roof of a new railway station. The rest came from the roofs of an untidy looking collection of wooden buildings that lined the shoreline to the west of the railway. This wood smoke smelt wonderful, and Bill was later to discover that the smell heralded the glorious taste of freshly smoked kippers.

Bill kept out of the way of the crew who busied themselves about the deck after he had roused them. He had learned early that they were not at their best when first awakened!

He took the opportunity of having a look around the harbour as they crept slowly in; admiring the new wooden pier that had, he later learned, been built by the railway company to service the steamers that now ran between Mallaig and some of the Outer Isles. The small rocky bay, which he reckoned could almost have been encompassed by a ring-net, was sheltered from the prevailing south-westerly winds by the new pier. The rough, heather-clad ground, dotted with sheep, rose steeply to the east. It would, he thought, be a veritable sun trap on a good day. There were a handful of low-lying crofters' houses scattered sparsely around this bay, hens scratching busily among the crazily tilted haystacks that lay close to each house. About a dozen new houses, a small bank and a very few shops constituted the beginnings of the budding village, just yards east of the railway station.

There was a substantial—if dour looking—two-storey building to the south of the railway station buildings. This, Bill later learned, was a dormitory for the railway workers. A small hotel had been built close to the station. On the southern outskirts of the budding village there stood two white-painted churches.

The entrance to the harbour lay to the northeast, giving a view across the mouth of Loch Nevis. The youngster deduced, correctly, that this would be the weak point of the entire layout as it left the harbour exposed to the winds that would blow—fortunately rarely—from that quadrant.

There was no wind at all this morning however, and the still water reflected truly the rough landscape that was revealed to Bill. Although it was still very early—smoke came from but a few chimneys and there were few humans to be seen around—the day promised heat.

Bill scrambled ashore up a ladder as soon as the boats were safely berthed and set off to look for the baker's shop. His curiosity drove him first along the wooden pier though, towards the area from which he had seen the steam and smoke of the railway engines.

He didn't have far to walk. The entire harbour system had been designed from a railway point of view, and it was simply a case of following the glistening rails that led him to where he saw, for the first time ever, a steam engine. It lay there panting lazily beneath a pall of black smoke that rose straight into the still clear air. Its black paint was shining, steel oil-coated pistons gleamed, and steam hissed from a number of pipes all—though motionless—evoking a feeling of tremendous latent power.

"You shouldn't be here, you know!" The petulant sounding complaint came from a young lad—no older than himself—who had arrived unnoticed around the front of the engine. He wore railway uniform, and carried in one grubby hand an oil can which sported an inordinately long spout. The other hand clasped a big bundle of oily rags with which he occasionally polished the already shining metal.

On his head he sported, at a reckless angle, a greasy black cap which had a glossy scoop at the front, just below a railway worker's badge. An unruly crop of wiry red hair protruded from below the cap.

Bill immediately went on the defensive.

"I'm not doing any harm, am I?" he retorted. "I just want to have a wee look at an engine."

"I see. Well, that's all right," replied the new arrival in a conciliatory tone, adding somewhat self-importantly, "It's just that I'm in charge here now, and if you got run over, I'd be held to blame. You must be a fisherman, where are you from?"

"Yes, I am a fisherman. My name is Bill Martin," replied Bill, choosing not to challenge the newcomer with the obvious retort that it would be indeed difficult to get run over by a stationary railway engine!

"I'm mate on a Campbeltown ringer. We have a spot of engine bother, and need a spare part. That was us that got towed in a wee while ago," replied Bill, feeling that the lie about his position on the boat would restore some of the kudos he felt he had thus far lost in the exchange.

"Mate eh? You're a mite young looking for being a mate," retorted the lad, doubt showing plain on his face. "Anyway, I'm Ian MacPherson, and I'm a fireman. Have you ever been on the footplate of an engine like this? Come on. Jump up and I'll show you the controls."

So saying he walked rapidly towards the rear of the engine, and clambered up some steps.

Now Bill had no idea what a footplate was, but he had no intention of revealing this to his new-found friend, so he followed the lad up the steps to find him opening a small steel door, revealing the raging inferno inside.

"It's all right, there's plenty fuel on the fire just now. We don't use much when the engine isn't working. It's a heavy job keeping her in coal when she is being worked hard though. I have to shovel it from here." Ian indicated an aperture at the rear of the compartment that Bill now felt sure was the footplate to which Ian had just referred.

"It gets shovelled onto the fire, through this wee door. It is no easy task, I can assure you, when we are moving. This beast jumps about all over the place! Anyway, you will know all about movement, I'm sure. This is the throttle, you push it this way to give more power, and this here is the whistle. I'd give it a blast, but some of the lazy folk will still be sleeping, and they'd be sure to complain. If you wait a wee while, you'll get a spin if I ask the driver, he's not a bad lad really."

"No thanks," replied Bill, reluctantly. "I'll have to get going; I have to get some rolls for the breakfast." Then, remembering his earlier lie he hastily added, "The cook will have it ready soon. I'll see you later though."

"Wait a wee," retorted Ian. "You said you had bother with your engine. If it's a Kelvin, I'm your man. There's not many around here that knows more about Kelvin diesels than I do. I was born here; my father comes from here so I'm a local. My mother came here from Fort William when she married my father. If you want me to have a look at your engine, just say the word."

"Thanks for the offer, but our engineer knows what the trouble is, so we're just here to get the spare part. It's the fuel pump that's wrong, apparently. We'll be away in a few hours if we get the bits."

So saying Bill jumped lightly to the ground and set off in search of the bakery. Truth to tell, the last thing he wanted was for Ian to discover that he was really the cook, and not the mate!

His nose led him unerringly to a small shop from which came the mouth-watering aroma of freshly baked bread.

"What can I do for you? Have you many herring? Are there any more boats coming today?"

These rapid-fire questions, posed in an obvious east-coast accent, came from a small, round, rosy-faced lady who stood, bare, flour-coated arms akimbo, behind the counter.

"Eh, a dozen rolls please. No we have no herring, we were towed in with a broken-down engine, and I have no idea if there are any more boats coming at all," replied Bill as soon as he had gathered his wits.

"Oh, that's a pity," said this lady, absent-mindedly. "It is fine to know how many boats are coming; we can bake more rolls if we think we'll need them." Then, realising that Bill had told her of his boat's misfortune, she added, "Sorry your engine is broken. I hope you get it fixed soon. What is wrong anyway?"

"It is the fuel pump. If they have the bits here, we'll only be an hour or two, but if we have to get a new one up from Glasgow, we might be another day or so. Do you know a family called MacDonnell; I think they live up Loch Nevis somewhere? I think they had a daughter—maybe her first name was Theresa—that was learning to be a doctor."

"MacDonnell, you say? Well that is a common enough name around here. Do you know anything else about them? A doctor, did you say? Never heard of anyone local doing that. Are they local? I'm not, I come from Fraserburgh," replied the lady, now giving all her attention to Bill, who in turn realised that this was a lady to whom gossip was second nature, and with whom he was totally out of his depth!

"No, I don't really know anything about them," Bill replied casually. "Anyway, it isn't me that knows them; it is another lad on my boat."

"Hmm, well if this other fellow comes up and tells me more about them, I might be able to help," mused the unconvinced baker.

At this, satisfied that he was no match for her guile, Bill paid for his purchases and left the shop, almost bumping into a bleary-eyed Jim who had followed him on the same errand and who had obviously just been roused from bed. They exchanged greetings, and then parted.

Back aboard, the crew made short work of scoffing the unaccustomed fresh rolls with their equally rare bacon and eggs.

As soon as breakfast was over, old Archie stretched himself, and announced that he was going ashore to make enquiries as to how he would go about getting the engine fixed. "You can haul the net forward while I am away, and mind and lay out any wee holes you come across. Mending them will keep you from wearying," he added mischievously.

This task was ended, and Bill had the dishes washed before Archie came back, accompanied by Dan, who had followed him ashore as soon as he had been fed.

"Well lads, I'm not sure just what we should do," began Archie. "We found a fellow by the name of Macbeth, who has set up as an engineer here. He certainly seems to know what he is talking about. He says that we really need a new pump, but he doesn't have the one we need. Worse still, when he telephoned Glasgow, he was told that there isn't a pump for this engine in the whole works, and they won't be able to get one for about four days. That's an absolute disgrace; they should always have spares for engines they have sold. This engineer lad has a pump, but it is for a two-cylinder engine. He says that there isn't a three-cylinder engine in the local fleet. I would suggest leaving the boat here, and going home till the engine is fixed—that would give us a break at any rate—but I am not too keen on leaving her here unattended, and Dan feels the same. We are not too sure of this harbour. It's a pity though; we could have been home tonight. The train would be at Arrochar just about the same time as the bus from Glasgow to Campbeltown."

"How would it do, Archie, if Jim and I waited behind?" blurted out Bill before he had given it any real thought. "We're not married, so we have no wives to miss us, and we could make sure that the boats were looked after properly. There's not much that a full crew could do that we couldn't. We've no engine after all, and the weather is settled looking anyway."

"Have you asked Jim if that's all right with him? Anyway, I'm not too sure about this, it would be a big responsibility for two young lads," answered Archie, weakening visibly despite his protests.

The intervention of a lively looking, stocky young man with a strong East Coast accent who had made his way down into the forecastle and who now spoke—resolved the issue.

"I'm Willie Mair," he announced. "I'm the new fish salesman here; can I be of any help at all?"

As soon as this dynamic chap heard their story he immediately sprang into action.

"You've spoken to the local engineer? Macbeth is a good lad. He knows his business. If he says you can't get spare parts for a few days that'll be correct, so you'd be as well to get the train right away. You get little enough time at home as it is, so why waste the opportunity of giving your wives a treat! Wait you here, and I'll get your train tickets organised for you if you like, and you may rest easy, skipper; if the young lad here wants any help with anything at all while you are away, he need only ask. I've got a phone up in the office so if there's anyone you want to speak to, don't hesitate. You'll be all right moored here alongside the steps; I don't think anyone will need to get alongside them."

Jim, when he was consulted about whether or not he was willing to stay behind with Bill, took little time in deciding that he would forego the thrill of his first trip on a train, preferring the sense of power he would get from being left in sole charge of the boat!

When the decision had been made, it took no time at all for the crews to get their cases packed, have a quick wash, and set off light-heartedly towards the station from which, Willie Mair told them, the Glasgow train would soon depart.

In no time at all, the youngsters were left alone, sitting in the forecastle of the *Bengullion*, digesting all the warnings on the care of the boats that had been issued by the departing skippers.

"Why don't you take a trip up the loch, Bill, to see if you can maybe find that lass? I'm sure someone here would give you a loan of a wee boat, and it's not very far to that bay where the shop is?" asked Jim quietly. "If you can't get a loan of a boat, I could quite easily take you up in the *Silver Birch*."

He now knew Bill well enough to recognise that he was somehow different to the others of his kind. Someone who was, he felt sure, destined for greater things. He also was wise enough to tease Bill very gently when he spoke about Theresa.

"I would love that, Jim, but she's at school in Inverness just now. Either that or she is at university. I don't hear much from her at the moment, she's studying very hard," he added defensively.

"I'm sure the schools and universities will all be on holiday. We're the only ones that work all the time. Let's ask that salesman lad, Willie was his name. He'll be able to get us a boat, I'm sure."

"Well, maybe, but not just now. What would you like for your dinner? I've a good idea, why don't we take turn about of cooking, that way we'll each get some time off."

"A capital idea, Bill," cried Jim. "Just you go and have a wee snooze on the deck. I'll make up some sandwiches just now. We'll have them with a cup of tea in an hour or so. There's some of yesterday's soup and a wee bit of boiled lamb aboard my boat. We'll have that for our tea tonight. How about trying to get some nice fresh kippers for tomorrow?"

Bill went up on deck into the warm late morning sunlight. He was a bit weary, he realised. The past twenty-four hours had been eventful ones. He lay on his back on the net that had been spread over the port side to dry, and closed his eyes.

"You shouldn't be lying at these steps you know; they're for small boats only and anyway, sleeping in the sun at this time of day isn't good for you!"

Bill woke with a start at these words and sat up, to be confronted by the vision that had dominated all his dreams for so long. His sleep-fuelled confusion was made the worse when he sat up and looked into her smiling black eyes. Not for the first time, they seemed to transfix his entire being.

"Theresa! Where did you come from? How did you get here? I thought you were still away. You haven't changed a bit. You're so beautiful. How are you?"

His stuttered questions seemed to amuse Theresa greatly, but her voice was soft and kindly as she answered, "I'm on holiday, Bill, and have just sailed down from my parents' house. Our boat is tied up alongside the boat that is outside yours. My mother and father have just gone ashore to do some shopping. I made an excuse and waited behind for a bit when I saw you—what a surprise I got—but I can't stay long. I have been watching you sleep for a minute or two. You looked really peaceful there; it was a shame to waken you. Where is everyone, are they all asleep below?"

"No, they've all gone home on the train. Our engine is broken down and we won't get spares for a day or two. There are only two of us left, Jim and I. We're looking after the boats. Jim is making tea just now, would you like a cup?"

"Yes please, Bill, I'd love a cup of tea, but I cannot wait very long. We have to be at the church in about an hour. I am sorry you are having trouble with your engine. "

"Right, Theresa, come down into the forecastle—but you'll have to excuse the mess, it's not as tidy as you would have it. Can I come up the Loch and see you sometime? There's a man, Willie something or other, I think I might be able to get a boat from him. What are you doing after you come out of church? Why are you going to church anyway? This is Friday, not Sunday."

Bill tried to cover his confusion by chattering.

"I'm going to confession, Bill. I won't be long. This afternoon I will be busy with my parents. We have given up trying to run the shop at Tarbert; all the boats are landing their fish in Mallaig now that the train has started running. We are living in the upper loch now, on the croft, and we are going to be doing some clearing work at the old place this afternoon, on the way home."

Seeing the disappointment clearly etched on Bill's young face she continued, very hesitantly, "Perhaps I could come back to Tarbert tomorrow by myself for a wee while and see you then. I could think of some excuse to go back there, but are you sure you would be able to borrow a boat?"

"Oh yes," Bill answered. "If I can't get a wee boat here, I'll take the *Silver Birch*, that's our neighbour boat, and her engine is all right. I'll be there; I really must see you. When will you be there?"

Theresa smiled at Bill's eager face. "I'll arrive about eleven in the morning. If you are going to be there then, will you bring something to eat? We could have lunch together. My father would not like it if he knew that you were coming up, Bill, he is quite old-fashioned in some ways. That's why I won't be able to take food for the two of us. I'm sorry, but he is very protective of me. I am the only child they have. I hope you understand?"

"Yes of course, Theresa. Now come on and get this tea I promised you."

Bill dropped down the steps into the forecastle, relieved to discover that Jim was not there, and watched as Theresa followed him. He tried, rather half-heartedly, not to look as she revealed quite a bit of her lovely legs during her unpractised descent down the vertical ladder.

"I'll just get a clean cup for you and make some fresh tea."

"Never mind the tea, Bill," Theresa said as she settled herself on the wooden locker, gazing around the small, but tidy, forecastle. "I'd rather hear about you. Come and sit beside me here."

Bill did as he was bid, perching himself awkwardly in the corner below the hatch. "What do you want to hear," he began. "I haven't really been up to much at all, just working and learning. What about you?"

This was a mistake. To listen to her he felt compelled to look at her, and the close proximity of her dark gaze caused complete turmoil in his head. He was totally unable to cope with the emotions that flooded through him.

Theresa reached out and grasped his hands, turning so that they now faced one another. "Bill," she breathed. "I have missed you so much. I never dreamed that I would care for anyone as I care for you—and yet I don't know you at all. We only met once but it is amazing, I feel as though I have known you all my life."

Bill's face drew slowly nearer to hers until at last their lips met. Her hands still held fast to his so that they were pressed against the youthful firmness of her breast. He felt as though his blood was on fire and when the power of thought eventually returned, he hoped that this moment would last forever.

Theresa leaned towards him so that she now lay in the cradle of his right arm, her body twisted awkwardly with her legs below the table. She eventually broke the embrace and sat up, still holding his left hand against her breast. "Which is your bed, Bill?" she asked. "I want to know where you will be sleeping."

"Theresa, I think I love you, and I want to marry you. I've hardly been able to think of anything else since I saw you. Nobody has ever affected me like this before, and I'm just not interested in any other girls. Don't waste time talking of petty things. I want to marry you. Could we get married in another Church when we feel that the time is right, or would that be impossible for you?"

"Oh, Bill, why could we not both be of the same faith? My parents would be devastated if they heard that I had even thought of marrying outside of the Church, and I would hate to hurt them so much. Could you not come with me? Is your Church as unyielding as mine? I am having a struggle with life as it is. University is much more difficult than I had imagined and if there weren't so many problems involved, I would leave and marry you now. We just cannot do that, though. There are so many things to think of."

"Yes, we'll have to think long and hard, Theresa," Bill answered. "But why is it always the Protestant that has to change? Can you not all tell your Church what you want?" Then he added, smiling, "Come and sit on this other side. There's more room, and you won't be sitting so twisted. Apart from that, anyone passing on deck will be able to see us if we stay here!"

They moved across the small forecastle and Bill pulled Theresa down towards him, his eager lips seeking hers. This time she nestled in his right arm, and he slid to the floor until he was kneeling beside her as she now lay on the wooden locker. She had both arms around his neck and, amid thundering in his ears, his left hand found its way to her breasts. His hand probed until it found access through the neck of her blouse. His hesitancy was relieved when she moved slightly, to allow him more freedom. Unfastening two buttons, he slid his hand along her smooth young skin until it encountered the swell of her breasts and continued between her flesh and the hindering brassiere, until it encountered the totally different feel of her engorged nipple.

Theresa's mouth opened beneath his and she moaned slightly as his unpractised fingers caressed her.

The thump of someone stepping heavily on to the deck caused the pair to jump apart. Theresa sat up—her face flushed—and hastily buttoned her blouse. Bill stood awkwardly, facing away from her to hide the visual evidence of the effect of their encounter.

"I must get up the pier, Bill," Theresa said breathlessly. "My folks will be looking for me soon, and I don't want to be late. And how am I going to confess this?" she added, looking at him archly under her eyebrows.

On deck, Theresa smiled and pressed his hand again and Bill watched, scarcely able to breathe, as she went up the steps and onto the pier. He could hardly believe his good luck—of all the weeks to get engine trouble, it had to be this one—if the spares had been held at Castlebay, he wouldn't have been here—if this engineer here had a spare pump—if there had been a pump at Glasgow! As he watched the trim figure of the girl he was now certain he loved and would marry, walk off the pier and up the hill to where he assumed the Catholic Church was situated, he knew beyond all doubt that their lives were meant to be linked through all time.

Shortly after, in the forecastle of the *Silver Birch*, an excited Bill told Jim as they drank their tea, of his plans to borrow a boat from the salesman who had visited them.

"Listen, Bill," said Jim quietly. "I saw you with Theresa. I was up on the pier when they arrived. She stood watching you for a good few minutes before you woke up. You are young and yes, so am I. Now I know that this girl is really beautiful, and she certainly is fond of you but don't you go making a fool of yourself. It is none of my business, but there are a lot of differences between you—different backgrounds, religion, upbringing, and work—even language!" He hesitated, and then continued in a self-conscious way, "I like you a lot, Bill, and I'd do anything for you. I know you are going to go far further in this life than I will, and I'd like to join you when you start out on your own. If I didn't like you, I wouldn't be speaking this way."

"I know you mean well, Jim, thanks for your concern. I'll remember what you have said," replied Bill. Then, by way of closing the matter he continued, "What was the name of that salesman again?"

Willie Mair, the salesman, greeted Bill in his little office on the pier, and in answer to his request for the loan of a boat told him that he would fix that "No bother!"

He sat behind his desk and eyed the young man opposite him with a shrewd look. Much later, Bill realised that Willie had been appraising him carefully as he talked, and that Bill's responses to what had been said, had been carefully noted

"My task in life is to market the fish that the boats catch," he began. "But you see, this place is only just starting up. One thing I am aware of is that we salesmen have to try to see all sides of the problem. I am certain that this ring-net is the coming thing, although there are doubts to be resolved before it is accepted everywhere, as I am sure you will realise. I am trying to develop the shore side of the industry here. There will be more firms who will come in, I am sure, to smoke kippers—bigger firms than we have here now. The railway will get the kippers to market quickly, but we must be in a position to offer them some sort of continuity of supply. One way of doing this is to get more locally owned boats. The big East Coast drifters are fine, but they can be here today, and in Yarmouth three days later."

"I know from experience that I am a sound judge of character," Willie continued. "I have never met you before, but I know that you are just the sort of young man we need here so whenever you want a boat of your own, just get in touch with me. The Company I work for trusts my judgement, and they have the money we need to do the job. You are a mite on the young side, so I would suggest that you wait for a year or two, learn all you can, and then get yourself up here. This is where your future lies. Meantime, I'll get my runner—helper to you—to have a wee boat alongside you first thing in the morning"

Bill sat quietly through all this. He knew that this man had had a vision that closely resembled his own, but that he had managed to put it all into words—something that Bill had so far failed to do.

"Thank you, Mr Mair, for your faith in me," he said, feeling strangely devoid of embarrassment for once. "There are a lot of things I need to sort out, but these few words from you have helped me more than I can ever say. I will certainly be in touch again, soon, and I can assure you that I will not betray any trust placed in me. Thanks too for getting me a boat for tomorrow morning."

"That's no problem; I know you will look after it. Now I don't know why you want it, and it is none of my business, but be careful, that is all—but before you go, the name is Willie to my friends—and that includes you."

The older man stood up, thus signifying that the interview was now over, but Bill hesitated. "Tell me, Willie, what does your job as a salesman mean—just what do you do?"

Willie sat down again, smiling as he did so. "Well done, young Bill, that's the stuff. If you don't know something, ask! You see you fishermen here on the West Coast have been in the habit of looking after your own affairs for a long time. You go out and catch the fish, then try to sell them. I do all of the selling for the boats that agree to work through my Company. I also look after paying all the bills for them and sort out the squaring up, I think you Clyde men call it dividing—I pay out the crews, in other words. This industry is going to get bigger, you mark my words, but that means that there will be some unsavoury characters around on the buying side. They'll promise you the earth, get your catch, and then you'll never see them again. If the herring were sold through me, I would insist on having some sort of guarantee from them so that you fellows would get your money for whatever you sold through me, no matter what the buyer might do. Sometimes buyers can get caught out too, Bill. They send fish on to an inland market in all good faith, but the payment for them never turns up. If that happens too often, the buyer can go bankrupt while they owe you money. We'll look out for that sort of thing. Another benefit for you lads is that my Company is quite big, so it can sometimes save you money when you are buying gear. If we buy ten nets, for example, we can get a discount from the manufacturers. We pass some of that on to you. We charge you a small percentage of your gross earnings, for our services. I told you that this industry would expand. Well, part of my task is to see that the shore side keeps up with the catching side. Does that answer your questions?"

"Yes, Willie, that's all quite clear to me. I overheard two buyers talking at Castlebay recently, and one of them certainly was of the opinion that Mallaig would grow because of the railway. That ties up with all that you have told me today. I think you are the sort of man that will go places, so I will certainly keep in touch, and I might well take you up on your offer of help. Thanks again for everything."

Chapter Five

Saturday dawned bright and calm, with the promise of much heat to come. Bill busied himself by going up to the baker's shop as soon as it opened, buying rolls and pies, food that he thought would be acceptable for the venture ahead. His excitement had meant that he could not eat breakfast, despite Jim's light-hearted protests.

His promised boat, a small motor launch, was alongside by nine am, and after a short course of instruction on just how the engine should be managed, he got under way out of the harbour and round the corner into the Loch. His last words of farewell to Jim were that he might not be back for a couple of days!

He turned east into the loch and soon passed Mallaig Vaig, the first tiny settlement on the south side, relishing the calm of the morning and the rugged beauty of the steep hills that bordered the loch. He could not help contrasting it with the wind, rain and utter bleakness that had greeted him on his first visit—what a difference some sunshine could make! The wake from his boat stretched unbroken for as far as he could see, the only marks on the still waters, and he amused himself by trying to keep it as straight as possible. As he neared Tarbert and drew closer to the shore, he slowed the boat and stood up to get a better view of where he was going. He didn't know these waters, and the very last thing he wanted to do was to strike a rock!

Tarbert now presented a totally different face from the thriving wee hamlet he remembered. There was no smoke rising from any of the chimneys, and the whole place looked deserted. He could not see the sign that had marked the shop and surmised, correctly, that it had been removed. Nor was there any evidence of Theresa but then he was early, he told himself. She might not be there for an hour or more yet.

As he drew slowly closer to the land he saw a small mooring buoy. From it there stretched a rope that passed through a metal ring on the rocky shore. He saw that this was the same sort of contrivance that his mother used to hang clothes out to dry at home. It was in fact an endless loop, so he was able to come alongside it gingerly, and make it fast on the mooring cleat on the tiny foredeck of his wee launch. This done, he stopped the engine and it was an easy task to pull the boat shoreward. He then clambered ashore onto the seaweed slippery rocks with his two bags of food, and pulled the boat out carefully until she nestled snugly by the buoy, about thirty feet from the beach. Having made the rope fast so that the boat was now firmly and safely moored, he turned and clambered up on to the sward that lay above high water mark, where he placed the bags on top of an old wooden box and looked around.

Bill wondered what to do next. He decided that he couldn't very well explore the houses even if they gave the impression of having been deserted and there was of course, no one to talk to, so he decided to climb to the top of the hillock that bounded the west side of the bay. From this vantage point, he decided, he would get an earlier sighting of the boat that he felt sure would soon be bearing Theresa towards him.

The top of the hillock did indeed give a wonderful view up the loch, but there was nothing stirring its placid surface, not even a gull!

He lay down on his back and closed his eyes, relishing the heat that the sun's rays now brought, and slowly fell into a state of total relaxation.

The sound of low singing brought him back to consciousness. Rising to his knees he saw Theresa walking barefoot toward the burn that bubbled its way past the west side of the houses, crooning to herself as she went. She presented such a beautiful picture, clad as she was in a white blouse and blue skirt, that Bill was unwilling to break the spell by making his presence known.

As he watched, she stood by a shallow man-made pool in the burn and turned away from him, both hands sweeping through her long unbound raven hair as she did so. She then slipped the blouse off and tossed it carelessly on the turf behind her. As she turned Bill caught a glimpse of her proud, heavy, dark-tipped breasts, the first he had ever seen. His breathing stopped, such was the power of the emotion this sight stirred in him, and it took a conscious effort to start it again.

She then knelt by the water and, still with her back to Bill, tied up her hair and washed herself slowly in the clear burn water.

Bill watched the looping curve of her white back as she did so. He was powerless, quite unable to turn away. Closing his eyes against the beauty that confronted him, or fleeing the scene was totally beyond him.

Her toilet completed, Theresa stood again and raised her arms to the warm drying rays of the sun. She stood there motionless, like some deity from the past, for what seemed an age then turned, arms still raised, her eyes closed, this time facing Bill.

He could not believe the beauty she revealed. The dark, almost black aureoles on her breasts were crowned by large dark red nipples, nipples that were stiffly erect—no doubt from the stimulation of the cold water that had so lately been flushed over them. He relived the emotions that had coursed through him just yesterday when he touched those very nipples. As he watched, transfixed, she undid her hair again and let it fall over her shoulders, thus partly obscuring Bill's view of her body. Then she leant far forward and slowly shook her hair.

This action made her pendant breasts appear even larger and Bill at last closed his eyes, unable to cope with the emotions that surged through his young body. He felt the first stirrings of shame course through his veins. Why had he behaved like a peeping Tom? How could he ever look her in the eye after this? The puzzle of where she had appeared from was the least of his worries now.

These thoughts he put to the back of his mind after a struggle, and he quietly and carefully descended the back of the hill until he had reached the shoreline again. There he sat until he had judged it safe to make his appearance around the front of the hill, close by the boat's mooring.

Once there he made a needlessly noisy fuss by the rope, whistling tunelessly through dried lips as he clattered over the stones. He then climbed up again until he was able to retrieve the bags of food, and then wandered aimlessly through the close cluster of rude houses.

As he went his eyes were darting everywhere. Where had Theresa gone? Were her parents perhaps here somewhere too? Then he noticed that a thin plume of smoke had started to rise from the chimney of one of the houses so he headed for that, but first he hid the bags of food again.

"Who's there," he called as he neared the house with the smoking chimney.

"Bill!" The cry came from a seemingly delighted Theresa as she appeared in the open doorway, white blouse reinstated over the blue skirt. "It is lovely to see you. You must have been very quiet; I never heard your boat's engine. You didn't row here, did you?" she added with a mischievous smile.

"No, of course I didn't row. I came in slowly because I wasn't sure if there were any rocks around. It is lovely to see you, Theresa. How did you get here? There isn't another boat in the bay."

"We were coming up the loch yesterday when I told my parents that I wanted to come back here today so they suggested that I come ashore then and stay the night. That meant that they didn't have to take me back down the loch again today. They will come and get me tomorrow. Come on in. I have just lit the fire, so it won't be long before the kettle boils. As soon as it does I'll make you a cup of tea."

"Just give me a minute; I have a few bits and pieces of food in a bag. I left it just down there," said Bill, turning away from her and starting back down the slight incline.

After the bright sunshine outside, Bill found it relatively dark when he returned and entered the small front room of the house. As his eyes grew accustomed to the gloom he saw that it was sparsely furnished. There was a small wooden table with three chairs around it, placed below one of the two front windows. A small white sink was situated below the other window. On the table was a container, suspiciously like a jam jar, that held a few fresh primroses. There was an old brown leather settee to the right of the fire. A small split in it revealed that it was stuffed with what looked like horsehair. On the dark varnished wood-lined wall above the fireplace, there was a heavy-framed painting of a small herd of deer, drinking from a loch that lay below a heather clad mountain. A dark wooden dresser sporting two ornamental plates completed the furnishings. A metal crucifix was attached to the wall above it. Through the open door in the wall opposite the dresser, Bill saw a metal-framed bed, complete with brass knobs. Above it was a print depicting Jesus, his heart exposed and bleeding. The bed was unmade, so was obviously where Theresa had spent the night. The thought of her lying asleep there made him again aware of what he had so recently seen of her.

"There's not much left here, Bill. We moved most of our treasures up the loch to the other house," remarked Theresa with a teasing smile, as she busied herself taking a battered old teapot from the inside of the dresser.

"I wasn't thinking any ill," replied Bill, blushing furiously at the thought that he had been caught scrutinising the bed where Theresa had so lately lain.

They sat at the table when the tea was ready, Theresa making much of the fact that she was able to have a fresh roll—"Thanks to you Bill"—but he was slightly disconcerted when she lowered her head and said grace before she ate. This reminded him again of the difference in their faiths.

Bill broke the silence by asking her how she was getting on at school.

She told him that she had now finished her second year in medicine at Glasgow University. She had come home just three weeks before, for the summer break. She was, she told him, in lodgings in Glasgow, living with her mother's cousin.

"Glasgow is fine, as I told you in my letters, Bill, but I'd far rather be at home here. The city life is not for me so if I qualify as a doctor I'll want to get a practice here—or maybe in somewhere like Campbeltown." The last she added with a demure smile from below her lowered eyes.

"What about boys at the university, there'll be plenty there, I suppose?" Bill asked, knowing well that the answer might further fuel the first pangs of jealousy that he was even now experiencing.

Theresa looked directly at Bill, her gleaming black eyes seeming once again to see right into his heart. After what to Bill seemed an age she said, "I am at university to study, Bill. Yes, there are boys there, many more boys than there are girls, but if I was interested in any of them I wouldn't be sitting here with you. I've told you what I want to do with my life. If I am able, I want to stay there until I am qualified. My parents are sacrificing a lot by allowing me to do this—they could just as easily have insisted that I get a job somewhere. They aren't getting any younger, and they are back on the croft now. They'll miss the income they made here from the shop, even though it wasn't much."

"I'm really sorry, Theresa," Bill said. "I suppose I am a wee bit jealous, thinking of you amongst all these men. They see you every day, and I can't."

"Oh don't be daft, Bill. Come on; let's not sit in here in the dark. There's little enough sunshine in this Loch, and I spend most of my time reading in dusty libraries. It's all right for you; your life is lived in the open air!"

Outside they went to sit on a grassy knoll just a few steps from the door.

"Tell me about yourself, Bill. What are your plans for your life?"

"I met a fellow in Mallaig," Bill began. "He's a fish salesman, and he seems to know just what is what. He wants me to come to live at Mallaig, and says that he will help me to get a boat of my own there. We both think that Mallaig will grow a lot now that the railway has arrived, and it makes sense to get in on the ground floor of this growth. There are lots of markets for herring in England, and the railway is the way to get them there. I have thought a lot about it since I spoke to him. I think that the boats we have just now are far too small. We would have to cross the Minch to get to Mallaig and with boats like the one I'm on we'd miss too much fishing time because we were unable to cross in bad weather. That's another problem I've been thinking about. Our neighbour's cook, Jim, is interested too, and I think he would join me. He is a good lad, and I can trust him."

When he realised that he had a very good listener in Theresa and that she was genuinely interested, Bill told her more of his plans for the future. He talked to her more openly than he had ever talked to anyone—perhaps because he instinctively felt that he could trust her neither to mock his grand plans, nor to tell anyone else of them.

The day wore on and grew hotter until eventually Theresa suggested that they move inside saying, "It's time we had some lunch now, I'm famished."

Inside the house she busied herself around the table whilst Bill sat watching her movements intently. She was without doubt the most beautiful girl he had ever seen, and he noticed that when she passed the open door, that the brightness of the sun outside made it possible for him to see the dim silhouette of her legs through the thin skirt. This sight provoked thoughts that made him feel distinctly uncomfortable.

"I have some cold mutton here, Bill," she said, head bent over a small pie dish that she had taken from inside the dresser. "Come and tell me what you would like."

Bill got up from the settee and came towards her.

He was close enough to touch her when she turned quickly to face him. Her hands instinctively went out in a gesture of defence, but they remained on his waist, where they had landed.

"Oh!" she exclaimed smiling, "I didn't know you were so close. You startled me."

Bill looked into the dark pools of her eyes and was lost instantly.

Their faces drew together slowly until their lips met. Her lips were cool and moist and they parted slowly under the insistent pressure of his. Her hands crept slowly up his back until they met behind his head. Then they gently pulled his head closer.

He could feel the gentle pressure of her firm young breasts against his chest; the breasts that he had so recently seen unbound before him. Her young eager body strained against his, and he felt as though his entire being was on fire.

His hands, grasping her eagerly to himself, closed over her crisp hair—hair that reached to her slim waist. Her face smelt of a faint perfume and her skin was soft beyond belief.

His brain was lost in an intensity of emotion that he could never have imagined possible and reasoned thought disappeared, lost in a blaze whose heat defied belief.

Theresa was the one to break the embrace. She leaned her upper body away—a movement that had the effect of intensifying the contact between their lower bodies, and her hands moved back to Bill's waist. Their eyes met and slowly, very slowly, reason began to return.

Theresa moved away from Bill and sat at the table, her head bowed. Bill stood over her, still not trusting himself to speak.

"I've never kissed anyone else before yesterday, with the exception of my parents," she said slowly. "Please don't think badly of me."

As Bill stared down, he saw her tears spill on to the table. He grasped her shoulders roughly and dropped to his knees beside her chair. Her beautiful dark eyes were misted with tears, and misery clouded her lovely features. He sought her hands and pressed them to his cheeks.

"Theresa my beloved," he started, but words seemed to fail him. "Theresa," he eventually continued, his voice choking, "I don't think I have ever had any doubt, not since the day I first saw you here at Tarbert. I love you more than life. I would never do anything to hurt you. I want to stay with you forever. I'll go anywhere and do anything for you. And yet, I am ashamed of the thoughts that I have had. I have never kissed a girl before you. Not anyone!"

With this, his head dropped and he felt tears well up in his own eyes.

Her hands clasped his face firmly and she lifted it so that once more their eyes met.

"Bill," she whispered, and then she murmured a few words in Gaelic, "I am sorry. When I'm upset I revert to my mother tongue. I love you. I share the same feelings with you. I want to marry you so that we can be together forever. I will never love anyone else, no matter what may befall."

Bill shook his head free from her gentle grasp and as it dropped, the sheer intensity of emotion took over and he felt his tears flow free.

Theresa stood up, pushing the chair back as she did. She bent and once more cupped her hands around his face. As she lifted him slowly to his feet, he smelt the warm perfume of her envelop him. Standing, he buried his face on her shoulder, sobbing.

She backed away slowly, drawing him with her. Through his tears he saw that her eyes were fixed upon his and he followed her—transfixed, incapable of speech, and lost in the depths of her unblinking gaze.

Through the door and into the bedroom she led him, her face unsmiling and grave.

Inside, she turned him around and, still gently, pushed him backwards until he felt the edge of the bed behind his knees. He sat on it facing her. She stepped back a pace and began to unbutton her blouse.

Free from this encumbrance, her gloriously proud breasts confronted him again.

She stepped forward and he smelt the wondrous musk of her, as she began to unbutton his shirt.

His hands seemed powerless and he was incapable of movement or of reason, his senses transfixed by the nearness of these wondrous orbs.

Her task in removing his shirt over, she slowly bent forward, grasped his hands, and raised them to her bosom. He felt, and wondered at their soft heaviness.

Slowly she came yet nearer, and with her soft hands guided his mouth to the large erect crimson nipples that crowned her breasts. She crooned and cradled Bill as though he was her baby.

Her hands now firmly on his shoulders, Theresa stepped away, breaking the comforting contact. She slowly undid the belt at the waist of her skirt and, as it fell to the floor, she stepped out of it to stand erect, proud and unashamed before him, naked.

Bill's eyes fell unbidden to the black mass of hair at the apex of her legs. This bore no resemblance to his experience with the child Kate, so many years ago. This woman, his Theresa, was beautiful beyond belief.

She stood there for what seemed to be an age then slowly moved nearer to him again. This time she did not stop, but bore him backwards until they fell on to the bed together. He felt her hands, slowly eager, at his belt and then she knelt beside him, eyes on his, and drew his trousers down. They landed on the floor beside the bed and then her softly insidious fingers moved to his underwear. He groaned then in futile protest as she drew them over his erection, but she hushed him into immobility again.

Theresa kissed him now, as they lay naked together. He was frantic with desire, but she would not allow him to take charge. Again she led his hands to her breasts and as he explored them, she raised herself and straddled him.

He could feel the moistness of her core close to him, and was amazed at the heat he felt there.

Her hand sought him—and again she stilled his protests. Slowly, ever so slowly, she lowered herself on to him. Their eyes were locked together now; this was the supreme moment of their love for each other. Theresa flinched slightly at the tightness she felt as she descended and paused, but only for a moment, continuing until he was fully inside her. Then she leant forward and kissed Bill with a tenderness he could hardly believe, before she started to move.

Bill's eyes closed then for the first time since they entered the room. In the darkness he felt his entire conscious mind descend through his body until his whole being was gathered in a welter of the most intense feeling he had ever experienced, concentrating where her body was moving—now quickly—on his. This intensity gathered until he could bear it no more, and he screamed and bucked upwards in the burning ecstatic pain of relief. Vaguely he sensed that Theresa also was screaming, her head thrown back as she sat over him, but forever after he was convinced that he had lost consciousness for a time.

They dozed peacefully in one another's arms until they came slowly back to wakefulness, facing one another as they lay side by side on the softness of the bed. Theresa smiled at Bill, shyness returning to her.

They told the same story that lovers have told since time began, softly, unashamedly, and unhurriedly caressing and exploring as they spoke, until again they made love, Bill taking the lead this time.

Later, Theresa was the first to stir, getting out of bed and quietly insisting that Bill follow. She stripped the sheet and took it outside. Bill saw that it was stained with blood and then, looking down at himself, saw the same stains on his body. Theresa calmed his alarm and explained that this would only happen once, and that it was quite natural. She made fun of it saying, "That's the best of having a doctor in the family!" She then washed the sheet and spread it in the sun to dry as Bill, at her invitation, displayed his prowess as a cook in preparing a very late lunch.

As they ate, Theresa, with downcast eyes, asked Bill if she had shocked him by her behaviour.

"Me shocked? No, not really," his bravado made him lie. "But I certainly was thrown a wee bit, you see, I had never seen a naked woman before."

"Oh yes you did!" she smilingly replied.

Again Bill protested his innocence, and again she stated her disbelief.

"Did you not see me this morning as I was washing?" she laughed.

"You knew I was watching! How did you know I was there?"

"Your engine wasn't that quiet when you came into the bay. I heard you and then saw you climb the hill."

"You horror," cried Bill. "You enjoyed teasing me. I'll get you for that."

They spent the rest of the day in closer communion than either of them had ever felt with anyone, talking unashamedly of their fears and their hopes, and reiterating their love for one another. Bill didn't want to let her out of his sight, feeling lost as soon as she went anywhere.

"I feel terrible saying this Bill," said Theresa as the day wore on. "You could stay the night if you want, but only if it doesn't mean that someone will be out looking for you."

"There is nothing I'd like more. Jim is the only one that might worry, but I warned him that he was not to come looking for me until tomorrow night. I said that in case I had an engine breakdown," he added hastily. "I had no idea that we—you know."

As evening came they sat on a bench outside the house, gazing across the still calm waters of Loch Nevis to where the sun's dying rays bathed the mountains of Knoydart in a glory of red.

The blissful calm encouraged Bill to now unburden himself totally in Theresa's willing ears—all of his hopes and dreams came out. He wanted to settle in Mallaig and to become a successful fisherman. He would not be content with owning one boat, he told her. He had visions of himself being a shore owner eventually, directing his fleet's operations from the house he would some day build. Reading, as he had, some of the many tales of the Klondike days in the Yukon, he had realised that the people who made the real money were the ones who supplied the miners' needs, not the men who actually did the digging. He had seen how his own family life had been curtailed by the prolonged absence of his father, and how neither he nor his brother had got to know him well as a result. He did not want his wife to have to be father and mother to his children, nor did he want to have children until he had established himself.

"What about a wife?" asked Theresa quietly. "You mentioned that, do you have anyone in mind?"

"You know full well that I'm going to marry you, Theresa—that is if you'll have me," he added quickly. "You are very much a part of the life I want to build for myself here. In fact, I would need you beside me to help me to achieve all these goals. What about you though, you've heard me ranting on about myself long enough."

Theresa paused before she replied. "I very much want to become a doctor, Bill. You know that already. My parents have given up a lot for me, and it isn't very often that a girl from my sort of background can get to University. I don't want to let them down if I can possibly avoid it. I would never marry anyone but you, Bill, and if I could get to be a doctor in or around Mallaig, I could help you achieve some of your goals. I have known since I first saw you that you are the only one I will ever love but there is a snag that you are forgetting—we spoke of it yesterday. I am a Catholic, and when I marry, it will have to be in a Catholic Church, and our children will have to be brought up as Catholics too. You are a Protestant, but all I know about your religion has been learned from my friends at University. My mother and father have never spoken to me about this, but I know beyond doubt that they would not be happy to see me marry a Protestant even if he did change. Being older, they are much more set in their ways. We will just have to face up to them together when that day comes. Things will change sometime, I am certain, but we are stuck with the present. I'd like you to think about it all carefully, Bill, but in any case, we cannot marry before I graduate. I owe my parents that. Unless of course I get pregnant as a result of what we have been up to," she added mischievously.

"Well, if that happens, you will be able to do something about it, you could get rid of it—you are almost a doctor now, aren't you?"

"What do you mean, 'Get rid of it,'" retorted Theresa sharply. "If I was pregnant would you want me to murder our child? That is what it would amount to!"

"I was only joking, Theresa," he added slowly—but his hesitation told the lie. "But how could it be murder if you got rid of it soon? It isn't as if the thing was alive, is it? You know you won't be pregnant—will you?"

The last bit was added rather apprehensively, Theresa thought, but nevertheless she assured him that it was highly unlikely. It was the wrong time of the month for her to become pregnant, she told him archly.

They sat silent for a long time. She was much more perturbed by his talk of getting rid of an unborn infant than she was willing to show. This was something that was utterly repugnant to her and it went against her every instinct. She was also bothered by his remarks that he hoped that she knew what she was doing, and that she would not become pregnant. Gradually however, they each became content in the closeness that they shared, until the gloaming chill chased them into the house.

They spent the night locked in each other's arms, exploring each other's bodies and making love with the quiet content that only people who are true soulmates can ever experience.

Chapter Six

When morning came, the weather still windless and settled looking, they went outside to wash in the burn. Bill said, reluctantly, that he really should get back to Mallaig in case the engine parts had arrived, so after a Spartan breakfast they made their way down to the rock to which the dinghy was secured.

There they took their leave of one another tearfully. Bill promised that he would write to her in Glasgow, not to Loch Nevis. This, they agreed, would keep her parents from worrying about this fisherman who might steal their daughter away. She in turn said that she would not be able write to him until after she returned to her studies, as it would be impossible, while living up the Loch, to hide the fact that she had letters to post.

On his way back down the Loch, Bill went over the events of the last day or two. He thought of Theresa's part in the consummation of their relationship. He had never before thought that a girl would, or could have behaved in such a fashion, and thinking about it troubled him greatly. It startled him initially when the thought that she had behaved quite shamelessly, came into his mind. Girls simply didn't feel or act in that way, he reasoned! Gradually however, he reached the conclusion that he really shouldn't have been surprised at her actions. She had been brought up on a croft where it was not at all uncommon to see animals mating. Such things were simply a part of farm life, and there would be no mystery about them. His own existence was due to what was, of course, human sexuality. Why should girls not have the same sort of feelings as men? Were they not also human?

His doubts were further eased when he realised that yesterday had been the first time that either of them had ever had real sexual contact with anyone. He knew that Theresa must have had the same sort of opportunities to have sex as anyone else, and guessed that such happenings would not be unusual when healthy young men and women were in close contact daily as was the case in universities. The knowledge that they had somehow saved themselves for one another finally reassured him about their lovemaking.

Back in Mallaig, Bill warned Jim that he must never even think of asking what had happened. Work, he declared grimly, was all that would count for the next five years.

"I'm off up to see Willie Mair now, Jim, and I think you should come with me. What I am going to ask him, could well involve you too."

"It's all very well for you to tell me not to ask about what happened yesterday, Bill, but you have changed somehow. Is everything all right?"

"Sorry, Jim, I'm going too fast," replied Bill. "Yes, everything is fine, but maybe I have been a wee bit hasty. Tell me, would you be willing to join me if Mr. Mair can get us a boat? Not right now, but soon. I think there is a lot of money to be made here if we can get in before the rush starts. This is the place where all the herring caught in the Minch will be sold in the future, or I'm a Dutchman. What do you say? Are you willing to take a chance?"

Jim thought for a time before replying.

"There's a lot of sense in what you are saying, Bill. Our skipper was on about that just recently. He won't move here though; he is too old, and too set in his ways. I'll come up with you and see what this man has to say, but I'm not promising anything till I hear the options." The pair then set off up the pier to the salesman's office.

"Your engine parts will be here this evening, and we'll get them fitted tonight. Macbeth, the engineer, will do a good job, you may be sure of that. As soon as he has done all his tests, we can let your skippers know. They'll be desperate to get back to sea now, or my name isn't Willie Mair!"

This was said as soon as the two young men had been seated before the big wooden desk in the inner office. Willie, with the inbuilt sense of a man well used to the ways of fishermen, had sat himself formally behind this rather forbidding desk. His instincts told him that this was not an idle visit.

"So, is there anything else I can do for you?"

"Yes, Willie. Jim and I have been talking, and we feel that we might like to settle here—if the deal with a boat is the right one," Bill added quickly. "We are not married, we both are hard workers, and we can make a go of it, of that I am certain."

"I don't think you could have possibly timed this visit better, lads," said Willie. "There is a man from Lochboisdale who is keen to take up the ring-net, but he has no experience of it. He has a boat that belonged to his father. This poor man died, very young, just last month. They have been fishing with drift nets, but this fellow thinks that the ring-net is the thing of the future. I don't know if he would be willing to go neighbours with you—he may think that you are a bit on the young side even though he is not much older himself. This would all depend on us getting you a boat, that is. Have you any of your own money to put up?"

"Money of our own? You must be joking, Willie. We're far too young to have saved up any money," said Bill. "Jim and I just started getting a full share about six months ago; we were on half shares until then. I might be able to get a loan from my parents, but that would all depend on how they felt about me leaving home. Jim's parents are both dead—he has been brought up by his aunt and uncle. Would they be able to help, Jim?"

Jim laughed at that. "No, they certainly don't have money to throw about, and I think far more of them than to cause them embarrassment by asking."

"Hmm, we'll have to see what my head office has to say about this," said Willie, thoughtfully. "They usually want the applicants for a loan to put up half of the total, but I'll see what can be done. Nothing will happen in a hurry though; there is a lot to be sorted out. I'll get in touch with the Lochboisdale chap—he's a fine lad and a good fisherman too. The only problem I can foresee is—as I said—that he might want someone older. You'll need to talk things over with your parents, Bill. You might well be more of a free agent, Jim. Will you be moving here if things go the way you want them to go?"

"We haven't talked about that," said Bill, with a sideways glance at Jim. "It would be inevitable, though, if we get all we need," he concluded with a sly glance at Willie from below his eyebrows.

"Aye, aye, you are a fine pair all right," laughed Willie. "Off you go now and talk it all over. I'll be in touch with my bosses, and with the man in Lochboisdale, and I'll write to you at your home addresses as soon as I have something to tell you. I hope you enjoyed your trip up the loch, Bill. It can be a cold place at night on your own, even in the summer!"

Was Bill's imagination playing up, or was there a laughing glint in Willie's eye as he uttered the last sentence?

The intrepid pair spent all afternoon discussing their foray into the world of high finance. Jim took a little persuasion before he finally entrusted his fate to Bill's pleadings, but agreed following the enthusiastic portrayal of the oceans of herring that were there for the taking. "It couldn't be better, Jim," Bill cried. "Think of all the local knowledge we'll gain from this Lochboisdale lad. He will be well acquainted with all the wee lochs and bays, and that is where the herring will be in the winter months. You'll see—I bet he knows every rock and shoal in the Hebrides! Besides that, Willie Mair is desperate to get us signed up. His job is to get this place up and running and he knows perfectly well that he can't do it without the likes of us. How many married men would be willing to move here? What would their wives say if they suggested leaving Campbeltown or Girvan, to settle here, tell me that? There's nothing here but a few sheep and a railway line but mark my words, folk like Willie Mair, aye and like that baker too, they can see the future that is possible in this place. And, in case you think I just want to move here to be near to Theresa, I can tell you that she is going to be busy at University for a good few years yet. We'll not even be thinking of getting married till after she qualifies."

He paused then before adding, thoughtfully, "That's if she still wants a common fisherman after mixing with all these doctors and lawyers that she will be meeting."

They sealed their pact in a cup of tea, and sat quietly planning and plotting until Macbeth the engineer arrived with the new fuel pump, then went down to the engine room with him, to watch just how these things were fitted.

The crews arrived back on the following night's train, and whilst they were preparing the boats to sail off west towards the fishing grounds, they related stories of their enjoyment of the bright lights of Campbeltown. "Not like this dump!" they said to the youngsters. "Did you enjoy meeting all these sheep?"

Bill and Jim held their tongues as they had previously agreed. There was no sense in risking getting the sack from a good berth if they told their skippers that they might be leaving soon.

Their time in the North was limited. There had been reports of an appearance of herring off the Cock of Arran while the men had been home, Bill learned, and the apron strings were pulling the married men homeward again.

On the long passage south and east to the Clyde a few days later, Bill shared a watch with old Dennis.

"Tell me, Dennis," he said quietly, "What do you think of a Protestant marrying a Catholic? I'm serious about it; it means a lot to me. I've asked you already, I know, but I don't know who else I can talk to about it."

"Well now, Bill, as you say, this isn't the first time you have brought the subject up and I think you must have a good reason for asking me." He took out his old pipe, and again took a long time filling and lighting it. "I did a wee bit of research after the last time you asked me—for my own benefit, you'll understand. I like you a lot, so I will tell you exactly what I think. The current rules are that the powers-that-be will not allow a Protestant to marry in a Catholic Church. He must renounce his faith, and become a Catholic. Now, before you—or anyone else for that matter—do that, you should consider it very carefully. To someone who has no real faith of their own, it is probably a good thing that they join a Church. To someone who has a deep faith, it might well lead to trouble in the future. For example, a young man might agree to change in the flush of passion—and we were all young, so I can remember how strongly I once felt about the girls. In that case, he might start to rebel when he got a bit older, and that would lead to trouble between him and his wife. In a mixed marriage my Church says that the Protestant must agree that their children should be brought up in the Catholic faith. That too could lead to bother. For example, how would your father react if his grandchildren were Catholics? I think that in time our two Churches will grow closer together, but they are so divided just now that I would even have to ask my Priest for permission to attend the marriage of a friend in a Protestant church. It is by no means certain that he would allow me to do so either! I think that, sadly, we should marry into our own Faiths unless, as I said before, the Protestant does not have a strong belief. Then it wouldn't matter. It might even do some good!"

The kindly words from old Dennis were so obviously wise and well-meaning, that Bill sat quiet for a long time, then he asked, "When you said that in time the Churches would come closer, did you mean that this might happen soon, say in five years?"

"No, Bill, I would say that fifty years would be nearer the mark."

After another long silence Bill asked, "What if the girl was a Catholic. Could she not get married to a Protestant in his Church?"

"Yes she could, but as I told you already she would be living in sin as far as the Catholic Church is concerned. She would not be able to take communion—oh no, there would be nothing but bother ahead for the girl who did that. She would be cut off from her Church, and that would be a recipe for disaster. I don't know what is bothering you Bill, but I hope you can get it all sorted out. You are a fine young man with a good future ahead of you. I would be delighted if you wanted to marry a daughter of mine but oh dear, I would dread what might happen. If you want to know any more, you should ask your own Minister and a Priest too, but beware what either of them says. Your own conscience, aye and your prayers to the good Lord, will give you a less biased answer."

His next comment, "Is that Ardtornish light I see flashing ahead?" ended the conversation, but Bill was to recall his wise words many times in the future.

Chapter Seven

Between them, Bill and Jim decided that they would not say anything at all about their plans until they had heard something concrete from Willie Mair, but they were not kept in suspense for very long.

The letters they received from Mallaig were identical, and were filled with good news. The fish-selling firm had agreed to back the pair financially on Willie's recommendation, provided they tied themselves to the firm legally. All of their catches were to be sold through Willie, and all returns were to be made to his office even if the catch were landed somewhere that this firm did not have a representative. A fixed percentage of the boat's gross earnings were to be paid over, and in return, all of the routine paperwork would be dealt with, the boat's bills would be paid, and crew wages calculated. The loan—for such it was—on the boat, was to be paid off as soon as possible. Equally importantly, Willie told them that Alex John MacDonald, the Lochboisdale man, was happy to try out working with them for a season. His boat was called the *Mystical Rose*. He would also be able to get men from the island to help to crew their new boat if necessary. That was good news, as Bill had been quite concerned about the lack of suitable men around Mallaig.

As soon as they had signed agreements to the terms set out, the letter continued, Willie's firm would set about finding a suitable boat—although he personally had an idea where he could lay his hands on just the craft they would need. He suggested that Bill and Jim respond as quickly as possible to this letter. It would be better, he reckoned, that they start teaching Alex John the art of ring netting in the summer months, before the winter season got under way.

Bill and Jim met in the street. They had been en route for each other's homes to discuss the contents of the letter.

They set off down the pier together and got themselves comfortably settled in the privacy of the forecastle of the *Silver Birch*. The kettle was soon boiled on the Primus stove, and when they had a cup of steaming tea in their hands, they began to talk excitedly about the new development.

Everything, they agreed, seemed fine. There was nothing in the letter that raised any doubts.

"You'll need to talk to your parents about this, Bill, before we write back to Willie and as soon as we decide when we are leaving, we'll need to tell our skippers. It wouldn't be fair to just up and leave, they should get some warning."

"Aye, Jim," replied Bill. "It has been on my conscience that I haven't told anyone about our plans—except for Theresa of course. She won't have mentioned it to anyone, I'm sure. How will your folks take this?"

"Well, it isn't as if we are going to the ends of the earth, Mallaig isn't that far away really. My aunt and uncle are good people. They'll try to talk me out of it, I'm sure, but when you think about it, Bill, we have nothing to lose really—except our pride if we have to come back here again with our tails between our legs!"

"That won't happen, Jim. There is a good future ahead of us. We're not daft—we may be a bit young yet, but neither of us is afraid of hard work. The opportunities are there; it is up to us to make a go of it. I would like to think that we would be able to buy another boat for you to skipper, in a few years' time. We'd be rich in no time," he laughed.

"I think we should get this partnership off on the right footing though," Jim said hesitantly. "There's something that has been bothering me a bit, and I want to say it now. It is about Theresa. You just seem to fly off the handle whenever her name comes up. I want to ask you something about her now—see—there's that wild look in your eyes again! That is not going to do, Bill, I'm deadly serious. We need to be able to talk sensibly about everything, and that includes her. We are all mixed up in this deal together."

Bill sat silent for a moment, and then replied. "You're right, Jim, I'm sorry. I just don't want anyone to tease me about her, and the whole situation has maybe been getting on top of me. I suppose I have been too secretive. What is it that you want to ask?"

"Well," Jim paused for a long time, thinking hard about what he would say. He had thought of it often, especially in the last few days, but didn't want to send the wrong message to Bill.

"How much of a part does she play in your wanting to go and settle in Mallaig? That is what we are going to do after all, settle there. Would you still want to go if you had never met her, and will you stay if she disappears out of your life?"

Bill laughed out loud at this. "Is that all? I thought there was something about her that was bothering you. In answer to your questions, yes, I would still want to go there even if I had never seen her, and if things don't go well at the fishing I'll be the first to suggest that we leave again." Here he hesitated for a bit. "Jim, I love her, and I want to marry her, but I will never let that love influence me in any way as far as fishing is concerned. If I was thinking only about her, don't you think that I would be trying to get a job in Glasgow, where I could be near her whilst she is studying? It is over two months since I saw her now."

"I'm sorry, Bill, I don't want to pry into your private affairs. I am a bit worried because she is a Catholic though, it would have been better if you were the same religion."

"But we are the same religion, Jim," Bill said. "We are both Christians!"

Jim didn't reply to this, but privately he sensed a disaster ahead. Bill was not, he thought, treating the whole business of differing beliefs seriously enough and therefore was not being fair to Theresa, but he was not about to interfere further.

As soon as he and Jim had agreed on their future ahead, they composed a reply to Willie, agreeing to the terms set out in his letter. Bill then wrote a long letter to Theresa. He had heard nothing from her since they had arrived home, but by now, he reckoned, she should be back in Glasgow and would be free to reply.

In this letter, which consisted largely of imparting the good news about the boat, he also told her of his long conversation with old Dennis.

Perhaps it was his excitement with the knowledge that he was on the verge of realising his ambition, of becoming skipper of his own boat, that clouded his judgement; perhaps he had not yet realised that Theresa's faith was a major part of her everyday life whereas his was nicely contained within a couple of hours on an occasional Sunday, or perhaps it was just the plain, crass thoughtlessness of youth that caused him to write what he did. Bill suggested that thought that the 'slight problem' that their religious differences posed could be simply overcome by their being 'hitched,' as he put it, in a Registry Office!

He then compounded the major errors he had already made by referring lightly to the possibility of her being pregnant, writing that he was glad that she did not appear to be 'in the family way' or that if she had been, she had taken steps to remedy that. Such problems, he wrote, should be dealt with by the women concerned!

These personal parts of the letter were not written to be cruel nor were they meant to attempt to deal in a business-like manner with personal differences. They were written as an afterthought to conveying to Theresa what was foremost in Bill's mind; his fishing career. If he had written it thoughtfully, he would have realised that he had taken no heed of her strong beliefs and had totally disregarded her dreams of becoming a doctor. As it was, it must have seemed to Theresa that he was repeating the views he had already expressed in the cottage, this time deliberately disregarding the feelings that she had made abundantly clear on that occasion.

Whatever the reasons for it being written, many, many years would pass before he understood just how big a mistake he had made; a mistake that would affect not only their lives, but the lives of many other, totally innocent people.

Perhaps it was his natural excitement at the thought of his life's dreams being made possible that clouded his thinking; or perhaps in the matter of the girl he so loved his fundamental honesty would out. Or perhaps he had not fully realised that though faith rested lightly with him, Theresa's faith was profound. Whichever, he carelessly wrote that he thought the matter of the religious objections to their marriage could easily be put aside, perhaps with a Registry Office wedding, and then, in a gross error that he much, much later came to realise was the biggest single mistake he ever made, wrote of his gladness that Theresa had not become pregnant, or that if she had, would have made arrangements to deal with the matter.

He wrote this not in a moment of cruel harshness, but as a practical man planning to build a good life with the woman he loved, and about how a pregnancy would without any question compromise this and put an end to Theresa's dreams of being a doctor as well. Nevertheless, in ink on paper, his real feelings were revealed as they had been in those moments at the cottage when she had sharply rebuked him for them.

After he had posted the letters, he plucked up enough courage to speak to his parents, a duty he had been avoiding for too long.

As he had feared, they were united against his plans, saying that he was far too young to be thinking of leaving home. His father was particularly vociferous in his objections. He had, of course, been planning to get Bill aboard his boat where he could train him to take over when the time came. Bill had suspected that, but knew his father well enough to know that he would hang on to the reins for as long as he possibly could—far longer than Bill was prepared to wait.

They talked for a long time, and then Bill said, "Dad, you will have Donald leaving school this year. He is different, and he may well be content to stay here with you."

Then, in an attempt to split the unity of the ranks arrayed against him he continued, "If Mam allows him to go to the fishing, that is."

"Donald will not be a fisherman if I can possibly talk him out of it. You and your Dad being at the sea is enough. I want one ashore with me." Tears began to roll down her cheeks as she choked back a sob. That was enough to make Bill ashamed of his ploy and he impulsively threw his arms around her.

"Mam, I'm not going to the ends of the earth," he said, close to tears himself.

"Mallaig isn't that far away, it is only a few hours by train from Glasgow. If it is the chance of me being drowned that is worrying you, Dad will tell you that the North is a far safer place to work than just about anywhere else; all the fishing is done in sheltered lochs." He said this with an appealing look to his father.

"He's right enough, lass. The boy's right enough. Maybe we should let him go with our blessings. Men need to do their own things in this world, you know that well."

Then to Bill he said, "You must promise us that if things don't work out, you will come home. Give it a try, your best try, and I hope that you succeed. If you don't, there will always be a berth waiting for you. Old Archie speaks well of you, and his blessing goes a long way in making a man's reputation. He will be disappointed to lose you though."

Bill's mother dried her tears, having returned Bill's embrace, and started to busy herself aimlessly around the kitchen, dusting and rearranging the few ornaments she owned.

"I suppose that I'll just have to accept what you want to do, Bill. If you are going away soon, I'll have to get busy. There is a lot to be done you know, clothes just don't clean themselves!" Then she added tearfully, "How will you get your washing done, and who will look after you at the weekends? Are you going to stay on the boat all the time? You men, I just can't keep up with you, you are as changeable as the weather."

The rest of Bill and Jim's time in Campbeltown was spent busily sorting things out prior to their departure. Their respective skippers had expressed their disappointment at losing good men, but they assured them of their best wishes and allowed the pair to leave as soon as their replacements were chosen. This didn't take long—berths aboard good boats were soon filled.

Very soon after Bill had told his skipper, old Archie, that he was leaving, Dennis O'Hara sought him out.

"I've just heard that you are away to leave us, boy. Off to the North, I hear. Well, I don't want you to go without my blessing. You have been a good lad and a good shipmate too. I am sure you will put all your learning to good use." Then he added, with a twinkle in his eye, "I hope so anyway, I would hate to think that all I taught you was going to be wasted!" He paused for a moment then continued: "Did you ask your minister or a priest about yon other thing that was bothering you?"

"No, Dennis, I didn't. I think I'll just let it lie for a bit. Thank you for coming to talk to me though. I appreciate all you have taught me and you may rest assured, I will not waste any of it."

"Aye, boy. It may be just as well not to let the clergy in on any of your problems. Sometimes they will try to get you to toe the party line, rather than tell you what may be best for you."

He looked long at Bill, and then held out his gnarled hand. "Anyway, take the blessings of an old man with you. I hope it all goes well for you, and I hope to see you in the North before too long."

He turned then and walked away. Bill stood alone, and watched the old man until he disappeared out of sight behind the herring barrels that lined the top of the pier. He knew that he would miss him greatly.

Before long the awaited letters arrived from Mallaig. When they opened them the new partners were delighted to read that Willie had put in an offer for the boat he had earmarked for them, and that he wanted them to come to Mallaig as soon as possible. A net, or nets, had also to be bought, and he felt that they should say just what sort of nets they wanted. On that subject Bill was ahead of Willie. He had spent some time with the manager of the local net factory and had two nets tentatively ordered. All that was needed to get the work started was written confirmation from the fish salesman who would pay for them.

Bill had specified nets of different depths so that they would be prepared for fishing just about anywhere. Whilst speaking to the manager, Bill had told him that Alex John, skipper of their new neighbour boat, would also need two nets. He was certain that the Uist man would not have a ring net in his gear store. If this new order were confirmed, Bill said, he would expect commission in the way of a reduction in the price of his nets. This was agreed readily enough. When Jim first heard of this deal he was shocked, then, as he realised that this was their baptism into the ways of the world, he laughed and said, "I knew you would make a success of things, Bill. This confirms my thoughts. You are a hard man!"

Bill wrote again to Theresa, bringing her up to date with all the news and telling her that he would be leaving in two days, for Mallaig. She should, he continued, write to him care of Willie Mair.

On the morning of their departure they met at the bus terminal in the town and caught the early bus to Glasgow. They had earlier agreed that they did not want anyone to see them off. Tearful farewells were the last thing they wanted.

The journey to the rail station at Arrochar took four hours, but they were busy planning ahead, so they didn't feel the time pass at all.

They boarded the Mallaig train in some excitement. This was, after all, the first time they had ever travelled by this means. At Fort William, they had a wait of almost half-an-hour before starting the final leg of their trip. Whilst stretching their legs on the platform Bill spotted Ian MacPherson, the man he had spoken to in Mallaig on his first visit. He was leaning out of the engine, and recognised Bill at once.

"Aye, there," he roared, jumping down with his hand outstretched. "Are you one of the Campbeltown men that are coming to get a new boat for the ring net in Mallaig? If you are I wouldn't mind a berth; I am fed up with this railway lark, up and down the same bit of track, day after day. I'd like to try fishing before long, and ring netting for herring would suit me just fine. It'll be a change of scenery anyway!"

Bill was initially shocked at discovering that their mission was known outside the salesman's office but when he had recovered his wits he replied, "Well, nothing is finalised yet, Ian, but yes, maybe we will need a man. We'll let you know. Are you really good with diesel engines? An engineer might be useful—if we go ahead, that is."

"Any good with diesels, you say? Can a bird fly? There's not a lot that I can't do with marine engines—they're my hobby. Far better than the dirty old steam kettles I have to work with. What make of engine is in your boat?"

"I'm blowed if I know, Ian," admitted Bill. "We haven't seen her yet, and we're not even sure that we have got one. It seems that you know just about as much as we do about it—by the way, this is Jim, my partner. Jim, this is Ian MacPherson. It looks as though he might be our new engineer. If we have a boat, that is!"

"Aye, but if we don't get on the train now, we'll all be spending the night in Fort William. There's old Jimmy the guard getting ready with his flag and whistle. See, that's him looking at his watch. I'll talk to you in Mallaig."

With that, the irrepressible Ian skipped off down the platform and up on to the footplate where his first action was to give a cheery tootle on the whistle.

"Well, Bill, that's us on the last leg. It won't be long now. How do you feel?"

"I'd be telling lies if I didn't admit to being just a wee bit nervous, Jim. I'm not certain that we did the correct thing in letting Willie Mair choose a boat for us but then, beggars can't be choosers, and this is just a start."

Willie Mair was waiting for them on the platform when they finally arrived, and after welcoming them, he helped them load their luggage on to a small barrow.

"You will be staying with a friend of my wife for as long as you want. She's a fine lass. I just don't know what your long term plans are—if you want to stay on the boat all the time or not—but this lady will do your washing for you in any case, if that is all right with you. In my opinion, you could do an awful lot worse than lodge with her all the time, though."

Ian roared at them from the front of the train as they left, telling them that he would see them in the morning, a comment that caused Willie to ask quizzically if they knew him and then add, "He's not a bad lad beneath all the racket he makes!"

They arrived at the door of a small, whitewashed cottage that was not far from the centre of the village. It was of a more modern design than its neighbouring houses. For example, it had slates instead of a thatched roof. The small garden, viewed through the gathering gloom, seemed to be well cared for and was ringed with a substantial fence that appeared to the lads to be much higher than they would have thought necessary.

A small, chubby, white haired woman met them at the door and ushered them in. "Come away in, boys, come away in," she cried in a broad East Coast accent. "The kettle is boiling. You'll be hungry after your long trip, I'm sure. Come through here, this is where you will be sleeping. You can get rid of your luggage in here and get a wee wash while I make the supper."

Willie took his leave of them, saying that he would see them in his office in the morning, and left the pair alone in the neat tidy room. There was a small washbasin in a corner, with two fluffy towels arranged neatly to one side of it. A pair of hand-embroidered bedspreads covered the twin beds that were placed on either side of the window, and the room seemed immaculately clean. On the small cabinet that stood against the wall opposite the beds there was a framed photograph. Closer inspection of this revealed the lady of the house and a man sitting beside her, who, Bill guessed, was her husband. An attractive fair-haired young girl who appeared to be of a similar age to Jim and himself, stood behind them, a hand on each of their shoulders. The final decoration the room boasted was a religious text in the form of a sailing ship. Each of the sails on this square-rigger—called the 'Gospel Ship'—had a biblical quotation inscribed on it.

"Well, Bill, home was never like this," said Jim quietly after lifting the bedcover to reveal spotlessly clean linen sheets and pillowcases.

"Aye, Jim, the landlady seems to be really nice. I hope that Willie's taste in boats is as good as his taste in landladies. That lassie is not bad looking either, I wonder if she is their daughter," said Bill as he stripped off his jersey in preparation for a much-needed wash.

When they finished their toilet they joined their landlady who promptly sat them at a well-laden table. When they had eaten as much as they could of the feast that Mrs. Ritchie—or Meg, as she assured them she wanted to be called—had put before them, they pushed back their chairs. Jim sighed contentedly and thanked her.

While she washed the dishes in the kitchen sink she told them, calling over her shoulder, that her husband, George, was a fisherman also but currently he was a mate on a klondiker which was now moored, she thought, at Stornoway. He didn't make a lot of money, she said, but at least he got paid regularly, and that was something to be grateful for. He hoped to be a skipper some day. She augmented their income and passed her time profitably, by taking in lodgers. They had a daughter, Lisa, who worked in an office on the East Coast. Meg was, she said, always delighted, when her visitors were young people—"Like you two"— she beamed, adding, "I hope you will be regulars; we need young blood in the village."

"Did you see the garden on the way in?" she asked. Then, not waiting for a reply she continued—"You'll have spotted the height of the fence, no doubt? That is to try to keep these blessed sheep out; they're all over the place. Two minutes in the garden, and they'll have the work of a season just ruined. The beggars will eat anything, but they seem to be very fond of flowers. Anyway, I mustn't blether all night, you must be tired. Off you go to bed now; I'll call you in the morning."

They needed no further bidding, so said their goodnights to the good lady on their way into the bedroom where they fell, exhausted, into the soft warm beds.

Next morning, well slept and after a big breakfast, the lads made their way to the harbour and Willie's office.

"Come in, lads. Were the digs all right? I'm sure they were. No one has ever complained about the way Meg treated them. She is a proper gem," said Willie as he rearranged some papers on his desk.

"There are a few things we'll need to get you to sign before we go any further. I'll sign them too where necessary. Jessie, my clerkess, will witness our signatures. These are just the agreements we spoke about earlier, the amount of commission you will have to pay us, loan repayments, and of course the agreement that this office will handle your accounts no matter where you land your catches. They are all in legal jargon, but they are the same as you agreed to in your letter. You will find them all in order. I have checked them myself. I am on the spot here, and I am the fellow you would fall out with if something were wrong, so you can trust me. When we have finished, you'll come down the pier for a wee stroll."

After a perfunctory look at the papers, they signed them, Bill saying jocularly, "I expect we've signed our lives away now, Willie!"

"No, Bill. These papers are for the protection of all of us. They will stop any arguments or disagreements that might crop up in the future. Anyway, let's go. I have something to show you."

Down the wooden pier the three of them went, Willie leading the way until he stood above a trim-looking boat about sixteen metres long. She was painted black, unlike the cleaner-looking varnish that adorned most of the other boats that Jim and Bill were used to seeing, but she looked well cared for. The registration letters BRD, for Broadford and the number 97 were painted on each quarter, and again on each shoulder.

"What do you think about this one then? Will she do you?"

"Is that her?" blurted out Bill, excitedly. "She looks braw," he continued, "But she'll look even better when we have finished with her. There are a few things we'll need to change before we are ready to go to sea, but that won't take very long, really. What do you think, Jim?"

"She certainly looks good! Let's get aboard, and see what she is like up close. By the way, Willie, that fellow that spoke to us in the station last night, Ian MacPherson, says that he would like to come with us as engineer. Is he all right?"

"By Jove, you lads don't hang about! Yes, he is a steady enough lad, and I've heard that he is very good with engines. I believe that some time back, Macbeth, the engineer, wanted him to serve an apprenticeship with him, but Ian joined the railway instead. If you get him aboard with you he'll do a good job, I'm sure."

The two lads set to immediately exploring and examining the boat at some length. Everything seemed to be well cared for and the engine room, with the eighty-eight horsepower Kelvin engine, was exceptionally clean and tidy. She was a little bigger than the *Bengullion*—not much, but it showed in the forecastle and engine room particularly.

They agreed that the name, *Misty Isle,* was acceptable, but in any case they were influenced to a degree by the thought that it was considered bad luck to change the name of a boat.

It was mid afternoon when Jim, as they were exploring together in the tiller flat, asked Bill plaintively if they were on a diet. "We've had nothing to eat since breakfast!" he complained.

"Right then, Jim. You nip up and get something from the baker; I'll boil up the kettle."

Jim arrived back shortly bearing a large white paper bag. The size of it caused Bill to ask in amazement if they were going to feed the five thousand!

"The baker gave me all this free, Bill," said Jim. "She heard that we have just bought this boat, and said that this was for good luck!"

Bill looked at Jim for a while before he replied. "We've got off to a good start, partner. Let's hope that everyone is as kind as the ones we have met so far."

They had just started tucking in to the pies and pasties that the bag contained when there was a clatter on the deck, followed by loud comments on the state of the boat. Fortunately, they were all favourable.

"Is anyone at home?"

This question was followed by the sudden arrival—before they had time to answer—of Ian as he almost fell down the hatch.

"Good, I'm just in time for a snack. I'm ravenous. I've been shovelling coal all day. What sort of engine has she? There's a Kelvin steering wheel and gear in the wheelhouse anyway. I hope it's a Kelvin engine, I'm well acquainted with them, and they're good. I'll go and have a wee look!" He then grabbed a pie from the table and disappeared back up the hatch, stuffing it in his mouth as he went.

Bill and Jim looked at one another in amazement.

"Well, we'll never weary with that lad aboard, he's a proper live wire," said Bill.

"Aye and we'll never get any peace either. That fellow's voice must be close to perpetual motion, I think," replied Jim, just before loud cries of approval came from aft as Ian examined his new charge.

Very soon a few muffled clatters were heard faintly from aft, then the engine sprang into life, the initial roar settling to a steady even beat as Bill and Jim arrived on deck, concern showing on their faces. Ian emerged from the engine room and looked over the side at the exhaust. "Look at that," he roared. "There's not a hint of smoke in that exhaust, and she started first swing!"

He later voiced his approval more quietly, telling them that he was very impressed with the way the boat's engine had been treated. "There is new oil in the crankcase, and the batteries are clean and well filled up with distilled water. Whoever was the engineer aboard her knew how to look after an engine. If I see the outside clean, I feel confident that the inside will be well looked after. The tanks are full of fuel too; I checked all that. By the way, when are we going to sea, and which is my bunk? I've finished with the railway, and I'm eager to get going."

Willie appeared above the boat later, and asked Bill and Jim up to the office. They sat down, and then Willie produced a bottle of whisky from a cupboard and asked if they would like to drink a toast to their future together. They both refused the whisky, but lest they offend Willie, they offered to drink a glass of something non-alcoholic with him.

"Well done, lads. I much prefer men who can cope with life without having to depend on alcohol. I very rarely touch it myself—but everyone to their own."

They sat contentedly discussing the events of the day. Bill asked when the nets would arrive, as he wanted to get theirs aboard. He also suggested taking the two nets that had been ordered for Alex John on board for delivery to Lochboisdale. "We will need to get together to see just how much he needs to learn, so the sooner we start, the better," he said. "We'll need three men from Uist too, Willie. Will you warn him about that? We'll need the men, unless you have anyone lined up here, for crew, and Alex John is not the only one who will need to get used to the ring-net. We'll need to get some practising done as well!"

"I'll do all that, no bother, Bill."

Then he continued somewhat hesitantly, "I'm glad you mentioned the nets. You negotiated a price reduction on your own nets. That is not really on, I'm afraid. You see my firm expect that discount. They are paying the bills, after all."

"I see, Willie," replied Bill. Jim knew from the quiet intensity of Bill's demeanour that he should just listen, and not interfere. "Well in that case there will be some mention of that in the papers we signed this morning."

"No, Bill, that is just recognised business practice in this trade."

"Well, I don't recognise that practice, Willie, and you didn't warn me about it, so it is just not on. We had better get these things straight, from the beginning.

You play fair with me, and I'll play fair with you. I did all the negotiating with the net factory, and planned the nets. I didn't get any money from them, all I got was a discount on the bill, and you were bound to see that. Now, if there are any other 'discounts' that your firm gets, we'd rather know about them from you now, before we go any further."

There was a long silence in the office, broken only by the cries of the ever-squabbling gulls.

Willie eventually broke this silence. "You're a sharp young lad, of that I am certain. We'll let this go then, but I am not exactly happy about it. I'm the one that will have to explain it to my bosses. There's nothing else that I am aware of that you should be told about, but if anything crops up, I'll let you know. We won't fall out about it."

"I'm sorry, Willie, the last thing I want to do is cause trouble, but after all's said and done, our work is what's going to pay for these nets. You know as well as I that everything's paid for out of the hold! If you have any problems with your bosses, please let me know about it. I'm not going to ask anyone to fight my battles for me."

Willie laughed. He had now had long enough to recover his composure. "I suppose I am quite pleased really, that you are obviously not an easy mark. There will be plenty of times where you will have to stand up for your principles, especially as you are so young, but you have proved today that you are well able to look after yourself. Now, let's talk about the crew side of things. I am quite certain that there will be an influx of men from the East Coast as soon as we get this operation going properly. I think you'll get your pick of good time-served men when that happens. I'll get Alex John to get some men gathered together on Uist in the meantime, however. Anyway, off you go now. I'm sure you still have plenty to do. I'll see you both in the morning. Off you go and have a good night!" Chuckling quietly, he saw them both to the door.

There was nothing said between the pair as they walked back down the pier until, just as they reached the boat, Jim spoke.

"I admire you for what you did up there Bill. I must admit that when you started on about the nets, I was worried. I thought you had blown the whole scheme, but Willie seemed to take it all right in the end."

"Well, Jim, I didn't want to cause any bother, but I have no intention of letting anyone walk over us. We may be young, but we're not daft. I think we've set the boundaries for our dealings with Willie, and I'm sure he'll respect them in the future."

The next three days were busy ones for the three young men as they readied the boat for the sea, for there was much that had to be done. On the morning of the fourth day, the nets arrived on a large lorry. One of them, the one Bill had designated their 'winter net,' was stored in a small wooden shed that Willie Mair had made available for the purpose. The other three were hauled aboard the *Misty Isle*. Their own one was laid on to the port quarter, ready for use. The remaining two—belonging to Alex John—were hauled aboard and spread over the deck. Then, after getting some last minute stores, they set off in the early afternoon, heading west towards Sleat Point.

Bill stood alone in the wheelhouse, steering his boat through the calm seas. He had arrived at the point in his young life that he had been aiming at for some time. Apprehension and some disappointment filled his thoughts. Apprehension because he knew that there would be difficulties ahead, and he was uncertain of how he would cope with them. Disappointment because he had hoped that Theresa would have put in an appearance somehow, or that he would have received a reply to the letters he had written, but there was nothing. He had thought of these things quite a lot in the last few days, but had decided to make a conscious effort not to dwell on them.

Instead, all of his energy would be devoted to the task in hand; a task that he knew would not be an easy one.

Once round Sleat Point, Bill steadied the boat on a course that would take them close by the north side of the Island of Canna.

Jim arrived up on deck just then and offered to let Bill go below for a cup of tea, an offer that was gladly accepted. As Bill went forward, he heard the sound of music coming up from the forecastle. Ian was enjoying one of his great loves, playing Scottish Country-Dance music, on his mouth organ, and was playing it quite well. Bill turned and called aft, "It sounds as though we'll never weary with this lad but how do you get him to stop!"

Ian did stop playing when Bill took his place at the table, and poured him a cup of tea from the teapot that sat at the edge of the stove.

"It's good to get a start, Bill. I hope we get some herring this week, you must be a wee bit bothered about getting the first shot aboard. Are your nerves bothering you?"

"Aye, Ian, but there'll have to be a lot of things sorted out this week. Remember that we all have to learn how to walk, before we can run. There aren't usually a lot of herring around at this time of the year either. Autumn will be the first real chance for us."

Then, changing the subject, he said, "Do you know a family called MacDonnell? They live in Loch Nevis somewhere, and used to have a wee shop at Tarbert."

"MacDonnell?" answered Ian pensively. "Yes, now wait a minute, I think I do. They have a daughter if I'm thinking of the right ones. I can't remember the daughter's name, but she is at University. Coming out as a doctor I heard. She's a really good-looking girl. Is that family you mean?"

"Yes, that's the one. I sort of know her—the daughter that is. Have you seen her recently?"

"I saw her a good while back, on the train to Fort William," said Ian. "She was probably going off back to the University after her holidays. I was on the early shift that week. Here, wait a minute; didn't she come back home again not that long afterward? Ach, maybe I'm blethering. Do you want me to make enquiries for you?" Then, awareness dawning in his eyes he asked, "How do you know her? It's her that you want to find out about, isn't it, not the family?"

"Well, yes," Bill replied. "I suppose it's all right to tell you. I sort of know her a bit, but I'd rather not talk about it just now."

"I don't really know anything about the family. I think they moved from Loch Nevis though. I'll maybe find out something later on. Aye, I know someone who might be able to tell me something about them. My lips are sealed, Bill, rely on me. Here, do you know this one —?" He then applied himself once more to his mouth organ.

Chapter Eight

At last, after around six hours steaming, they arrived at Lochboisdale and made straight for the pier where they were supposed to meet their new neighbour. Sure enough there was a boat, roughly the same size as the *Misty Isle*, lying at the pier, smoke curling lazily from the galvanised chimney. As they drew nearer they saw that she had the registration letters CY on her sides, signifying that she was registered at Castlebay. Nearer still, and they saw, just before the first head—drawn by their engine noise—emerged from the forecastle hatch, that her name was indeed the *Mystical Rose*.

Her crew were all on deck to greet them and catch their ropes as they came slowly alongside. Bill just had time to register how dark, almost swarthy, most of the men appeared before one of them called to him.

"Welcome to Lochboisdale, Bill. I am Alex John." He jumped aboard the *Misty Isle* and came toward Bill, hand outstretched. "It is good to meet you."

Bill grasped the offered hand and shook it warmly before releasing it and coming out of the wheelhouse.

"This is Jim MacInnes, my partner, and Ian McPherson. Ian is our engineer. He's from Mallaig. We'll need a wee while to remember all your names lads," he laughingly continued as Alex John started to introduce the others. "Just be patient with us!"

Introductions complete, the two crews set about removing the nets that belonged to the *Mystical Rose*. One of them, on Bill's advice, was laid on the *Mystical Rose*'s quarter. This was the one designated for use now. The other was hauled on to the pier with some difficulty, as the height it had to be lifted—because of the low tide—added to the problems already posed by the inexperience of the men doing the job.

It was late and almost dark before all the work was done. The three men assigned to Bill as crew took their bedding below and began to make themselves at home before they set about eating the pot of Irish stew that Jim had made on the passage from Mallaig

Alex John and Bill clambered on to the pier and went for a stroll along the rough road that led west—not that there was any choice of roads; this was the only one in existence!

"What have you in mind, Bill?" asked Alex John in his soft highland accent. "Are we going out tonight, or what?"

"No, I don't think that would be a good idea," replied Bill. "We'd be better to wait until tomorrow. We can go out and if you show us somewhere, preferably in deep water where there are no rocks we could tear our nets on, we will get some practice done in daylight. It is far better to make mistakes when it doesn't matter and to learn from them, than to make a mistake and maybe lose a shot of herring."

"That's good thinking, Bill," replied Alex John. "I am a wee bit apprehensive about a few things. Do you think it might be a good idea if your partner, Jim, came aboard with me for a few days? He'd keep me right."

"I'll need to think about that," replied Bill thoughtfully. "There are only the two of us who have any experience at all, and if he goes with you, I will be left with the greenhorns—sorry Alex John, I don't mean to be disrespectful to the lads you have rounded up, but you see what I mean. I'll have a word with Jim about it. Maybe it would be all right, but we'll need to play it by ear."

They walked on, each learning a little of the other as they walked and chatted. Bill heard how Alex John's father had died leaving his son with a boat that was only half-paid. Alex John and his mother now owned the boat between them. Although he was only five years older than Bill, Alex John was very happily married, and had two sons upon whom he obviously doted. He and his family lived in a small croft house near Daliburgh on the west side of South Uist, about five miles from Lochboisdale. His wife, Mary, would look after the cow and the hens, Alex John laughingly said. She was well used to having to fend for herself like that, and she was happy doing it.

"I notice that your lads are all very quiet. I've seen that in all the island people," Bill said. Then he hastened to add, laughing as he did, "That's no bad thing, we Lowlanders make far too much noise. Your way is better—just be patient with Jim and me!"

"Oh yes, we are a naturally quiet lot, but just you wait until everyone gets to know you. Then you'll see some fun—especially when we let our hair down at ceilidhs!"

They arrived back at the pier in the deep dusk. Alex John said his good nights and clambered aboard his boat, which had now risen as the tide came in, until its deck was nearly level with the pier.

Bill paused, and then wandered slowly toward the far end of the pier. He sat down on an old packing case and gazed out at the still, darkened waters of the loch. Only the occasional feeble splashing of the tiny fish they called cuddies, close to the pier, broke the silence. The evening stars were showing faintly in the cloudless night sky, their reflection dimmer yet in the still water. Bill felt the deep peace of the scene filter slowly into his soul. He realised that this was where his destiny lay and as he relaxed, he once again felt the serenity that the certainty of this knowledge brought. Time ceased to exist as far as he was concerned and it was only when someone came on deck on one of the boats and urinated over the stern, that he came back to reality and went aboard to his warm bunk.

Next morning dawned fine, and they got under way early. Bill followed their neighbour as she turned north from the mouth of Lochboisdale. They passed the small group of islets called the Stuleys, and continued north until eventually, the *Mystical Rose* slowed and came to a halt in the middle of a bay called Corrodale. This bay contained one of the many caves in which the Young Pretender had allegedly hidden after Culloden.

Bill took the *Misty Isle* slowly alongside her neighbour.

"I've spoken to Jim," he called to Alex John. "He has no objection to coming aboard with you for a spell, so one of your lads will have to change places with him."

This done, there commenced a period of intense activity. Jim stood forward on the bow of the *Mystical Rose* and as she steamed along he would, without warning, throw a small float into the water. This signalled Alex John that his task was now to shoot the net around the float, encircling it. It had to be done in such a manner that the net was up-tide from the marker, and the centre buoy of the net had to be very close to the marker.

Time and again they tried, and still Alex John was finding it difficult to judge the positioning of the net. If he got the centre buoy close to the float he would sometimes be, as Jim said, "Across the tide!" which meant that the net was not shot so that the tide would sweep it down over the imaginary shoal.

Late afternoon came and as the crew of the *Mystical Rose* busied themselves once again in laying the net aft in readiness for another attempt, Bill steamed slowly north and west, toward the centre of the bay. A lone gannet took his attention as its wings flashed in the sunlight. He watched the bird intently for a time and then went back, at full speed, toward his neighbour.

"What is the ground like close in, just north of the centre of the bay?" he called to Alex John. "There's a gannet looking well in there but from its antics, I would say that it is mackerel he's seeing."

"I'm not very sure, Bill," replied Alex John. "If it is clear of any of the wee points, it should be all right. The ground should be mainly sandy in the bights, but there will be fasteners off the points."

"Well, I'm going to have a go at it anyway. Jim, just you stay where you are, you'll be needed there to catch the end of my net. Just everyone take their time. Don't rush at anything, and we'll be all right—it's probably a waste of time anyway, but at least it'll be more practise for us all."

So saying, he put his engine into gear and set off shorewards. Following Bill's instructions Ian turned on the engine-driven hose, and told one of the Uist men to play it on the net. This would wet it and so lessen the time it took for the brand new net to sink. As they neared the land, he coached Ian on what would happen. "Just do as I say, Ian. There won't be anything happening in a hurry, so relax and you'll get it all right."

The lone gannet was still circling as they approached, beak pointing straight down. He would stoop quickly to one side, then recover to circle and hover once more. He was right in the centre of a small bight that Bill gauged would be just about the right size to encircle with his net.

Bill steered the *Misty Isle* slowly into the bay and, when he judged he was in the correct position, he called softly to Ian to drop the end of the net overboard.

Still going dead slow ahead, he turned the boat around in an arc to port. As he had anticipated, the bight was just about tailor made to take the length of the net. If there were any fish inshore of them, he thought smugly, there was no way out; they were as good as dead! He said a silent prayer, asking that the ground be good, and clear of fasteners.

Jim had seen to it that Alex John made a good job of picking up the other end of the net, and was gently towing it shorewards. Bill soon called to him to—"Close her."

The two boats came slowly towards one another, thus completing the circle, and as soon as the two boats touched, the *Mystical Rose*'s crew jumped aboard the *Misty Isle*.

They set to hauling with light hearts; this was no longer practising, this was the real thing.

As they hauled away, Bill's eyes were eagerly darting about all over the place. His vigilance was rewarded when he saw a glint of silver. Up it came, a large mackerel caught in the wider meshes low down in the net.

"We're not going home empty handed!" was his excited call.

"No, by Jove," Jim called back in great glee. "Look! There they are buzzing at the centre buoy—just look at them, boys. Isn't that just beautiful? We'll never be poor again!"

At last they had the haul dried up, around fifty crans of beautiful mackerel. The trapped fish dashed furiously from one side of the net to the other, showering the delighted men with spray.

Mindful of the unwritten rule that 'killer naps'—meaning that the catch, and therefore the task of unloading them, was usually brailed aboard the boat whose net had not been used, Jim called to Bill, "We'll have to use your brailer to get this lot aboard. We haven't got one rigged on the *Mystical Rose* yet. That's a job I had in mind for tomorrow."

"Aye, but just what are we going to do with them?" answered Bill. "Is there a market for mackerel in Mallaig?"

These sobering questions were asked of no one in particular, but the answer was vital. There was no sense in killing the fish unless they could be marketed, and mackerel had never been a favoured fish, for reasons that Bill had never heard properly explained.

"I think we could get them all sold in Lochboisdale, or in Castlebay," answered Alex John. "There aren't many fish being landed anywhere on the islands and it is Wednesday, so folk will be getting desperate." This was said in direct reference to the fact that to the mainly Catholic population of the southerly islands, fish was necessary on a Friday, as the Church frowned on eating meat on that day. Indeed, Bill had often heard old Dennis O'Hara call out in jest to a shipmate who had offended him somehow—"If it wasn't a Friday, I'd chew the balls off you!"

"Anything we can't sell for eating," Alex John continued, "we'll get rid of for bait. The men that fish lobsters and crabs on the west side of the Uists will be keen enough to get them salted down into barrels."

They then agreed that they should split the catch between them in order to share their catch between the markets. The *Misty Isle*, Bill decided, would go to Castlebay, and the *Mystical Rose* to her home port of Lochboisdale. Jim, he suggested, should stay aboard the *Mystical Rose*—there were a lot of tasks to be tackled aboard her still, tasks that required a degree of expertise that was as yet beyond Alex John's crew.

The still struggling fish were brailed aboard the two boats using the *Misty Isle*'s brailer. The men, now that they saw some rewards in sight, worked cheerfully at their tasks.

Before they got under way, Alex John came aboard the *Misty Isle* and went into the wheelhouse to talk to Bill. "You'll maybe not be too well acquainted with the entrance to Castlebay," he said quietly. "Black Dan is one of the local lads you have aboard now, and he will keep you right if you want. He was born in Northbay, just north of Castlebay, and he has fished up and down the shores here for more than twenty years now. You can rely on him as long as you keep him clear of the pub; he's fond of a few drams. I hope you don't mind me saying this, I'm sure you would keep me right if we were fishing down in the Clyde."

"Not at all, Alex John. I need all the help I can get, and I appreciate you coming and saying it all quietly. I'll keep my eye on Dan when we get to Castlebay. He'll not get much time in the pub; I can assure you of that. Now, it is time we were under way. When you get finished discharging tomorrow, just come south. We'll head north as soon as we are ready, so we should meet up somewhere. I expect it will take a good while to get clear of this lot, it isn't going to be a quick discharge, and we won't get started until the morning."

The two boats started steaming south and remained in close company until the *Mystical Rose* turned west into the mouth of Lochboisdale. By that time, the *Misty Isle*'s net had been laid back aft and was ready for use again. The teapot was filled once more and Bill, for the first time since they had left the pier (was it only eight hours ago?), went below into the forecastle leaving Ian and Black Dan on watch. He couldn't settle there however and soon he was back on deck again. This time he went up onto the foredeck where he lay looking over the low bulwark, his restless eyes ceaselessly scanning the sea and the heavens for what fishermen poetically called an 'appearance on the water,' which meant any sign that fish might be around.

He remained there for almost two hours until Ian, following Black Dan's instruction, turned the *Misty Isle*'s bow westward, and keeping the bulk of Muldonich Island on her port bow. Bill stood up then pondering, not for the first time, on the uncanny similarity in shape between the Muldonich and Davaar Island, which is at the entrance to Campbeltown Loch. As he went aft and approached the wheelhouse Ian, obviously slightly nervous at approaching a shore that was completely unknown to him, asked Bill to take the wheel. His Kelvin, he explained, would be in need of a wee drink of lubricating oil!

It was late evening when they eventually slowed down as they passed close beside Kismul's castle, the ancient island stronghold of the MacNeil clan, and moored up alongside the pier at Castlebay, which at this late hour, was deserted.

As soon as the boat was secured, Black Dan came aft to the wheelhouse. "I think it would be a good idea if I went ashore and let everyone know that we are here, and tell them that if they want some mackerel they'd better get down early in the morning. What do you think, skipper?"

Bill knew instinctively that this was an important moment for him. If he didn't take this opportunity to stamp his authority on his crew now, it would be doubly difficult at a later date. "Aye, Dan," he began slowly. "That might be a good idea. Where would you be thinking of going to spread this news?"

"Ah well, skipper, there's only one place in Castlebay where you'll find anyone at this time of night. They'll all be in the pub."

"Right, Dan, just you go away up and see who you can find—but there's one thing you better be sure of before you go. We'll have a busy day tomorrow, so if you take enough drink tonight to keep you from pulling your weight in the morning, you can just make your own way home to Northbay. There's no room aboard my boat for people who take too much booze." Then, in order to soften what sounded like a harsh-sounding ultimatum he continued with a smile—"There'll be plenty of opportunity for fun at the weekends, I'll maybe join in, you never know. Then you can teach me some Gaelic songs!"

"Oh now, skipper, I take a wee dram at times, but I've never let anyone down yet. Just you wait and see. I'll be back in an hour at the most."

So saying, he climbed nimbly but carefully up the ramshackle metal ladder that was attached to the one of the wooden legs of the pier, and disappeared from view.

The rest of the crew had barely finished their tea and were in the process of getting into their bunks when Dan arrived back aboard. Bill had remained on deck awaiting his return, concerned that he had sent someone else to do what he felt was the skipper's job, but not quite certain of what the other options had been. Perhaps, he thought, he should have asked Ian to go with Dan for company—or should he have gone himself?

A call from the pier made Bill switch on one of the lights on the side of the wheelhouse to illuminate the deck for Dan as he started down the ladder.

"By Jove, skipper," he announced as soon as he was aboard, "There's plenty of interest here for our catch. They would have come down right now and started in at them, but I thought that maybe we would be better to get everyone together in the morning, and get rid of them all at once. I told them that we would start at seven o'clock. Did I do the right thing?"

Bill, leaning out of the wheelhouse window, smelt a hint of alcohol from Dan, and noted in the gloom, just the slightest glint in his eye.

"Aye, Dan, that is just fine. You did a good job. Now we'd better get a few hours shuteye before daylight. There's tea left in the pot, away and help yourself to a cuppa." Then, still feeling guilty about his warning regarding drink he laughed—slightly self-consciously—and continued, "I think I'll leave all the cash transactions to you in the morning. You will have a far better idea of how we should handle that side of it and I've no doubt that the people will be happier talking Gaelic with you. I'm not very good at bargaining, either. Anyway, that's for the morning. Come on away below, I'm for going to my kip."

Early morning preparations included Bill supervising the raising of the mast and derrick that were required to discharge their fish. This was carried off with fewer snags than he had anticipated; the islanders had worked with similar rigs in their drift-net boats, and very soon overcame any differences with a minimum of interference from Bill. The mast was hardly up however when the first of their customers arrived, and before they had grabbed a hasty breakfast, the pier was swarming with potential buyers. Some pushed small handcarts, most carried hessian bags, and a few who, being unable to get their small horse-drawn carts through the mass of people, had left them further up the pier.

In what seemed to be no time at all, the hold was emptied of fish. Bill, feeling unable to cope with the rabble of Gaelic speakers, had relegated himself to a task that he felt more at home with—down in the hold where he filled the mackerel into baskets!

When they had finished Dan came aboard clutching an old biscuit tin that was fairly brimming with money. "See that, my lads; no bother to me, eh! They were sore needing fish of just about any kind at all, especially as tomorrow is Friday." Then with a sly grin in Bill's direction he added, "What will I do with this pile of money then, will we get a wee dram out of it, skipper?"

"No, no dram!" replied Bill, aware that this was yet another moment when he would have to assert his authority. "We'll get some grub with some of it but the rest will be squared up as normal. There's a boat and nets to be paid yet."

As soon as they had the boat cleaned up and ready for sea they left the pier and headed out again. Bill suggested to Dan that he should go below and help Ian to count the money, as he was confident that he would manage to take the boat out of Castlebay on his own. Before he went however, Dan told Bill that the market in Castlebay was now probably flooded for the moment, especially as the few men who required mackerel to salt for lobster bait, had now bought almost enough for the year.

As they cleared the buoy that marked the rocks to the north of the approaches to Castlebay, Bill saw a boat in the distance, coming toward them, and as it drew nearer, he recognised their neighbour. Alongside, they excitedly exchanged tales of their experiences—tales that were remarkably similar.

"I think we'll go south for a wee look, Alex John," said Bill. "We're not very far from Barra Head now; we may as well carry on. You never know, we'll maybe come across a spot of herring on the way."

Their brief run of luck seemed to have deserted them, however, and they were to scour the seas between Barra Head and Loch Skiport, at the north ends of South Uist for over a week without a sign of anything, not even mackerel.

In Lochboisdale for the weekend, a despondent Bill spoke by telephone to Willie Mair, in Mallaig.

"I have heard that there were gannets seen at Canna, Bill," said Willie. "The skipper of one of MacBrayne's steamers reported them to a drifter that was lying in Tobermory, but the drifter was on her way south to Ireland. A cousin of mine is aboard her, and he telephoned his mother in Banff and told her to tell me. It's amazing how news gets around, eh? It wouldn't do any harm to have a wee look there, I think, but you please yourself."

This news cheered Bill up enormously and to everyone's delight it heralded a steady fishing at Canna that lasted for over five weeks. They didn't get any big shots, but they had regular small ones, and they were only three hours' steaming from the market at Mallaig. These modest but regularly landed shots of good quality herring were just what the few small firms that smoked the herring needed, and their smoke houses were drifting their aromatic smoke over Mallaig for twenty-four hours every day. The railway swiftly conveyed the succulent product as far as London and kippers were eaten in fancy restaurants in the capital city not much more than twenty-four hours after the herring had been swimming at Canna.

The time spent fishing there gave Alex John the perfect opportunity for learning and perfecting the skills required to be a successful skipper of a ring net boat, under Jim's supervision. They tracked and caught the shoals by following the gannets, using the feeling wire, and by watching for the red streaks of plankton on the surface. There was little time for rest now, and their every waking hour was spent among herring, either discharging them, or seeking them in the unusually calm weather that prevailed.

This spell of regular fishing at Canna confirmed Bill's love for the island, a feeling that had been conceived while he was on the *Bengullion*, and which was never to leave him. He pondered over this feeling often. He simply felt totally at home there but could offer no idea of why he loved it so much.

On the rare occasion that allowed time off, he would climb up to the 'jail.' This is a small pinnacle of rock that raises itself over a lovely sandy bay just to the north of the harbour. The remains of some sort of wooden structure on top of it seemed to confirm the story that it had been used to imprison the errant wife of the laird, many generations past. When he reached the top, Bill would lie on his stomach and gaze for hours into the clear waters of the small bay that lay below him, as he drifted in that mood that lay between sleep and wakefulness.

Bill was totally happy with his lot; he felt that his destiny was being fulfilled. The thoughts that marred his happiness was when he wondered what had become of Theresa, and he was usually so tired that he had little time to spend in fruitless worrying. She must, he believed, have met someone else, perhaps someone who—like her—was going to be a doctor. Well, he dolefully concluded, if that was what she had decided, there was nothing he could do about it. Thoughts of her ate away at him like a cancer, though.

When they made their first landing of the Canna herring at Mallaig, Bill took his half of the money they had earned from the mackerel up to Willie in the salesman's office and handed it over, explaining where he had got it. Willie looked at the notes, and then looked straight at Bill.

"I knew you were an honest lad," he said quietly. "Many another man would have squared it up among the crew, and would have said nothing to me. You won't lose by this."

As autumn approached the herring shoals deserted Canna, and they went through a leaner time, searching along the west coasts of Skye and for a time returning, with little success, to the eastern shores of the Uists and Barra.

Neist Point, on the West Coast of Skye, was where Bill had the worst experience of his life to date. They had been searching, without success, for a long time when Bill spotted a gannet circling just off the Point.

"We'll have a go at this, lads," he called. He was well aware that the tide was strongest just off these rocky points, and that there were very often fasteners, or spines of rock, there too.

They shot and their neighbour caught their end but as soon as they had the spring ropes on the winch, they became aware that they were in serious trouble. The soles were fast on the bottom and the tide had the corks and buoys wrapped around the boat. The spring ropes were cracking with the fearful weight that they were suffering.

In desperation, they let one end of the net go, trying to decrease the strain by hauling the net 'end on,' but the tide—which was bubbling furiously around them—was far too strong. Despite their efforts, the spring rope broke, and in no time at all the corks and buoys disappeared below the surface, never to reappear. When all the chaotic action was over, all they had left on the boat was a few fathoms of rope. The unseen rocky peaks that lay below the sea had claimed everything else.

Everyone was completely stunned by the speed of the disaster and at the rate at which they were swept north, past the Point. The two crews stood speechless, eyes searching to no avail, for some sign of their net.

Bill went into the wheelhouse and stood silent for a few moments. He knew full well that he had been foolhardy in risking their net in such a dangerous spot, but soon decided that self-recrimination was not the way ahead. He put the engine into gear and went alongside their neighbour. Before Alex John had a chance to speak, Bill suggested that they go into the bight that lay just to the south of the Point, and anchor until slack water, which was just two hours away. Then, he hoped, the buoys would resurface and they might get at least some of the net back.

It was useless. No one would ever know what happened to the net. It had simply disappeared. The buoys had probably burst with pressure when the net went down. It was with a heavy heart that Bill at last gave up the fruitless search and told Alex John that they would need to go into Mallaig to get their spare net. They would also need to order another one, to replace the one they had just lost.

The trip in to harbour was an unusually quiet one. Even Ian was subdued by what everyone perceived as a tragedy. Not until Bill was in Willie Mair's office, did he properly come to terms with what had happened.

"There'll be bigger losses than that, Bill," began Willie. "At least there was no one lost or hurt. We'll soon get another net, and I don't think you'll do that again in a hurry. Everyone needs a lesson in life—perhaps you have had a cheap one!"

Back at sea again, the search for fish continued but there were simply no herring to be seen anywhere. Eventually the two skippers, Bill and Alex John, got together with Jim and had a long talk about their efforts, and it was decided that they should take a break for a week or two. This would give them time to prepare for the coming winter herring season. They would have to get the winter nets ready, and the boats' bottoms would have to be cleaned and coated with antifouling paint. Having agreed on this, they parted company. Jim returned to his berth aboard the *Misty Isle* while all the islanders, with the exception of Black Dan, went aboard the *Mystical Rose* to go home to Lochboisdale. Jim set course for Mallaig. Dan explained to all who would listen that he wanted, "A wee spell among the bright lights in Mallaig!"

Chapter Nine

When they got to Mallaig their first task was to haul the net onto the old stone pier and then, as soon as the tide was high, they put the boat as far onto the beach as they could.

Although the net had been little used, they would have to get it barked. This process involved firstly boiling cutch—an extract from the bark of the Acacia tree—in a large tub of water. The tub had to be big enough to contain the entire net. When this dark brown solution, which prolonged the life of the already tarred cotton net, had cooled sufficiently, the net was steeped in it for an hour or so, then removed and hung up to dry thoroughly.

Bill and Jim took advantage of this event to bark their 'canvas carseckies.' These were over-garments made of light canvas that were worn to protect the knitted jerseys, and steeping them in the same solution as was used for the nets helped to preserve them. Their East Coast fishing companions called these garments 'slopies,' but perhaps they were better known all over as simply, 'barkit jumpers.'

Bill was intrigued to hear when he used the word 'carseckie' aboard the boat, that it might well have come from the Gaelic words 'cartadh seic.' 'Cartadh,' he was told, means the act of tanning or barking and 'seic' means a skin, or hide. "I would say," said Dan, his informant, "That these garments were originally made from animal skins, and not from canvas."

Willie Mair had organised that they could all stay in Meg Ritchie's if they wished, but although Bill and Jim accepted without hesitation, Dan stated that he would rather live on the boat. He would, he averred, "Get more peace that way!" He did agree to have his meals in Meg's, though, after being assured that he would rue missing the chance to "Eat like a king," as Jim put it.

Meg was delighted to see them again, and they had hardly got into the house when she began plying them with hot buttered scones. As she fussed around them she told them that she was expecting a visit from her daughter, Lisa, in two days' time. "That'll not bother you two at all, she has her own bedroom, so there's plenty of room. She is coming for a wee holiday, but I'm always hoping that she will settle down nearer home. I miss her a lot," she concluded quietly.

There was much to discuss with the salesman, and Bill spent most of his first full day ashore in his company, leaving the others to get on with the bottom scrubbing and painting. Ian was busy stripping down the Kelvin, cleaning and checking everything as he went.

One of the things that Bill wanted to discuss with Willie was the distance that the boats would have to travel to and from the market in the coming winter fishing. If they were catching herring regularly—and that was their main purpose in life—then they would of necessity spend a lot of time either crossing the Minch, or discharging at Mallaig. That enforced lack of fishing time bothered him. He was also concerned that if the boats were stuck in Mallaig because of bad weather, then they would be unable to take advantage of any sudden lull in the weather on the fishing grounds. A quiet period lasting only a couple of hours might, he knew, be ample time to fill both boats.

With that in mind, he asked Willie if he thought that it might be a good idea to charter a boat such as the one that George, Meg Ritchie's husband, worked on. If they had access to this much bigger boat on the fishing grounds, they could employ her to ferry the catches across the Minch.

"Aye, Bill, that is certainly possible," replied Willie thoughtfully. "It would just be an extension to what these boats are doing already when they are employed in the klondiking trade but instead of salting the herring aboard, they'll take them fresh to the market. Aye, that might work. The winter fishing is when you will have to make the bulk of your year's earnings and as you say, the more time you spend fishing, the better. Leave it to me, I'll telephone around and see what comes up. Have you thought how you would pay this boat?"

"Well yes, that seems simple to me, Willie. They would get a third of the money that was earned. They will be out a lot more in fuel expenses than we will; they'll be back and fore across the Minch all the time—that is if we are catching herring—but they won't have the expense of buying fishing gear. That way would also mean that if we have a slack spell, we'd not be crippled with the cost of having to pay him for just lying there. I am sure that Alex John will agree. I have spoken to him about it already, but you should have a word with him too, just in case."

Willie eyed Bill thoughtfully for a spell. He was delighted that his initial summing-up of the lad was now being completely justified. The foresight and business acumen that one so young was displaying, amazed him.

"Right, Bill, I'll get on with that. Now have you seen the new wooden huts at the back of the railway? Well they are houses for the lassies that the kipper merchants have brought here to split the herring for them. They are all from the East Coast, and I am certain that if we get this port off the ground, they will bring more of their relatives through here to work. I am talking now about men with experience of fishing, so it will be far easier to get a crew here in the future. Now how about you? Are you quite happy with the way things are going?" Then he added with a quizzical look at Bill, "You'll need a girl friend; everyone needs a woman to look after him—or is there one somewhere in the background that I haven't seen yet?"

Bill thought for a few moments before he replied. Willie had been good to him and Bill trusted him so he hesitantly began to tell Willie about Theresa, and about his distress at not being able to trace her. "It is a long time now since I first wrote to her and I have written several times since, but there has never been a reply. I wondered if I had the correct address for her, but my own address was on every letter so that the Post Office would return them if she were not there. That hasn't happened, so I think there's something wrong, and I don't understand it."

"Let me try to see what I can find out, Bill. I remember a local man having a shop at Tarbert right enough, but I have no idea what happened to him. The shop will be closed, and as you well know there is nothing there now except empty buildings. In my opinion it is time you knew what is going on. You cannot be chasing ghosts all your life."

Bill left the office and wandered quietly down the pier. There was a lot of sense in what Willie had said. Maybe it was time he recognised that Theresa had found someone else. With that in mind he sought out Ian McPherson, thinking that as a local he would be more likely to be able to find out something about her whereabouts, although his previous efforts had borne no fruit.

In the *Misty Isle*'s engine room, an oil-stained Ian listened to Bill's hesitant story then, on seeing that Bill was so serious that he was having difficulty talking about it, he promised to find out what he could. "My priest will maybe know about her. If, as you say, her family is Catholic, he should be able to trace her quite easily and if they are still in Loch Nevis, it'll be a dawdle. Just leave it to me. I did try before, but got nowhere. I'll try harder, this time, now that I know that it means so much to you!"

That evening, Bill set off alone on a long walk on the rough road that led south from Mallaig. There was no wind, and the beautiful late autumn evening had an unusually balmy feel. This peace provided a medium that was made for reverie and his thoughts at this time were of Theresa. His head was convinced that she had met someone else, but his heart thought otherwise. If only he could see those clear black eyes, he would see the truth in them. They could never lie to him!

He gradually persuaded himself, as he walked on the deserted road, that tonight he must make up his mind what he was to do. He could not spend the rest of his life chasing someone who had rejected him. He must make a success of his career as a fisherman. Slowly a sad bitterness came unbidden into his young soul and with it the determination that he would show everyone what he was really made of. There would be no more 'nice guy.' From now on he would do that which he knew must be done, no matter what the cost might be. There was money to be made in this place, of that he was certain. If ruthlessness would carve him a share of it, then he would be ruthless. If he could not have love, he would have success.

Once again, thoughts of the gold rush 'Klondike' of the Yukon came to his mind. His reading of some of the poems of Robert W. Service had kindled his interest in this area of the world. Reading factual accounts of these stormy times had revealed that the people who made the fortunes were not the miners who endured the hardships, but rather those who had provided the services on which the miners depended. The men who ran the shops, hotels, brothels and gambling dens—they were the ones who made the real money. Could he emulate them here? Not with brothels or gambling dens of course, but there must be some way of making capital out of the herring bonanza he felt sure was coming.

His face became set in a bitter mould as he walked on. He would wait until he heard what Ian and Willie had to report and if these reports confirmed what his head was already telling him, then his course was obvious.

It was already dark when he arrived back at Meg's house. He refused her motherly offer of a "Nice cup of tea," and went to bed, glad that Jim was not there to quiz him.

Sleep came late that night; he tossed and turned and when eventually he dropped off it was to a fitful dream world where herring were raining down on fields, to be picked up by girls whose naked breasts were covered in scales. His mind was in such turmoil that he didn't notice Jim's continued absence.

Meg woke him in the morning with a steaming cup of tea. "Where on earth is Jim?" she asked, looking pointedly at his undisturbed bed. "I hope he's all right. Was he going to be working at the boat?"

Bill was suffering from the results of a very restless night, but he slowly gathered his thoughts. "No," he answered sleepily. "He wouldn't have been at the boat. At least I don't think so. Anyway, Black Dan would have been aboard and if there was anything wrong, he would have raised the alarm. I'll go down as soon as I get dressed, and see what is what. Maybe he went for a dram, and didn't like to come home here."

Less than an hour had passed before he hurriedly arrived on the pier, relieved to see smoke already curling from the zinc funnel that led from the forecastle fire but when he dropped down into the warm den, only Dan was there to greet him.

"Cup of tea, skipper?" he cried cheerfully.

"Aye, Dan, that would be nice, but first of all, do you have any idea where Jim is? He didn't come home last night, and I'm getting worried. It isn't like him to go somewhere without telling anyone about it."

Dan opened a locker, took out a mug and busied himself pouring tea. "Well, skipper, I don't like telling tales, but I can see you are bothered. The last time I saw Jim he was with one of the gutter lassies, but that was early on in the evening. I dare say you'll know her, I've seen them talking more than once." Then, seeing concern growing in Bill's eyes he continued, "She was a real bonny lass, and they seemed to be getting on well together. I wouldn't be surprised if they ended up spending more time with one another last night—you know what I mean?" The last was said uncomfortably, as Dan obviously didn't want to appear to be talking ill of a shipmate.

They sat together sipping tea in silence. Bill's concern was tempered by his knowledge that Jim was a careful lad but if he didn't show up soon, he was going to have to do something.

Barely ten minutes of this uncomfortable silence had passed when there was a clatter on deck and Ian half-fell into the forecastle.

"Is the tea hot? Where's Jim? What's to be done today, skipper? I'll need to have a wee yarn with you later." All this was said as he grabbed a clean mug and filled it from the battered brown metal teapot.

They had hardly begun telling him of their concern for Jim, when a quieter step announced the arrival of the subject of their thoughts.

Jim helped himself to tea when he arrived in the forecastle and then he spoke quietly.

"We'll get the starboard side of the bottom painted this tide, lads, and then as soon as she floats again, we'll turn her so we can get the other side done tomorrow. You'll need to get another couple of brooms for scrubbing, Ian, and while you are about it, you could get a couple of tins of red anti-fouling paint and a wee tin of white gloss for the waterline. We'll need paint brushes too; get three big ones for the anti-fouling, and one smaller one for the waterline. You go and help him Dan, as soon as you've finished your tea. I'll have a word with you in a wee while Bill. There's one or two things I want to tell you."

When the pair had left to carry out Jim's bidding he turned to Bill and said, "You'd better be the first to know, Bill, I think I'm going to get married," he said hesitantly.

"Get married! You think? What do you mean, you think? Who are you going to marry?"

"Well, I mean I definitely am going to get married. I'm not sure when, but the sooner the better as far as I am concerned. I've been seeing this girl—Mary Flett is her name. I haven't been out with her very often I must admit, but I know I want to marry her and she wants to marry me; and we would like you to be best man. She is from a wee place near Buckie and she works in one of the kipper yards here. That's it," he concluded somewhat lamely.

"That's great news, Jim. I'll be delighted to be your best man. When am I going to meet this lucky girl? Are you going to get married here, or are you going to Campbeltown?"

"Neither, we're going to get married quietly in Buckie. We don't want any fuss and no, she isn't pregnant! I saw the look in your eyes, but I can assure you that is not why we want to tie the knot. We spent all of last night talking about getting married. Then, when we did eventually go to bed for a couple of hours, we were not in the same one. We thought we'd maybe get it all over with whilst the boat is ashore. You'll meet her very soon. I think you'll agree that she's a lovely girl. Will you manage without me for a week or so?"

"For goodness sake, Jim. You didn't need to ask that. You're rushing it a bit, are you not? I would guess that there'd be a lot of organising to do. Of course you can have a week off—in fact, why don't you take two or three? There's not likely to be much doing for a wee while yet. There's never a lot happens before Hallowe'en and that is weeks away yet. Now come on, there is plenty to do here if we are all going to a wedding, and you needn't think you are going to keep me away from that celebration. Let's get on with it! Here, wait a minute, what about Mary's parents, do they know anything about their daughter getting married?"

"Oddly enough, Bill, she is like me on that score; her parents are both dead.

Her father was a fisherman and he was lost when he was washed overboard from a drifter at Yarmouth a few years back. Her mother didn't last long after him; Mary says she probably had a broken heart."

When they went home that evening, tired from all the scrubbing and painting, Meg Ritchie was fussing around them as usual. As soon as she had placed the steaming plates of stew on the table before them she announced that she would be going to the late train to meet her daughter, Lisa.

"Oh aye," said Bill, casting a sly sideways look at Jim. "She'll maybe be going to the wedding as well, what do you think, Jim?"

Jim, despite his obvious embarrassment at the wedding subject being raised managed nevertheless to retort, "Aye, she'll be a good partner for you at it," before Meg abruptly sat down at the table and demanded to know what wedding they were talking about.

She sat open-mouthed and silent until she had been advised of the plans, then she announced that she knew the lass personally and that more importantly, she had known her parents. "They were hard working, God fearing, honest fisher folks. You couldn't have chosen better, Jim. She'll make you a real good wife; you need have no fears on that score. Now," she continued—talking more to herself than to her company—"There is a lot to be done. You'll need a new suit, aye, and new shoes too. There's no-one getting married out of this house but they do it properly. Just you leave that all to me, I'll keep you right."

Jim and Bill exchanged amused glances. They knew that Meg would thoroughly enjoy all the planning and, more importantly, all the innocent gossip that would be exchanged before the 'big day,' as she termed it, arrived. They agreed that they should invite Ian and Dan to the pub for a wee dram that very night where they could tell them of the forthcoming wedding. This was important for they knew enough of the looseness of women's tongues to realise that the whole village would be in on the news before very long, and Jim didn't want his shipmates to find out from anyone else. Bill also announced that he wanted to meet Mary as soon as possible, but that would have to wait until the following day, they thought.

It wasn't until they set out for the bar that Bill remembered that Ian had wanted to talk to him alone, so he told Jim of this and said that he would go outside with Ian as soon as he arrived, to see what it was all about.

"Well, skipper," began Ian when they were sitting alone on a stone wall outside the bar, "I have spoken to the priest as I promised I would, but there isn't a lot he will say about it. He knows the family quite well but says that they left his parish a few years ago, and he thinks that they might possibly have gone to Canada. He says that the daughter was at the university in Glasgow studying medicine, but he has no idea if she qualified or not. That is all I was able to find out. I'm sorry. I just don't know where you could go to find out more. I'm quite sure he knows more than he is telling, but there's nothing more I can say to him about it. There may be something that he has heard as a priest, that he isn't able to repeat to anyone."

Bill had listened in silence to all that Ian had to offer, and sat for quite a while with his head bowed before stirring himself. "Thanks, Ian, for your help," he said in a very quiet voice. "There's nothing more you can do. They went to Canada, eh? Let's get inside now. I think Jim has something good to tell us."

The news of the wedding went down well with Ian and Dan, who seemed prepared to make it a night of celebration but Bill had other ideas and as usual, his will prevailed. The little alcohol they permitted themselves that night was enough to have them in bed and sound asleep before the late train arrived so it was morning before Bill was introduced to Lisa.

She was a lovely girl, inclined to be slightly plump, with a mass of reddish fair hair that hung below her shoulders. Her fair skin was a mass of beautiful freckles and she had very clear blue eyes. She was obviously a very quiet and shy lass and she busied herself helping her mother in preference to chatting to the two lads. Meg announced that she was going to see Mary right after breakfast and was going to ask her to come for a meal that night. This, she said, would give Bill the chance to get to know Mary, the bride-to-be. Although Lisa had already met her on a few occasions, they would also, no doubt, get better acquainted now.

The first impression Bill got when he was introduced to the bride-to-be was that she was painfully thin. She was very neatly and conservatively dressed in a dark blue skirt, topped with a similarly coloured woollen twin set. She was of a very dark complexion, and had a rather disconcerting habit of gazing unblinkingly at the person she was addressing. Her straight black hair was set in a rather old-fashioned bun. She was quiet, but Bill was in no doubt that she would be a very determined young lady indeed, and that she would work very hard to attain the goals she set herself.

When they got round to the matter of arranging the wedding, it transpired that Mary wanted Lisa to be her bridesmaid. "I left home a long time ago, and have been working ever since," she said. "I haven't formed a strong friendship with any of the other lassies, they all have families at home that they keep close to, but I have neither brother nor sister. My cousins were never very helpful after my mother died."

She then turned and gazed directly at Jim, "So, it looks as though we are going to mean an awful lot to one another; we are in the same boat in that we have no close relations. You have a very good friend in Bill, and I hope that Lisa and I will grow closer after our wedding. I'll not want to leave here now."

The evening wore on and many indeed were the plans that were laid—mainly by Meg, who appeared to be getting a great deal of pleasure from taking the part of Mary's mother.

Mary had decided that the wedding would be held in the church in Buckie where her parents had been married, where her father's remembrance service had been held and from which her mother had been buried. Indeed, she had already written asking that the banns be called there. They all agreed that there should be an informal lunch in a nearby hotel for the guests before the young couple set off on their honeymoon. The guest list, written by Lisa on instructions from her mother and Mary, was deliberately kept short, as money was not plentiful. Meg offered them a room with her when they returned to Mallaig but Mary refused, telling her that she had the promise of a hut—one of the ones erected for the gutting crews—from the man she worked for. She wanted, she said, to take Jim back to what would be their home for the foreseeable future. It had, she added, all the necessities a young couple might need.

Bill went to see Willie Mair first thing in the morning and told him of the wedding plans. Willie listened to the story and then commented that he knew Mary, and had known her parents also. "Jim is getting a fine lass, one who will make him a good wife." Then he hesitated and continued; "I've tried to trace that family you asked about, Bill. It seems they gave up the wee shop they had at Tarbert. It wouldn't have been viable for them to continue after the railway arrived and the boats all started to land their herring here in Mallaig. The lad I spoke to says that he heard that they went back to their croft at the head of Loch Nevis but thought that they didn't last long there either. He has no idea where they are now and he has no idea if their daughter went with them or not. He seemed to be of the opinion that they cut off all contact with people they knew around here, but he stressed that this was only an opinion."

Willie looked keenly at Bill as he spoke of the daughter, but this mention provoked no reaction.

"Do you want me to make any more enquiries about them, Bill?"

"No, Willie," said Bill slowly. "Never mind them, they aren't really important now."

They sat in silence for a moment then Bill said, "I think I'll ask George Ritchie about getting a drifter to run the herring for us—he'll be coming to the wedding so that will be as good an opportunity as I will get. I think he is going to be giving the bride away."

"Well, that would be a good idea, Bill, if that is the road you want to go down. It will be better to be dealing with someone we all know. It won't be long now until Hallowe'en and the winter herring might be taking the shore sooner than you expect, so we may as well be prepared for them!"

The trip to Buckie for the wedding was a long one, being of necessity a mixture of travelling on a variety of trains and buses, but the company was quite a large and cheerful one, so the time did not drag.

Bill had, of course, already met George on several occasions when George's rare weekends at home in Mallaig coincided with Bill being there and had formed the early opinion that he quite liked the man. Since getting the idea of asking him to run the herring, he had thought long about it and had formed the opinion that he could work well with him.

George was quite a tall, sparsely built fellow with a large hooked nose, but his face was dominated by his very pale blue eyes—a throwback, Bill reckoned, to his Viking ancestors. Lisa had certainly got her eyes from her father, but her fair colouring must have come from her mother, as George was quite dark complexioned. Quiet by nature, he smoked a pipe. This was often used as a device to gain thinking time when he was asked a question that required some thought. Then the pipe suddenly needed very careful scraping out and refilling—a job that took some time. He used this ploy when Bill asked him for his views on the subject of carrying herring.

When he eventually had his pipe lit and drawing well, he gave a very well reasoned reply, but it was one that consisted mainly of questions! How long would the season last, what would his boat do when the winter herring season was over and how would the money earned be shared out, were his main queries.

Bill told him of his talks with Willie Mair, talks in which, thankfully, most of George's questions had been anticipated and catered for. He explained that his planned joint enterprise would only be valid for the winter, approximately five months in all, and put forward the thought that at the end of that time George would be free to pursue whatever fishing he had been involved with in previous years.

George ended the discussion after some time by saying that whilst he thought that the idea was a sound one he wanted to think about it before saying yea or nay. There was, he said, something else on his mind—something that would be settled whilst they were in Buckie, so he would give Bill his answer after this had been dealt with. They spoke for a long time on fishing matters in general, finding that they shared a lot of common ground on the industry and its future. It was a pleasant yarn that was only ended by the bus's arrival at its final destination.

Thanks to Meg's organisational skills and contacts, friends and relatives in and around Buckie were housing all of the wedding party so a slightly apprehensive Bill found himself being whisked off by a blue-jersey clad young man who appeared to be about his own age.

"I'm Albert Cowie, but they call me Ally because my father has the same name" he announced as he grabbed Bill's case. "You're staying with us in my parents' house whilst you're here. Are you from Mallaig? What size of a place is it? I've never been there. You're a fisherman like me, but what kind of fishing are you at? Ach, never mind my chattering, we'll have plenty of time to get acquainted later on. You must be tired after all that travelling. I'd far rather haul a hundred cran of herring in drift nets than travel from Mallaig to here I'll tell you. I hate buses!"

Most of the time between their arrival and the wedding passed in a blur for Bill. His kindly hosts whisked him on a quick tour of the harbour, which seemed to be filled with hundreds of boats, and the nearby boatbuilding yard where he saw a new drifter nearing completion.

Jess, the lady of the house, was a typical fisherman's wife. Though somewhat short in stature, she was broad in the beam. Her clear-eyed, smiling round face was crowned by silver hair that was done up in a bun, and her spotlessly clean white short-sleeved blouse showed off her burly arms. Her long black skirt was well covered by a dark-coloured checked apron and her kitchen seemed to be permanently blessed with the mouth-watering aroma of something baking.

The first evening was spent with Ally and his parents sitting cosily before a roaring fire in the rather fussily furnished front room. Jess was busy knitting—but listening intently—whilst the men spoke of fishing.

The furniture and brasses in this room glistened in witness to the oft-applied polish whose pleasant smell pervaded the air. Ally took the opportunity when his mother left the room to make tea and his father was busying himself with the fire, to whisper laughingly—"You are honoured, Bill. This room is normally only used for marriages, births and deaths. We are not allowed in here at any other time!"

It took Bill some time to become used to the broad Buchan accents they used but he very soon felt quite at home with people whose background was so similar to his own. He encouraged Ally's father to tell tales of his life at the fishing and was horrified to hear of the loss of life that prevailed amongst the drift-net fishermen. Whilst he could not recall any men being lost from the ring net fleet since he had left school, it seemed almost a monthly occurrence that these people were burying some of their workmates. It quickly became apparent that the majority of the loss of life on this coast was due to the dearth of natural harbours that served the waters they worked. Boats were lost, or crewmen were swept overboard in the often-horrendous sea conditions they faced at their harbour mouths. Fishing in the North Sea and at Yarmouth and Lowestoft, Bill decided, was not something he would relish at all.

For their part, the two Cowies expressed disbelief at what they perceived as the serious lack of lifeboats on the West Coast. Albert senior was second coxswain on the Buckie lifeboat and his son was also on the crew, so this was a subject that they were keen to discuss. They were amazed when Bill told them that although he knew very little about it, as far as he was aware there were lifeboats at Campbeltown and Islay but that there were no more until Stornoway, an area that covered the entire West Coast of Scotland! He reassured them somewhat when he described the multitude of harbours and sheltered anchorages that abounded there, havens that were conspicuous by their absence on the East Coast.

The morning of the wedding dawned fair, if a bit chilly and Bill, assisted by Ally and Ian, whose help he had sought, was kept running with the last-minute arrangements that had to be made. The ceremony was held in an austere grey granite church that overlooked the harbour. Jim and Bill sat alone for a short spell in the sparsely furnished vestry, while the minister kept watch for the bride's arrival.

"This is where Mary's parents were married. Her mother was buried from here, and her father's memorial service was held here also. She told me that his body was never found," said Jim thoughtfully. "It will give Mary a thought, being here again."

He then turned to Bill and said, "I love her a lot, Bill. She is a wonderful girl. I want you to promise—if anything happens to me—that you'll do whatever you can to help her."

Bill's assurances that he would look after her as he would a sister, were cut short by the busy little minister darting in. "Come now. The bride has arrived. She's not very late!" he called as he ushered them to their positions in the church.

Bill turned as the organist struck up the Wedding March to see Mary, a vision of loveliness, come down the aisle on George's arm. She wore a very plain white dress that contrasted beautifully with her black hair and her naturally dark complexion. Obviously awe-struck, he whispered to Jim, "You're a lucky man. That's the bonniest lassie I have seen in a long time. She is just beautiful!"

After the service they all walked, led by a piper, to the nearby hotel where the speeches after the simple luncheon were thankfully short. The hotel manager surprised and delighted the guests when he presented a cheque to the groom and the bride and read out the congratulatory message that had accompanied them. The message and cheque were from Alex John, skipper of the *Mystical Rose*, who expressed regret at not having been there but passed on his own and his crew's best wishes. This kind and thoughtful gesture visibly moved Jim.

The bride changed into a simple grey costume and left with her new husband soon after the meal. Their guests escorted them to the railway station where, showered in confetti, they caught a train to Aberdeen.

Back at the hotel, Ian and Bill had a dram together. "You'll be next, skipper," said Ian. "I hope you get someone as nice as Mary. She's a super lassie. By the way, Dan and I didn't get dispensation to come to your church today. We deliberately didn't ask. That priest we have just now is not the most understanding man in the world. Don't tell anyone in Mallaig we were here!" He then produced his mouth organ and began to play happily, attracting the company of other music-lovers among the group.

Most of the guests spent the rest of the day back in the hotel. Nearly all of them were from the fishing community and apart from enjoying—and joining in—the music, they spent much time in exchanging fishing yarns. At one point Bill found himself in George's company.

"When are you going back to Mallaig, Bill?" George asked.

"Tomorrow, George. There's a lot still to be done to the boat, though the bulk of the work has been finished. I want to be sure that she is in the best of order before we start the winter season." Then he added with a grin, "We'll be a man short for a week or more now too."

"Right, Bill," said George, starting to fill his pipe again. "Meg and I will be staying here for a day or so yet. I told you there was something I wanted to sort out before I answered your question. Well, the next few days will probably see all my sorting out done, and I'll give you your answer when we get home. Lisa will be going home with you fellows, she'll see to it that you are fed until Meg and I get back. She's a good lass, our Lisa."

He refused to countenance Bill's protests that he would be quite happy to sleep on the boat, telling him that it had all been sorted out between the ladies.

The company who left Buckie the following morning was tired and not nearly as lively as they had been when they arrived, so the majority of them spent a good part of the journey asleep.

"What's for eating when we get home, Lisa?" said Bill laughingly when he took a seat beside her on the bus from Inverness.

"If I were you, I'd get a fish supper in Fort William when we get there. I am not in the mood for cooking," replied Lisa with a smile. "Were you not late to bed last night?"

"No I wasn't, not really. I sat for a spell with Ally and his Dad, Albert. Jess made us a cup of tea and scones and then she went off to bed. We weren't long after her. They are a grand family, and they just don't drink alcohol often. They're very hospitable people too."

"Yes," said Lisa. "They are a lovely family. My Dad says that he might be working with you this winter. How do you think it will work out?"

This overture gave Bill the opportunity to go over once more his plans for the future, this time with someone who was not directly involved in fishing. Lisa listened intently, interrupting but rarely to ask questions whenever something puzzled her. When he had finished they sat silent for a time, then Lisa said, "I hope things will work out for you, but it all depends on the herring. Willie Mair seems to think a lot of you."

"When were you speaking to him?" Bill asked.

"He asked me down to his office the other day, and asked if I would like to work for him."

This was a surprise to Bill. "Are you going to accept his offer?"

Lisa thought for a time before answering—a trait she had displayed before and which Bill assumed she had inherited from her father. "I suppose I will," she answered eventually. "He seems certain that the port will flourish, and I would like to be part of its growth. Apart from that, I am fed up with working away from home—oh, I forgot, you are away from home all the time. I shouldn't have said that."

Bill looked at her and smiled. She had blushed slightly, and her eyes dropped from his gaze. He thought for a moment that she looked particularly beautiful, and then he too averted his eyes and looked unseeingly at the road ahead, his mind a welter of mixed emotions.

Ian stood up just then, stretched himself and then announced that they were very nearly at Fort William. Did anyone, he asked, fancy a fish supper. There was just time to buy one before catching the train on the last link of their journey home.

There was a slight awkwardness between Bill and Lisa when at last they arrived in Mallaig; neither of them was quite comfortable with the fact that they were alone in the house. Lisa busied herself by rushing around tidying up and emptying the contents of her case—unused clothes back into the drawers—used ones into the laundry basket.

Lisa called through from the bedroom, asking Bill to put on the kettle. His reply, "Huh, you're ordering me about as though we were married," was a comment that was meant to tease, but the words were hardly out of his mouth when he realised that in fact they only added to the uneasy atmosphere. This led him to say, in order to hide his confusion that no, he did not want any tea. "I'll just go straight to bed. It's late, and there's a lot I have to do tomorrow."

The rest of the week passed quickly and by the weekend, the boat was just about ready for sea. Bill had quite enjoyed the new experience of being looked after by someone his own age, and it soon became apparent that as far as cooking was concerned, Lisa had little more to learn from her mother.

"You know"—he began one evening when he had taken his seat by the fire, watching Lisa as she busied herself tidying away the dishes from which they had just eaten—"You know, I think I'd be as round as a barrel in no time at all if I was ashore eating your cooking!"

Lisa blushed at the praise, something that Bill had realised that she did very often, and again he noted just how attractive she was.

"Mum and Dad will be home tonight, so you better make the best of it. There'll be more mouths to feed then. When are you going back to Campbeltown to see your parents?"

"I saw them not too long ago, and I hope to go there every New Year. There isn't much there for me now, I am far more at home here. A lot of the lads of my age are married and have their own pals now, and we don't have much in common at all."

There was a pause and then Lisa continued hesitantly, eyes downcast, "What about a girl friend? Have you not got someone special there?"

"Girl friend?" answered Bill after a time spent gazing thoughtfully into the flickering fire. "No, I never really had a girl friend in Campbeltown," he replied truthfully. "I left home as soon as I left the school, and I have been far too busy ever since, to think of girls. Well," he added hastily, "I think of girls all right, but I never seem to meet any."

He sat, still gazing at the fire, for a long time. Then, coming back to the present, he turned to face Lisa. She was staring at him with a strange look on her face but as he turned she blushed furiously and started into the kitchen. "I'd better get these dishes done right away," she muttered as she went.

Bill sat by the fireside for a few minutes then, hearing the clattering of dishes in the sink he went through to dry them. Lisa had her back to him and did not hear him approach. As he leant past her to where the dishcloth lay she turned sharply, startled by his presence. For a long moment they stood very close, eyes locked together, and then she dropped her head on to his chest. He put his arms around her and pulled her to him. She then raised her head and looked straight at him, and their lips met. She felt very soft in his arms, and he felt as though he could melt into her flesh.

Lisa was the first to break away.

"I am sorry, Bill, I don't know what got into me. I have never kissed anyone like that before. I don't know why I did it."

Bill put his hand below her chin and lifted it gently until he once again looked into her face, a face that was now crimson with embarrassment. "You are blushing again," he teased, then said, "You didn't do anything. It was something that just happened between us, and I for one do not regret it. In fact," he continued as his lips neared hers again, "I think I want to do it again."

They stood locked together for a long time until reluctantly, Lisa pulled away from him, saying that she really ought to get the dishes finished and stored away. They worked on in silence for a time then Bill spoke.

"You know, Lisa, I think a lot of you. You are a lovely girl and a man could do worse than have you for a girl friend," then he broke off in confusion. "What I mean is that I didn't just kiss you because you were there. I really like you.

Lisa turned and gazed at him for a moment before she replied, "You have got that slightly wrong, Bill. You didn't kiss me—we kissed one another. There is a difference. Anyway, I think we should get finished here and then we could maybe go for a walk before we meet the train. What do you think?"

"That's a good idea. Apart from anything else, it will keep us from getting up to any mischief. We're better not to be alone for too long, you might haul me off to bed!" Bill ducked just in time to avoid the wet dishcloth that Lisa threw in mock anger and ran laughing from the room.

They met Meg and George from the train and helped them carry their luggage the short distance to the cottage. Once inside the two women busied themselves in the kitchen chatting happily while making the inevitable cup of tea, leaving the men by the fire.

"How are you getting on with the boat, Bill?" began George.

"She's just about ready now; we could be off before the middle of the week. I spoke to Alex John yesterday. He is ready to go now, but then he didn't have a wedding to attend, and he had more men working at his boat. That's something we are short of; we need more men to set up their permanent homes here. I told Alex John to take a wee look along the shore over there on Monday to see if he could see any appearance."

George looked at him speculatively as he played at filling his pipe. "You are a hardy lad right enough," he began. "Not many of your age would have thought of getting their neighbour to do that. Anyway, you'll maybe get another man through here looking for a berth soon; you seem to have made a good impression on young Albert, and his father too. He says he will be thinking along those lines. Now, I've got more news for you. There's a man on the East Coast that wants me to skipper his boat. That's what I was hinting at when we left here, and that's why we didn't come home straight away. I had to meet him and I've talked to him about your idea of getting us to run the herring. He is quite keen on giving it a trial. What do you think about that?"

"Man, that's great news, but what are you going to do after the winter season is over, have you talked to him about that?"

"Yes I have, and we agree that when we finish working with you, we'll just go fishing for ourselves with the rest of the drift net fleet. This man has heard all about the ring net, and seems to think there is a future in it all right. I am going back through to Macduff—that's where the boat is lying—on Tuesday, and with any luck I'll be on the fishing grounds with you on Thursday. Maybe Jim will come out with us if he hasn't arrived home before you sail."

They were shaking hands on the deal when Meg and Lisa arrived bearing the tea and of course, scones.

"I see you've told Bill the good news. I'm delighted about it; we'll see more of one another if he is running the herring in here. I just hope there are plenty of them," she added quietly. Then, busying herself with the cups she looked mischievously at Bill and said, "I hope you two young folks have been behaving yourselves." Then, seeing the confusion on Bill's face she paused for a moment and then added, "I mean that I hope you have been keeping yourself busy with the boat, and not spending all your time blethering with Lisa by the fireside!"

Her keen eye was on Bill all the time as she spoke, and there was a knowing smile on her face.

George saved the day for Bill—who had felt his face flushing—as he said, "For any sake stop your teasing, woman, and leave the lad alone! Take no heed of her, Bill. Get your tea and we'll all be able to get to bed—it has been a long day and I'm tired. It's a good job it's the Sabbath tomorrow, we'll all get a long lie."

Bill had a fitful sleep that night. When he was awake his mind was filled with thoughts of Lisa, and of how closely she had clung to him. When eventually he fell asleep he kept waking from dreams in which he was being embraced by a beautiful woman whose face was never visible but whose warm body seemed to flow insidiously over his. He was relieved when the grey light of a late autumn morning crept through his curtains and soon after, the noise of someone raking the fire told him it was time to think of rising.

They all went to Church together in the morning. It was the first time that he had been there with the whole family, and he did enjoy it.

"I don't think the weather looks very promising for tomorrow, Bill," remarked George on the way home for lunch. "If I were you two young ones, I'd be away for a walk before the weather breaks. There won't be many chances for quiet strolls when you go back to sea. I'll give Mam here a hand getting the meal ready tonight, so you needn't hurry back."

The pair of them set off out along the railway line together. This was a favourite walk on a Sunday—the only day on which trains did not run—as it was the only length of level ground for miles around. Although the sleepers never seemed to be placed a regular stride length apart it was still much easier going than being on the hilly roads. Neither of them was aware that they were holding hands until

Lisa shyly relinquished his when she saw someone approaching. They chatted happily as they walked, he of his plans, she of her coming start with Willie Mair. At last Lisa said with surprise, "Here, Bill, it is time we were turning back. We'll soon be at Arisaig if we carry on, and we'll be crawling over these sleepers in the dark before we get home!"

They stopped and turned towards one another. Bill took both of her hands in his, looked her straight in the eye, and slowly pulled her close. Her eyes closed before their lips met and it was with obvious reluctance that she eventually pulled away saying, "Someone will see us, Bill."

"I don't care," Bill announced in a show of male bravado. "We have nothing to be ashamed of," but he let her go nonetheless.

On the way back they were quieter. Both of their minds were obviously filled with thoughts of the feelings they had aroused in each other's bodies.

"I would like you to see if you could help me to get a piece of ground for a house. I'd like to build one."

This statement from Bill caused Lisa to stop short in surprise. "What do you mean, build a house?" she demanded.

"I don't want to be in lodgings all my life, not even with your mother, and if more people come here the price of ground will go up. Anyway, if I get married my wife will need somewhere to stay!" The last was said with a sideways glance at Lisa, whose hotly flushing face, she knew, was now betraying her thoughts.

"I'm serious, Lisa. I would like you to think of where you would like your own house to be built. Oh listen," he continued hastily, "I am not proposing marriage to you—not yet at any rate. I just think that I'd like a house here. Will you help? I like you a lot—an awful lot and..." Bill stuttered into silence.

"I think I understand what you are saying, Bill, and I will certainly help. I think that we would have to get to know one another a lot better than we do before we even thought of getting married, even though I do like you a lot too. What size of house are you thinking about?"

Bill stole a sideways glance at her before answering, "A big one. We'll have lots of babies in it!"

He only just ducked below her swinging hand and scuttled a little way off, saying in mock terror, "I'm only joking."

Chapter Ten

It took a good deal of concerted effort to get the boat ready for sea by the Wednes-day, but they managed it. The weather had not been good and as they left the harbour at around midday there was still a strong westerly breeze and a heavy sea running, so everyone aboard was pleased when Bill took the boat into the relative tranquillity of Canna harbour in order to get a cup of tea in peace before crossing the Minch. Although no one admitted it, nearly everyone's stomach was feeling decidedly queasy as the motion and smell of the boat took effect after the spell ashore. There were only three of them aboard; Jim wasn't due back until later in the week

It was seven o'clock and quite dark before they made their landfall at Uishnish light, and saw the lights of the *Mystical Rose* in Shepherd's Bight, the bay just north of the point. They came alongside in the lee of the land and the extra men that Alex John had brought out, jumped aboard the *Misty Isle*.

"Did you see any appearance at all?" queried Bill.

"We left Lochboisdale early this morning and went south as far as Castlebay," replied Alex John. "It was a very poor morning, Bill, and we didn't see as much as one gannet. There were gulls gathered on the Stuley Islands just an hour south of here, but a man who lives in Loch Skipport here was telling some of the lads in the pub that there were herring in the loch, just below his house. He heard them jumping in the evening when he was down at the pier for something or other. I didn't go into the loch yet; there was no point in disturbing any herring that might be there, before you arrived. What's the news of George? When is he due here with the drifter—what's her name?"

"The *Silver Searcher*. He reckoned he'd be here some time today, but this weather will maybe keep him back a bit. He might possibly have Jim aboard. We had a poor day crossing; it was quite bad at the West End of Canna. I hope he isn't too late; it is nights like this that will prove the worth of a bigger boat if we do get a shot. I told him that I thought we'd be somewhere between here and Lochbois-dale. Did you see any other boats at all?"

"No, Bill, you are the first boat we've seen since we left this morning. Two Castlebay drifters were out at the end of last week. I think they shot a few nets at the Curachan, just outside Northbay, but they drew a blank. Did you hear of anyone else starting yet, yourself?"

"There are three Kyle boats rigged for the ring net now, and they were telephon-ing Willie Mair just yesterday, asking for news, so they are ready to start, but I don't know if they have left yet, or not. The salesman at Tarbert, Loch Fyne, was on the phone too. There isn't much doing in the Clyde just now, so I wouldn't be surprised to see some of the Clyde fleet appearing. As soon as they hear of a landing in Mallaig, they'll be up like a shot. One or two of the East Coast fishermen are starting to get interested in how we get on too, so that'll be more competition for us, I'd say. Anyway, let's get these lights off, and see what's to be found along the shore."

They crawled, dead slow, along the shore north from Shepherd's Bight and into Loch Skipport feeling all the time with the wire for the elusive shoal of herring. It was nerve-racking work—they had to be very close inshore, yet far enough off to avoid running aground. Striking a rock was quite a common event with just about all ring-netters. It usually happened in a sheltered loch and the slow speed at which they grounded, coupled with the fact that there was almost always another boat in close attendance to help tow them off, meant that there was seldom any great damage.

However, to strike a rock on such a night out of the security of the lochs would be a costly business. Although the wind was offshore, there was a constant swell surging off the rocks, and an accident would certainly cause a lot of damage to the boat. It was all but impossible on such a dark night to be certain of just where the shoreline ended and the shadow of the hills above began; the craggy skyline, showing black against the lighter sky, was the only visible clue to where they were.

Not one herring was felt on the wire, nor did they hear any jump during the long, bitterly cold night. They scoured Loch Skipport and Loch Carnan and then headed south again, still at dead slow speed, past Uishnish Point and into the long stretch of Corrodale Bay where Bill's first shot of mackerel had been caught. They were now well into Bonny Prince Charlie's country—there was a cave in Corrodale where, it was said, he had hidden from Cumberland's troops. South still they went, into Loch Eynort where Prince Charlie's helper, Flora MacDonald, had been born; past the Stuley Islands and into Lochboisdale.

Their fruitless search led them south again. They sailed past Eriskay, the island where the Prince had taken refuge, and across Barra Sound. The wind had eased to a gentle breeze but Bill was so tired that his eyes would have needed, in old Dennis's words, "matchsticks to keep them open," by the time they reached Northbay. There, daylight overtook them and ended their quest.

"We're wasting our time now, Alex John, daylight is well in," called Bill, as he steered the *Misty Isle* close to the *Mystical Rose*. "We'll follow you in here and get the hook down for a few hours."

"What about the *Silver Searcher*, Bill. What will he be doing?"

"Well, he'll have enough sense to realise that we are getting a bit of shuteye somewhere, and will do the same—that is if he has arrived now. We'll run across him somewhere tonight, I'm sure of that. Lead on Macduff, it's bedtime!"

Bed was a welcome respite for tired eyes and limbs that ached from the long hours standing in the wheelhouse, but it was a temporary respite—the alarm was set for one p.m., a mere five hours away. Bill explained that he thought that they should search south for a bit to see if there were any gannets or gulls around. He then passed the comment he had often heard in his time with old Archie Blair: "Sleep? There'll be plenty of time to sleep when you're in Kilkerran!" This was a bizarre reference to Kilkerran graveyard, in Campbeltown.

Thus began what Bill was to think of later as the worst part of his life to date. Day after day and night after night they searched fruitlessly, ranging from the Sound of Harris in the north to Berneray—on top of which stood Barra Head lighthouse—in the south. They were joined in their searching by George in the *Silver Searcher*. He had found them as they came out of Northbay and had come alongside to reunite Jim with his shipmates. Jim was subjected to a fair deal of teasing on how married life was treating him. This lasted only for the first day or so, and was the only light-heartedness they were to share for some time.

Bill did ask Jim if he had a good time, and just where he had gone on the honeymoon, but he was so disconsolate and disinterested that he could not really recall what the replies had been.

As the days passed and still the herring shoals eluded them, everyone began to get worried. They showed it in different ways. Jim, who wanted to get a chance of running to market to see his new bride, apart from earning some money, spent the daylight hours standing or lying forward, avoiding conversation. At night, he stood aft with the feeling wire in his hand for hour after hour, again shunning any idle chatter. Bill rarely took time below, even eating his meals in the wheelhouse, his eyes straining for the longed for glance of the white flash of a gannet in daytime, striving to keep as close to the shore as possible, at night. The *Silver Searcher* did her bit also, ranging further offshore than the much smaller ringers, adding several pairs of experienced eyes to the search.

The only thing there was to be thankful about was that the weather was extraordinarily good. Day after day dawned calm and were it not for the strain that everyone felt, they would have appreciated the magnificent scenery through which they steamed.

Several of the men commented that the weather was too good. "We need a good stiff breeze to stir them up!" they said.

There was one event that stirred up a deal of interest amongst the boats' crews, the appearance of a rarely seen phenomenon they called a 'moonbow.' This was seen one showery night when the moon was quite large. It was in fact the nighttime equivalent of a rainbow, being lit by the moon instead of the sun, however, and was different in that it was very pale indeed—showing little or no sign of colour.

There were no other boats to be seen. It would at least have broken the monotony if they could talk to someone else. Probably, Bill thought, cynically, they were still at home waiting for some herring being landed. They knew that there were boats searching already, and there was no sense in their spending money on fuel when they could sit at home and let someone else do the looking.

Bill could feel himself withdrawing from his crew and looking ever more critically at himself. Had he done the wrong thing in moving from his birthplace? Had he involved not only himself but also others, in taking on debt that looked now as though it would never be cleared? The weekend was the worst. They remained at sea on Saturday. Sunday was spent lying alongside the other two boats at a desolate pier in Lochboisdale. In bad weather they would have been lying at anchor in a bleak anchorage—an infinitely worse prospect.

Could luck have something to do with the lack of success? Bill thought of the scores of superstitions he had heard but the only one that he could recall them breaking recently was when their neighbour had turned 'widdershins'—anticlockwise, or 'against the sun'—when they were leaving the pier at Lochboisdale.

He thought of the Carradale fishermen, who paid more heed to such things than most. In the spring they would put their boats into Carradale River, locally called 'The Burn,' for their annual refit. The burn ran east into Kilbrannan Sound, just a mile or so south of Carradale and in it the boats were moored heading south, their bows facing the road that followed the course of the burn. When the time came for them to go back to sea the simplest way of exiting the burn would be to turn them ninety degrees to port, so that they were headed east, toward Kilbrannan Sound. As this meant turning widdershins however, they laboriously hauled the boats to starboard against the flow of the river, through two hundred and seventy degrees! This, they thought, placated the ancient traditions of their forefathers and hopefully ensured a good season's fishing.

The usually irrepressible Ian, who more often than not kept them amused by playing medleys of Scottish dance music on his harmonica, was now more likely to be found in the engine room, disconsolately polishing the brass pipes that adorned his beloved Kelvin. On the rare occasion when he was heard playing, it was something slow, and mournful.

The comment, "Eat up; the best fed man is the best paid man," was heard often at mealtimes.

Conversations in the forecastle were predictably morose. "I'm going to put an anchor on my shoulder and start walking inland, when we get back to Mallaig. When someone stops me and asks—'What is that on your shoulder?'—I'll set it down and stay there for the rest of my life. I'll be far enough from the sea then!" This gem, designed to try to lift their spirits, came from old Hector, one of the *Mystical Rose's* crew, and that statement brought a smile to even Bill's lips.

"What would you do, if you had the choice of any other job?" was another favourite.

"If I had the money I would buy a wee hotel somewhere in the country, miles from the sea," said Ewen, another islander. "I wouldn't want a big one; just about four bedrooms would be fine. I would tend the bar myself—there would be maybe ten regulars that came in every night without fail. We would lean on the counter and yarn away just fine until about ten o'clock, and then off to bed I'd go. I wouldn't be worried about herring then!"

"I'd settle for a job as the janitor in a girls' finishing school away out in the country somewhere!" said big Ian, laughingly. "Think of the fun you could have, being the only man among all these lovely lasses."

They were just into their third week of this unrewarded and soul-destroying labour when at last the breakthrough came. Alex John came aboard the *Misty Isle* one Sunday, in the late afternoon. He excitedly told Bill's crew, who had been disconsolately playing cards, that he had met a man at mass that morning in Dali-burgh, a village about three miles west of Lochboisdale. This chap, he said, lived in a remote house at the entrance to Loch Carnan, just north of Loch Skipport, and had told Alex John that there had been a good appearance of herring there on Saturday afternoon.

"He knows what he is talking about," said Alex John. "He works a few drift nets in the loch there in the winter months. His wife helps him to salt the herring he catches into wee barrels and they sell them to the locals. He came down to Daliburgh on Saturday night to spend a couple of days with his sister and brother-in-law, so we only met by accident this morning. This could be the start of the winter fishing, couldn't it, Bill? He said there was plenty of it in the loch".

Bill, who had been lying in his bunk alone with his thoughts for most of the afternoon took his time in replying, thinking again of the odd-sounding 'it' that the Gaelic speakers used when referring to herring. George Ritchie, who had fol-lowed Alex John down into the forecastle, spoke up excitedly.

"You are right there, Alex John. They have to hit the shore somewhere and if, as you say, this man is a fisherman—even a part-time one—he'll know what an appearance looks like."

"I hope you are right, boys," said Bill. "I am just about ready to jump into the water with desperation. Put the kettle on lads, this news calls for a cup of tea!"

Bill, with George and five other crewmen, walked out the dark, wind–swept road with Alex John that evening for some exercise after their supper. They got little exercise during the week; the only parts of their bodies that had been getting any work of late were their eyes and the walk, George pointed out, would help them get a good night's sleep.

Monday morning dawned foul. There was a stiff breeze from the southwest, and it was raining. Not heavy rain, but that soft deceiving stuff that soaked re-lentlessly through the best oilskins. Their nets, which had as usual, been hauled forward for an airing, were laid aft again ready for use. There was an air of pur-posefulness about their work and the men, Bill was relieved to notice, were laugh-ing and teasing one another—something they had not done for some time.

They got under way at midday and headed north, running before quite a heavy quartering sea. The rain that usually accompanied such weather had started in earnest and was really heavy, but at least that was usually the forerunner of the wind going into the north-west, and easing. When they reached Uishnish Point Bill slowed down and steered close inshore before turning for the entrance to

Loch Carnan, followed by the other two. There was not a gannet or gull to be seen anywhere.

As they went up the sheltered loch a small half-decked boat, less than half the size of the two ringers, came out of a small bight below a house—the one man aboard waving his sou'wester.

He went alongside the *Mystical Rose* and started a long conversation in Gaelic with Alex John. Bill, who had steered close by the small boat, couldn't understand a word of what was being said but he knew from the faces of the men who could, that the news was not good.

"Donald is saying that he hasn't seen any appearance today at all, Bill. It is puzzling him. He says that there was plenty of it here on Saturday. His exact words were—'It came in with the flood and went out with the ebb and it didn't come back again!' Maybe they'll come in when the darkness comes on properly," he added hopefully.

"Aye, maybe that," Bill answered, a note of despair in his voice. "We'll just have to wait and see. It isn't very promising, though, there isn't a gannet or gull to be seen anywhere."

"The only gull I saw since we left this morning was the one that was sitting on the south point of Shepherd's Bight," remarked Jim, in a voice that matched Bill's in despair.

"I didn't see that!" said Bill. "Are you sure?"

"Aye, I'm sure all right, but it was only one wee gull, and he was sitting quite contentedly on the rocks. They need to sit somewhere, don't they?" Jim retorted rather crossly.

"I think you're seeing things, Jim. Maybe you're missing your wee gull at home; you haven't seen her for a long time!"

"Aye, maybe she has a big gannet on the nest with her now, just to keep her warm!"

Jim's reaction to this good-natured teasing from his shipmates was to go rather huffily below into the forecastle. This was not quite what the others had expected from a man who was usually so easy-going, but it caused Bill to realise that they were all feeling the strain of so much prolonged and fruitless searching.

They lay alongside one another, waiting until darkness settled. The small boat left and went back towards the bight from which it had emerged.

"I think we'll try the searchlight in along the shore of the lochs, up as far as Petersport," said Bill. "You'd be better to drop the hook in here, George. This is not a place to be prowling about in the dark in a big boat like yours. If we get anything, we'll soon rouse you. No doubt you'll leave a man on watch in the wheelhouse."

The searchlight to which Bill referred was going to be shone over the bows as they hunted. It was used mainly in shallow water and could be put to use with the boat steaming at full speed—something that did not apply to the wire—but none of them had much faith in it, fearing that it chased as many herring as it revealed. Certainly the herring, if there were any, would be seen quite easily as they fled before the boat but Bill was convinced that the light only revealed their presence, and would never countenance its use when he knew that there were herring around. Then, stealth and silence was the rule. One point in its favour was that they were less likely to strike one of the sunken rocks that abounded in the area, as the men forward might spot it in time to warn the skipper.

The two boats set off, leaving the *Silver Searcher* at anchor, and spent the next three hours fruitlessly quartering the wind-whipped waters of the lochs until they had gone as far north as was sensible. Bill slowed the *Misty Isle* down in the lee of a small islet after they had passed Petersport, and switched on the deck lights, a signal for Alex John to come alongside.

"There's not a single herring to be seen, Bill," said Alex John. "What have you in mind now?"

"We're just the same as you. There's more life in the graveyard," replied Bill. "I just don't know what to say; we can't go on like this for much longer, that's for sure. The only thing we can do now is to go south again. We'll be at Lochboisdale by daylight, and we'll have a good talk about what we should do then. The flood tide will be on now, that might take a wee spot in somewhere, and the wind will probably ease too."

"Right, Bill. Lead on and we'll follow!"

Off they went, headed south now into the wind and driven rain, searchlights still glaring down into the black water below them.

They came alongside the *Silver Searcher* just after midnight and whilst the men on the ringers enjoyed some food and a brief respite in the warm dry forecastles, they reported their lack of success to the equally despondent crew of the big boat.

The wind had eased somewhat, and was now blowing gently from the northwest when the three boats came round the point and turned into Loch Skipport. The two ringers searched slowly now with the wires—searchlights having been banished into the forecastles again—along the shores. Not a single herring was felt by either of them and it was with a heavy heart indeed that Bill led the way out of the loch and south into Shepherd's Bight.

"There were a couple of wee taps on the wire there, Bill. That's the first I've felt in a long time," said Jim from his position on the starboard quarter.

They were just about fifty feet from the shore, on the west side of the sheltered bay as Bill, more to relieve the monotony than anything else, said—"Right lads, we'll have a go at this." He switched on the small dim light above the winch as he spoke, thus signalling their intentions to their neighbour, and turned the boat slowly to port.

"What did you feel there?" Alex John asked as he came alongside and his crew jumped aboard the *Misty Isle*. He had quickly caught the end of Bill's net, and his crew was quite excited at the prospect of some action at last.

"Not a lot, Alex John," Bill replied. "Jim felt a couple of wee taps and I thought we would have a go. We'll maybe get a fry out of it; it's a while now since we had fried herring!"

"These corks are heavy here, boys!"

The call came from forward shortly after they had started hauling as Hector, one of the *Mystical Rose*'s crew—more alert than the rest—spotted that one of the buoys appeared to be settling slightly.

"It's your imagination, Hector, that or wishful thinking," cried Black Dan.

"No, you are right, Hector. Get these soles up as fast as you can, lads. I think we've got a shot of herring here!"

A great and heart-felt cheer greeted this instruction from Bill, a cheer that was followed by a deal of excited and good-natured chatter among the men.

The working lights were switched on as soon as the soles were aboard and the herrings' last avenue of escape was closed and it immediately became obvious from the weight on the buoys, that they had indeed secured a good ring of herring. The excitement that greeted this sight was followed by another cheer as the first glister of a meshed herring was spotted.

"Get ready to come alongside, George," Bill called to the skipper of the *Silver Searcher*. "Be careful, though, we have a good shot here."

This call instigated a great deal of scurrying to and fro on the decks of their companion boat as her crew removed hatches in preparation for taking the catch aboard.

When they came alongside and had the centre of the net securely strapped to the drifter's side, the work of brailing the catch aboard began. This was done using the *Misty Isles*' brailer. It was more difficult than usual, due to the relatively high sides of the bigger boat, but the men set to with the high spirits of men who had searched long and hard for this moment.

"How many herring would you think we have here, Bill," asked George, wanting to know how to distribute the load evenly in the *Silver Searcher*'s hold.

"There's better than three hundred cran, George, I reckon," Bill answered. "Will you manage them all?"

"Aye and more. Just you catch them—I'll carry them!"

"What was it you guys were saying about the gull I saw this afternoon on the Point over there? Who is daft now, eh? My wife will be out with two shopping bags in Mallaig tomorrow when she hears about this shot. Aye, the gannet will be thrown out of my wee nest! That gull I saw on the point there could smell the herring before they arrived. They know more about fishing than any of you lot!" Jim had his opportunity of teasing the others now, and he made the most of it.

The last few baskets of herring were taken aboard the *Misty Isle* on Bill's instructions. "We'll give them to that fellow in Carnan, what was his name? Donald, wasn't it? If it wasn't for him we might not have got this shot. It won't do any harm to keep on the right side of lads like him; he will be a good lookout for us here."

Then, turning to George, he suggested that he should get his boat's hatches lashed down firmly, and make his way to the market. "I don't think there is much sense in hanging on here in the hope of getting more herring. We'll keep looking and if we get any more, we'll take them aboard ourselves and we'll see you in Mallaig. Mind, though, don't tell a soul in Mallaig where we got this shot. These guys have been lying in their beds waiting for us to find the herring for them. Well, we're not going to make their lives any easier than we need to. They'll have to search a bit, the same as we have. Tell them nothing!"

The crews quickly set about their tasks and soon the *Silver Searcher*'s stern light was all that could be seen of her, bobbing up and down as she cleared the sheltering point and felt the Minch's swell beneath her as she set course for Mallaig. The *Misty Isle*'s net was laid aft again, ready for action and the pair, after a perfunctory look around the bay, set off north again finishing up, just about an hour from daylight, in Loch Carnan. They had found no more herring and were weary men when the anchor eventually went down in a sheltered bight. Sleep came readily to Bill; he had shed most of the cares that had kept him from sleeping well, and now had renewed confidence in the immediate future.

They were awakened in the late afternoon by the bump of a boat coming alongside.

"Are you awake, boys?" came the call in slightly awkward English from their newfound friend, Donald, as he came clumsily into the forecastle.

"Aye, Donald, we're awake—the boat that just came alongside saw to that! Anyway, poke that fire up and put on the kettle, it's time for a cuppa."

While they waited for the kettle to boil they told him of their luck the previous night.

"We've kept a few baskets for you," said Jim. "You'll get them as soon as we get ourselves sorted out and get a cup of tea!"

"Oh now, that's just lovely, you are very kind. It's been a long time since I had a fresh herring. Look," he continued, "I've brought out some fresh milk and some scones. My wife says that you will enjoy them and I know you will. She makes the best scones in the whole of the Western Isles. I had a good look up along the shore this morning. There aren't many signs of herring, but they are around—I could feel the smell of it strong around the mouth of Loch Skipport. I think you'll get another shot tonight!"

Bill noticed again that Donald, like the rest of the islanders, referred to the herring as 'it,' and he was soon given another insight into the difficulties experienced when men who thought and spoke in Gaelic, had to resort to English. "What," he asked Donald, in an attempt to better his local knowledge, "is the bottom like in this bight?"

"Well, it is nearly all sand, with a thin covering of rock!"

Bill realised that he meant that the bay was sandy with an occasional outcrop of rock, but it was with some difficulty that he refrained from commenting on the mistake, or laughing at it.

They yarned for a time over their tea and scones—which were as delicious as Donald had boasted—and then at Bill's behest, they opened up the hold and quickly lifted the herring in baskets on to the deck and emptied them into Donald's boat. As soon as they had finished, Donald, grinning from ear to ear, set off homeward saying, "This will keep me and my wife busy for a long time, gutting and salting!"

It was growing dark before the anchors were lifted and the pair set off out of Loch Carnan and into Skipport. There was very little wind now, and the night had a strangely mild feel to it. Donald was right; there were no immediate visual signs of herring. Jim wandered aft from his place on the foredeck as they steamed into the loch, in readiness for getting the feeling wire out as soon as they slowed down. He paused beside the open starboard window of the wheelhouse. "If they're not in here, we'll get them somewhere else," he offered, smiling at Bill as he spoke.

"Aye, maybe so. Just you get that wire out and see if you can feel another two or three hundred cran," said Bill, wondering how Jim was able to read his mind so accurately. Then he added, "The flood won't be on for an hour or two yet, and remember, we never saw or felt a thing last night until it started."

They scoured around Skipport fruitlessly for a couple of hours, then turned south toward Shepherd's Bight. Jim wound in the wire as Bill increased speed when they cleared the south point of Loch Skipport, and quickly dropped down into the warmth of the forecastle. He was intent on grabbing a warming cup of tea before they slowed in the bight, and the wire had to go out again.

"That's our neighbour's winch light on!" came the cry, just as he was stirring the sugar into his tea.

"Aye, there's his winkie away."

The winkie was a small wooden float that held a metal tube containing three batteries and a small bulb. It was tied to the end of the net, marking it for the shooting boat's neighbour. In use—thanks to the corks attached to its sides—it floated upright in the water; a mercury switch made contact and the light lit. It tended to switch itself on and off as the motion of the waves caused the mercury to move. This explained how it came by the name, 'winkie.'

Jim quickly made his way aft.

"Is the bottom not supposed to be bad in there, skipper?" he asked.

"Aye, Jim," replied Bill. "I hope he knows what he is doing. We'll soon find out, but just leave him alone. He knows the ground far better than we do."

"Close her up right away!" was the cry from the *Mystical Rose* as soon as they had lifted the winkie aboard the *Misty Isle*. "The bottom isn't good here."

Once aboard the *Mystical Rose*, Alex John explained to Jim as they hauled, that they had felt a good spot of herring on the wire. "I know we're taking a chance, the ground isn't good at all here, but we've been too long without herring to pass up a spot like this.

"You might be lucky, Alex John. I've been told that when you get round a good spot of herring they tend to lift the net clear of the ground. If the soles don't fasten, you might be all right." Then he roared—"Heave away, lads, get this net in before it catches or we'll be mending for a fortnight!"

The winch was groaning under the increasing strain that the cracking spring rope was putting on it and Jim's spirits fell. He was certain that the soles were fast and that they were in for what was commonly called 'a wiping'—a really badly torn net. This fear was confirmed in his mind when he noticed that the buoys, instead of being evenly spaced out around the net, seemed to have gathered together in an untidy cluster. Even the report of the first herring being seen meshed, failed to change his conviction.

Suddenly the boat, which had been listing to port under the combined weight of the two crews and the downward pulling action of the winch, lurched into a more upright stance. The strain on the ropes eased immediately and the buoys moved out into a more regular pattern.

"Heave in now, boys, as hard as you can," Jim shouted desperately. "That felt like the sole rope breaking. We could get a proper wiping if she has started to tear—it'll run right up to the corks, and we'll lose any herring that are in the net."

The men pulled away frantically, driven by the hope that they could save something from what was beginning to look like a disaster.

"The soles are broken here, but the guard isn't torn!"

This call came from the man who was hauling the after sole rope. It meant although the rope had broken, the heavier meshed net—a fathom or so deep—that 'guarded' the vulnerably lighter net above had served its purpose.

Jim pushed the man aside roughly and held the net in his hand, interrogating it with hands that had gained much in sensitivity during his time at the wire. "I don't feel the net tearing, lads. Heave in the fore sole, we might get away with this yet! Just go canny hauling in the net until we get the other end of the break aboard."

The task now facing them was getting the guard aboard without putting too much strain on it. Once the lighter net above started to tear, nothing would stop it.

Jim and Alex John, who was now looking a very worried man indeed, pulled as gently as they could, one on either end of the bare edge of the net.

A tremendous cheer of relief broke out spontaneously when they finally got all the guard aboard, gathered the net together into several rope-like handfuls and started to pull up the centre of the net.

"Heave ho now, my hearties, let's see what we've got here. Put your backs into it, we could have a braw shot yet!"

When at last the net was dried up, they had a shot indeed. More, Jim reckoned, than they had taken aboard the previous night.

Bill came alongside gingerly, having first let go an anchor.

"I wish we knew where George was," were his first words as soon as they had the two boats positioned properly. "There are too many herring here for the two of us to carry. I wish we had those new-fangled radios I hear them speaking about. We'd be able to talk to him if we all had them fitted." Then he added—"You made a braw job of that, Alex John. You didn't take long to get on top of this job. There must be well over three hundred cran here. I thought you were going to get a week's work, mending, though."

They decided to brail away until the two boats were full, and then to try to hang on to what was left until the *Silver Searcher* reappeared with her empty hold.

It took them barely an hour until both boats' holds were filled, and still there were a lot of herring left—over a hundred cran, they estimated.

We'll just have to hang on for a while, Alex John," called Bill. "It's a good job it is a bonny night. When we get the decks squared up, we can grab a cup of tea—we're safe enough lying at anchor here. I think we should get your net repaired now and put out our deck lights as soon as we can. They might stop herring going into the bay. With any luck, we'll get another ring that'll fill the *Silver Searcher* too!"

Both crews busied themselves repairing the *Mystical Rose*'s net. They were able to do this as the damage was confined to the bottom of the net, and their work did not interfere with the haul of herring that remained alongside. Nearly two hours were to pass before they saw a single white light appear out of the darkness away to the east. The red and green sidelights of a single boat soon became visible below the bobbing white masthead light.

"That must be George; give him a blink with the searchlight," called Bill.

It was indeed the *Silver Searcher*, and George soon had his charge manoeuvred into position, taking the corks from the *Misty Isle*. This was no easy task as the herring had all died by now, and the weight was considerable. Brailing them aboard the *Silver Searcher* was not so easy either, as the herring were all lying in the bottom of the net like, as Ian put it, "a lump of cement!"

George told them that he had been very disappointed in the price he had obtained at the auction in Mallaig. They would, he told them, be lucky if they averaged £4 a cran. "It is still a good shot," he commented, "But I thought that we'd have got more for them than that—after all, they have been starved of work in the kipper sheds for a long time now. There were no lorries ready to cart any off to the East Coast, so there was no real competition among the locals. They just put their heads together and shared them out!"

Bill also was disappointed with the price, and angrily resolved that he would do something about it when they arrived the next day. He wandered back aboard his own boat, deep in thought. He returned quite soon, his face reflecting his anger.

"When we are finished here, we are going to see if we can get another shot to fill you up, George. If we don't, we'll discharge what we have aboard into you and let you go to market with that, and I'll come with you. If we do get enough herring for us all, I want to be first boat into Mallaig, so just you hang back with your faster boat. These guys aren't going to take a loan of us; just you wait and see." Then he called to his crew, "Come on, lads—let's get looking for more. They're nearly finished brailing here."

Their luck was certainly in. They were just approaching the head of the bay when Jim called out excitedly, "They're good here, Bill. That's as good a spot as ever I've felt."

Bill turned slowly and made his way back towards the still-brailing pair, switching on his winch light as he did. This was very soon spotted by someone aboard the other two boats, and provoked a deal of furious activity and shouting as they ran the last few baskets over the corks and made ready to catch the end of Bill's net.

This ring brought no repetition of the drama of the previous one although the men still shouted excitedly at the first sight of a meshed herring. They had taken four of the *Silver Searcher's* crew aboard and thanks to the extra hands, they soon had a fine shot alongside.

"I think there's enough here to satisfy you, George," Bill called. "Let's get them aboard and get away to the market."

As soon as they had finished, the three heavily laden boats set off across the unusually quiet Minch and those of the crews who were not needed on watch, crawled into their bunks for a sleep. It would take around six hours to get to the market, so this time was broken into two watches of three hours each. Two men were on each watch.

They arrived at seven in the morning and were greeted by several of the buyers, eager to know what they had, and what the quality was like.

Bill clambered up the ladder, ignoring the requests for information, and immediately sought out Willie Mair.

Willie's greeting—"That's another fine shot, Bill," was rudely cut short.

"I want a few words with you, Willie, away from these fellows!" Then he turned and shouted down to the crews of the three boats, "Don't take the covers off the hold just yet. I'm not sure what is going to happen."

He walked away for a bit, then stopped and turned angrily to Willie.

"I'm not at all happy with the price we got yesterday. These lads took advantage of us, and it is not going to happen again. We're not daft, and I am looking at what we can do to stop it happening again. There have been no herring landed here from the Minches for a long time, and if they can't do better then they'll have no herring from any of us for a long time. We'll simply go elsewhere with them."

"I'm sorry about that," replied a somewhat shamefaced Willie. "Why don't we tell them how you feel?"

"That's exactly what I am going to do, Willie. Get them up to the sale ring right now!"

Bill strode off up the pier to where the herring were usually sold.

Willie, still shocked at Bill's actions, went to the huddled group of buyers who had been staring at the pair of them.

"You'd better come up here; the skipper wants a few words."

Bill, when he saw them leave the side of the pier and come towards him, put one box on top of another and climbed up on them. As soon as they were close enough, he glared at them angrily from his makeshift platform for a moment, and began to speak.

"You lads took advantage of the lack of competition yesterday. You have been without herring for a long time now, and the price you paid just wasn't good enough. Well, I'm not daft, and I am telling you now that you will never do it again. We are young men, but we are not stupid. You can make up your minds now. If you are not going to pay a decent price, we're not going to land to you. There are other markets we can go to—Kyle is only an hour away, and we could easily make Oban our base from now on if Kyle cannot manage to cope."

One of the buyers, a sour looking, thin-faced man known only to Bill as 'Acky' looked around his compatriots. "He says that they are young, but they're not daft, eh? That's a matter of opinion, I say!" Then he cackled loudly at his own idea of a joke.

Several of the boats' crews had followed the buyers up the pier and Ian Mor, one of Alex John's crew, a very large man who had the reputation—like most large men—of being very placid and easy going, stepped towards Acky and took him by the scruff of the neck, pulling him irresistibly towards him. "If you ever speak to our skipper like that again," he said quietly, "I will throw you into the harbour, as far as I can!"

"Now, now boys," said Willie quickly. "There's no need for violence—nor is there any need for sarcasm, Acky. You would do better to keep your mouth closed. There's seldom much sense comes out of it in any case. Bill is right. You could have done better yesterday, and you know it. You'd better get off to your wee offices and think what you want to do today," and then, turning to Bill he continued, "That is, if Bill is willing to give you another chance."

"Get the samples up, lads," said Bill. "We'll see what they are made of this morning."

The crews, chattering animatedly among themselves, made off down the pier. Their task was now to take a fair sample from each boat's catch, consisting of at least 40 herrings, up to the sale point. They would label each basket with the boats' number, and an estimate of the amount each had to sell. These samples would be kept until the shots had all been discharged. This was done in case there was a dispute between buyer and boat. It was not at all unusual for the buyer—very often in order to get a reduction in the price—to claim that the herring were not as good as the sample had led them to believe. In that case, the sample would then be compared to the stock being discharged. If they were the same, then the buyer had to take them, and pay for them.

On the other hand, quite often the fishermen would throw any small herring out of the sample, making sure that only the large ones remained; so the system, developed over many years, gave protection to both sides.

Bill came down off his low platform and turned to speak to Willie.

"Excuse me, skipper, could I have a word?" This softly spoken request came from a well set-up, well-dressed, middle-aged man.

"This is Murray Buchan, Bill," said Willie. "Murray is a buyer from the East Coast. He is a member of the family who own Buchan Fish, and he might buy some herring here today. Murray, this is Bill Martin, skipper of the *Misty Isle*."

Introductions complete, Murray asked how many herring each boat had aboard.

"We have about 140 crans, the *Mystical Rose* will have a few more than that, and the *Silver Searcher* should have over 400 crans. They're quite good herring, thin, but there aren't very many small ones mixed through at all."

"I noticed that you were the first boat in, so you should be first sold. Would you sell the *Silver Searcher*'s first? You won't lose by it, I promise you."

"I don't know," replied Bill. "What do you think Willie?"

"Well, I don't know either, but you heard what Murray said. He is a man of his word; I can assure you of that. In any case, what do we have to lose?"

"I can tell you now that I have lorries parked just a couple of miles out the road. They have been there for a few hours now, but none of the other buyers are aware of that. They'll think that I have no transport. Just let's leave them thinking that. If you will trust me, I will give you my word that I will pay a minimum of £5.50 a cran, no matter what price they are sold at."

Bill looked at him quietly for a moment, and then held out his hand.

"We'll shake on that, Murray. You look like a man who will keep his word. I'll go down and organise that right now."

As soon as the samples had been brought up, Willie summoned the buyers by ringing on an old ship's bell.

"Right now, lads, say away on the first sample. We have 400 crans of lovely fresh herring in the *Silver Searcher*. Who'll offer £4 for them?"

"Wait a minute, Willie. The *Silver Searcher* wasn't the first boat in! Why are you selling them first?"

"Acky," began Willie quietly. "Some day your mouth will get you into trouble that your legs won't get you out of. Will you just bid on the herring and keep your comments to yourself!"

"I'll give you £4 for them."

"Thank you, Murray. Can anyone better that?"

"Let him have them. He hasn't got any transport." This remark came from Acky's direction but Bill, who was watching proceedings closely, couldn't be certain.

Despite this comment the bidding rose slowly until it reached £6.

"No-one better than £6? Right, Murray, they're yours, how many do you want?"

"I'll take the lot!"

"Right gentlemen," Willie called to the rest of the buyers—who were visibly stunned by what had just happened. More than half of the day's landing had been snaffled from beneath their noses, and they could hardly believe it.

"Say away on this lot. We have 150 crans here in the *Mystical Rose*. Who'll give me £6 again?"

"I will," called Murray. "There's none of you will get a tail at less than £6 now, you can rest assured of that."

"Where are you going to put them? You have no transport!" This remark came from Soogan, as he was known to all and sundry. He had a small kipper house that he worked single-handed, and would be happy with 3 or 4 cran.

"I am happy with the transport arrangements, and so are the skippers," said Willie. "Now will anyone give me £6.20, or do I knock them down to Murray again?"

Gradually the rest of the buyers were forced to toe the line. Not one of them was brave enough to take the gamble of calling Murray's bluff, but the sale of all of the herring concluded with a degree of ill will between the buyers.

"That's what I'd call a good night's work, Bill!"

"Aye, Willie. It's a relief to pay off all the debt we've got ourselves into over the last few weeks. Now all we have to do is get them discharged and get ourselves back to sea for more." Then, seeing Murray approaching he added, "Will your lorries be here soon? We need to be back to sea as soon as possible."

Murray assured him that the transport would be on the pier within ten minutes, and added that he hoped that this would not be the last time they dealt together.

"I'm sure it won't, Murray, but we'll have a yarn later. The herring need to be discharged, that is the first priority," Willie answered. "Now, Bill, we have one or two things to talk over. Let's get up to the office. There's someone up there who'll be glad to see you and make you a cuppa! I have a man standing by to take your place on the boat if you want, helping with the unloading. We'll be well able to pay him out of today's gross."

The warmth of the welcome Bill got from Lisa as she rushed around excitedly, making tea, eclipsed even the warmth of the salesman's office. "It is nearly three weeks since we saw you, Bill. That's a braw shot today—and yesterday too. Are you going back out today? There was a man on the telephone from Ayrshire, Willie. He wanted to know if there were any herring in. I told him that he'd have to call back after nine as you would be in the office then. Do you want anything to eat, Bill, or do you just want a drink of tea? We have some nice new-baked rolls! Do you want to go up to the house for a bath? Oh, I don't mean that you need one—I'd better get someone to run up and tell Mam that Dad's in again!"

So saying she rushed out of the door in some confusion.

"She's not usually like that," said Willie, a big grin on his face. "I think you have her all hot and bothered, Bill. Now, do you want me to square up this weekend—will you be in on Saturday, do you think? If you want, I'll get all the bills in and get them paid. It wouldn't be a bad idea to keep a wee bit of money back, though, in case we need it for the next lot of expenses."

"I hadn't really thought about it, Willie, but maybe the boys could do with a day or two at home, and they'll need the money. Aye, just square us up. I certainly could be doing with a bath, myself! If we get a shot on Friday night, then everyone that wants to be in Mallaig can come in with the boat that has the herring aboard; the rest can stay out there. Aye, just you go ahead and square up, but we're not going to have any long weekends off, we're here to catch herring, and make some money. There's a boat to pay off yet. I expect that Jim could be doing with seeing something of his new wife," he added with a laugh.

"Aye, Bill, but if you keep on fishing like this until New Year, there won't be much left to pay. Anyway, that brings me to the rest of the news. How do you feel about getting another boat? There's one on the market in the Clyde, and the way the fishing has been there, they won't be looking for a fortune for her. She has a Gardner engine in her, and they're supposed to be very good. Do you think that Jim would do as skipper? Maybe not—he seems to be content with his lot. Maybe you would want to get her all on your own. Think about it," he added, seeing the slight frown on Bill's forehead. "Just think about it and let me know."

"I will that, Willie—I will that. You've really given me something to think about. Anyway, I've finished the tea, and I didn't get the roll I was promised!" Then he added with a laugh, "I think I'll get away down and maybe let Jim home for a wash—or something."

"Before you go, what am I to tell this Ayrshire lad, when he phones? Do you want him to know where you got the herring? If so, you'd better tell me—I don't know myself!"

"Aye, Willie. Maybe you are better not to know everything," Bill laughed. "What you don't know, you can't tell. He can find the herring himself if he comes up. Tell him nothing. I'm not doing any of these lads any favours—I don't think they'd do me any!"

On his way along the short corridor out of the small office, Bill almost bumped into Lisa. The closeness of their bodies brought her perfume strongly to Bill, and he was once again reminded of the Spartan lives he and his colleagues led. She laid a hand on his arm, and the touch was enough to cause Bill to gather her to him in a close embrace. They kissed and Lisa was the first to break away. "Bill," she stammered. "We are in a very public place here—I've missed you a lot—I don't know what gets into me—I'm sorry."

"Don't be sorry, Lisa. It is only natural. I've missed you a lot too." Then, gathering her close again he whispered, "We'll maybe be in this weekend. I want to spend some time alone with you. See what you can do. Remember about the house, now."

Then, brushing her flushed cheeks with his lips, he left and made his way down to where the boats had started to discharge.

Amid many good-natured catcalls from his shipmates, Jim blushingly took up Bill's offer of an hour off to go home and—as his pals put it—see to his new wife!

The two smaller boats finished discharging by mid-afternoon and as soon as the holds were washed down they left for the fishing grounds. George, who had more herring aboard, told them that he expected to be finished in less than three hours. Because he had a much faster boat, he reckoned that he should be not much more than an hour or so behind them when they reached the fishing grounds. They all agreed that they should not switch their navigation lights on in the interest of secrecy as they approached Uishnish Point, in case there were boats already in the area. Bill told George that he would flash a searchlight into the sky to reveal their position to him, but only if they needed him.

They all grabbed a bite to eat and then four of them that were not on watch, crawled wearily into bed. They were bone tired after the hard labour involved in discharging, but would get little more than a couple of hours sleep before the next two were called for their watch. Ian, although he had now regained all of his natural ebullience, was too tired to give them a tune on his mouth organ! Bill had no chance of discussing the news of the possibility of another boat with Jim—sleep was the greater necessity.

As they approached the land they saw that there were boats' lights in Corrodale Bay, south of Uishnish, but they appeared to be heading south towards Lochboisdale. When they finally made their way into Shepherd's Bight they saw, to their disappointment, that there were drift nets already anchored there. They assumed, correctly as it turned out, that they had been shot by some of the Uist boats. It was going to be difficult, Bill saw, to get room to shoot a ring net anywhere in the bay if they felt a spot of herring, so they spent very little time there before heading north.

They drew a blank in Loch Skipport, but whilst there, they saw the anchor lights of the two drifters whose nets had filled Shepherd's Bight. They rounded the point and turned into Loch Carnan just about an hour after the flood tide had started and hadn't gone far when they saw ahead of them the frantic flashing of what they soon discovered was a large torch. The *Mystical Rose* was slightly ahead of them and went alongside the boat that was signalling to them.

"Donald here is telling me that there's a big lump of herring lying close in along the rock face just ahead of us, Jim. He has just dropped his anchor. He is going to shoot his nets in a few hours, just before the ebb tide starts," Alex John reported.

"Well, they're no good to us if we leave them lying there; just you have a go at them! Don't run through the water where the herring are, you'll frighten them off; just start shooting as you get near where Donald says they are lying. We'll need to flash our searchlights to scare them off the shore and into the net, after you get it shot. The lights will show George where we are, if he is close at hand."

Jim finished by calling, "If there's as big a spot as you say, Donald, you won't need to shoot any drift nets tonight. Alex John will fill your boat for you!" Then he added, "As soon as Alex John gets shot, would you take your boat out to the point, Donald, and flash your torch towards the east? George might be close. If you find him, guide him in here to us. We'll need him if we get herring. He isn't acquainted in here and might strike a rock. We want him full of herring—not full of water!"

Alex John shot and before they had the ring of herring –a big one—alongside, the *Silver Searcher*, whose navigation lights were still unlit, hailed them from the darkness. The *Mystical Rose* brailed the herring aboard the bigger boat until she was almost full, reserving the last few crans for the jubilant Donald.

The *Silver Searcher* set off immediately for the market—still without navigation lights—but before he left, George told them that he too had seen quite a few boats' lights to the south of Uishnish. "I think that there are a few Clyde boats up now, and the Kyle lads are at sea too," he said.

After George had left, they searched without coming on another spot. Daylight was almost in before they finally gave up, and dropped their anchors in a small sheltered loch close to Petersport.

That night, Thursday, they again searched fruitlessly. The herring seemed to have deserted the coast once again. They did come close to another four boats in Corrodale Bay in the course of their quest, and spoke to them briefly. They were from Kyle and, in their own words they, "Hadn't seen a scale all week." They reported that there were several Clyde boats working south of Lochboisdale, but that they hadn't had any luck, either. They also discovered that the Uist drifters had drawn a blank with their anchored nets in Shepherds Bight.

They had one ring in Loch Eynort for a few crans of very small herring, which they ran over the corks—thus allowing them the chance of growing up properly, as Ian put it.

Friday night brought a fresh breeze of southerly wind, so they ran back north again.

Alex John had a ring for about twenty crans in Shepherds Bight, and then Bill got another fifteen or so, in Loch Skipport. The wind had freshened, and it was a very poor night when, just after midnight, the three boats came together to discuss what they should do next. It was decided that the *Silver Searcher* would set off right away for Mallaig with the few crans they had aboard. Alex John suggested that Bill, Ian, and Jim should go to Mallaig with George. He would take the *Misty Isle* into Lochboisdale and would, he assured them, look after her for them. Not much coaxing was required before they agreed to this!

That Saturday afternoon, Bill found himself alone in the house with Lisa. Her parents had gone to Fort William for the day and were not due back until late evening. Bill had turned down Willie Mair's suggestion of a meeting that afternoon, pleading tiredness. It was arranged however that Bill and Lisa, with Jim and his new wife Mary, should have their lunch with Willie and Maggie, his wife, on the Sunday after church. Bill sat on the sofa in front of the hissing fire; conscious of the cosiness it afforded against the wind and driving rain outside. Two plates of Meg's soup accompanied by several of her scones and butter had left him replete. He was pleasantly drowsy although he had slept well on the way in. No watch keeping for him, he was a guest aboard the *Silver Searcher* and had used George's bunk, at his insistence.

He was aware in his subconscious mind of Lisa washing up in the adjacent kitchen, but came awake properly when she came to join him.

Bill put his arm across the back of the sofa and pulled Lisa close. She in turn cuddled her head down on his shoulder and sighed contentedly. Bill was aware of the delicate clean perfume of her hair and it was not long before their lips met. Their positions were awkward as they were sitting side by side, so Bill slipped on to the floor and knelt on the carpet, still kissing Lisa.

His hand went slowly to her breast and caressed her softness. Lisa made no complaint until his hand insinuated itself inside her blouse.

"We shouldn't, Bill," she murmured, but her obvious enjoyment of Bill's gentle caressing gave the lie to that.

Bill now had his hand inside the soft satin of her brassiere, and was in direct contact with the hardened nipple he found there. He had loosened her blouse, but now his other hand went behind her back to where the brassiere was fastened.

Lisa moaned in pleasure, and raised herself to ease the passage of his hand but Bill was unsure of just how this fastening worked so eventually, she had to do it for him.

She now lay on her back, naked to the waist, and Bill had free access to her gloriously firm young breasts.

His hand started down her body, caressing as it went, and pushed inside the elasticated top of her skirt. Her hand reached for his but she didn't make a serious attempt to stop his relentless progress. Bill felt her suck in her waist to allow him easier access to the mysteries below and then his hand, freed from her restricting hold, was between her firm flesh and the silken panties; then among the thin blond hair that covered the pulsating wet heat below.

By now Lisa was moaning aloud and Bill was aware that his painfully engorged penis was being uncomfortably constrained by his trousers.

Lisa whimpered quietly as Bill withdrew his hand from the spot that was giving her so much pleasure, and then she started slightly—but said nothing—when she became aware that he was in the process of removing his trousers.

When he had accomplished this, his hand pushed her skirt upward until he had it all bunched at her waist, then he pulled at her skimpy underwear.

Lisa's breathed protests at this latest move grew stronger, but when Bill ignored them and continued his pulling, she eased herself upward to ease his task.

At last she lay still, naked but for the skirt bunched at her waist, and Bill's hand resumed its quest between her legs, legs that parted to allow access to her most secret part, a part that was now so hot that she could barely endure it.

Her body started to writhe and her hand, seeking support from the floor, made contact with Bill's erection. At first she withdrew it with a gasp but then, as curiosity took over, her cool hand returned and began, hesitantly, to explore the length of his throbbing shaft.

It was now Bill's turn to feel as though he would explode. He eased himself upward and over so that he was now above Lisa, supporting himself on both of his hands.

Their lips were still together as he gently lowered himself between her open legs.

Lisa was still holding him gently with her right hand and she was now almost sobbing with a mixture of desire and apprehension.

Bill felt the tip of his penis touch the scalding heat of her and, with her hand still holding—now it was guiding him—he lowered himself on to her and his being sank deep inside her.

Lisa cried out wildly and thrust her hips upward so that Bill was now fully in the white-hot core of her and the spasms started. Bill was shouting something unintelligible; his whole being on fire as he bucked on top of her in a welter of emotions that seemed to go on for an eternity.

Gradually their passion subsided and they lay motionless together. Lisa began to sob quietly, her tears flowing freely down her cheeks. The realisation of what they had done dawned slowly on Bill. What could he say to ease the pain that Lisa was now feeling? He felt ashamed that he had betrayed her trust, and the trust of her parents. He turned his head to her wet cheeks and began to kiss them gently.

"Please don't cry, Lisa. I don't ever want to do anything to hurt you. I love you so much."

At that moment he did feel an overwhelming mixture of love for the girl who lay beside him, and guilt for what he thought he had done.

Lisa stiffened and she pushed herself up on to one arm.

"Don't ever tell me you love me unless you mean it!" she sobbed, anger glinting in her tear ravaged eyes. "I love you—I have since I first saw you. I am not sorry for what happened just now. I wanted it to happen just as much as you did. I was meant for you, but I know that there has been someone else in your life. I can sense it. Telling me that you love me will only hurt me more if you decide to leave me for her. Tell me the truth, or stay quiet." Then she pushed herself off the sofa and stood unashamedly before him, glaring at him angrily as she shook her skirt down from her waist.

"I'll need to clean myself up," she continued, after what to Bill seemed an age. "Someone might call and I couldn't face anyone like this." She turned and almost ran from the room.

She obviously hadn't gone as far as the bathroom because she returned very quickly, bent and kissed Bill tenderly. "I love you, Bill. With all my heart I love you."

Then she left again, more slowly this time.

Bill sat alone on the settee. His mind was in a whirl. What if Lisa became pregnant? His thoughts went to the only other occasion when he had thought the same thoughts and he realised that perhaps Lisa was not as knowledgeable as Theresa, with her medical training, had been.

Thinking of Theresa only served to increase the turmoil in his mind. How could he resolve the dilemma he now felt himself enveloped in? Where was this calm voice that had spoken so clearly to him in the past? He tried to relax and will himself into a state in which he could resolve his feelings.

Perhaps, he thought, he had never been intended for Theresa. Yes, that might be the answer! He had assumed that the feeling of belonging and fulfilment that he had always felt in Mallaig was due to his having met Theresa. Maybe not, he now reasoned. She had deliberately shut herself away from him and that had opened the door for what had now happened with Lisa.

The more Bill thought, the more he convinced himself that this was indeed the case. His future, he now saw with absolute clarity, was with Lisa. She was from the same fishing background as he was and, more importantly, she worshipped in the same church. Why, he asked himself, had he not seen this before? It was all perfectly simple—he would marry her. It would also save a lot of explaining, he thought, if he refrained from mentioning anything about Theresa, to Lisa.

He rose to his feet when Lisa came back into the room, eyes downcast, and went towards her, both hands outstretched. He took her hands in his, pulled her close, and looked deep into her eyes. "I do love you, Lisa, and I want to marry you. Please will you marry me?"

"You aren't just saying that because of what happened just now, Bill?"

"No, Lisa. I want you to be my wife, and to have our children. Please say you will?"

Lisa looked long at him before lowering her eyes. Intuition told her that there was something in Bill's past that he had not told her, something that had hurt him deeply but for all that, she loved him dearly. Raising her eyes again she again quietly told Bill that she had loved him since the day they had met and that yes, she would marry him.

Bill felt a great surge of happiness mingled with relief, relief that no longer would he feel the loneliness that had blighted his young life at times, and happiness that now he had someone he could trust implicitly and in whom he could confide his innermost thoughts. He started to talk excitedly of wedding plans until he saw the smile on her face. "Am I allowed a say in this, Bill," she asked mischievously. "We will have to tell our parents before we do anything else about it. Is your dad fishing up here yet, or is he still in the Clyde?"

"The last I heard he was on his way here, Lisa, but I don't know where they will be right now. I'll send a telegram to my mother, and ask her to telephone your office on Monday. You can break the good news to her then. It'll be up to her to tell my dad. My brother, Donald, is aboard with him now. He is too young to be best man, isn't he? He's only eighteen, and unless he has got himself a load of common sense in the last year or two, I can't see him being much use at all."

"Let's just wait a wee while, Bill. There's no need to rush at anything. Things will work out just fine, wait and see."

"Talking of rush," Bill began hesitantly. "Is there any chance that you will— you know—could you——?"

"Yes, Bill. I could be pregnant, but I really don't think that I will be. I have no intention of rushing into a quick wedding just in case, though. We'll do things properly. I want to get my parents' agreement to us getting married, that's the first thing."

Chapter Eleven

The wedding took place in the spring of the following year, after the very successful winter fishing had closed.

Before this, however, there were several important developments on the fishing scene. Earnings had been so good that the debts that Bill and Jim had incurred when buying the *Misty Isle* were almost cleared. After Bill had long and detailed discussions with Jim and Willie Mair, they decided that they would buy the Clyde boat that Willie had earlier heard was for sale. The *Marguerite*, as the boat was named, was owned by a family who lived in Maidens in Ayrshire, and that fact alone convinced the young pair that she would be well kept.

"The Maidens men keep their boats better than any other fishermen we ever heard of," they told Willie. Ian expressed some concern that she had a Gardner engine. "I don't know anything about them," he said.

This apprehension was very soon put behind him when he gained some experience of the one in their new acquisition.

"Look at this, lads," Ian called delightedly as he discovered how to operate the sea water pump, which was driven by belt from the Gardner engine. It was different from the reciprocating pump on the Kelvin in that it was centrifugal, and therefore gave a constant pressure to the hose. This was unlike the pulsating stream that came from the Kelvin powered one. It also had the ability to both supply clean sea water for washing the hold and to pump out the bilges at the same time—a major advance when the men were washing down the hold after discharging a catch. A firm whose initials were G.G.G. manufactured this pump and so it was initially nicknamed 'Gee Gee.' In time, it was referred to as 'the donkey.'

Several east-coast fishermen had arrived in Mallaig over the winter months, attracted by the good landings of herring that the port had enjoyed. Some of them came to join their womenfolk who had found lucrative work in the kippering factories. This influx of experienced fishermen helped to solve the crewing problems that were being experienced, as they soon adapted to the use of the ring net.

Bill and Jim had, of course, kept Alex John fully informed of all their intentions and decisions, and reassured him that their purchase would not affect the smoothly running partnership that had evolved since they had got together. They all agreed that three boats working together might well be better than two, on occasion.

Lisa's dad, George, had remained with them over the winter fishing and when it ended, he sought out Bill and Jim.

"I think that I'd rather stay here than go off somewhere else to fish with the *Silver Searcher*. I think I've become too used to spending so much time at home, so I will deliver her back to the East Coast—if that is what the owner wants. You will not need another boat to run your herring until the next winter season starts. Meantime, if you need another man, I would be quite happy to come with you as a deckhand. What do you think of that?"

There was silence for a time as the pair digested this news, then Jim spoke.

"I think it would be great if you joined us. I'm going to be a skipper for the first time ever, and I'd love to have someone like you with me, to keep me right. What do you say, Bill?"

"Well, Jim, if you would be happy with George keeping an eye on you, then that's that. While we are on the subject," he continued hesitantly, "Which of us is going to get the new boat?"

Jim smiled at first, and then laughed out loud.

"You are the man for the new boat, you'll enjoy that."

"No," replied Bill, joining in his laughter. "I think you should take her. George has experience of Gardner engines for one thing, and for another, Ian will be staying aboard the *Misty Isle* with his Kelvin. This way, we'll each have someone we know well with us, someone we can rely on."

He did not voice his other reason for his decision. He did not want Lisa's father to be with him on the boat for exactly the same reason that his own mother had objected to his going to sea with his father—it was not good to have too many of the same family on one boat!

The following morning, Willie Mair asked Bill to come to his office. When they had both settled down with their coffee, he began: "I had a call this morning from a man who wants to sell you an echo-sounder. He works for a firm that makes them, and will be here tomorrow with the lunch-time train. What do you know of these things, and would you be interested in getting one?"

"I don't know much about them, Willie, but I have heard about them. They were originally designed to chart the seabed but apparently they can be used to find herring, also. I think they send some sort of electronic signal downward and read the signal that bounces back up from the bottom. There are a few boats in the Clyde that have had them fitted but they haven't been on the market for very long, and I don't know just how successful they are. I know that one skipper in Carradale had one put in to please his son, but he switches it off as soon as his son isn't looking! He reckons that it frightens the herring. Anyway, we'll see what this salesman has to say about it before we do anything."

The meeting with the echo-sounder salesman was not nearly as difficult as Bill had feared, there was certainly no great pressure put on them to buy one so, after a short discussion, Jim and he agreed that they should fit one on a trial 'sale or return' basis. They thought that it should go into the *Marguerite*, as she was a newer boat than the *Misty Isle*. If it worked as the engineer promised it would, Jim said, they would want one fitted in the *Misty Isle* too, and he couldn't see Alex John being the odd man out—he would want one also.

The Maidens men happily delivered the *Marguerite* to them in Mallaig, and

Bill felt well satisfied in every respect—well, nearly every one. He was still not absolutely clear in his mind if he should be marrying Lisa. They had both spent an anxious few days, months ago, before she was able to tell him that she was not pregnant, and immediately afterwards, Lisa told Bill in no uncertain terms that she would not allow them anything like the same intimacy again!

Bill passed quite a few unhappy hours in the last few days before the wedding thinking of Theresa, and agonising over whether or not he had made the correct decision. How could he tell if he loved one more than the other? The end result of his deliberations was always the same, though. Theresa had disappeared from his life. He had no idea where she had gone, nor why. He would never, he convinced himself, see her again.

Bill's parents and several of his uncles and aunts attended the wedding. All agreed loudly that Bill had made a good choice in his bride. Donald, his brother—now a fisherman himself—who was to be the best man, told Bill that he would never contemplate living in such a 'dead and alive hole.' Bill ignored that comment, thinking only that he should probably have stayed with his first inclination to have Jim as his best man. He had not, he thought, come to Mallaig for nightlife; he was there to make money!

Bill had written a personal letter to old Dennis O'Hara, inviting him to the wedding. Dennis had, his father told him, retired from his fishing career and now filled his days working part-time in the factory in Campbeltown that made the ring nets. The reply was disappointing. In it Dennis wrote that he felt that the long journey would be too much for him as his health was not very good, but he went on to wish Bill all the best in his married life.

"I assume from reading your invitation," he wrote, "that you are no longer concerned with the problems you would meet by marrying outside your own Church. That is a good thing. I doubt that I will live to see the day when any of us are able to marry as we please."

Without thinking about it at all, Bill passed the letter to Lisa to read. Had he thought about it at all, he would have realised that Lisa would be puzzled by the parts of it that referred to marrying outside the Church.

She read and re-read Dennis's letter, realising that in it there lay another clue to what had happened to Bill before she met him. She thought about asking Bill about it again, but after a lot of careful thought decided not to pursue the matter further. Bill would, she reckoned, tell her what had happened, when he was ready.

The young couple had decided that they would try to build a small house for themselves and to that end, they had—after many trials—eventually managed to prise a piece of land from the titled man who owned all the ground in the area. Lisa had, of course, been looking out for a site for some time and had set her heart on this spot. It had a very good open view to the west, overlooking the south end of Skye. The islands of Rhum, Eigg and Muck were also clearly visible. Until Bill managed to get some financial help for the building secured, however, they would live with Lisa's parents.

Bill spent several nights before the wedding in Willie Mair's house, it being considered incorrect that he should be married from his new bride's parents' home.

It was a bonny day, but a clouding sky promised rain. In the harbour lay the *Mystical Rose*, bedecked with flags. She had arrived that morning from Uist, complete with her full crew and their wives or girlfriends. It touched Bill greatly that they had gone to the trouble to see him and Lisa "properly wedded," as they put it!

After the ceremony, they all walked from the church, led by a piper, to the small hotel that had been opened after the railway line reached the village. There they had lunch, and listened to the speeches before Bill's new father-in-law announced that—"It is nearly time that Mr. and Mrs. Martin made their way to the station. The train will leave soon!"

This announcement, which of course contained the first reference to them as husband and wife was greeted with loud cheers from the guests and provoked furious blushing from the lovely bride.

Lisa looked into Bill's eyes, her face filled with happiness, as she asked to be excused while she changed into her 'going-away clothes' before hurrying upstairs, accompanied by her mother, to the room reserved for that purpose.

Jim approached Bill and motioned him to step aside from the crowd.

"There's something you should maybe know," he began. His worried face caused a feeling of dread to come over Bill.

"What's wrong, Jim," he asked, fearfully.

"Well," began Jim hesitantly. "You see—we think—no, we are sure—well, you see, Mary is going to have a baby! We have known for a wee while, but we thought we'd keep it a secret until after the wedding. The baby is due in the late summer."

"That's brilliant!" cried Bill. "Just wait till I tell Lisa, she'll be delighted—but I think I'll keep it from her until we get on the train. You know what these women are like, she'll probably start crying!"

The happy pair set off on their honeymoon to Inverness but Bill had made sure that the boats would be well cared for in his absence. He had, with Jim's full agreement, decided that they should use the few weeks before the spring fishing started, trying to scrape the hull of the *Misty Isle* clean enough to varnish. Neither of them cared for the black paint job they had inherited and when finished she might, they hoped, match the beautiful varnished hull of the *Marguerite*. Ian would use the time, he said, to give the *Misty Isle*'s engine a complete overhaul, saying—rightly of course—that it was much better to correct any potential faults before they caused damage.

The new echo sounder would be fitted before Bill and his new wife returned, but the engineer who was to install it had promised that he would come back to Mallaig when they went to sea, so that he could show them just what his machine was capable of, as he put it.

Chapter Twelve

So Bill's married life began.

Back in Mallaig after the brief honeymoon, Bill threw himself into his work with his usual gusto. In time, Mary had her daughter, calling her Margaret, after Mary's late mother. Soon after Margaret's birth, Bill and Lisa built their three-bedroom house, with financial assistance from the Bank. Lisa took great delight in keeping it spotlessly clean and tidy, and she dearly loved to welcome Bill's mother into it, when she came to visit.

The new echo sounder had proved its worth as soon as it was switched on. Bill and Jim were both amazed at being able to see the image of the seabed being inscribed on the special paper that had to be loaded into it. The marks that appeared between the line that marked the boat's keel and the bottom of the sea were, the engineer who had installed the echo sounder told them, shoals of fish. They both realised that this machine would be invaluable not only as a fish finder but also as an indication of the type of bottom that lay below them, and that facility would certainly save them from tearing their nets so often.

They were so impressed with its performance that they ordered another one for the *Misty Isle* before the week was up, and Alex John was not long behind them.

However, some of the older men were not in favour of the sounders. They noticed that if they were sitting in the forecastle whilst lying in a quiet harbour alongside a boat that had its sounder switched on, they could hear the distinct loud clicking noise it emitted as it sent its pulse out. They were convinced that this 'racket,' as they described it, would frighten the herring, especially in the shallow lochs they often worked in.

The first radios that were fitted to any fishing boats were medium frequency transmitter/receivers. They had a range of around one hundred miles in good reception conditions and they soon earned their keep as they enabled the boats to stay in touch with one another at all times and of course, were used to keep the skippers advised of the best markets for their catches. On more than one occasion Willie Mair called them through a coast radio station, advising them to go somewhere other than Mallaig with their catches.

Bill had kept up the friendship with Murray Buchan that had started when Murray had helped him out in his dispute with the buyers in Mallaig. They spoke on the telephone often at the weekends and Bill had, on several occasions, landed herring to him at ports such as Gairloch, Kyle and Oban when, for transport reasons, these places were more suitable to the buyer. They had built up a good working relationship and Bill was able now to call Murray—again through one of the coast radio stations—advising him of what herring they had, and how the fleet had fished that night. Information like this, Murray told Bill, was invaluable to him as he worked in the ever-changing marketing scene.

When they spoke of the coming winter fishing, Bill and Jim talked of getting a replacement for George's drifter. After a lot of discussion they agreed that they should perhaps try doing without one. The money that had been paid out over the last winter would now be kept among themselves and this, they reckoned, would more than compensate for the extra work.

Jim announced, almost apologetically, that Mary was pregnant again, just five months after wee Margaret's birth, and asked Bill's help in getting ground to build on. "It looks as though you should be building a hotel, instead of a house!" Bill said as he laughingly agreed. In his quiet moments, Bill wondered why Lisa had not become pregnant. Plenty of time yet, he told himself and anyway, the money she earned working, came in useful.

Bill and Jim had a long discussion one morning in Willie Mair's office, about what should be done about George. Jim was quite happy having him aboard his boat, but they both wondered just what George wanted to do and of course, what was the best way forward for them all. Although they had decided that perhaps they should try doing without one, they needed to know if George wanted to get another drifter to run their herring, or was he happy where he was? Eventually they all agreed that Bill should ask him straight out but for various reasons, they both had reservations about his getting another boat.

George, when Bill asked him, thought for a time before he replied.

"Well, Bill, I am not sure myself. I have been quite happy working with Jim, and I'm not sure now that I would want to go back to having more responsibility again. I am not as young as I once was, and it is fine being at home with my wife and being at ease, with no boat to worry about. I would be quite content to stay as I am, and I might be handy if any of you want a relief skipper at any time. How do you feel about that?

Bill, inwardly relieved at the way things had gone thus far, replied, "That's just fine, George. I'm sure that Jim will be delighted too; he relies on your support quite a lot. We'll just carry on as we were, then"

The fishing continued to prosper, and more boats appeared in the port. Bill was delighted one day when Albert Cowie, who had been such a good host to Bill when Jim got married in Buckie, appeared with his son, young Ally. Bill had thought of them often, as he had grown to like them well in the very short time he had spent with them and he was not really surprised when Albert told him that they wanted to try at least one season fishing with a ring net boat out of Mallaig. If it was successful, they told him, they fully intended to make their homes there.

Bill suspected that they had already been in contact with Willie Mair, but that made no difference; experienced men were always appreciated so he bade them welcome, and told them that there were berths available on either his or Jim's boat. This offer was accepted immediately! The relatively easy summer fishing would, they said, break them in for the rough winter they knew lay ahead. Bill was aware that if they liked the job, and felt that they could master it, they would soon have a boat of their own. They would not, he recognised, be content to work for someone else for the rest of their lives.

Jim came to visit him one Saturday afternoon some months later. They were both soon comfortably seated in front of the wonderfully aromatic peat fire that Bill loved so much, mugs of tea in their hands.

"I've taken on another hand today, Bill. He's a young fellow, just out of school. He has no fishing experience but he seems a very likely lad and he looks as though he is not short of strength. MacDonnell is his name, Francis MacDonnell, and he comes from somewhere up around Loch Hourn. We didn't really need another hand at the moment but I don't think we'll have the Cowies with us for all that long. I'm sure they'll be off in a boat of their own soon. In any case, we need all the good hands we can get if the fishing continues as it is."

Bill laughed. "You don't need to justify everything you do, to me, Jim. You're skipper of your boat and if you need something, man or equipment, just you go ahead and get it. How did you meet up with him, anyway?"

"He came down to the boat on Thursday, when we were in with herring, and asked for a berth. I said I'd think about it, and would see him at the weekend. He seems very keen."

Jim paused for a bit then and looked at Bill quizzically. "MacDonnell, that was the name of that girl from Loch Nevis, wasn't it?"

"Yes it was," Bill replied, quietly. "I don't suppose there is any connection, though. It isn't an unusual name around here. In any case, as far as I can tell she left here for Canada a long time ago, with her parents. Has he any brothers or sisters?"

"I asked this lad about his folks, Bill," Jim said. "I did wonder about a possible connection, but he says that he lives with his mother and grandmother. His father was long dead, he said, and his grandfather died three years ago so there's just his mother and grandmother left. They are living on a wee croft now. He has no aunts or uncles and so has no cousins either. He's a very quiet chap, and I think he'll be a good hand."

They sat silent for some time, gazing into the fire, Bill once more feeling that great sadness that came over him whenever he thought of Theresa, and what might have been. There was no way that there was any connection between this lad and Theresa, Bill decided.

They sat quietly until Lisa came in and asked them if they wanted any more tea, whereupon Jim announced that it was past time that he went home to his bairns.

Francis was duly welcomed aboard and very soon proved his usefulness. He had obviously spent much of his life in or around boats and his worth was enhanced when it was realised that he spoke fluent Gaelic. They had at least one

Gaelic speaker on each boat and it became common practice to have them talk in that language to their neighbour boats on the radio when anything sensitive had to be discussed. More than once Bill was approached by the skipper of a Clyde boat who said, "Aye, lad, we know fine when you are among the herring. You only talk Gaelic, then!"

Lying in bed one Saturday night, Bill broached a subject that had been festering in his mind for some time. "What do you think would Willie Mair's answer be if I suggested that he might start out on his own, Lisa?"

Lisa didn't answer right away, but lay silent for a time. "What exactly did you have in mind on that score? There's more to that question than you are saying," she said.

Bill laughed. "You know me too well. I was thinking that the firm that he works for is making money out of the port, and out of me. If they weren't, they would soon clear out. What would be wrong with Willie and me starting out on our own? Then we would keep the profits, instead of handing it to some strangers. I have counted up how much commission our two boats have paid out, and that alone would be enough to pay Willie's salary. There would be plenty left over to pay the rent for an office too and if we could get a few more boats to sell with us, we'd be quids in! I think I'll have a word with him about that."

"Are you not making enough money, Bill," Lisa asked quietly. "Is it worth making enemies of powerful men, just for the sake of making money that you don't really need? Are you making a God out of money and power?"

"Who is going to make enemies? All I want to do is to get everything on a sensible footing. I don't see why a fair bit of the money we are making through damned hard work, is going to people who don't even know our names! I'm going to have a word with Willie anyway. There's no harm can come from that."

The heated tone of his reply indicated to Lisa that he was determined to get his own way, but she was concerned that he was succeeding in this too often for his own good. She had heard him talk more sharply to others than he used to, and this apparent change in his character worried her at times.

"If he agrees, will Jim be in on this too?" was Lisa's next question, her voice betraying the sarcasm. "If your scheme does go ahead, I don't see why Jim should be part of it. You shouldn't be carrying him any more than you already are."

"Oh yes," snapped Bill, who had missed the point completely. "I was the one that was making a God out of money, was I? Now you're the one that wants to keep others out. Jim has a family to support, and that's more than we can say!"

As soon as he had said that, Bill regretted it, but his anger remained. Lisa turned on her side, facing away from him. He knew that he had hurt her deeply. After a few moments a muffled sniff confirmed that she was crying. Well what of it, he consoled himself. He had told her the truth and if she couldn't take it, then that was her problem. It wasn't his fault that she hadn't become pregnant. Why, his flawed reasoning continued, even his mother had expressed some surprise and disappointment that they had not yet made her a grandmother. He convinced himself that he was right and the more convinced he became, the harder grew his thoughts. This train of thought, although he did not yet realise it, was a descending spiral that could only cause great harm to everyone.

He turned away from his wife, and fell asleep, his mind still full of his totally arrogant self-belief.

He woke in the morning to the familiar sounds of the fire being cleaned out and rose to see Lisa bent down arranging kindling.

"Will you bring in some coal for me, Bill, please?"

She spoke quietly but the strain she was feeling was made clear by the awkwardness in her voice, and in the set of her shoulders. She did not turn to greet Bill with her usual smile, but remained kneeling. She was hurting very badly inside herself. It seemed to her that the Bill she had married so recently had changed considerably, and she could not be certain why this had come about. He had, she thought, become more determined to get his own way in many things and although she was young herself, she knew that in any marriage there had to be a lot of give and take. She tried to make excuses for him—he had been working very hard, and had been under a lot of pressure in many ways, but still she thought that he should be much more considerate of others.

"I'm sorry, Lisa," Bill began. "I shouldn't have said what I did last night. Let's go to the doctor and find out why you aren't getting pregnant." Then, in a poor attempt at levity he added smilingly, "It's not for the want of trying, is it?"

Then, realising that it would require time and patience before the situation grew easier to deal with he went back into the bedroom to put on his clothes, and then took the coal scuttle outside to fill, as he had been asked.

The strain between them carried into the Church that morning. Bill saw Meg look quizzically at her daughter's face and saw the worried frown that replaced her usual smile.

"Yes, of course I'm all right!" was the snappy reply from Lisa after her concerned mother had asked if all was well, as they walked out together after the service.

Her next statement, however, that she and Bill would not be coming to lunch that day, a regular event on Sundays, "I have a bit of a headache!" being her excuse, did nothing to relieve Meg's concern, and certainly didn't help the awkwardness that Bill felt.

The walk home was completed in total silence, unbroken until they had entered the house and had taken their coats off. Then, as Lisa started toward the kitchen, Bill spoke.

"I don't know how long we are going to continue this silence for, but it all seems very silly to me—" That was as far as he got.

"Silly! Is that what you think all this fuss is about? I don't think it is silly. Don't you think that I have been wondering and worrying just why I'm not pregnant? I'm the one that is left alone here in this house all week, every week. You're among your friends all the time. I'm alone. Can you understand that?"

Then the tears started. "I can't even spend any time with Mary," Lisa sobbed. "She has her work cut out trying to look after her children. Every time I see her and her kids I am reminded that I have let you down. I don't want to be childless any more than you do. I didn't tell you that I have been to the doctor already; I thought that you had enough on your plate with running the boats. I tried to talk to my mother about it, but she doesn't seem to understand how important it is to me. I have tried to be a good wife to you, Bill—"

Lisa sat down heavily on the corner of the settee, sobbing her heart out, seemingly unable to continue talking.

Bill sat down quietly beside her, turning sideways to face her and although she resisted his efforts to put his arm around her, he laid it gently across her shoulders.

"I am sorry, Lisa. Please forgive me; I had no right to say what I said last night. This is our first real quarrel, and I had to start it through my thoughtlessness. When did you go to the doctor, and what did he say? I'm asking that because I love you, and I want to be with you. Troubles should be shared. We're both guilty in that we haven't shared our thoughts about kids."

They both sat for a time. Neither of them spoke, but gradually Lisa calmed down, her sobbing eased and she allowed Bill to hold her close. They sat there silently in an embrace for a long time, and then Lisa told Bill that she had spoken to the doctor around three months previously. His initial examination had revealed nothing obvious wrong with her that would prevent conception, and his advice had been that she should wait a little longer, around a year perhaps, and then if nothing had happened, she should return and he would get her an appointment with a specialist. She suggested, and Bill gratefully agreed, that they were both under strain and that this was why they had reacted so badly. She brought up again the thought that had sparked it all off, Bill's possible approach to Willie Mair. Had Bill, she asked, talked it over with Jim?

His answer surprised her greatly.

"No I haven't, Lisa. This has really got nothing at all to do with him, it is my idea and I don't see why I need to talk to him about it. We're in partnership with the boats. That has worked out well so far, thank God, but trying to talk Willie into leaving the firm he works for is my idea and mine alone. Jim's a fine lad and a very good friend and I enjoy working with him. He's as honest as the day is long but I know that if it weren't for me he would probably still be a share fisherman. I think it would be fair to say that so far, he has had more out of the partnership than he put into it. I think that if we—that is Willie and I—decided that we would have a go at setting up a fish selling company, that Murray Buchan would be interested also. He could lay his hands on as much money as we would need, if the Banks wouldn't help out. I've always had a good relationship with Murray. We've always played fair with one another and besides, he knows the fish business inside out. Now, how about making a nice cup of tea—but I think you should wash your face first. Your mother knows fine that there's something wrong, and I wouldn't be surprised to see her appear any minute now."

That evening, after they had spent the afternoon cosily in front of the fire, each trying to make up to the other for the row, they both called on Willie Mair. Bill insisted on Lisa coming along. It was, he insisted, her future as well as his that was going to be discussed.

Willie and his wife, Maggie, another Buchan lass, made them welcome with the obligatory cup of tea. Bill wasted no time in launching straight into outlining the reasons for the visit.

When he had finished, Willie, who had heard him out in silence told him in a very definite tone that he would not under any circumstances consider leaving the firm that he worked for.

"They gave me my first job, and they have given me a free hand in setting up the office here. They have backed me in all I have done. I am well paid, and I just will not let them down—and that is what I think I'd be doing if I set up another office in the port. They'll see me all right for a pension when it comes time to retire and in any case, I just don't want the hassle I'd get if I left."

He then paused for a moment and, after a long look at Maggie, told Bill that he was suffering from heart trouble. He did not want this information to go any further, he said. It had been diagnosed three years ago and was not immediately life threatening, but he had been told to avoid as much stress as he possibly could.

"I understand your motives in coming to me, Bill, and I appreciate all of the thoughts that have led you here tonight. I know that you are not alone in thinking that the men who catch the herring are the ones that generate the money. It is easy to come to believe that we on the shore side of the industry are creaming off more of the profits than we should. If that is what you believe then so be it. I hope that I don't need to remind you that you got your start with the help of my company. There are others that are getting the same sort of help in ports all over Scotland. You've worked very hard and have been successful. Your loans are just about clear, but not everyone will be so fortunate. Some of these other fellows will go broke, owing us money. Thank you for your honesty in coming to me first. It won't make any difference between us as far as I'm concerned, and I am sure that you will feel the same way too. Now, let's have another cuppa, Maggie!"

Bill was disappointed at the reply from Willie but in fact, he was not too surprised. He knew that Willie had high standards of loyalty and that this would stand in the way of any move away from the firm he had been with for so long. Both he and Lisa expressed their concern for his health. They did like him, and their regard for him was plain for all to see.

"Don't worry about turning down my suggestion, Willie. It won't make any difference to our dealings. Let's pretend that it never happened. I had to ask, but I respect your feelings."

At home that night, Lisa asked Bill how he really felt adding, "You know that I will always want the best for you, but I think I am glad this is not going to go ahead. I think that you have enough on your plate as it is."

"I told Willie the truth, Lisa, I'm not too disappointed. I am not saying that I've closed the door on the subject, though. You heard what Willie said about his heart. What if we should lose him? I don't necessarily mean that he is going to die, but he might be told to cut down, or even stop working. Who is going to take his place? Will it be someone as honest and hard working? We could easily get someone we don't like or trust. I'd like to be in a position where I could have some say in choosing the person that is going to be appointed to look after our business. We'll just let it lie for now. It's time we were in bed."

Chapter Thirteen

The weather was always a prime consideration in fishermen's lives and they treated the elements with a great deal of respect. This was particularly true of the ring net men, because the boats that they used were much smaller and less heavily built than the drifters that worked alongside them. This difference in size was because of the ringers' need to be able to get really close inshore.

Every skipper had a tale to tell of being caught out in a storm at sea. This was a common experience in the Minches because boats, deep-laden with herring, leaving the shelter of the eastern seaboard of any of the Hebridean islands where they fished were exposed to the open sea for at least three hours, until they gained the shelter of Canna. The weather could, and often did, change dramatically for the worse in this short time.

On dirty nights, eyes would be strained looking through the spray and rain for the reassuring three flashes of the lighthouse on the low-lying Oigh Sgeir islands that lay some six miles to the south of their course. Often though, the poor visibility meant that they failed to see the light and the first sign that they were near the shelter of Canna would be when they felt the motion ease somewhat.

They had all learned that even in good weather, the boats had to be well prepared before setting off. The nets were securely tied down and a heavy tarpaulin was carefully lashed over the hatches that covered the hold. If they had herring aboard, the baskets used for discharging were pushed upside down into the herring. This helped to stop them moving around and becoming de-scaled or 'washed,' as the buyers would have it.

Because of these careful preparations and the watchfulness of the men on deck, it was rare indeed for any boat to get into severe difficulties. Although no one would have dreamed of boasting of it, no man was ever lost off a ring-net boat. This may have been because they were taught from a very early age to be at one with the sea. They did not fight the elements; they lived with them.

One Saturday afternoon Bill was taking his ease, sitting at the head of the pier on an upturned wooden box, enjoying the spring sunshine when Albert Cowie joined him. Bill moved over to make room for him and in response to the usual greeting, "What's doing, Bill?" he replied, "Not a lot Albert. I'm just enjoying the sunshine. What's doing with you?"

"Just the same as yourself, Bill. It's a bonny day now."

There was an easy silence for a time. Bill was of the opinion that Albert had something on his mind, and he believed that he had a good idea what it was.

"Ally was thinking of getting a boat to himself, Bill. He has enjoyed his spell at

155

the ring net with you—and so have I—but now he is of the opinion that he should maybe branch out on his own. What do you think of that?"

"Well, there are a few answers I'd need to have before I'd commit myself to answering that, Albert. Is he going to set up home here, and if so, where? What about you; are you going in with him on buying this boat? We'll be sorry to lose you, but I can understand that he won't want to spend the rest of his life working for someone else. I didn't."

"Well yes, Bill, I'll go with him. I'd want to be with him for a spell anyway. He hasn't got the money to buy a boat outright and, in answer to another of your questions yes; we will be moving here permanently. That means that I'll have to build a house somewhere here and at my age, I am not sure that I want to spend the rest of my life at sea. Jess has been at me to come ashore for a while now and I thought I might just set up a wee kippering yard here. I wouldn't make a fortune at it, but I think I could make enough to live on, anyway. Jess has been here for a few months, as you know, and she thinks that she could settle in the village all right. It's just the same sort of environment that we have lived in all our lives, anyway. She's talking of starting a wee tearoom. There is a need for somewhere for people to go when they come off the train, and have to wait for a steamer. Visiting fishermen might well use it too—there's only the pub available to them now, and not all of them drink. What do you think of that?"

"That's all good news so far, Albert. You have all been thinking quite a lot, and I am pleased that you are talking the way you are. The village does need more facilities, as you say. Jim and I will be sorry to lose two good men, but that's the way it goes. What about a neighbour for this boat of yours, have you thought about that?"

There was a pause before Albert answered.

"Well, Bill—that is another point. We wondered if we could team up with you. There are three of you already and I thought that it might be better sometimes if there were four. Then there would be two pairs, and they could split up and search in different directions if the fishing was slack. I don't want to be pushy, but it might be a good idea—"

"Aye, Albert, I see what you mean. Well, I am only one part of the act. There are others we'll have to think about, and I can't answer for them. I'll have a word and see what they think. You won't get an answer before next weekend, though."

"That's just capital, Bill. Ally will be delighted with what you have said. Now, there's something else I wanted to talk to you about. You know that I was second coxswain on the lifeboat at home. Well, it has bothered me for a while now that there isn't a lifeboat here and I was speaking to one of the lifeboat guys—he's on the management side—and he agrees with me. There is a long stretch of coastline here without any cover from lifeboats. I think we could get one stationed here without too much bother. Do you think that would be a good idea?"

Bill laughed out loud. "You surely have been doing a lot of thinking, Albert!" he said. "I don't know anything about the running of a lifeboat station but there are several points that you will need to think about. Will you be able to get people to man it? What about the shore side, there must be something that needs to be done there? Will it all be feasible?"

"You're right, Bill. I have spoken to the stationmaster here, and he is willing to help. He hasn't got much idea about the sea but he's very good with paperwork, and I think he'd be perfect as the secretary. He would be in charge of the shore side of the running of the boat. The manager of the bank would take on the job of treasurer. I haven't asked him yet, but I'm sure he'd do it. It would mean another account being opened in his branch and he'd like that, I'm certain. We would need someone to be the mechanic on the boat. He would be a full time employee, the only one needed here. I'm sure that we could get someone to take on that job, without much trouble. How are we doing so far?" he laughed.

"You're doing fine, Albert. Just you go for it! I'll back you any way I can. What about a coxswain for her? Is that something you want to keep for when you come ashore? That is a pretty responsible job; you'll need someone who knows what they're about."

"Well yes, Bill, it is. You are correct, I would like to take the job myself, but I'd want a year or so with Ally before I swallow the anchor. I wouldn't want to do it for very long, though. I've spent nearly enough time on boats now. Anyway, there's no real rush about it: we've been without a lifeboat here for a long time now. Another year won't mean the end of the world!"

The pair sat silent, deep in thought, for some time until the chill—as the low sun dropped behind some buildings—forced them to move.

When he got home Bill thought long about what had been confided in him. He was well aware that Albert knew that if he, Bill, was in favour of taking another boat into the partnership that the others wouldn't stand against him. He was also aware that there was a possibility of making some capital out of the situation. Why should he do someone else a favour without reward? As he thought of it, he became determined that he would agree only if he were to be allowed to buy a share in the Cowies' boat. That way he would make some money out of the deal—provided they continued to catch herring. The cash to buy his share of the boat would be available from the bank, he was certain. He had made sure that he had kept on the right side of the local manager in all his dealings with him thus far.

Lisa knew that something was on Bill's mind. She had learned all of his moods and was worried only because she did not know what was now troubling him. Bill had not brought up the question of the lack of children again. She knew that it was still distressing him, but had made up her mind that he would have to be the one to open the subject again. She had talked to her mother about it, but the only advice she had been given there was once again limited to "Just give it time!" She had been to the doctor again, unknown to Bill, and was now waiting for him to come back to her with a date for an appointment with a specialist. Her husband's silence and the lack of help from those from whom she had sought it meant that the whole affair was weighing ever more heavily on her mind.

On the Monday morning, before they set off to sea for the week, Bill spent a few minutes with Jim on the subject of taking young Ally as a neighbour. As he had thought, Jim was in favour of this. He had become quite friendly with both the Cowies, and respected their ability as fishermen. They had, Jim thought, adapted very well to what must have been a completely alien way of fishing. They had been drift net men for most of their days and the only other mode of fishing they had tried until their move to the west coast, was 'ripping' for cod, not too far from Buckie harbour. This method of catching fish involved the use of hand-held lines and was, of course, pursued in daylight only. Crawling along very close to the shore at night had been a new experience for them.

Bill did not get the chance to talk to Alex John until later in the week when they were lying at anchor in Polteil Loch. He raised no objections at all—in fact he thought that it was a great idea. Four boats working together would be a definite advantage, especially during the winter fishing when bad weather meant that it was possible for one's neighbour to be stuck somewhere.

On the following Saturday afternoon, Bill arranged to meet up with the Cowies in Willie Mair's office. He had spent a couple of hours that morning in an informal meeting with the bank manager, Ian Johnston. Ian, who was of Orcadian fishing stock himself, understood that there were times when his fishermen customers could not get to see him during normal office hours and had made it plain to them that if there was something urgent, they should contact him at home.

Ian listened to Bill as they drank a cup of tea.

"I don't see any problem, Bill," Ian said. "You have always kept your word in the deals we have done together and if the fishing keeps up, I'm sure I can rely on you to pay off any loan you get, quite quickly."

Bill thought that there was a hint of warning in Ian's voice and that what he was in fact meaning was that he had better pay off loans as soon as possible, but he wisely said nothing. He simply thanked Ian, and left.

By common consent, Willie sat in on the meeting with the Cowies, acting as a sort of chairman.

Bill got straight down to business, telling Albert and Ally that there had been no objection to their joining the company. He would, he said, want to buy a quarter share in the boat—"Just to keep things right!"

He knew that they must have discussed this possibility during the week and instinctively felt that Ally would much rather have had his father as his only partner.

"Well, I don't know about that. We're going to get a new boat built, Bill," said Ally rather defiantly. "We think that this is the best thing to do. There is a shortage of boats on the second-hand market just now—that is driving the prices up."

Bill caught Ally giving his father a sideways glance and thought that Albert nodded his head slightly in reply. Bill was slightly surprised at being told that they were after a new boat, but tried to hide it as much as possible. He had been sure that they would look for a second-hand one.

"Where are you going to get her built?" was the next question.

"We thought that we would go to Weatherhead in Cockenzie. He has a reputation for building a good boat, and has lots of experience in building ringers," replied Albert. "We want a Gardner engine in her; they're the ones we're used to running, and they are very reliable."

"Yes, that's fine," said Bill. "Ordering a new boat means that you won't have her before the winter fishing starts though. I had been hoping that you would be up and running before then. You should ideally have a boat very soon—that would give you some time to get used to her before heavy fishing comes on."

"That's right, Bill," said Ally, with a slight grin on his face. "But you see, there is a partly built boat on Weatherhead's slip now, ordered by a fellow from Girvan. He has run into some kind of trouble with finances, and we can have her if we want. She'll be ready by late August if we grab her now!"

Bill, after a pause, gave a slight laugh. "You're great guys, sure enough. You certainly play your cards close to your chest." Then he continued in a quieter tone, "Just don't be keeping too much from me; I don't think I'd like that very much. I'll need everything to be up front between us if we're going to get on together. Am I to think that the deal is on for me to have a quarter share?"

Albert replied hesitantly, "Yes, Bill, that should be all right. We would have preferred to be all on our own, but I can see why you would want an interest in her. On our side, it will guarantee us that we won't be left on our own—we'll always have a neighbour."

Bill rose abruptly saying, "I'll leave you to sort out all the details, Willie. You know what I'll want done."

There was an awkward silence after Bill had left—a silence that Willie broke. "Now lads, you have annoyed Bill, I know, but he'll get over it. He just likes everything to be correct, and he feels a wee bit angered that you kept some things from him."

Then, seeing the protests form on his guest's lips he added, "He just doesn't like to think that someone has put something over on him, that's all. He'll be fine."

"I don't think we put one over on him, Willie," Albert said. "We wanted to get a boat of our own. We could afford it and I'm still not certain that we have done the correct thing by letting him buy a share. We didn't know until today whether we were going to be welcome to join that group or not, so I am not going to apologise for anything. I feel that we may have started off on the wrong foot, but that is Bill's fault for being so touchy. Maybe we should stop right here."

"I think I know Bill well enough to be certain that he is annoyed with himself," said Willie. "He will be all right about it in the morning, I am sure of that."

Then in order to cool tempers a bit he continued; "He is probably a bit jealous at the thought that you will be starting off with a new boat while he had to make do with a second-hand one. Just carry on as though nothing had happened. In any case, I think that there is something else bothering Bill. He hasn't been himself for some time now. It has nothing to do with the fishing in my opinion—maybe he just isn't getting on well with his wife. You know how it is at times, Albert?"

"Yes, Dad, let's just get on with it," said Ally. "I would like you to talk to Bill though, Willie. There was no way that we could tell anyone that this boat was available. We found out about it by pure chance and if we had made it public, someone else might have moved before us. I would like you to call Weatherhead right now, and tell him that we want to go ahead. As for anything else, I am quite happy to let you look after our interests. You won't let us down, I am sure."

Chapter Fourteen

The summer fishing went well enough. No one made much money at it but they made enough to keep the wolf from the door and more importantly, they kept their crews together.

Jess started her wee tearoom in a small wooden shop she had built just a few steps from the station. Much to her delight it proved very popular not only with travellers but as she and Albert had hoped, with visiting fishermen also. Jess's home baking was the main attraction, but she had been wise enough to reassure the baker that she had no intention of stepping on her toes—the tea-room goodies would all be consumed on the premises!

The village continued to expand rapidly. It now boasted three grocery stores, two of them facing one another across the rudimentary main street, and the same number of pubs. A fairly large hotel had been built close to the road on the southern outskirts and another Presbyterian Church was opened. There was now an established building firm run by an enterprising young man who catered for the continuing demand for housing.

True to his word, Albert contacted his acquaintances on the Lifeboat front. A small deputation from the Lifeboat head office, in London, visited the village and after a preliminary meeting with Albert they convened a public meeting that was held in the village's small dance hall.

It was held on a Saturday afternoon and was well attended. The officials later confided in Albert that they were very pleased with the response when they asked for the names of those who would volunteer their services if a Lifeboat were to be stationed there. Albert agreed to take up the position of Coxswain. This offer, in view of his experience, was met with general acclaim by all present. The final decision as to whether or not a boat would be sent to Mallaig would be conveyed to the Hotel owner who had been appointed Chairman of the meeting.

The stationmaster, James MacBride, offered his services as the Honorary Secretary as he had promised he would, and the officials gladly accepted this. They did warn Albert privately, after the public meeting, that they didn't think that a boat would be available for at least a year, a time scale that suited him to the ground—he would now get the winter fishing in with young Ally.

As usual, Halloween heralded the first herring being landed from the Minches and before long the pier was a hive of activity every morning. The season had barely got under way however, when the *Misty Isle*'s engine packed in. They were *en route* to Mallaig with a good shot aboard and Bill was sound asleep when there was a sudden crash from the engine room, followed by silence when the engine stopped. A connecting rod had broken and part of it had burst through the crankcase.

This was not something that Ian could fix in a hurry—this was a major breakdown. Fortunately, the *Mystical Rose* was also on her way to market and was not far from them so a frantic radio call brought her alongside and a tow was rigged.

In Mallaig, the local engineer, who had increased his workforce to keep pace with the bigger fleet, set about dismantling the stricken engine immediately. The herring were discharged using the *Mystical Rose*'s winch, as soon as her own cargo had been unloaded.

The engineer reckoned that it would be around a week before he completed the repair so Bill arranged for four of his crew, who lived on Uist, to go back home with the *Mystical Rose*. This arrangement was changed however. George, who had been suffering for some time with a sore back, took advantage of the mishap by staying ashore for a few days, and his place on the *Marguerite* was taken by one of Bill's crew.

Francis MacDonnell, who had some urgent dental work to be seen to, also stayed ashore, another of Bill's crew taking his place. Bill then had to suffer the frustration of seeing boats coming in with herring every morning, while he remained unable to fish.

It was the following Wednesday when, after trials, the engineer—and Ian—stated that they were satisfied with the job and Bill could go back to sea. Ian's mother had been taken to hospital for a check up, so Bill insisted that for his own peace of mind, Ian would remain ashore. A full gale had blown up on the Monday night, and continued to blow right through until the Wednesday, so no herring were landed. Bill, however, was for going to sea, gale or no gale.

This decision didn't go down well with his crew, who now faced as they put it, "Getting battered stupid," for at least six hours. They had been looking forward to another night safe in port!

After rounding Sleat Point, the southernmost point of Skye, they headed toward the north shore of the island of Rhum, getting dubious shelter there from the raging gale. Both of Bill's crew, Hector and Francis, were outside, huddled together, sheltering behind the wheelhouse, preferring the cold and wet there to the warmer but smellier confines of the wheelhouse. They took infrequent trips down into the engine room to check the level of water in the bilges and to add oil to the engine. George was still ashore in Mallaig, waiting to have a specialist examine his back.

"What sort of ship is that, Bill?" asked Francis, opening the wheelhouse door unexpectedly.

"What ship? Where is she?" asked Bill, whose visibility was impaired by the spray-lashed windows.

"Look there, away down to leeward, near the mouth of Loch Slapin."

Bill slowed the engine down to idling speed and turned to starboard, opening the starboard window as the boat turned.

There was a ship there all right, he now saw, headed roughly into the wind. She was smothered in foam, and did not appear to be under way. As they watched, they all agreed that she appeared to be listing badly to port.

Bill tuned the radio to the emergency frequency and called Oban Radio, the coast radio station for the area. When he had made contact with them, he asked if they knew of a ship in difficulties anywhere in the Minches, but they replied that they did not. No one, they said, had sent out a distress signal.

Bill told them what they were seeing, promised to keep in touch with them and lifted the throttle again, heading downwind toward the ship. As they drew closer, they saw that she was indeed listed to port, and that she had an anchor out.

"She must have engine trouble, lads," said Bill. "There's no other reason they'd be anchored there!"

"I don't see anyone aboard her," cried Hector from his position on the foredeck, where he had a firm grip on the halliards that were used to raise the mast. It was telling that both he and Francis had, unbidden, donned their lifejackets. "She looks abandoned, to me!"

Bill called them aft as they drew close to the ship. She was, they now saw clearly, a fine looking Swedish coaster of around one thousand five hundred tons. She appeared to be very well looked after; the paintwork was clean and everything looked to be in good order. She looked heavy in the water, but because of the list, they were not certain if she was fully loaded or not. They circled her carefully, going as close as Bill dared—tumbling and tossing in the confused sea.

Their presence did not awake any response from the ship, nor did the noise from their hand-cranked foghorn—hastily brought up from its usual place in a spare bunk in the forecastle. Not a soul was in sight.

"I think that the crew has abandoned her," said Bill. "Look, there, that looks like the place that the life raft would have been. See—the fastenings for it are just hanging loose. We'd better run down before the wind and see if we can sight them. Stay up forward, the two of you, and keep a sharp lookout. Be careful, though, I don't want to be left aboard here on my own!"

They set off slowly downwind, following the direction that anything drifting from the boat would follow and Bill went on to the radio to report what they had seen, and what they were now doing. He also reported her name, *Katerine*, and told them that Stockholm was the port of registry of the stricken ship.

They were within a mile of the shore, which was a mess of white, broken water when Francis, whose eyes were sharper than most called out, "Look there, Bill! Just off your starboard bow. There's something orange in the water, not far from the breakers."

Bill opened up the throttle and turned the boat downwind, in the direction of Francis's pointing finger.

"You two had better come aft again," he instructed. "If there are any survivors in that raft, we'll have to take them aboard. Get a light line and tie a couple of lead weights to it. That'll have to make do for a heaving line if we need it. If you do throw it, for God's sake try not to hit anyone, though! Get yourselves attached to the boat too—use a bit of that line. If you do go overboard, then at least we can get you back again."

As they approached what they now could see was indeed a life raft, they saw a hand waving feebly in the air.

"At least there's someone alive there," Hector roared. "Thank God for that."

A thin rope led up to windward from the life raft. That rope, Bill correctly assumed, would be attached to a sea anchor and he reminded himself that he would have to be very careful not to get it into the *Misty Isle*'s propeller. If they were to be disabled, there would not be much time to do anything before they were among the breakers.

He slowly passed the raft and when he judged that he had enough space, he warned his crew, turned the *Misty Isle*'s wheel hard to starboard, and gave the engine full power. She answered like a thoroughbred, throwing her head defiantly in the air as she came round into the wind. As soon as her head was pointed straight into the wind, Bill centred the rudder and eased the engine down again. He was now able, using combinations of rudder and throttle, to claw his way upwind towards the raft.

As they approached, he saw that it would be extremely difficult to put his boat alongside the low-lying, heaving and pitching raft without the *Misty Isle* coming down on top of it.

"Get these survivors to jump into the water," he roared to his crew. "We'll get them aboard that way, a lot easier than getting them out of that thing! Hurry them up too; we'll be into the surf in a minute."

It then dawned upon Bill that there could be a language difficulty, but all he could do was hope that somehow they could make the occupants of the raft understand just what was required of them.

As they drew nearer, the aperture in the raft opened and a man, clad in what appeared to be some sort of survival suit, stuck his head out. He took it back in just in time, as the *Misty Isle*'s stem reared above him.

Bill cursed as he threw the Kelvin into reverse to avoid striking the raft, aware as he did of his crew screaming something over the bow.

As he struggled to get the boat under some sort of control, he became aware that Hector had now turned and was shouting aft, to him.

"They can understand us, Bill. There are four of them. Turn her to starboard, if you can. We'll get them on the port side." Then, after a quick glance upwind, over his shoulder he turned again and screamed, "That's two of them in the water now!"

He and Francis now scrambled, on their hands and knees, over the slippery foredeck as they made their way aft to the lower part of the boat.

As the seas threw their stem to starboard, Bill got a fleeting glance of two orange-clad bodies in the water. He had all the wheelhouse windows open now, but was completely unaware of being soaked by the spray—and solid water—that was coming aboard. His feet were apart, jammed on either side of the wheelhouse floor as he wrestled and juggled with the steering wheel and engine controls.

The *Misty Isle* came lurching round, driven by another breaking sea, and Bill was aware of himself screaming oaths as he tried to keep sight of the two men in the water. Only afterwards did Francis tell him—"My God, she rolled to port and we just grabbed them, one each, and they fell aboard! Her rail just went under them, and scooped them up like two big herring. You never saw anything like it!"

Bill saw the survivors aboard, and continued his struggle to keep his boat's head into the wind. He watched Francis in particular, admiring his sure-footedness as he scrambled around the heaving deck. Not for the first time he thought that Francis's actions reminded Bill of his own, in his younger days.

"Get the heaving line into that raft if you can, and get the other two to tie it around them before they go into the water," he shouted.

The two survivors lay for a short time on the deck just in front of the wheelhouse, then one of them, a slightly built man, Bill thought, crawled aft into the slightly better sheltered spot between the net and the wheelhouse door. The other, after a short pause, crawled forward after Francis and Hector and joined them in shouting instructions to the two remaining in the life raft.

This time things went better. The men forward scrambled their way aft, taking the end of the heaving line with them. As the *Misty Isle*'s head fell off to starboard they pulled heartily and very soon had the two remaining men alongside. Taking advantage of the boat's rolling, they hauled them aboard.

"Check with them that there aren't any other survivors anywhere," Bill cried. "Make sure we have them all!"

"That's all there are, Bill," called Hector after a short conversation with one of the men. "What about the life raft?"

"If you want that raft, you can come out some other day and get it," replied Bill. His relief at having the men safely aboard, was uppermost in his mind—now he wanted to get upwind, clear of the lee shore and then get into shelter somewhere, as soon as possible.

"We'll go round into the wee harbour on the north side of Soay," he told Hector. "That's about the best shelter we'll get here. You'd better get these people down below and get something hot for them if you can. Stoke up the stove anyway; they must be freezing. I'll dodge slowly in that direction until you all get below."

When they had all cleared the deck, Bill closed the wheelhouse windows again and turned to the radio. He had shut it off as they ran down towards the life raft and had fortunately remembered to drop the heavy oilskin cover—made by Ian—in front of it. If he hadn't, it would have been completely waterlogged and as it was, he said a few words to his Maker quietly, before he switched it on. To his enormous relief, it hissed and crackled into life, and he was able, after a few repeats, to relay to the authorities that he had the crew of the ship safely aboard.

Only then did the reaction set in as the adrenaline left his system. He started to shiver—not from the cold—and he was glad that none of the others were there to see his distress.

It took less than an hour until they were in the lee of Soay and, sensing the reduced motion, Francis and Hector came up from the forecastle.

They stood by the open starboard wheelhouse window.

"Aye, it's a great pity he missed that!" said Hector, looking at Francis but obviously talking to Bill.

"By Jove, yes. It's not often you see a sight like that," replied Francis. "Aye, that was something to remember. Wait 'till we tell the rest of the boys."

The two of them giggled.

"What on earth are you two on about?" queried Bill.

"Oh, ach well, nothing much, really," said Francis. "You tell him, Hector. You're older than me!"

"Well, you see, skipper. You see—we stoked up the fire—as you said. Then we told these folk to get their wet clothes off." He stopped, in a fit of laughter.

Seeing the glints of anger appear in Bill's eye, Francis quickly blurted out, "One of them is a woman!"

"Aye," continued Hector, "And she just stripped off—right in front of us. Right down until she was naked. She is the cook aboard that ship. By Jove, she is a beauty! Did you ever see anything like that before, Francis?"

"And where is she now?" said Bill. "Are they all right?"

"Well, we have tried to hang up their clothes to dry; they are just sitting down there with our blankets wrapped around them. We gave them a cup of cocoa, to warm them up a bit."

Bill at last saw the humour in what he had been told. "I'm telling you fellows. If you ever let something like that happen again without shouting for me, you'll be looking for a new berth," he laughed. "Anyway, the tide should be high enough to allow us into the wee harbour. Get up forward and get the anchor ready to drop—I could use a cup of something myself, a nice cup of tea—with plenty of sugar in it."

"Aye, OK, skipper. We'll get the new cook to make something for you as soon as we get in," said Francis, as he set off forward.

They soon anchored in the tiny, almost landlocked harbour that lay on the eastern side of Soay. The wind was howling overhead and it was still raining, but the low hills screened them from the worst of the blast. Bill waited for a short spell, checking that the anchor was holding before he made his way forward and dropped down into the warmth of the forecastle.

"We must thank you for saving our lives, captain," said one of the blanket-draped men, in excellent English. "If you had not come along when you did, I fear we would be drowned."

This statement brought forth a torrent of thanks from the other three, moving Bill to wave his hands in an effort to quieten them down. Eventually, he got a chance to ask what had happened.

"We are on our way from Glasgow to Kiel. We took a cargo of salt to Glasgow, and then we took aboard a half load of whisky. At first I thought to come up the centre of the Minches, but the weather grew so much worse, and I turned my ship to come to the inside of the Island of Skye—there it would be so much less stormy, I think. The seas grew worse as we came to shallower water, we took some very large seas on board and the cargo has moved. We had a very big list, and I feared that the ship would capsize, and we should all be drowned so I told my men to drop the anchor, and set our life raft into the water. The anchor was not holding so well at first, so we took ourselves into the raft from which you delivered us. My radio would not work, so I was not able to call for assistance from anyone. I think the seas must have damaged the radio or the aerials."

"I was able to tell Oban Radio that we had you safely aboard," said Bill. "They also have the name of your ship, so they will be in touch with the authorities in Sweden. As soon as you feel that you are able, we will go to the wheelhouse, and you may call anyone you wish. You may need a tug—they will organise that if you ask."

"Thank you, Captain. I think we might do that after I have a drink of hot coffee, with much sugar in it. Perhaps it would be good if we had some of your very nice Scottish whisky, to add to it, but we took none with us. We wanted our lives when we got into the raft, nothing else."

"Stop calling me Captain, please; my name is Bill. Francis, make some coffee for the men, aye, and for the lady too. Hector, have a look around in the spare bunks. There is bound to be enough clothing of some sort lying around between them all, to give these folk some decent cover. Get their own clothes hung up above the fire; it won't take long to get them dry, in this heat! I'll need some gear for myself, too!"

After they had laid out a motley collection of bits and pieces for the survivors to wear, Bill took the skipper aft to the wheelhouse. Lifting the oilskin cover from the front of the wireless Bill switched it on but when he pressed the 'transmit' trigger on the handset, there was a loud 'crack' and a puff of acrid smelling smoke arose from the transmitter.

"That's the end of that," cried Bill, angrily. "Water must have got into the works despite the oilskin. There is nothing we can do about that now. This is a job for an electronics engineer. We were damned lucky that it worked long enough for me to report that we were all safe."

They gazed at one another despairingly.

"I would have liked very much to have talked to someone at home, just to reassure them that we are all well. When can we go to a harbour, Bill?"

Bill stood silently for a time. He was conscious of the time they had lost through the engine trouble. Now there was the probability of an expensive repair to the radio! Although there was absolutely no chance of fishing in the sort of weather that prevailed at the moment, he was well aware that a short lull might provide an opportunity to fill the boats. The very last thing he needed at the moment was a run back into Mallaig with an empty boat.

Then he remembered something.

"There are people on this island, and I read recently that they had just had a telephone installed. If I remember correctly, it's powered by electricity that is made from sunlight." Then, looking around at the lowering skies he laughed, "That means that it probably won't be working now! I am going to put you all ashore here. You will have access to a telephone to make all the calls you need and as soon as the weather improves, a tug will come here for you and your ship. The people on the island will look after you; they are good people and you'll be more comfortable with them than if you were to stay here with us. We will also be able to get to our fishing grounds as soon as the weather improves. Yes, that is the best option now."

Francis and Hector reluctantly put their oilskins back on. They had been looking forward to spending more time in the company of the woman they had plucked from the sea. "Ingrid is her name, Bill," said Hector, jokingly, when they were on deck again. "She is from Sweden you see, and they are all for free love there, aren't they?"

When they had the anchor lifted, they cautiously made their way to the small, rickety pier, a relic of Soay's owner's unsuccessful foray into killing basking sharks for their livers. This business collapsed when the price of the oil from the livers fell.

The two or three houses that were still occupied were, although out of sight, just a few hundred metres away over the hill so when the boat was safely secured, they got the four survivors clad in oilskins and boots that belonged to the remainder of the crew. The oilskins and boots, Bill explained, would have to be brought back to the boat when the wearers had been successfully handed over to the islanders.

The Swedes shed tears, and addresses were exchanged along with promises of financial recompense and lifelong friendship before Bill, anxious about the fall-ing tide, was able to get them all ashore. "Mind now," he called to Francis and Hector, "Don't hang around. As soon as you hand them over, get back here. And don't come back without the oilskins and boots!"

True to their word, the pair were back in just over an hour, accompanied by the owner of the island. "Don't you worry, skipper," he called. "We'll look after our guests all right. You might get a wee lull in the morning, but I think it is going to blow up again soon after that. You should get a good sleep now. You did a good job out there today—we'll look after the rest. I'll telephone Mallaig and let them know there that you are safe, but that your radio is not working."

Bill silently cursed himself as he thanked the islander. Why had he not thought of getting someone to telephone Mallaig?

When they had the anchor down again, they set to tidying up the boat. The violent motion they had suffered had upset most of the contents of the lockers which now had to be tidied up; the wet blankets were hung around the stove in an attempt at drying them, and Francis busied himself making a pot of mince, well garnished with onions. The stove was almost red-hot and the door into the hold was open in an attempt at getting a through flow of air, although they knew full well that there was little chance of getting anything really dry in the current weather.

Bill, wearing a rag-tag of whatever reasonably dry clothes he had been able to garner from the others' bunks, lay back on the seat locker, thinking on the past few hours. He was feeling really tired now, a reaction, he thought, to the stresses he had undergone.

"You did a really good job back there, Bill," said Francis. "If we hadn't got to them when we did, they would have been up on that rocky shore, and the lot of them would have been drowned, for sure."

"Aye and it is a good job you spotted them when you did," replied Bill. "Your eyes are sharper than mine. How's that mince coming along?"

After a feed of mince, onions and potatoes—all cooked in rich, thick gravy, they agreed that bed would be a good idea. "That wind could ease any time," said Bill. "As soon as it does, we're off. We'll get no herring while we are lying here!"

Chapter Fifteen

Bill woke some four hours later, roused by the torrential rain that was drumming on the deck just above his head. He clambered from his bed and realised, as sleep left him that the wind had eased.

"Come on, lads! Time we were getting that anchor up again. It's a bonny night now. The herring will be swimming up soon!"

His two crewmen reluctantly crawled out of their bunks. The superhuman efforts that they had put into the rescue had tired them out far more than they had realised at first, and they could well have done with a few more hours. Habit dictated that they obeyed Bill's command without question though, unpopular though these demands might be.

Bill went aft as soon as he had dressed and dropped down into the engine room. It was warm there, the old Kelvin still retaining a few degrees of heat. It started first swing, and soon settled into its steady beat.

Bill went into the wheelhouse and switched on the deck lights as Francis and Hector busied themselves at taking the anchor chain to the winch.

As Hector got a few turns of chain on the winch and began hauling, Francis dropped down into the engine room and turned on the pump in preparation for hosing off the mud that would inevitably be clinging to the chain and anchor.

Bill waited until they had the anchor aboard and safely stowed before he switched off the lights whose glare that would prevent him from seeing the exit from the harbour.

"You'd better get that searchlight up forward, lads. I don't think there will be enough water to let us get out of here just yet; it'll be touch and go for a while."

Coached by instructions from the pair on the stem, Bill edged the boat slowly along the shingle bank that marked the entrance, looking along the searchlight's beam for the part that seemed to have most water over it. Even with those precautions, the *Misty Isle*'s keel touched lightly and she came gently to a halt.

"Away below and make a cup of tea," said Bill. "Another half hour will float her over—the tide will be making quickly, now. She won't come to any harm here."

A few minutes later, Hector appeared on deck with two steaming mugs in his hands and came aft.

"I'm coming in beside you, skipper. A wooden oilskin is the only one that'll keep this rain out!"

Bill laughed at this reference to a wooden oilskin. Disgruntled deckhands who were jealous of the skipper sitting in a relatively warm and dry environment often used this phrase, referring to the wheelhouse.

"It won't be long till she floats," said Bill. "I'd like to get across the Minch while this lull lasts. I don't think we'll get very long; it got too calm too quickly, for my liking."

"I was just saying to Francis, I wonder what will become of that ship. She will be worth a lot of money, for sure," said Hector.

"I suppose that a tug will be under way right now, Hector. These guys never miss a trick! There's always one on stand by in the Clyde. They'll have her somewhere safe in no time after they get here. They'll have a dram out of her cargo too, I'll bet."

Hector waited for just a moment before he spoke.

"Do you not think that we could have a go at saving her, Bill? It would be an awful pity if the wind came away again and she came to grief before the tug gets here."

"We've only got eighty-eight horses down below here, Hector. The tug will have over a thousand, I'm sure!"

"Aye, skipper, but there's no wind just now and you know yourself that when you get a tow moving, it doesn't take an awful lot to keep her going. There's no one aboard her now. She has been abandoned as far as marine law is concerned, and whoever gets her into safe harbour will have a huge claim on her insurance. There's the anchor to think of—we would have to get rid of it but I'm sure you could figure a way of getting round that problem!"

Bill looked at Hector, suspicion dawning on him. He had been among the island people long enough to have a lot of respect for them but he was also aware that they were very good at manipulating people. Hector, he thought, might be doing just that now!

"And just how do you think we would cope with the fact that the ship is anchored, Hector? I think you have an idea ready to offer me right now. Is that correct?"

"Well yes, skipper," replied Hector, uncomfortable with the thought that his scheming had been spotted. "I think that we could sweep up her anchor with our heavy anchor rope. If we did manage that, we could tow her with our rope fouled around her anchor flukes. That way also, if the wind came away and we couldn't manage her any more, we could just let the rope go and she would be anchored again."

Bill was silent for a while as he thought out the possibilities. Hector was correct in his summing up of the salvage opportunity, he thought, but he was well aware that neither of them was a lawyer. Nothing in this world was ever simple, and there could well be problems of which they had no knowledge. Once again he silently cursed the lack of a radio. With that working he could have called on his neighbour boats to help. He could also have called someone ashore, for advice. One thing was not in dispute; the ship was worth a lot of money.

"Right, lads, we'll have a go at it. We've got half-an-hour before we'll get over this bar—if you have everything ready before that we'll give it a go. One thing you seem to have forgotten, Hector. Is the casualty's rudder amidships? If not, we have no chance of steering her with this wee boat, so it'll be a non-starter!"

These words sparked off a period of intense work. The anchor rope, commonly called the cable, was used instead of the chain in reasonable weather simply because it was lighter to handle. This rope, or cable, was spliced into about six metres of heavy chain on the end that was attached to the anchor. They unshackled this from the anchor and tied their next heaviest rope, the sweep line, to it. This now gave them two long lengths of rope with six metres of chain in the middle. Various other lighter ropes were made ready for possible use in the operation that lay ahead.

The gear and the boat were soon ready and Bill was able to nudge the *Misty Isle* gently over the bar and into deeper water clear of the harbour.

As they approached the ship there was still quite a heavy swell running, although there was still no wind at all. They circled slowly around her, searching for any trailing ropes that might foul their propeller, or any other dangers. Satisfied that all was clear, Bill told his two crewmen just what he intended.

They came in as close as they dared to the ship's bow and Hector threw a light line with a small bunch of corks attached, into the space between the ship's bow and her anchor chain. Four times he tried before he got the result they needed— the line was now well through the gap and the corks were floating clear on the opposite side of the ship. Bill now had his work cut out getting the *Misty Isle* quickly around the ship's bow to where Francis could grab the corks with the boathook. Meantime, Hector's task was to ensure that the rope he was paying out as this manoeuvre was conducted did not get into their spinning propeller.

When Francis had brought the line aboard, they now had a circle of rope around the ship's chain. While Bill went slowly astern, keeping his boat stem to stem with the casualty, Francis and Hector hauled frantically in on one side of the line. The other end had been secured to the sweepline, which ran out over the side as they pulled. They continued hauling after the chain had rattled out over the side until they guessed that they were now in a position where they had the chain positioned roughly under the ship's bow.

Bill now had to turn his boat until she was headed in the same direction as the stricken ship. Both ends of the ropes that had been attached to the chain were taken aft, and were securely tied, one on each quarter.

They went ahead slowly, the ropes pointing almost straight down, and Bill gradually increased the engine speed. Hector had his foot on one of the ropes and he shouted—"I think I can feel our chain running along hers, skipper, I can feel it rattling!"

Bill knew exactly what Hector meant, and this was what they were hoping for.

The downward angle of the ropes gradually decreased as the *Misty Isle* crawled ahead—the ropes cracking under the strain. Suddenly they felt a terrible lurch, and the engine revolutions slowed noticeably.

"That's us fast on her anchor now, lads. Pray that it hasn't got such a hold that we cannot get it out of the mud. Francis, you get the axe up from the forecastle. We might need to cut that tow rope in a hurry if that ship capsizes."

Still they kept full power on the engine. The boat was shuddering and vibrating terribly.

"Try twisting her one way then the other, skipper," Francis called. "That might break the anchor out."

"A good idea," said Bill as he hauled the wheel round. Hard over to port—then hard over to starboard, went the rudder.

Another shudder transmitted up the towline after perhaps three applications of the wheel, bringing roars of delight from all three men.

"She's away, the anchor is out now. Well done lads!"

Hector had been keeping a careful watch on two of the high Cuillin Mountains and he came closer to Bill. "I think we have her moving, skipper. That peak there seems to be moving against the other."

Bill looked where Hector was pointing. "I believe you are right, Hector, the angle does seem to be changing," he said after watching intently for a time. "But is she following us in a straight line?"

Then he called—"Francis! Get the wire out. Let it out till it is touching the bottom. That'll prove if we are moving or not."

This was quickly done and yes, it did prove that they were moving the ship. Painfully slowly, it is true, but she was moving. The trusty old Kelvin sounded healthier also, it didn't sound quite so laboured. Equally importantly, it appeared that the rudder had been centred, on the casualty, before her crew had left her.

"Away down and make a cup of tea, someone," said Bill. "We better get some grub into ourselves as well; if the wind comes away before we make Sleat Point, we'll be in big trouble. At the speed we're making, it will be four or five hours before we get Mallaig in sight, and my guess is that the wind will be with us as soon as daylight comes in."

As they continued towing Bill thought that their speed was indeed increasing. Whether or not this meant that they would get round Sleat Point before the expected gale arrived remained to be seen. Looking all around, he did not see any boats' lights anywhere. He also noted that although their tow was rolling considerably in the swell that was now on her starboard side, her list showed no appearance of increasing.

Francis arrived on deck bearing a steaming mug of tea and a plate that bore two huge bacon sandwiches. Handing them through the wheelhouse window he asked Bill where he intended to take their tow.

Bill, his mouth full of bread and bacon, answered that this was in the lap of the Gods. If there were any weight of wind, he would not dare to attempt to get her alongside the pier at Mallaig. Nor, he added, did he want any help from anyone unless it was absolutely necessary. That would mean sharing the reward they hoped for!

Nearly three hours had passed before they reached Sleat Point and the sky to the east was showing a very angry looking redness over the hills as dawn approached. The sky to the south was filled with black and angry looking clouds.

"I've just felt a light puff of wind from the south-west, skipper," said Hector. "I doubt that we're going to get another gale from that direction, very soon."

"Yes, Hector, I think we are in for it. The tide will be against us if we try to run up the sound toward Kyle and at the speed we are making, we won't get very far if we go against it. We'll carry on toward Mallaig while we can and hope we get there before the wind arrives. I don't think we have any other options."

Within the half-hour, their worst fears were confirmed. Rain started, and very shortly afterward, the wind arrived. It grew in strength rapidly and very soon the seas, which had not really had time to calm, were giving them all cause for great concern. They had already wrapped greased hessian bags around the towropes in order to save them chafing on the boat's rails. Apart from that, all they could do was watch the increasing rolling that their tow was being subjected to.

"No, boys—this is no use at all," cried Bill. "We'll have to run before this sea or she'll capsize, for sure. I don't know where we'll fetch up, but I'm beginning to wish we had never thought of this scheme!"

So saying, he turned the *Misty Isle* carefully to port, and headed her into the north- east.

"One good thing, Bill," said Francis. "The wind is right behind us now, and the help we will get from that will overcome the tide that is against us. Another thing in our favour is that we'll be getting into more sheltered waters all the time as we approach the narrows of Kyle Rhea. We'll manage yet; just you wait and see! I'll go and make some more tea now."

Running before what was shortly to become a full gale, was never going to be easy. Their tow would run ahead off a sea, causing the towrope to slacken. Then, when its momentum had expended itself, the towrope would tighten and the little ringer would shudder yet again. Eventually Bill had to get Hector to stand on deck beside the open wheelhouse window looking astern, telling him when to reduce power.

The short day was nearly over and dusk was falling when at last they reached Kyle Rhea. The tide had slackened to almost nothing as they went through the narrow channel below the darkening hills, and still the gale raged. The narrow confines of the channel meant that there were now no big seas to trouble them.

"There's a bay just up ahead there, on the Skye shore," said Bill as he turned the *Misty Isle* north toward the welcoming lights of Kyle. "I think the only thing we can do is to head into it, get as close to the shore as we can, and slacken the tow rope down completely. The anchor will reach the bottom then and with any luck, it'll hold her there safely. It is about low water now, so we can get in quite close. We daren't risk trying to get her alongside at either Kyle or Kyleakin in this sort of weather; we'd sink her or wreck the pier!"

This was what they did, although Bill thought that they would never get the ship close enough to the shore. Altering course meant that they now had to tow the ship against the wind. Only the fact that they were now close to the shore and so got quite a lot of shelter from the worst of the blast saved them from getting into serious trouble.

When Bill judged that they were close enough, he slowed the engine down to idling speed, and then stopped the propeller. The weight of the anchor and chains took over, and the ship's anchor reached the bottom in around three fathoms of water. Hector and Francis slackened out the towrope and before they finally cast it overboard, tied both ends to a large buoy that they had removed from the net.

Clear at last from the burden of the tow, Bill was able to exploit the manoeuvrability of the ringer and spun the *Misty Isle* around the casualty's stern.

"I'll go alongside her low side. Jump aboard with a rope as soon as you can. We'll tie up here until this weather abates a bit," said Bill. "We'll get aboard her and see if there's anything left aboard that's worth eating!"

When they were securely tied alongside, Bill had Hector drop the wire once again. This was, he thought, the most foolproof way of checking if the anchor was holding and that they were stationary. Only when they were satisfied that this was the case, did Bill leave the wheelhouse and venture out on deck. The rain had eased off a bit and they were certainly out of the worst of the wind, but when Francis stopped their engine, they could hear the loud gale moaning above them.

They then gingerly stepped aboard the *Katerine* for the first time. It was strange being on a surface that was not horizontal, and they had to claw their way aft and up onto the bridge superstructure. From her wheelhouse they were able to look down on the diminutive shape of the *Misty Isle* and all expressed wonder that they had been able to take her as far as they had done.

The crew rooms and messdeck showed signs that they had been vacated in a hurry. Clothes and other gear lay where the rolling of the ship had left them.

Inspection of the immaculately clean engine room revealed that the bilges were reasonably dry. This was fortunate indeed as none of them had any idea of how to activate any bilge pump that might be fitted!

When they had explored all they wanted, they went back to the more familiar surroundings of the *Misty Isle* and over a cup of tea discussed what had to be done. Eventually, it was decided that they would lie overnight astern of the *Katerine*, tied to her stern. They would stand a watch of two hours each, giving them all a much-needed rest.

Bill, knowing that the excitement of the day had generated so much adrenaline that he would certainly be unable to sleep immediately, took the first watch.

Next morning, well rested, they sat at breakfast. This was the first time they had eaten a proper meal since they left Soay—how long ago was that? The wind had eased quite a bit since daylight had come in, but it was still blowing hard from the west.

"Will you be comfortable staying aboard the *Katerine* while we get to a telephone, Hector? You can take some bread and anything else you think you might need. I don't think we should leave this ship unattended, do you? We'll need to let the Coastguard know what we've done—they'll have a tug searching all over for her if we don't."

"That'll be no problem, skipper. If you are away too long I'll get into the hold and open a bottle or two of her cargo, so just take your time, there's no need to hurry back!

Bill laughed easily at that remark; he knew full well that Hector was not likely to take alcohol under any circumstances, as he was one of the few total abstainers among the fishing fleet.

Then Hector continued, "I don't know about leaving the ship unattended, but I wouldn't want to chance it. Don't you worry about me! There's bound to be plenty of grub aboard her, and I can always get a wee snooze in the cook's bunk. She won't need it for a while, and I'm sure it'll smell better than my bunk aboard here. I think I'll have pleasant dreams in it!"

They dropped Hector off on the *Katerine*, and within the half-hour, were tied up at the pier in Kyleakin. Just a few yards from the quayside, they found the familiar red telephone box they were seeking and Bill asked the operator for a transfer charge call to Willie Mair's office.

"Where in God's name are you, Bill? Is everything all right? There are boats searching all over for you. I've been on the radio all night trying to contact you."

Bill started to tell Willie where they were, and of their radio failure but Willie interrupted him.

"Listen to me Bill; I have something to tell you. First of all, is there someone with you?"

On being assured that Francis was there, Willie continued; "I have some bad news for you, Bill. Lisa has been in an accident. She was in Fort William yesterday and was struck by a car. She is in the hospital there. Her mother and father are both with her. She is pretty badly injured, Bill. You'll have to get there as soon as you can. That is all I can tell you. Put Francis on to the phone now. I'll get something sorted out with him."

Bill, his face ashen and his mind in complete turmoil, handed the telephone to Francis who, though he had not heard what Willie had said, knew from Bill's face that something dreadful had happened. He listened to what Willie told him, answering "Yes," occasionally. After a time, he handed the telephone back to Bill at Willie's bidding, and went outside where he sat, head in his hands, on a low wall.

He stood when Bill replaced the receiver and came out. Throwing his arms around his skipper's shoulder he said, "Come on, Bill. I'll take you over to Kyle now. By the time we get there Willie will have a car waiting for you. You'll be in Fort William in no time at all. Don't you worry about anything here; Hector and I will sort it all out."

Bill cried then and had to be led, unseeing, back to the *Misty Isle* where, at Francis's bidding, he had a perfunctory wash and shave while Francis started the engine and took the boat across the few hundred metres of water that separated Skye from the mainland. True to his promise, Willie had a car waiting for them and Francis put Bill, who had still not uttered a single word, into the back seat.

Chapter Sixteen

When the car drew up outside the hospital in Fort William nearly two hours later, Bill's father-in-law, George emerged from the porch where he had been waiting since shortly after Willie Mair had let them know that Bill was on his way. Bill, alighting from the car, shuddered visibly when he saw his father-in-law's face. It disclosed all that Bill had feared and dreaded since his conversation with Willie.

George faced Bill and, looking him straight in the eye said, "I'm so sorry, Bill. My wee lassie didn't stand a chance. She was too badly injured." Then the floodgates opened for both of them and they stood in the wind and rain, embracing one another, sobbing bitterly.

A nursing sister came out and without speaking, drew them gently into the hospital and into a small room. "Sit you down there. I'll get you both a cup of tea," she said, in a soft island accent.

"What happened, George? Why was she in Fort William? She didn't tell me she was coming here."

"She had an appointment with some sort of specialist, Bill. Meg knew nothing of it either. We only found out when they gave us her handbag, and Meg found the appointment card in it."

This news plunged Bill's heart into even deeper despair. He knew now that he was the one that was to blame for his wife's death. "I want to see her, George," Bill said eventually.

"Meg is with her just now, come along, I'll take you there."

"I want to be alone with her, George. I need that."

"I can understand that, Bill. Come along."

They walked unspeaking along a silent carpeted corridor then George stopped outside an unmarked door.

"Her head was badly injured, Bill, but they have bandaged it all up." Then his control left him again and he sobbed bitterly. "Why did Our Lord have to take my wee lassie?" he cried. "Could He not have taken me instead?"

The door opened and an ashen faced, but dry-eyed Meg came out.

"I'll take you to her, Bill," she said, taking him gently by the arm. "Then I'll leave you. There will be things you want to say to her. I'll be back out in a minute, George."

They went together through the door and Bill saw his wife's familiar face lying on a white pillow. Her lovely golden hair was concealed beneath the swathe of white bandage that framed her face.

"Her face wasn't hurt, Bill, it was the back of her head. She didn't feel anything; it was over in a flash. Isn't she lovely, my wee pet? She's just asleep for a while."

At that, Bill's grief boiled over once more and he threw himself across the bed, sobbing uncontrollably.

Meg left the room then, quietly closing the door behind her.

Bill would never know how long he lay there, or what he said to the cold body of his wife. He came back to reality when the door opened again, and a nurse came in. She took him by the arm and gently led him outside. Years of experience of dealing with the bereaved came to her aid as she took him to the small room where Meg and George waited.

"We'll need to leave her for a while," said Meg. "We have to get home—there's a lot that must be done. The nurses will send her home to us, soon." She was acting like an automaton, only her ashen face and trembling hands betraying the depth of her hurt. "Willie Mair is outside. He drove here after he talked to you in Kyleakin, Bill. He will take us home. I want to talk to the doctors and nurses; they looked after Lisa so well. I must thank them before we go."

Bill was later to wonder at the tremendous inner power that Meg displayed that afternoon. He would never understand just where she got the courage and strength to keep going when both he and George were so hopelessly drained.

Outside, Willie opened the doors of the car for them, saying nothing. They were well on to the Mallaig road before he spoke, and then it was to tell Bill that he had been in touch with his mother. She was making arrangements to come to Mallaig as soon as she could. Bill's father and brother had been traced to where they lay at anchor in Castlebay, he said, and they were on their way in to Mallaig as he spoke.

Bill could never fully recall all that happened in the days that followed. His mother arrived to join him, his father and his brother, in his house. He must have eaten, but he could not recall what or when. Funeral arrangements were made, but he could only remember agreeing to them, he did not know who decided what.

On the day of the funeral Bill went into the church flanked by his father and his brother. They were beside him at the graveyard also. He was aware of Jim's presence, but could not remember talking to him at any point. Alex John and all the crews from the islands were there. They must, Bill thought, have been given permission to attend. Perhaps this was one sign of the easing of the divisions that marred the Christian faith.

After the funeral they went, as was the custom, to one of the local hotels—the one that not long ago had hosted the reception after their wedding. Tea was served to those who wanted it, and the bar was open. Most of the people there talked to Bill but they were hazy figures, and none of the platitudes they spoke meant anything at all. He did recall thanking Murray Buchan for attending, thinking that it was kind of him to have travelled so far.

Leaving the hotel, the immediate families went to Meg and George's home and Bill found himself alone with them. George produced a bottle of whisky and poured out a large dram for the men present. This was a rare event indeed; Bill had never known George to take a dram before. Bill had seldom tasted whisky, and the alcohol soon took effect. After the second one, his eyes closed involuntarily and he fell sound asleep in his chair. His father and brother took him, at George's insistence, into the room that he had shared with Jim when they first arrived in Mallaig, and put him to bed there.

He must have been totally exhausted, because the first thing that wakened him was the sound of Meg raking out the fire. He got up and washed—his head still fuzzy from the effects of the whisky he had taken the previous evening, and went through to the living room.

"Good morning, Bill," said George, from his seat in front of the fire. "Meg has just gone down for the rolls. You must be hungry—you haven't had anything to eat for a long time."

"Aye, George, I am a bit peckish. Did the others go to my house last night?"

He hesitated then before adding, "I almost said 'our house' there, George. I'll have to get used to being alone!"

"Bill, it will take a long time for any of us to come to terms with what has happened. We are going to have to make an effort to get on with life. None of us will ever forget Lisa, but she would want us to get on with things. That is life—and death."

Meg arrived back just then carrying a paper bag filled with freshly baked rolls.

"Good," she said to Bill. "You are up. I won't take long frying up a bit of bacon and some eggs. You need some nourishment."

"Wait a bit, Meg. I want to talk to you both. I must tell you some things. Lisa and I had a few rows, lately. We both wanted a baby and it just wasn't happening. That must have been the reason for her being at Fort William to see that doctor. She didn't have to go—I didn't ask her. It was my fault that she was there though; I think she felt that it was all her fault somehow."

"Stop right there, Bill," said Meg. "She and I talked about this several times. Perhaps if I had been more helpful she would have confided in me more and then I would have been with her. Perhaps then it wouldn't have happened. Maybe if George had gone with her—where will we stop! It has happened, and there is an end to it all. We could all say, 'if only,' but that is nothing more than a form of self-pity. We have lives to live out, and the first thing I have to do is to fry some bacon. Now, how many eggs do you want?"

Meg then returned to her kitchen leaving Bill and George alone.

"She's right, Bill, we have to get on with things. One of the things that you don't know is that Albert was telling me that he has had some of the lifeboat people after him. They want to put a lifeboat here as soon as possible. This is one result of your job with that ship. It fairly put the place in the headlines!"

"Well, George, that reminds me of one of the first things I will have to sort out. I saw Francis and Hector here, but how did they get on with the *Katerine*? Is the *Misty Isle* still in Kyle, or what?"

"None of us wanted to bother you with any of that stuff, Bill. The *Misty Isle* is here, and the *Katerine* is at Kyle pier. Willie Mair sorted everything out in no time. He has a lawyer looking after the legal side of things. After you left, Francis spoke to Willie, and then Hector and Francis towed the *Katerine* to Kyle. The wind had eased away by then, and they said that they had no trouble with her, really. They had to let the anchor and chain go, though. They couldn't tow her to Kyle using the same method as you used—the anchor would have taken the ground before they got to the pier. They couldn't lift the anchor, as they couldn't get the *Katerine*'s winch to work, so they had to let the lot run out. They have buoyed it though, so it isn't lost. They did a really good job under the circumstances."

"Jim came in as soon as he heard about Lisa," he continued. "He was on his way to Kyle with the *Marguerite* to help, but he met Hector and Francis coming south through Kyle Rhea. Willie spoke to the Coastguard. The tug was on its way, but they were able to turn her back. I know that it is of no interest now, but the lawyer thinks that there will be a lot of money in it for you all."

"No, George, money is the last thing on my mind at the moment. They are all great lads. Jim has been hovering at my shoulder since—well, since he came ashore. I think he has deliberately kept his kids away from me. I expect he doesn't want to remind me of some things. I need to be alone for a while. As soon as we get our breakfast I'd like to go for a long walk by myself. I don't mean to hurt anyone, but I do need to be alone."

At that moment, Meg came in to tell them to come through to breakfast. Bill looked at her intently as she stood in the doorway. She was very pale, he noted, and seemed to have lost that verve she had always shown. In fact, he thought, she seemed to have aged twenty years in the last few days.

The meal was eaten in silence and as soon as he had finished, Bill made his excuses and left the house. He walked across the rough ground, heading directly towards the railway line and the sea, shunning the road that led downhill to the pier. He did not want to be seen by anyone or, more correctly, he did not want to talk to anyone.

Reaching the tracks of the railway, he turned south, walking on the rough ballast beside the single line. It was a reasonably bright day, a good day for walking although that fact simply did not register with Bill. He followed the railway track until he reached Morar where he left it for the bright sands that lined the estuary of the river.

To reach where he now was, he had passed within a few hundred yards of the graveyard where just yesterday he had laid his wife to rest, but he could not face going there again just yet.

The tide was out and he walked west on the glistening white sand until he reached the rocky point that marked the southernmost limit of the estuary. There he stopped, seating himself on a convenient rock. He gazed west, seeing but not heeding the wonderful aspect that lay before him. The Cuillins of Skye were stark against the skyline to the north and west. Further south were the slightly softer hills of Rhum and further south still was the dramatic rocky Sgurr of the island of Eigg.

What had happened to him, he wondered? What had he done to anger a God who would wreak such a horrendous blow in revenge? What would become of him now? Who could he talk to? Who would listen to his plans and dreams, and who would correct him when he went wrong?

Was there any reason for living?

Sitting there alone, Bill finally reached depths of despair that he had never imagined could exist. Tears came; deep racking sobbing that came from the heart, a heart that was broken.

He would never know how long he sat there but gradually the sobbing ceased and his mood changed. He became aware that he had never told Lisa of Theresa's existence. He should have done, he thought. She knew that there had been someone in the past: if he had been honest with her he would have told her all that had happened. Anger—at himself—grew within him. He could not tell her anything now: she had gone from his world!

He now felt the beginnings of anger against himself. Why had he married Lisa while he still harboured feelings for Theresa? Should he have made a bigger effort to find out what had happened to Theresa, and where she had gone? If he had behaved as he now thought he should have, Lisa would still be alive. He had, he thought, placed too much emphasis on financial success and not enough on those who had loved him and who had given so much to him. He had no chance now of telling Lisa so many of the things that he should have told her.

His despair and self-esteem had reached depths that were beyond anything he could ever have imagined. His mind could no longer cope!

In the dark semi-consciousness it came to him that the only thing he could do was to carry on as he had been doing. Too many people had placed their trust in him; he could not let them down! Gradually realisation came to his tortured mind that somehow, at some time, good would eventually come his way again.

When he became aware of his surroundings again, he realised that he must have sat there for a long time; the path he had walked dry-shod over the sand, was now covered by the incoming tide.

He clambered up over the rocks until he was able to walk through the rough heather to regain the road.

Darkness was not far off when he arrived back in Mallaig. He called first of all at Meg's but only remained there long enough to assure Lisa's parents that he was well. He needed, he told them, to go back to his own house; this was something that he had to face. It would not be so bad whilst his parents and his brother were there—beyond that he didn't want to imagine.

Chapter Seventeen

Bill went back to sea on the following Monday. He knew that he needed a catharsis of some sort; life on the boat, with the men he knew so well would provide that, he felt, and he didn't want to be in the house any more than was necessary. His mother would stay for a time—as long as he wanted her to, she said.

The crews were shy of him at first; not knowing just how to treat someone who had suffered such loss, but gradually this difficult time passed and eventually they were able once more to relax in his company. The fishing was good and of course this meant little time for idle thinking. When they were not working they were trying to catch up on lost sleeping time.

He had still not taken any part in the legal wrangling that had started over the salvage claim that his lawyer had laid at the door of the owners of the *Katerine*. He had left Willie to take complete control of the choice of lawyer, and to sort out the mundane matters that arose from the processing of the claim. He felt totally disinterested in how much they might get, or when they might get it. All of his energies were concentrated on catching herring.

The four boats were working well together. The skippers had settled down to working with Ally, whose new boat, the *Solan*, certainly was admired by many. Although she was only a few feet bigger than the other boats, she seemed huge in comparison. Her forecastle was larger than her neighbours' were and incredibly, there was a tiny galley incorporated in it! Although it was only just big enough for one man to stand in, it boasted a stainless steel sink and, wonder of wonders, a gas cooker—complete with an oven! Her six cylinder Gardner engine gave her the edge on all the others as far as speed was concerned and to see her under way on a sunny day, varnish still gleaming, was a beautiful sight.

Bill found himself looking at her often, and he realised within himself that it was nearly time to think along the lines of ordering a replacement for the *Misty Isle*, the older of the two boats that Jim and he owned.

Bill's mother went back to Campbeltown after a few weeks. She offered to stay on for a time, but Bill knew that he had to come to terms with coping with an empty house at some point in time; delaying the inevitable would not make things any easier.

Meg was able to find a lady that would look after the house while Bill was at sea and who would do his washing. She was an elderly widow who had come to Mallaig to work in a kippering yard, and was delighted to be offered what was in effect a much easier job.

"She is getting on a wee bit but she is a very clean housewife, and is as honest as the day is long!" said Meg. Bill was never to witness anything that gave the lie to that statement; the house was spotless, and it was not long before she accepted Bill's suggestion that she move in permanently.

It was well into January when Willie Mair sent out a message that Bill should come ashore as soon as possible, as he would like to talk to him. The only herring they had that night were all aboard Jim's boat so Bill swapped places with him, and took the *Marguerite* into Mallaig.

"Come away in," said Willie when Bill presented himself at the office door on the following morning.

"There's a man wanting to see you, he arrived last night and is in the hotel now. He is the lawyer who has been handling the salvage case for you; I think he has an offer to put to you. Do you want to go home now and have a wash, before we go to the hotel?"

"I think I'd like to talk to him here, Willie, if that is all right with you. I'd rather meet these guys on my own territory if possible; there's no good in giving them any advantage at all. Just you stay with us, there's nothing going to be said that you can't hear, and I'd appreciate your company, and advice. As far as me going home for a wash is concerned, if he can't stand the smell of herring he shouldn't be here!"

Bill had hardly finished his obligatory cup of tea when the lawyer, summoned by telephone, arrived carrying a bulging briefcase.

Bill took stock of him quietly. He seemed to be somewhat older that Bill was and looked to be very fit.

"Good morning gentlemen," he said, holding out his hand. He took off his dark coloured woollen overcoat as he spoke, revealing that he was dressed in a black pinstripe suit. "You must be Mr. Martin; I'd like to call you Bill, if I may. I was so sorry to hear of your loss, it must have been an absolutely devastating blow to you. You are so young to be left on your own. Willie, I've talked to you on the telephone several times—I'm glad to meet you in person. My name, Bill, is David Murray. Call me David, please. I am a partner in Macrae and Davis. I am a QC and I specialise in marine law. I am very good at my work. That is not just my opinion—it is the opinion of the legal faculty in general." This speech, for that is what it sounded like, was delivered at machine gun rate.

"Yes, David, I'm Bill. Thank you for your condolences. I'd rather not talk about it though, if you don't mind. I am skipper and owner of my own boat. I also have shares in another three boats. Let's hear what you have to say and then I'll see if I agree on just how good you are."

David laughed out loud. "Well said, young man! I like a man that states his mind. Willie, may I borrow your desk for a time? This bag gets heavier by the day. I swear I'll need a carrier for it soon."

He then spread several files on part of Willie's cluttered desk, muttering to himself as he did so. At last he seemed satisfied with his preparations.

"If you're happy for Willie to remain, and I think you will be, I will move round here behind the desk. If you two take your chairs closer together, I'll be able to deliver the letters to you both in the proper order."

"Wait a minute, David," said Bill. "I have to get back to sea, and I'm also very tired. I haven't got time to study a heap of letters. There's only one that I am interested in at the moment—that is the one with the final offer in it."

"Bill, that's fine by me," David smilingly said. "I would have loved to have led you through the haggling that went on, but I will admit that this would only be in order to let you see how clever I've been on your behalf, and to justify my considerable fees! I will say that I wish that all my clients were like you. The ones I usually meet stutter and prevaricate—it is an honest pleasure to meet someone that says what they are thinking. Here's the letter you want."

Bill picked it up and looked at it. When he had got over the initial shock at the size of the sum that was mentioned, he handed the letter to Willie and stared at him.

"Don't look at me, lad," said Willie. "I am thunderstruck! David, how on earth did you come to that amount?"

"Gentlemen, I don't often get cases like this to deal with. It really has been a pleasure. Bill, you did a wonderful job in getting the crew from their life raft. Without doubt, you saved their lives. To then tow a ship that size with your little boat and in the weather that prevailed at that time, well, I'm simply unable to find words to describe how I feel. This case has dominated my life since it landed on my desk and after I read the facts I was absolutely determined that you should be adequately reimbursed for the risks you took. Apart from the ship itself, there was also the value of the cargo—very expensive whisky—to take into consideration. May I assume that you are pleased with the figure you see there?" he concluded, smiling broadly.

"Give us a couple of minutes alone, David," said Willie. "I'd like a few words with Bill, if you don't mind."

"Certainly, gentlemen. I shall see if I can charm a cup of coffee from your young lady assistant. Take your time, please."

When he had left, Willie and Bill, both grinning from ear to ear, stood and hugged one another.

"If I was you—and right now I wish I was—I'd grab that offer, Bill. That's more money than a lot of men will make in a lifetime."

"Yes, Willie, you are right. I don't want this thing dragging on any more than it needs to. David has worked wonders in getting this far in the time he has had. He really must have been going hard at it! Let's get him back in and we'll get it over and done with."

The rest of the meeting was taken up with the formalities that accompany any such transaction but then David asked Bill just how he was going to dispose of the funds.

"Do you mean to ask how the money is going to be shared out?" asked Bill.

"Yes," David replied. "There are guidelines laid down that state just how salvage monies should be shared among those who have participated in the salvage works. If you wish, I will send you a written guide as soon as I return to my office. That will enable you to conclude the transaction at this end."

"I don't know what rules there are, David, but with all due respect, I will make the decisions as to how this money is to be shared. There will be five shares. The boat and the engine will get one each—Francis, Hector and I will get one each also. All the expenses will come off the top, before the cash is divided. Willie has done a lot for us; I will want him to get something."

"Wait a minute, Bill," said Willie. "We're looking at a lot of money here. I can't see how you can justify giving your crew an equal share. They're just hired hands!"

"Willie, these men took the same risks with their lives as I did. So you see, they are entitled to the same share as I am. I realise that you are trying to look after my best interests, but that is how it is going to be! Now I need to be back at the boat; there's work to be done still."

Standing up, he shook David's hand and thanked him for his help. "It really has been a pleasure meeting you—you have changed my opinion of lawyers. Thank you for all you have done. I hope we will meet again sometime."

"I'll tell Francis and Hector the good news when we meet up with them," Bill then said to Willie. "I don't know what Hector will do, but I'd bet my last penny that Francis will be coming to see you soon about buying a boat for himself. Talking of that, you could start talking to one or two of the builders about a new boat for Jim and me. Weatherhead of Cockenzie would be the builder I would favour. One very like the *Solan* would be just fine, and I'd want a Gardner engine in her. I'll see you at the weekend. Just keep everything under your hat for the time being. Don't tell anyone about what happened here today."

The weather changed for the worse two days later and all the boats were lying at anchor in Loch Skiport. Bill had thought long about how he would broach the subject with Francis and Hector but hadn't said a word about it to anyone. He now took the opportunity of calling the pair of them into what was, with all three crammed together, the cramped wheelhouse of the *Misty Isle*. There he told them of his meeting with David Murray. He didn't mention the sum offered until he had told them of how he intended sharing it, and then he told them what their shares would be.

They took the news in stunned silence, and then Francis spoke. "I don't think that is fair, skipper. You should get a bigger share than we should. What about your partners? How are they taking it?"

"They don't know anything about it yet, I wanted you to be the first to know. They'll be fine with it, though. They are getting part of the boat and engine shares. I think we'll end up ploughing the money into a new boat. I'm jealous of the *Solan*," he laughed.

"How about you, Hector, what will you do with the money?"

"Well, I don't know for sure, skipper. There's a girl in Daliburgh, her father is dead and she has been struggling with her mother to run their croft. I'm quite fond of her, and well, maybe it's time I settled down and got married." This speech was made with downcast eyes. Hector, in common with many of his fellow islanders, was a very shy man. However, he lifted his head and looked Bill straight in the eye now.

"If this girl will marry me, I'll be leaving the sea. The croft will take a lot of work before it is as I would want it. After that, who knows, maybe I'll buy a wee boat and work the lobsters out the West Side—just to keep my hand in."

"Will you really be buying a new boat, Bill?" Francis asked.

"I think we will. This one lacks some of the comforts I am beginning to need, now. It would be fine to have a bit more room in the forecastle, more speed would be a great thing, and she would carry more herring! Why do you ask?"

"Well, Bill—I have been thinking along similar lines to Hector. I quite fancy getting a wee lobster boat of my own. Oh, I like the herring fishing fine, but I'd love to try being my own boss. There's enough money to get a wee boat, but not nearly enough for a ringer—not if you are starting from scratch and have to buy nets and everything. We'll see, though. I must visit my mother soon, I haven't seen her for nearly three months now so I'll go as soon as I get the chance, and talk it over with her."

Bill was quiet for a moment, and then said in mock anger, "Hell's teeth! If I'd known I might lose two good men, I'd have kept all the money to myself. I had you marked down as being a skipper yourself, Francis. I thought you might take over from me some day soon, but the choice is yours. Seriously though, there's nothing on fire just yet! I expect it will take months before these lawyers get through with their wrangling, and we get everything sorted out. Just keep all that has been said, to yourselves. There will be a lot of talk about it, but just keep quiet. Now, I'd better get the other shareholders together, I'll need to tell them the news also. The boat and engine shares will go into the company and we'll probably get a new boat as I said. My share—well, things might have been different, but—"

Both Francis and Hector grasped him by the hand, eyes downcast, and left quietly. Francis took only a few steps, turned, and came back into the wheelhouse where he embraced Bill, holding him close for a time without speaking. Then he followed Hector. Bill stood alone for a time, thinking. He knew that he did not want to lose Francis. For reasons that he could not figure, he felt closer to him than to any of the others, even including Jim. Perhaps, he thought, it was because he saw so much of his younger self in the lad.   Eventually, he shook himself and set off to get his fellow boat owners together, to tell them the news.

Chapter Eighteen

Mallaig's first Lifeboat arrived just a few weeks after the lawyer's visit. She was not a new boat, having seen service in Wales for nearly fifteen years.

There was a great welcome awaiting the crew who took her to her new home. A pipe band from Fort William was in attendance, and dignitaries came from all over Lochaber. She was busy for hours that day taking people, most of whom had never seen a lifeboat before, around the bay for a short trip.

Bill, although he did not voice his opinions, was somewhat disappointed with the performance of this boat. It was not really any bigger than the ring net boats that now used the port in ever increasing numbers and some of the newer boats were actually faster than the lifeboat. It had twin engines and Bill thought that this would make her very manoeuvrable, but to his surprise, this was not so. The fact that the propellers were protected from damage—should the boat strike a rock—by the hull design, meant that they were each enclosed in what was almost a tunnel. This gave a jet effect to the propeller's wash, and spoilt the 'twisting' effort of the two propellers. The lifeboat's turning circle, even using the twin screws, was far greater than any of the fishing boats. A mooring had been prepared for her in the bay, but so many people wanted to see her that it was dark before the crew was finally able to put her to rest on it.

The men who were to man the lifeboat had to be trained in her use. This involved the boat being at sea for most of the day and continued for almost a fortnight before the inspector announced that he was satisfied with the crew's abilities. He then declared the station ready for service.

Bill, who had always got on well with Albert, spoke to him one day in Jess's tearoom, asking how he was getting on. The boats had come ashore for their annual clean up now—the winter fishing was over. Albert declared himself well satisfied with the boat and the crew, but told Bill that he would have been happier if he had more fishermen aboard.

"It's all right, Bill, taking these lads out most of the time, but if we are called on a really bad night I'd like to have more guys that are less prone to seasickness. I'm not exactly sure that we've got the right lad as second coxswain, either. He is young, and is a wee bit too cocky for my liking. Anyway, it is early days yet, and things will settle down in time. So, how are things with you? You have had a good winter, I'm glad the silver darlings were swimming up for you!"

"Aye, Albert, the fishing has been good—and we've ordered a new boat. I'm sure Ally told you that. She'll be very similar to the one you got—I've always admired her. I'm disappointed with one thing; I fear we'll be losing young Francis.

I had him earmarked for being skipper of one of our boats, but he seems to be determined to get a boat of his own to go fishing for lobsters. He seems to have been quite happy at the herring, but I think he maybe wants to spend some more of his time at some wee croft up Loch Hourn. His father and grandfather are both dead, he tells me, and that leaves just his mother and his granny on the croft. It's not the life for me, but then, I'm not him! You should maybe have a yarn with him if you are unhappy with your number two. Francis will be available for lifeboat calls a lot more than he would if he stayed at the herring."

"Aye, Bill, that's worth remembering. I'll have a word with him some of these days and see if he would like to join the crew. As you say, he's a good lad, and he certainly knows his way around boats. How are you faring, yourself? You must feel lonely a lot. Remember, Jess and I will always welcome you, at any time."

Bill paused for a time, looking out of the window, seeming to stare at the railway lines that glistened in the rain.

"It is very difficult at times, Albert. I miss Lisa terribly, but I can't let my mind dwell on her too much. It is a cold empty house—old Margaret does her best, and the place is kept clean and tidy, but—"

"It is none of my business, Bill, but have you ever thought that maybe one day you could marry again? I don't mean that you should think of replacing Lisa, I know that would be impossible, but a man needs a woman sometimes."

"I appreciate what you are saying, Albert. Willie Mair said exactly the same thing just a week or so ago. I'm afraid that I am not very lucky with ladies—" Bill's voice trailed away, and the pair sat silent for a time.

"There was another girl, I thought at the time that we would get married, but I don't know what went wrong. She cleared out somewhere—I think she went to Canada, and I never heard of her or from her. Aye, I think I'll stick to catching herring, I've had more luck with that."

Bill shook himself, and stood up. "Anyway, I'm off now. I'm going up to Jim and Mary's for my supper tonight. Those kids of theirs will keep my mind off myself for a time. Five of them they have now, I don't know what they're thinking about. They're trying to repopulate the Highlands, maybe. I have a wedding to go to in Uist, too. Hector has decided to make an honest woman of his girl friend, at last! I'll see you later, Albert." He then called through to the kitchen where Jess, arms floury, was still baking. "Goodbye, Jess. Your scones are as good as ever they were!"

Bill's trip to Uist two weeks later proved to be an eventful one. There were several guests invited from Mallaig, so Ally took them across on the *Solan*.

Alex John had invited Bill to stay with them while he was there but Bill, sensing correctly that Alex John's house would be well filled with relations who had come from Barra for the celebrations, declined. He agreed to eat with them, thus settling the discomfort that the MacDonald family so obviously felt because he was staying in the hotel.

On his first night at Mary and Alex John's table, he spotted one girl who seemed vaguely familiar. She was rushing around with the other ladies, fussing over the many pots that filled the house with mouth-watering smells.

"Who is that girl, there, the one with the light blue dress on?" he asked Alex John.

"Ah yes, the pretty one, is it? That's Kirsty. She's a cousin of my wife, Mary. She comes from Northbay, in Barra, but she has been nursing in Glasgow for years now. A lovely girl, isn't she? She is staying in the same hotel as you are; of course she is here for the wedding."

He looked at Bill quizzically. "Do you like what you are seeing?" he asked with a mischievous grin. "She isn't married!"

"Not at all—well, yes, she is a lovely girl, but I was only asking because I thought I had seen her somewhere. Maybe I am seeing a likeness to your wife or perhaps it is because she is staying in the same hotel as me. I probably saw her there."

After they had eaten, the evening developed into a typical island ceilidh. Those who could sing—and some that couldn't—sang Gaelic songs. Hector and his bride-to-be were guests of honour but visitors kept arriving and of course, some of them had musical instruments so the night wore on in great fashion. There was whisky galore, bottles kept being passed around and Bill, not wanting to be a wet blanket, took a share of what was circulating. He even sang a song when requested—something he had never done in public before.

At breakfast the following morning, a late one because of the excesses of the previous night, Kirsty, seeing Bill sitting alone, asked if she could join him.

They ate together and Bill found her to be a most charming girl. Smiles came easily to her and the time passed quickly. However, she had a very disconcerting way of looking at him, Bill thought. She stared him straight in the eye, smiling as she did so. Apart from that, she was very easy company to be with and he was quite relaxed in her presence.

A very attractive girl, Bill thought.

"What are you doing today, Bill?" Kirsty asked.

Bill, who had given no thought to the matter, gave a non-committal reply whereupon she asked him if he would like to see around the island. "You have fished all around it, but I'll bet you haven't seen much of the west side, have you? I can borrow a car from Alex John's brother. He has a garage in Daliburgh."

"That seems like a good idea to me," said Bill. "I don't think I want to get involved in another night like last night—I don't have the head for whisky on that scale!"

It didn't take very long to drive round South Uist, Bill soon discovered, but they took their time about it, walking on some of the finest beaches that Bill had ever seen. They looked over the channels that separated North Uist and Benbecula from South Uist, marvelling at the beauty of the sandy bottom that glistened below the shallow water. Bill was able to point out some of the deeper areas where on occasion they had trapped a shoal of herring.

"It is a different place in the dead of winter and these bonny brown patches you are seeing out there among the bright sandy areas—that is seaweed. That is of no real interest, you might say, but it is to us. It is growing on rocks, you see, and that is important. If you hit one of these rocks with a boat, you are going to do damage! Funnily enough if there was a shoal of herring out there just now, they would look exactly the same as the seaweed. Aye, I don't know why the blue of a herring's back should show up that sort of reddish in the water, but take it from me, it does. They look just the same, really."

Kirsty looked at him quizzically. "Would you be able to tell the difference between a shoal of herring, and a rock, Bill, just by looking at it?" she asked.

"The only way you can tell, without getting really close, is to watch it carefully. If it changes shape, it is a shoal of herring." Bill laughed then; "Rocks don't change shape very often!"

"But I thought you only fished for herring in the dark hours?"

"That is usually the case, but sometimes they don't go off the shore when daylight comes in. Maybe it's because they swim up through all these shallow inlets in the dark, and cannot find their way out so easily—I just don't know. Can we get to the top of Loch Skiport, on the way back?

"Yes, I was going to take you down there and to Loch Eynort too. I thought you'd like to see all these places from the shore side—you've seen them often enough from the sea. Let's go now, Bill."

She took Bill's hand as they walked the short distance to where she had parked the car, an action that at first shook Bill slightly but as they walked and talked, he accepted that this was simply the gesture of a naturally friendly and open person. This reasoning didn't stop him stealing a sideways glance at Kirsty nor from admiring her smiling face, and windswept hair.

It was almost dark when they arrived back at the hotel.

"I'll get this car back to its owner, Bill," Kirsty said. "Are you going to see anyone tonight, or are you having a night off?"

"I certainly don't want to get involved in another session like last night. What about you?"

"I really must visit some more of my relations, I see them very seldom since I left the island, but I certainly don't want to be suffering from a headache tomorrow at the wedding, so I won't be late. I'll see you later, if you are still up and about."

She got back into the car and drove off, leaving Bill feeling strangely lonely.

He went to his room and lay on his bed, half snoozing but thinking of the time he had just enjoyed. He was aware that his was now a very lonely existence. Bitterness was no stranger to him. He had lost two women in his short life. Deep down inside he was aware that the real love of his life had been Theresa. Only the fear of being grossly unfair to Lisa's memory stopped him from consciously admitting this to himself. Below the surface of his conscious mind, he admitted that he had proposed to Lisa in a rush of guilt. Yes, he had enjoyed their all-too-brief time together but there had been something missing. It was all his fault! Where would fate lead him now?

His mind drifted deeper into itself. Things would change soon, and change for the better but he was also aware of darkness somewhere near. Something black, ugly and frightening lay close.

These thoughts were interrupted when the booming of the dinner gong rang out and he had to gather himself mentally. A quick wash sufficed and he set off downstairs. The short rest, although it had not led to sleep, had helped shake him out of the tiredness that the previous night's excesses had provoked and he was now feeling quite peckish. The sandwiches that the hotel had provided for lunch were but a dim memory!

A quick look around the dining room provoked disappointment. He had hoped that Kirsty would be there, but there was no sign of her.

"Are you ready to eat, sir?" the waiter asked.

"I think I'll just sit for a while with a glass of beer, if I may," Bill replied, hoping against hope that Kirsty would show before he started to eat.

Unfortunately, his hopes were not realised, and eventually he ate alone. After dinner, he wandered into the guests' lounge. He spent some time examining the book that recorded the fish that had been caught by the anglers who were the main source of income for the hotel. When that pastime palled, he found a comfortable armchair and looked at one or two of the magazines that lay around, but he could not help keeping a watch on the door in case Kirsty should appear.

He woke up as one of the magazines fell from his grasp, and admitted to himself that it was time for bed.

Despite the turmoil that confused his mind he slept soundly, waking only when daylight started through the east-facing window of his room.

To his surprise and disappointment, there was still no sign of Kirsty when he went to breakfast so when he had finished, he set off down to the pier. This was where he had first set his eyes on Alex John, he remembered. He thought wistfully of the time that had passed since then stopping himself when he thought of the sadder sides, preferring to dwell on happy events—like the very first fish he had ever caught, the mackerel in Corrodale Bay. Was that really so long ago?

Time was flying past!

The wedding service was held in the church at Daliburgh and that was an extremely happy event. Once again Bill wondered at the remarkable facility the island people had for making everyone around enjoy themselves—strangers were almost a challenge to them!

He had heard it said often before that when the older islanders were setting a table for a meal, they always set an extra place. They reasoned that no one ever knew when Christ might arrive in the guise of a stranger. Therefore the caller would be fed as one of the family.

Kirsty was there too; she was near the front of the church, chattering brightly with the people she sat beside.

The reception—perhaps feast would have been a more apt description—was held in the bride's home. All of the neighbours, friends and relations had brought along food and drink. There was food of almost every description and no matter how much Bill put on his plate, someone tried to offer him more.

Remembering his mistake of two nights ago, he refused all offers of whisky, taking miserly—but sensible—sips from a glass of beer instead.

A whiff of remembered perfume heralded the approach, from the crowd behind him, of Kirsty. He turned in time to see her near, smiling over a plate filled with cooked chicken and salad.

"Hi, Bill. Are you enjoying yourself?"

"Anyone that isn't, should see a doctor," Bill retorted. "These people are impossible to resist—but I'm not going to get myself filled up with that 'amber nectar' as they call it! Once was enough for me."

"Come and meet some of my old friends, I've been telling them about this rich fisherman from Mallaig so they all want to get to know you." Her open smiling face took away any evil thoughts that her invitation might have invoked, but still—

"Rich? Well, I might be wealthier than some, but none of it came easy so I hope they are not just after my money," Bill laughed.

Kirsty's face clouded slightly at that. "I didn't mean anything like that, Bill. I was only teasing."

"Sorry, Kirsty. Let's start again. I'd love to meet your friends—I just hope that they don't mind me sticking to sips of beer, though."

This was the start of a night that Bill would remember for the rest of his life. When everyone's hunger had been dealt with, they all wound their way to the long barn that lay behind the house. It had a hard-packed earthen floor and Bill surmised—correctly, he later discovered—that the animals it had held till lately had been taken by neighbours to clear the way for the dancing that would now start. Encouraged by two young lads on accordions, the guests lined up on the uneven floor and the fun began!

Up and down they whirled; reeling in the bright light that shone down on them from the paraffin-fuelled Tilley lamps that hissed on the walls. Beer was brought from the house in buckets that had been brightly scoured for the purpose, and Bill was amazed to see hands thrust into the buckets only to emerge clutching bottles of whisky!

After an hour or more of these strenuous exertions, Bill was glad to take advantage of the break between dances to go outside for a breath of cooling air.

"You shouldn't be out here with no jacket on, Bill. You'll get a chill. Your shirt is bound to be wet—unless you don't perspire!"

"Hello, Kirsty. I just had to come out for a breather. There's no way I could keep up with that lot in there. I'm not used to that kind of exercise."

Kirsty stood beside him and again he was aware of her perfume.

"You are a wee bit happier looking tonight, Bill," she said.

"Why do you say that? When was I unhappy looking?"

"I saw you during the wedding service. You were looking very pensive then. There were times yesterday too, when I could see that your mind was on something else."

Kirsty paused for a time.

"You must miss her terribly, Bill. Alex John's wife told me about your loss. That was awful."

"It isn't the sort of thing you can forget very easily, Kirsty. She was there when I left the house and then the next time I saw her—" Bill stopped and looked away.

"I'm sorry, Bill. That was stupid of me. I shouldn't have said anything that reminded you of what happened. Put on your jacket and take me for a walk. I'm not able to keep up with these youngsters either; I've been away from the islands too long. Wait here till I get something to put round my shoulders—I'll not be a minute."

They set off away from the sounds of revelry, walking towards the sea. They wandered across the machair, again hand-in-hand. Not much was said, but Bill didn't feel that conversation was necessary. He was quite content to simply be there.

When they reached the sand, Kirsty stopped, bent down and took off her shoes.

"There's nothing I like more than wandering across the sand barefoot," she said. "That's something else you cannot do in a city."

"What do you do exactly?"

"Me? I'm a theatre nurse. That means I am in the operating theatre when operations are going on. I love the work there; I see so many people come in suffering, and we are able to relieve so much of it. I am not so happy when we lose a patient though. It isn't quite so bad when they are older, but sometimes I wonder why it seems that so many young people are becoming ill now. When we lose someone young, it hurts, but I try to put that out of my mind."

"I went out with a girl who was studying to be a doctor. We were very close. She came from Loch Nevis. I don't know what became of her at all; she just disappeared. No one seems to know where she went."

"Something tells me that you were very fond of this girl, Bill. What was her name?"

"Theresa MacDonnell. How do you know I was very fond of her?"

"Oh Bill! You are like every other man I ever met. I can read you like a book! Why did you lose contact with her?"

"I don't know, really. She is a Catholic and I'm not, so I don't think her parents would have approved of her going out with me. I thought we would get married when she was qualified, but she just disappeared. Someone said that they thought she went to Canada with her parents, but I don't know."

"Things are changing in our Church now, Bill. A few years ago I wouldn't have dared to be seen walking with you, but now there is a bit more understanding being shown."

"I think you are right, Kirsty. There are some people on my side of the fence who are just bigoted beasts! Funny thing is that the majority of these people never see the inside of a church from one year's end to the other. Births marriages and deaths! That's what their attendances consist of!"

"You should surely be able to trace Theresa, Bill. No-one can just disappear without trace. If she emigrated there will be records; you would be able to discover if she graduated as a doctor, quite easily; I am certain that the Parish priest would be able to throw some light on it; have you thought of trying any of these contacts, or have you just given up?"

After a long silence, Bill answered; "I am not sure how to answer that, Kirsty. A friend asked the priest in Mallaig for me a long time ago, but got nowhere. Maybe I am afraid of discovering that she is happy with someone else … I just don't know."

They walked on in silence for a time, each lost in their own thoughts.

"I am sorry, Bill; I shouldn't be interfering in someone else's life. I just feel that you should perhaps have tried a bit harder to find her. There might be a simple reason for her having left without telling you where she was going. It doesn't make sense to me; there must be something else in this situation that neither of us is aware of. Anyway, we are at a wedding, we should be full of happy thoughts, not gloomy ones. Gracious, this water is warm for the time of year!"

Kirsty said this as she ventured onto the damp sand at the water's edge. The surge that is always present in the Atlantic had risen ankle deep around her before hissing back again. They stopped and looked out to sea.

"There's nothing between us and America, but open sea," Kirsty said. "I'd love to just sail away on a wee boat and just keep going west until I landed somewhere."

"That would be fine in weather like this, but it isn't always so calm. I don't fancy being out there in a westerly gale."

Kirsty, who was now standing close to Bill, shuddered.

"It's getting colder now. Take me back. I need to be in a warm place again. I'm not going to wait for long, though. I've been working hard all day."

"Where were you last night? I looked for you at breakfast."

"I stayed at my cousin's home. That is partly to blame for my tiredness. I was late getting to bed—and that was one that was made up on a settee in the living room. I'd have been far better going back to the hotel—I'd have had a decent bed there. When are you going back to Mallaig?"

"Tomorrow afternoon. Jim MacInnes is coming over for me. I don't want to be late either. I'll go back to the hotel with you. There'll be a lot for me to catch up on when I get back home; there are always papers of some kind arriving. What about you, Kirsty? When are you going back to Glasgow?"

"I'll be off to Castlebay tomorrow or the day after. I get the ferry to Oban on Tuesday and it's back to work on the Thursday."

As they spoke, Bill felt a touch of sadness. He liked Kirsty a lot, she was someone that he was able to relax with and he would be sorry to leave.

Back at the bride's house, they picked half-heartedly at the pieces of cooked chicken that were thrust upon them by the old lady that greeted them. "You'll be hungry now, after all the exercise." Then she smiled knowingly, cackled delightfully and added, "You'll need to keep up your strength, the night isn't finished yet!"

Within the hour they both took their leave of the party—which looked as though it was going to last until breakfast time, at least. They shared the taxi that took them the few miles back into Lochboisdale. Neither spoke on the trip. Kirsty looked out of the window on her side, her chin cupped in her hand.

They stopped at the top of the stairs that led to their bedrooms. Bill held out his hand to Kirsty saying, "I've really enjoyed the night, Kirsty." But she ignored his hand. Grinning widely she stepped towards Bill and boldly kissed him on the lips.

"Thank you for your company, Bill, today and yesterday."

Bill was totally unsure of himself, now. His male instincts told him that any advance he made might be well received, but fear of making a fool of himself meant that in his confusion he muttered something unintelligible and turned away in confusion toward his room. As he opened the door, he looked back to see Kirsty still standing at the top of the stairway. She smiled and raised one hand to him then turned, and disappeared along the dimly lit corridor.

In his room, Bill stood facing the window. Why had he not responded to what he perceived as her invitation? He no longer had a wife to consider. He would not have been unfaithful to anyone. Was his conscience making him behave this way as penance for the guilt he felt for Lisa's death? He was not, he told himself firmly, to blame. It had all been due to a dreadful accident.

Whilst his mind was thus engaged, he was taking off his suit. Habit made him hang it carefully in the wardrobe. His shirt, that had been soaked with sweat was now dry, but he threw it into the bottom of the holdall that stood at the foot of his bed. He had stripped to his underwear, and had decided to forego the pleasure of a bath until morning when there was a slight tap on his door.

He opened it cautiously to see an unsmiling Kirsty.

"What—" he began, but Kirsty pushed the door open and came into the room.

She stepped close, put both of her hands behind Bill's neck. Pulling his head down, she kissed him.

Feeling his reaction to the closeness of her body she leant back in his arms and looked Bill straight in the eye.

"This is a need, Bill," she said quietly.

Bill felt the warmth of the softness of her lower body against his male hardness. Reason had no place in this situation; instinct took over. He turned slightly and lifted Kirsty in his arms before laying her on the bed. He stood then and without taking his eyes from hers, started to undress her. She, for her part, eased her body as required until she lay naked before him. Then he let his eyes feast on the beauty of her body, the fullness of her dark-tipped breasts, the narrowing of her body to the slimness of her waist then lower still, to the fullness of her hips with their dark centre of age-old promise.

They came together slowly, Bill wanting the moment to last, savouring the sweetness of her lips before kissing his way down her neck to his goal, her breasts. He alternated kissing them with sucking gently on her nipples, whilst his hands roved gently around her waist. Up to her neck he explored then back down again, tracing a gentle path inside her thighs until they reached the incredibly hot wetness that lay at the centre.

Kirsty moaned gently for a time, and then her hands began their own gentle caressing, feeling down his back then, after a time, arriving at the centre of his desire for her. She grasped him, firmly at first then gently her hands fluttered along his length.

"Now, Bill. Please!" she murmured—her breath hot in his ear.

Bill forced himself to slow down, entering her gently, a little at a time. He countered her upward thrusting by withdrawing in return until at last the full length of him was in her. He replied to her frenzied actions then, reason leaving him as he soared towards his climax. Kirsty moaned something in her native Gaelic as she reached her goal, her body greedily taking his seed before she relaxed below him, sobbing slightly.

They lay together for a time then Bill raised himself and attempted to take the bedcover over them.

"I can't stay the night, Bill," Kirsty whispered. "Walls have ears in a wee place like this; it would be all over the island in no time at all."

Despite that, she roused herself and soon they were under the sheets together. Kirsty nestled close in Bill's arms, her breath on his neck, her hair pleasingly tickling his face.

"I don't want you to get the wrong idea about me, Bill. This is what I wanted to do and I think you needed it. Yes, I wanted it, but you needed it. I can see that you are hurting. You must try to let your wife go free now. You are still here, and must live as a man. I don't know what happened with Theresa. She must have been crazy to turn her back on the sort of happiness she could have had with you. We have had a few hours of happiness with one another. Let's be thankful for that, and let there be no recriminations. It is unlikely that it will ever happen again—I am married to my work. I should go back to my room now but first, I want you once more!"

Bill was confused by what she said, but her hands, wandering lightly over his body, soon put all his confusion to flight. He lived—and loved for the moment.

For all her protestations about going to her own room, the pale light of dawn was in the eastern sky before she finally left and Bill fell into as deep a sleep as he had ever known.

It was late before he finally wakened and by the time he had a much-needed bath, he thought that he would be far too late for breakfast. When he did eventually go downstairs, a waitress asked if he was ready for some food. "We are used to people being late on the morning after a wedding," she smiled.

There was no sign of Kirsty and he wondered if she was still asleep but the waitress, when she brought through his tea said, "The lady you were out with the other day has left. She asked me to wish you a safe trip back to Mallaig. She is off to Daliburgh to help with the clearing up after the reception."

Bill wandered down to the pier after breakfast. He felt lonely and very alone now, missing Kirsty's cheerful company. Even if he never saw her again, he would not easily forget her, he thought sadly. Then he realised that he could trace her quite easily. Alex John would be able to tell him where to get in touch with her. Glasgow wasn't so very far away from Mallaig—he could get there and back again in a weekend, quite easily.

These thoughts cheered him greatly so with a lighter heart, he went back to the hotel. Jim might have left early, and could be here at any time. He should be ready to leave at once.

Chapter Nineteen

Spring passed quickly but before the summer fishing had properly started, Bill attended his brother's wedding in Campbeltown. He spent several days there but realised that he was now really a stranger in what had once been his home town. His old friends had married and he felt out of place in their company. He discovered that his old friend and mentor, Dennis, had died during the winter. No one had thought to tell him of this, a fact that hurt Bill greatly. Old Ban was long dead also. Bill went to the old grey building where he had been brought up and sat for a time on the low wall that fronted it. Memories, good ones mainly, for the bad all seemed to be forgotten easily, came flooding back with the familiar scenes. He went to visit the graveyard, and quietly paid his respects to the two old men who had taught him so much.

Time dragged by so slowly while he was in the town, that it was a relief when he was able to return to Mallaig.

Their new boat, which Bill insisted should be called the *Girl Mary*, after Jim's wife, arrived in late August. Bill was greatly pleased with her. Ian MacPherson, who had in the past been a Kelvin man through and through, had of late been grudgingly admitting that the Gardner engines seemed to be less prone to trouble. He was delighted when the *Girl Mary* proved herself to be substantially faster than the *Solan*. There was one addition that was a first in the Mallaig fleet—she had a toilet in the engine room! True, it just sat there against the starboard side for all to view, but still, it was a most welcome addition!

"We're getting a new Lifeboat this autumn, an Arun class. They are beauties all right, and they are fast. She'll do twice the speed of your fastest ringer!"

This confidence came from Albert Cowie, who had called Bill into the tiny office in his small kipper yard.

"Aye, they do around eighteen knots, I believe," he continued. "The only thing that bothers me is that I don't know how long I'll be able to stay on as Coxswain. I think that this boat will require a younger man than me. I've had young Francis aboard as a crewman for a few months now. He isn't directly in line for the job, but I think he'll prove a better bet for a new Coxswain. Young Archie is a good enough lad, but I just don't fancy him to take my place permanently. He is a wee bit too fond of a dram nowadays as well."

"Eighteen knots is a big speed, Albert. That'll take a bit of getting used to. If that is correct, and I'm sure it is, she'll go to Lochboisdale before we could get to Canna in our boats! I look forward to seeing her. I've heard about these boats, they were talking of getting one in Campbeltown when I was at Donald's wedding, but I really didn't take much heed of what they were saying."

"They have proved themselves all right, Bill. A fellow called Alan McLachlan designed them. He works for a firm called G.L.Watsons. He is well known as a naval architect. They're bound to be good boats; they were designed on the Clyde! Anyway, do you fancy a kipper for your tea? They're at their best just now."

Francis was duly appointed second coxswain of the new Arun. During the working up period with the new boat, it had become glaringly obvious that he was the right man for the job. Archie Morrison, who had been second coxswain on the Barnett, and so should have kept this position on the Arun, admitted that he was having a lot of trouble coming to terms with the power of the new boat, so rather grudgingly gave way. He would not stay on the crew for very long after this but then neither would Albert, who also admitted to having difficulties. The difference in speed was the most obvious thing but getting used to handling the boat in confined situations was more challenging.

This was not to say that the boat was more difficult to handle—quite the opposite was true. She would literally turn in her own length by using the twin screws, stop on the proverbial sixpence, and could take off like a scalded cat! Some people found it difficult converting from the fishing boat type of handling. Francis took to it like a duck to water. The Lifeboat Inspector, who was there to oversee the training, said that he had never met anyone to whom it seemed more natural.

The other challenge to crews was a medical one. There were several men who had been quite at home on the Barnett, who were now shocked to discover that they were considered too old, or who failed the more stringent medical that was now required.

The first real service that the Arun performed, in late autumn, was when she was launched to assist the occupants of a small boat that had been seen to capsize off Sleat Point. They were there just twenty minutes after launching and took two young men aboard who had been in the water, clinging to the upturned hull. These men, who were not wearing lifejackets, agreed that they would not have been able to hold on for much more than a few minutes longer. That incident proved, if proof were needed, that the boat was a huge advance on its predecessor.

The winter herring fishing was not really under way properly when Albert again sought out Bill's company. This time it was to tell him that he felt that he should retire as Coxswain of the lifeboat.

"I really am getting a bit long in the tooth now, Bill. I think that Ally would like to take over as second to Francis if I do go, and no one on the boat would have any argument with that. He has attended all the exercises that he could, and is just as good as Francis is."

"But what about the fact that he is at sea most of the week, Albert?"

"That is a minus point all right, Bill, but I'd still be here and would be more than willing to stand in for him if needed. There's one other thing. I see that there are more big boats taking up trawling for herring. I don't think that this bodes well for the future, really. The drift net was in use for hundreds of years, and her-ring stocks stood up to that. The ring net almost drove the drifters out, but now I fear that the herring trawl will kill the fishing completely. We all know about these purse-seine nets too. The Norwegians have had great success with them. If they are next to arrive here, we have had it. There is no natural selection now, as there was with the drift net. That method only caught herring of a marketable size; the small ones swam through the meshes. With the ring net, and now with the trawl, everything that swims is killed."

"How would Ally being on the lifeboat help him in the long term, though?"

"That is another point, Bill. I hear on the grapevine that very soon the lifeboat will be paying wages to the crews. That may not come about, but if Ally is in on the ground floor he has a chance of being Coxswain. Francis has agreed that if this talk of payment comes about, he will step down in Ally's favour and continue as his number two. He is doing quite well at the lobsters, as you know, and he misses very few calls because he is working so close at hand. He can be in the harbour quite quickly from where he is working. You have been very good to Ally and me since we came here, so I didn't want to do anything without telling you first."

"I miss Francis's company a lot," said Bill. "I used to enjoy being with him, he's a fine lad and I get on very well with him. Thank you for telling me all that is on your mind. I agree about the trawling—sometimes I think I am getting too old myself. Maybe I should sell out and come ashore while I still have something to sell. We'll probably have to think again. It was good while it lasted. Francis could well have been the man to take over from me, but—"

Bill stopped there, looking down pensively.

"Don't get too downhearted, Bill. There are more fish in the sea than have ever been taken out of it. Come on, I'll treat you to one of Jess's scones—that'll cheer you up!"

January came in as wildly as anyone could remember. Gale succeeded gale and the boats were tied up at the pier for longer than they were at sea.

Bill was getting ready for bed one Monday night. The wind was once more into the southwest and was howling around the chimneys.

Because of the wind, no boats had left the harbour that morning. Bill had made himself a cup of cocoa and was taking it to the living room when he heard the deep growl of the Lifeboat's engines. The crew had just recently been issued with pagers that replaced the traditional maroons, an action that not everyone agreed with as very often the boat went out without the villagers knowing. He went to the window to see the boat's lights disappearing out of the harbour, heading west. She had hardly cleared the shelter of the west pier when the spray hid her lights from view.

"God help the poor soul that is in bother on the sea on a night like this," thought Bill as he watched her go. He sat for a while, but there was nothing to see, so he went to bed. He thought of telephoning someone to ask where she was going but decided against it. Finishing his cocoa and crawling into his warm bed was a better option.

The telephone ringing wakened him. Peering at the bedside clock, he saw that it was just after three a.m. His first thought was that one of the boats in the harbour had broken adrift but when he growled "Hello," into the handset Albert answered.

"Will you come down to the lifeboat shed, Bill? I think we have a problem."

Without wasting time on what he knew would be unnecessary questions Bill answered, "Right away, Albert." He knew from the tone of his voice that Albert was a worried man.

Bill hauled on the clothes that were, as usual, on a chair at the foot of the bed, and set off down the road.

The wind was still in the southwest and had eased just a little, he thought. There was no sign as yet of the heavy rain that usually arrived before the wind shifted up and eased, but there was enough to ensure that he was well soaked before he reached the large wooden shed that served as a store and crew room for the lifeboat.

The building was a blaze of lights and Bill saw James MacBride, the station-master and Honorary Secretary of the lifeboat, peering from a window.

Inside, he saw Albert and several fishermen, but Bill made straight for Albert.

"What's the problem?" he asked.

"You tell him, James," said Albert.

"I've had a call from the Coastguard, Bill. They have been told that a distress beacon has been heard somewhere near Canna. They think that it is from our lifeboat. They have been calling her on the radio for some time now, but cannot get a reply. They last heard from them over two hours ago, just before one o'clock. Every-thing was fine then, they were through Rhum Sound, and were going well."

"Where were they going?" Bill asked.

"A coaster called the Coastguard, saying that they had developed a list. They were about ten miles north west of the Cairns of Coll at that time. They are headed north through the Minch. They seem to be all right now, but still have a list. They haven't heard from the lifeboat, nor have they seen her."

"These men in the coaster would have been around the Hawes Bank when they sent out that distress call," said Bill. "That is a patch of shallow water where there are bound to be breaking seas, James, and it ties in with the position they gave. They would cope better as soon as they got off that Bank. We'd better get some men together, and get off out there. There is something wrong! What is the beacon saying?"

"It doesn't say anything, except that the recognition signal seems to belong to the lifeboat." James's voice was near to breaking, and the strain he was obviously feeling, showed clearly on his face.

Bill hesitated—"Is Ally aboard her?" he asked.

"Yes," said Albert.

"There are six aboard, Bill," said James. "Francis, Ally, John Morrans, Eddie Smith, Jim Roberts and Robin Stevens. They are all good lads, and they know what they are doing."

"Come on then, Albert. It's time we weren't here. Call Ian MacPherson right now, James. I want him aboard with us—I'm sure he'll come. Is anyone else here coming with us? You don't have to come, remember?" Then, before anyone could answer, he continued, "I'm off down to start the engine. The fenders will all have to come in, and the hold covers will have to be lashed down. Out there won't be the place to try to do something that should have been done in the harbour. Tell the Coastguard what we're going to do, James."

They left the pier some fifteen minutes later on the *Girl Mary*. When they cleared the harbour mouth, they felt the full force of the sea. The gales had been blowing non-stop for several days now, giving the sea plenty of time to build up. Bill had to ease the boat down to just over half speed—to charge into the seas at anything like full speed, would have done damage to the hull. The radio, tuned to the distress frequency, let them listen to the shore station calling the Mallaig lifeboat every fifteen minutes.

No reply was heard.

The crew of five—Bill, Albert, Ian and two of the men that had been in the lifeboat shed, were all in the shelter of the *Girl Mary's* wheelhouse.

"Some of the other boats will come out to help, Bill, as soon as they hear about the trouble," said Albert, whose voice betrayed the desperate anxiety he felt.

"I thought of asking James to call Willie Mair," replied Bill. "I didn't because this wind is going to ease soon, I'm sure. There's no use putting more men at risk just now; that's why I didn't call Jim. His family need him. At this speed, we'll take nearly five hours to get to where I think they are likely to be. I'm going to go to the north side of Rhum. We'll get a bit of shelter there, and will be able to crack on a bit faster. At least daylight will be in when we get to the search area. I don't like to say it, Albert, but from the plot of where the casualty was and where she is now, it's possible that when Francis was following her, he went too close to the Mills rocks. They are just two-and-a-half miles south west of the Hyskeir lighthouse, as you know. They might not see the light on a dirty rainy night. We can only hope that they have some sort of total radio failure. I don't trust these distress beacons either, though. They have been known to go off aboard boats lying in the harbour!"

"I hope you're right, Bill," said Albert. "Anything else just doesn't bear thinking about."

As they neared Rhum they gained some shelter from its bulk and were able to increase speed. Bill had two of the men go below to make some tea and corned beef sandwiches. It was fortunate indeed that their cook had taken some of the stores aboard before he discovered that they weren't going to sea.

"I think that wind is easing a bit now," said Albert.

"Yes," replied Bill. "Just wait—if we get a downpour, the wind will shift up to the north west, and will ease. That's what we need."

They had reached Kilmory Point, at the northernmost corner of Rhum when the rain did come with a vengeance. The wind eased within minutes of the rain starting, but it still clung stubbornly to the southwest quadrant.

"I think we should make for the north side of Canna, Albert. If they are drifting without power, they'll maybe come close by the west end of the island."

They were now up to full speed, but Bill still had to watch the seas very carefully, easing the throttle whenever he saw a big wave coming. The wind shifted into the north-west, as they thought it would, by the time they were passing Canna Harbour. About the same time, Jim called them. He had just left Mallaig, in company with five other boats, and told them that he had spoken with Alex John, who would, he thought, be leaving Lochboisdale very soon.

Bill cursed himself when he heard the news. Why had he not thought of calling Alex John himself? He would have reached the area they were going to search, far more quickly than they would.

A dismal grey daylight was now well in, and the wind was easing quickly. The coaster, whose call for help had started all the events, had now managed to reach a sheltered position nearer the shore of North Uist, and appeared confident of reaching the safety of Stornoway, without outside assistance.

Although the wind was now down to just a fresh breeze, the seas were still very confused when Bill judged it time to slow down, get men out on deck, and start the search.

The wind speed had been too great to send a helicopter to assist them, until now, but they were not long started their long zigzag searching, when they were joined by an RAF Nimrod aircraft. Albert's prophesy that this aircraft wouldn't take long to find the beacon was justified within the half-hour when they saw her turning in a narrow circle and dropping marker flares.

They turned toward these flares and their hearts all dropped when they saw the bright orange superstructure of the lifeboat and realised that she was indeed waterlogged. A call from the Coastguard that the Nimrod could see no signs of life aboard her hit them all an almost physical blow. They were also told that a helicopter should be with them very soon.

When they got close to the stricken lifeboat they were appalled at the sight that confronted them. Although most of the damage was out of sight below the water, they could see that the wheelhouse had been moved from its original position. It was immediately obvious to them all that there was very little chance that anyone could have survived the catastrophe that had happened here. They could plainly see the body of Eddie Smith—they were almost certain that this was who it was—as it washed around in the sea that was now level with the boat's deck.

Albert was beside himself with grief.

He knew at once that he had lost his only son here.

He was experienced enough to know that there was no sense in obeying his instinctive desire to be put aboard her. Damage would certainly be done to the *Girl Mary* and someone else would be hurt or killed if they tried to get a man aboard in these conditions. He went below to the forecastle.

Bill, seeing him go, waited for a few minutes before asking Ian to take the boat and to keep her running slowly before the sea, and went below to join him. The two stood there in the swaying confines of the swaying forecastle, holding one another, Bill in tears and Albert sobbing bitterly. After a few moments Bill spoke.

"When the helicopter arrives they'll drop a man aboard her, Albert. When he has done what he needs to do, he can take a rope from us and we'll tow her into the lee of Canna. There's nothing else we can do. Just you stay here for a spell—I think I know how you must feel."

Albert regained control of himself long enough to look at Bill through eyes that were haunted with grief.

"I'll leave it all to you, Bill. I know there's nothing else we can do for them."

The helicopter arrived within fifteen minutes and after surveying the scene for a time, began to hover over the wrecked lifeboat. The winchman was lowered aboard her and, after examining the body that was on deck, he disappeared into the wheelhouse.

He reappeared a few minutes later, waved his hands in a negative gesture and shook his head. He then spoke briefly into the handset of the portable VHF radio that he carried. These radios had not been fitted to many fishing boats so Bill, back in the wheelhouse now, closed the stricken hulk until they could talk to and hear what the man had to say.

He shouted to them that there were four bodies in the wheelhouse, plus the one on deck, and that there was no sign of life in any of them.

Which one was missing, Bill wondered?

The winchman agreed readily to Bill's shouted suggestion that he take a rope from them, and made it fast to the heavy bitts on the lifeboat's foredeck. Then, as they slowly and carefully started the tow, he secured the body of the man on deck. He spent some more time inside the wheelhouse and then, his tasks on board completed, was finally winched back up into the helicopter. The yellow aircraft circled them. The winchman, clearly visible in the aircraft's open doorway, saluted them, and then the helicopter left, flying east toward the mainland.

Alex John joined them shortly afterwards and kept close company with them as they made their way slowly to the east and the shelter of Canna. The boats from Mallaig had joined the sad procession before they started to gain less turbulent seas. Finally, it was judged safe enough to allow Jim, in the *Marguerite*, to get close enough to the lifeboat to let a man jump aboard, and secure a second rope to the bow. The man was taken back aboard the *Marguerite* safely and Jim gradually took the strain, thus increasing the speed at which they were travelling. They were escorted by the other boats that had joined the search, all of them trailing behind in what appeared to be a spontaneous gesture of respect.

It was dark before the lights of Mallaig finally came into sight. They had been told that all the arrangements for receiving them had been made and indeed, while they still had five miles to travel, a boat from Mallaig came alongside and put aboard three officials from the RNLI. These men were visibly shaken when they came aboard. They had, they told Bill, been astonished at the devastation the searchlight had shown them and they stood silent beside him until the harbour was finally reached.

As soon as he could, Bill left the scene. The boats had been safely moored and the lifeboat had been taken to the east side of the pier, where a berth that she would dry out at had been reserved. He went willingly with George, escorted by solemn policemen through the horde of news-hungry Pressmen to George's home, where Meg took over. She insisted that Bill have a warm bath before he ate. Food was probably the last thing on his mind but when the plate of steaming stew was put before him, he ate ravenously. The large dram that George insisted he drink was enough to send him to the bed that he had first slept in so many years ago, when first he arrived in Mallaig, and he slept the sleep of one that was mentally and physically exhausted.

Chapter Twenty

The grey morning light woke Bill. He had just one moment of peace, the aftermath of a long sleep, before remembrance of the previous day's horrendous events dawned on him. He lay for a time before rising, going over all that had happened, in his mind, hardly able to comprehend the magnitude of the disaster that had struck the village. He rose and went through to the kitchen where Meg, who looked as though she hadn't slept at all, was bent over her fire. Bill thought that she looked very old now.

"George is still down on the pier. He has been there all night. I expect he'll be home for something to eat soon. Did you sleep well, son?"

Bill sat at the kitchen table. Seeing the haggard look on Meg's face had twisted the knife of grief that was in his breast. He could not trust himself to speak.

Meg rose and took Bill's bent head to her breast. This broke the dam, and Bill shed the tears that needed to come.

"I'm sorry, Meg" he said eventually. "This has brought back memories of how I felt when Lisa—"

"Hush, now. You'll have to get yourself down the pier soon. There's a lot to do, although you did your part, and more, yesterday. I'll put on the bacon for you. You are not going anywhere without food."

Bill had not quite finished his bacon-filled rolls when George arrived, pale faced and shaken. He sat himself opposite Bill.

"There's a lot to tell, Bill. We've got all the crew now. John Morrans was the one that was missing, but we found his body in the engine room. It appears that they struck a rock. There's a fearful amount of damage below the waterline. I just don't know how on earth she kept afloat. You'll see this for yourself. They'll be taking her away but I don't know how, or when. They don't want her lying here for any longer than is necessary. All the bodies were taken to the lifeboat shed. There are doctors and nurses there and when their work is finished, they'll be taken to the churches. The only good thing is that they all seem to have died quickly."

He stopped there, stirring sugar into the tea that Meg had put before him.

"Aye, that would be the Mills Rocks," said Bill. "I thought that was where they might have been."

"Everyone seems to be of the same opinion, Bill. He must have cut the corner a wee bit, trying to get to the casualty as soon as possible."

"I think that his navigating system might have been out, George. They are prone to going wrong sometimes, especially in bad weather. That could have done it."

"You may be right. Nobody could call Francis reckless. We'll never know now, though."

Bill rose from the table.

"It's time you had a sleep, George. You have done enough. I'm away down to see what is happening."

"I believe you are right, Bill. I could use a rest. You'll see plenty of Press people around the harbour. They have been very good, really, but they have a job to do and they need news so they'll probably pester you a lot."

Bill reluctantly left the comparative quiet of the house and set off down the brae. Jim, who appeared to have been waiting for him, joined him as he approached the pier. The locals he met all had their heads down but without exception, they all shook his hand although not one of them spoke a word. When he reached the pier two men, one carrying a camera approached him.

"Are you Bill Martin?" the first man asked. The other busied himself taking photographs of him.

"Yes I am. I realise that you have a job to do, but so do I. If you will just leave me for an hour or so, I promise that I'll answer your questions. I do need some time to myself, though."

The reporter agreed to this, adding that he would ask his fellows to respect Bill's request also.

The lifeboat was moored in the area that was used by the fishing boats when they needed to be ebbed for any reason. The beach there was clean shingle, with no rocks protruding. Bill was shocked at the destruction that had been wrought on the lifeboat. The hull below the waterline was shattered and splintered beyond belief. He stood in silence, his mind unable to comprehend what his eyes told him.

James MacBride, the Honorary Secretary, approached. Bill thought he had aged years since he saw him last. He looked pale and haggard. He had a man with him who was a complete stranger to Bill.

"This is Donald Hammond," James began. "He is the Chief of Operations in the lifeboat service. Can you give him some of your time?"

"Surely," Bill said, shaking hands with the stranger.

At James's suggestion they went to the office part of the lifeboat shed. Bill could hear muttered conversation coming from the area in which he presumed the bodies lay.

Donald, who also looked extremely tired and pale, thanked Bill and Jim for all that they and their crews had done. He was a seaman himself, he told them, and knew well what conditions must have been like at sea.

His remit, he told them, was to try to find out just what had caused the disaster and, if possible, to take steps to ensure that it would never happen again. They talked over the possible causes but it was clear from the very start that the boat had struck a rock whilst under power. This pointed to a navigational error. Donald agreed with Bill that the most likely cause of the mistake was that the electronic navigation equipment had developed a temporary fault due to the weather. Bill stressed that he had great faith in Francis's capabilities but pointed out that he would have been trying to get to the casualty as soon as possible.

For his part, Donald told Bill that the Coastguard had informed him that the casualty had been guilty of keeping silent for long periods and had failed on several occasions to answer when called. They didn't know why this was, but Donald pointed out that these silences would have increased Francis's anxiety.

They went as far as they could go and then Donald stood up, shook Bill and Jim's hands and thanked them again.

"Before you leave, what is happening, when will the bodies—?"

"I think they will be released very soon now. The families have agreed that they should all go to their churches. They will remain there until the burial time is agreed. They have asked that it all be kept as low key as possible and I will try my utmost to see that their wishes are met."

"Right," said Bill. "That reminds me; I promised I'd say a few words to the press. They need something, and I feel that we shouldn't antagonise them. We'll need all the goodwill we can get."

That day passed in a whirl of activity. Only afterwards did Bill realise just what a tower of strength Jim had been. He remained quietly beside Bill during the entire day, speaking only when he felt that his views were needed, or when Bill faltered in any way. The weather had improved greatly and a weak wintry sun lit the scenes of destruction and sadness.

As night fell, Jim insisted that Bill accompany him to his home for a meal. His wife, Mary, greeted them unsmilingly at the door. Even the small children were subdued, tending to cling closely to their father's side. It was as though even they understood something of the depth of feelings that their elders felt.

Bill went home shortly after they had finished eating. The evening was now wearing on, but he found that it was impossible to rest. He didn't want to intrude upon the grief that the relatives of the dead were experiencing, but he called the recently arrived priest, Father MacNeil. Bill had formed the opinion that this was a very good man, although he had not spent a great deal of time in his company.

"Hello, Father, it's Bill Martin," he began.

"Bill! I was going to call and see you later. How are you? You did all you could for these poor lads. Thank you."

"I was calling to ask if Francis's folk have arrived. I'm sorry I didn't think of asking earlier."

"Yes, Bill, they are here. They are staying in the hotel at the moment but I will arrange for them to be with friends of mine until they want to leave."

"Good, Father. Remember, there is plenty of room for them here if they would want to come."

"Thank you, Bill. They may take you up on that offer. If so, I'll let you know."

They spoke until the priest remembered that he had work to do.

Bill sat silent before the fire. He just couldn't settle. It was late in the evening before he rose and put on his jacket. He set off slowly down the path and then, not wanting to meet anyone, took the back way up to the old church that stood on the hill. The outer door was ajar and he went through it into the dimly lit porch. There he stood for a time, dreading what he knew he would see inside, and then went into the church proper.

Right at the front of the church, arrayed before the communion table, lay five coffins. In time, before the service was held, they would all be draped with the Lifeboat flag but for now, they were unadorned. There were quite a few people sitting silent and anonymous in the gloom but Bill passed them by. He stood above the coffins and walked slowly along them, pausing at the head of each of them to read the names.

So young to die, he thought.

He then went to the rear of the church and sat for a while. The wind had ceased now, and the only sound was an occasional muffled sob from the pews in front.

Why were there only the five of them there, he asked himself? They had died together, why did they have to be separated now? Then he realised the futility of his thoughts. He stood and then left as silently as he had arrived.

He went down the steps that led from the church to the road and continued toward the village centre but before he reached that, he turned in toward the Catholic church. When he had almost reached the door he paused, feeling that there was something, almost a physical presence, stopping him from going any further. His entire being seemed to be almost overpowered by the sense of being close to something that was beyond his comprehension. He stood there, motionless, for a time then forced himself forward toward the entrance. Bill pushed the heavy door open. Inside the very dimly lit interior there was a heady smell of incense, and the place was completely silent. He walked slowly on the heavy carpet toward the altar, eyes downcast. When he reached the rail he paused, opened the gate and walked forward and to his right, to where the coffin lay.

He approached and laid both his hands at the top of it and then bowed his head until it also rested on the cold wood. He stood there for an age, then lifted his head again and looked down the dark length of the coffin.

In order to read the brass plate that was affixed below the cross, he walked to the foot. There he read—graven deeply into the brass—the legend, *Francis William Martin MacDonnell,* and the dates of his birth and death.

His brain was immediately thrown into turmoil.

William Martin?

How had the man he had known as Francis MacDonnell come by these names? He had seen Francis's signature on several legal documents, but had never seen William Martin as a part of it. What did this all mean? Could there possibly be any connection or relationship and if so, what and how? Could this start to explain why he had felt such an affinity with the young man whose body now lay before him?

As he stood there motionless, his thoughts in complete confusion, he suddenly became aware of movement behind him. He turned, shocked to see a lone female figure, clad in black from head to foot, moving slowly toward him. Her head—covered in a black lace shawl—was bowed.

As she approached, the strength left his legs, and he again grasped the coffin with both hands. He knew somehow, even before she raised the veil from her eyes, just what he would see. When she did, he saw that the ashen face now revealed before him was framed with black hair—now flecked with silver—but the eyes, Theresa's eyes, were still black and piercing. They still saw right into his soul.

She spoke quietly, and he heard her faintly through the roaring in his ears.

"Yes, Bill, he was your son. I came home from University to my parents as soon as I knew I was pregnant. I wanted our child. Getting rid of him was never an option. You should have known that, Bill. We moved to Loch Hourn to get away from the gossips. Perhaps I should have told you about your son, but I didn't want to put pressure on you. We talked about religion, remember, and I didn't want you to feel obliged to change for me. I never married. There was never anyone but you. There never could be anyone but you! He was a good son to me, and he was all I had of you. I did not tell him that you were his father, nor did he know anything of his middle names but he spoke of you often, and he loved you for the father he never knew. Forgive me—for I have long forgiven you. I am so sorry for all the tragedy you have had in your life."

Theresa turned away and started to walk slowly toward the door.

Bill fell to his knees beside his son's coffin and a great wail escaped his lips, a wail that came from the very depths of his soul.

"Oh Christ Jesus, what have I done—what have I done? Forgive me, please—please forgive me!" he cried—and then he fell prostrate, face down on the floor, a broken man.

Great sobs shook his entire body.

He sensed rather than felt a hand gently touch the back of his neck. Theresa had obviously turned back. "Don't cry, Bill," said Theresa, in a stronger voice. "You were not the only one to blame. We are both victims of a society that cares little for the gentle humility of Christ. We have to live within this society. Our son is free from this now. He died trying to help others. Because of that he is with our Father now. I know this!"

This statement caused the tears to flow more freely and Bill's body curled up on itself. Theresa knelt beside him then. At first she wiped the tears from his cheeks with her shawl, and then she gently kissed him on the head. "We will have to try to be strong for our boy, Bill; there are difficult times ahead."

Bill turned his tear-ravaged face toward her and wailed, "Why, Theresa, why didn't I realise what I was doing? I have never truly loved anyone but you. I married, but God alone knows I did not marry for real love. Your face was always there. I was told you had gone to Canada. Before the cold body of our child, I swear I never really loved anyone but you."

Theresa almost broke then, and it showed in her voice. "Bill, I know you love me. There has never been any doubt about that in my mind, and that knowledge kept me going through all the difficult times. We were meant for one another. God didn't keep us apart, it was the uncaring rules of man that did that. I have never stopped loving you. I gave up my work ... my entire life, for our son ..." She paused then, choking back a sob.

Bill lay still. They would never know how long they waited there; Bill curled in a foetal huddle, Theresa kneeling beside him, both their hearts broken.

Theresa was the first to stir. She stood silent beside her son's coffin, looking down on her lover.

Bill, sensing her movement, got to his knees. "Is it too late now, Theresa...?" he began, hesitantly.

"Bill, there was never another for me; I told you that, but it is too late. We have both suffered too much, you more than me. I at least had our son to support me and then, when he came here to work with you I heard of you from him. I had something of you; you had nothing of me. I am sorry. It is too late."

With these words of what sounded like her final decision, she bent and kissed her son's coffin and walked slowly away, through the gate and into the aisle then turned and genuflected before continuing toward the door.

Bill still knelt below the coffin. He had never before felt such pressure in his head. Then he felt this strange feeling, the one he had first felt so long ago at Macringan's Point, and a degree of calmness ensued. This time, however, it was not the future that was unravelling, it was the past.

Realisation of his own failings came into focus. He had been almost completely self-centred, he began to see. In his dealings with his partners and his co-workers, self had come first. He had treated Lisa very badly—he had known in his heart that he did not really love her when he married her yet he went ahead with it. Had it been a form of revenge on Theresa for her perceived abandonment of him, or had it all been yet another example of his obsession with his own comfort and wellbeing?

He had treated Theresa's faith with complete contempt. Dennis had warned him so long ago, that there would be difficulties yet he had, without any thought for her faith or for her feelings, blithely told her to 'get rid of' their son. At the time when she needed him most, he had abandoned her and left her to her own devices. He was more concerned at that time, with his own grand designs for making money! Theresa, on the other hand, had given up her lifetime ambition to be a doctor, in order to bring up their son: she had left the city, and had spent her best years in a lonely croft in a remote loch with only her parents and her son for company.

He had thrown away so many years when he could have been with his son. Even when Francis had hugged him after Lisa's tragic death, he had no knowledge, not the slightest inkling, of who this lad really was. Where had his precious insight been all those years? How had he not seen the tiny clues, the light in his eyes, the line of his jaw, that should have revealed the truth, or at least have made him suspect it? Was it the case that he had so completely believed that Theresa had forsaken him that blinded him—or was it that the truth was more painful and difficult than he had been prepared to countenance, too damning of his callousness and self-interest?

And the result of all his meticulous planning? A lifetime lost!

The creaking that came from the door as Theresa opened it broke the spell.

"Wait, Theresa, wait, please!" he cried after her.

Bill struggled to his feet and half-ran up the aisle to where she stood, watching him apprehensively. He reached out and took her cold hands in his.

"I am so sorry, Theresa. I have only now realised just how badly I have treated you. When you needed me, I was not there. Please, for God's sake, please give us both another chance."

Tears started again and Theresa turned her face away from him. "All those years I spent in Loch Hourn were spent because I couldn't risk seeing you again. Whilst your wife was alive I couldn't come to Mallaig because I could not face the risk of seeing you both together. After she died, I was simply afraid. I love you, Bill, I always have and I always will. I cannot resist any longer, I have no strength left."

Theresa stepped closer to him, turned up her tear-stained face, and kissed him.

"Let's go back now, and say 'goodnight' to our boy. Who knows what tomorrow will bring?"

They walked slowly, arms around each other, down again to where the lonely coffin lay.

Father MacNeil stood alone, right at the rear of the church, unseen in the dimness. He had heard all that had been said. He had heard many things in his time as a priest but he had never encountered a human tragedy that had moved him more.

He watched silently as the couple bent over the coffin, and as they walked slowly back and left the church.

He then knelt and prayed. He prayed that there might be reconciliation between Theresa and Bill; that they be given strength to get through the difficult days ahead and that there might some day be more understanding and less discrimination between the faiths. He was not yet aware that one day soon, he would be comforting the girl who was carrying Francis's child.

The End

Epilogue

In writing this book I have taken liberties with time. World wars do not exist within its pages, and it is not chronologically accurate.

There is an Arun class lifeboat in existence. It was designed by Alan McLachlan of G.L.Watson Ltd, Glasgow and it is still, in my opinion, the finest class of lifeboat ever built. Not one of them has been lost 'in action' and as far as I am aware, no crewmember has lost his life accidentally, aboard one.

Long may that proud record be maintained!

The book is, in part, a tribute to the men who learned, nurtured and cherished the wisdom, hard gained over many generations, that once was the backbone of the herring fishing.

It was a great privilege to have served with these men.

This irreplaceable lore was lost beyond recall in the few insane years that created a handful of millionaires, destroying entire communities in the process. Men who put their faith in electronics and who completely disregarded natural forces replaced fishermen who had worked with nature.

Nature has taken its revenge.

When I went to sea in 1950 around two hundred fishermen sailed from Campbeltown alone. They earned their daily bread fishing for herring to the exclusion of all else. Today, in the entire United Kingdom, not one person derives a living entirely from that source!

Mallaig was for several years, the premier herring port in Europe. Now, thanks to over fishing, to the unbelievable and uncaring incompetence of successive governments, and to the naiveté of the fishermen's own leaders it is, in common with the rest of the once proud fishing industry in the United Kingdom, a pale shadow of what it once was.

Lives and livelihoods have been sacrificed for the vainglory of a few.

All of the fishing operations described within these pages are factually accurate and are based upon my own experience, as is the description of the lifeboats portrayed.

The religious discrimination depicted is most certainly not exaggerated. In my time the divides between faiths were almost insurmountable. My mother's best friend was refused permission to attend my mother's wedding much less be, as my mother had wished, her bridesmaid. This divide is narrowing, thankfully, but it does still exist.

I have resisted the temptation to try to write in Doric or to try to use regional dialects as I have found that when reading other people's attempts, it can sometimes be embarrassing, and difficult to understand.

I do not wish anything I have written to cause any harm to anyone living, nor to sully the memory of the dead.

Also from PlashMill Press

Poaching the River

by

Rod Fleming

Price: £11.99   ISBN: 978-0-9554535-0-2

A hysterically funny, action-packed tale of love and life, humour and romance, played out by an unforgettable cast of genuine Scots characters, *Poaching the River* will make you laugh—and cry—out loud.

THE TOBACCONIST

by

JENNIFER DALMAINE

Price: £9.99   ISBN: 978-0-9554535-2-6

Jennifer Dalmaine grew up in Aberdeen in the 1950's and in her first "Easthead" novel she recreates the atmosphere of the city in that era with unerring skill.

A Boy's Own Offshore Adventure

by

Brian Page

Price: £11.99   ISBN: 978-0-9554535-1-9

Drawing on a lifetime's work in the North Sea oil industry, Brian Page tells the story of the "Offshore Tigers" in a refreshing and funny style.

Free Carriage!

Carriage anywhere in the world is free when you order direct from PlashMill Press. Please see our website for terms and conditions.

www.plashmillpress.com